TO THE DEVIL
A
SERPENT

GEORGE CORBETT

Dismissive of the odd, out of norm experience that defy logical explanation few of us give credence to the existence of the occult. That was how it was with Jack Sibley, until he became inadvertently enmeshed in the heinous doctrines of black magic and Devil worship. Now, hopeful of having shaken off the terrors of that encounter, he was looking forward to a lengthy vacation. His friend and erstwhile flatmate, Kyle Steinbeck, had suggested he spend a few weeks in the USA before having to worry about earning a living. But the promised holiday of a lifetime was destined to go terribly wrong.

CONTENTS

PROLOGUE

It wasn't easy, but with a few aggravated twists and turns he somehow managed to shift his body into a half-sitting position. Leaning back on his elbows for support, he wasn't at all sure it had been worth the effort. Faced with an abysmal landscape that threatened to swallow him in its vastness, Jack Sibley struggled to understand where he was and how he came to be here. It was too much too soon. It wasn't just a case of not knowing where he was, he had similar difficulty in coming to terms with who he was. But, as memory stirred and realisation dawned, he found it hard to believe he was still alive. It wasn't possible...he should be dead. The situation he was in: half buried in freezing snow, barely able to breathe? It didn't make sense. His chest aching with the effort of inhaling air from the clutches of a Scrooge-like atmosphere, he sought answers beyond his current level of perception.

How did he come to be in this hellhole, freezing cold and miles from anywhere? He winced. Failing to suppress a gasp as a sharp pain pierced his upper thigh. He tried to organise his thoughts. Pigeon hole them into some sort of chronological order. It was hard to think clearly with a mind clogged by half memories, but it was important he did so. There had to be an explanation, of how he came to be curled up like a gigantic snowball in the middle of nowhere.

Panic beginning to rear its ugly head he took a deep breath, as deep as his meagre ration would allow. Above all, he had to keep control. Get a grip; sort himself out. If he didn't he wasn't left with a lot of choice. He could freeze to death, or he could starve to death. On reflection, he got that wrong. The luxury of choosing which way to go was non-existent. The icy conditions would devour him long before lack of nourishment did the honours. He was rambling, taking the easier option rather than face the task of unravelling the mystery of how he came to be in this predicament and, more pertinently, how to get out of it.

Slow to respond in the near-arctic environment, his mental faculties stuttered into reluctant activity. The plane...the crash! Memories flooding back he recalled those final, fatal minutes. Out of control and heading fast towards the peak of one of the highest mountains in the Andes, a twenty-two thousand feet colossus in an aircraft out of control. That's why it was so cold, why breathing such a nightmare. He forced his mind back to his college days. Atmospheric pressure less than half that at sea level, temperatures well below zero. Bit of a wild guess but near enough to add to his despondency.

Kyle...he must find Kyle!

He turned his head slowly - even that small effort resulting in him having to force air into oxygen starved lungs - searching the stark and sinister, yet strangely beautiful, scenery. Near to its zenith, the Sun glared down at him from a startlingly blue sky. Querying his presence in a territory where all life was barred. Mocking him in his loneliness.

His eyes focussed on the awesome grandeur of the mountain peak and, not too far below, the shattered remains of the aircraft. Missing starboard wing and tail-plane but otherwise in one piece, it was no more than fifty-or-sixty yards away. The evidence told the story as clearly as if the script was written in the snow at his feet. The wing, which he could just about see protruding from the snow a couple of hundred yards off, had hit first. The impact would have been sufficient to spin the plane on its axis: finalising its last resting place...nose pointing the way to the stars. From what he could see, apart from the gap left by

5

the missing tail-plane of which there was no sign, it appeared to be largely undamaged and the right way up. He tried to stand but the effort required was more than that available. Head and frame both screaming the message that they needed more time to come to terms, for rehabilitation to be given a fighting chance. He studied the route to the plane. Assessing the difficulties in his minds eye. What bloody difference did it make? There was little, if any, doubt that Kyle was still strapped in the pilot's seat. Wherever he was, it would be a lifeless body that awaited discovery. So where did that leave him? Stuck at the top of an Andean leviathan with nowhere to go. Its name hammered into his skull…Huascaran. There to haunt him for as long as he had left. No mountaineering experience, a near non-existent atmosphere and extreme cold. Any one of which would see him off long before he reached civilisation. Had he been killed in the crash, death would have been that much more welcome... he wouldn't now be being asked to face the prospect of a long drawn-out melodrama. One man against the omnipotent might of nature. Dracula had more chance of becoming a Jehova's Witness than he had of survival. But there was one consolation. Nightfall couldn't be too far away and that would soon put an end to his misery. There was no possibility of surviving the hours of darkness in this desolate wilderness. Rendered intense with the sun's departure, the icy cold would adopt the role of Grim Reaper.

Reflecting on his unquestionable fate, sadness crept over him. They had enjoyed such great times together, he and Kyle. But what did any of it now matter? Come tomorrow he will have joined Kyle in the permanent darkness of oblivion.

"You wimp. You shameless bloody wimp." Delivered at the top of his voice the verbal admonishment proclaimed an authority he found hard to muster. Echoing back from the higher ground, his words repeated over and over in descending volume. Taunting him. Laughing at the ludicrous show of optimism. "So you're about to give it all up. To hell with the providence that has given you the glimmer of a chance to save your life. For Kyle's sake if for no other, pull yourself together. Use that thing you call a brain. Better to peg it knowing you did your damnedest than give up without a fight."

Addressed to the silent, inanimate monarchs of the Andes the outburst did him a power of good. Although singularly embarrassed as he came to the end of his tirade, its purpose was achieved. The self-imposed languor dropped away, replaced by a more positive attitude.

He'd take it easy. Time, energy and purpose were precious commodities, to be neither hurried nor ignored. He'd start by making a mental list of his priorities. A practical, working agenda to ensure he stayed on the right track. Number one...the plane. Had to get there well before nightfall. Obvious at first thought, but it didn't take top priority. To risk ploughing through the snow without first checking his body for any serious injury he might have would, at the vary least, be somewhat negligent. It was important he be aware of any encumbrance that might intrude on his ability to reach the stricken aircraft. If all was well, getting to the plane would move to the top of the list. To stand the remotest chance of survival he would need every bit of warmth and comfort the battered fuselage had to offer. Although no great distance, it wasn't going to be easily reached. The snow was deep, which would make walking difficult and play havoc with his breathing. There was also his physical state to consider...back to priority number one. No point at this stage deciding what to do and what not to do. That would come after he found out if there were any precautions to be taken.

Ignoring a blistering headache doing its best to rip his skull in two, he probed his body. A tear in the upper right trouser leg failing to hide a similar split in his thigh, there was no argument where to start. It looked nasty and, if the red stain on his trousers and surrounding snow was anything to go by, had bled profusely. That the bleeding had stopped was of little comfort. It was only a temporary respite and wouldn't take much for the flow to get going again. Not a good beginning. It was patently clear that something had to be done if death through loss of blood was to be removed from the list of murderous possibilities. A nagging ache in his left shoulder was another concern. In an awkward position, it in some respects worried him more than the injury to his thigh. Unable to reach the nucleus of the pain, he could only guess at the cause...anything from a pulled muscle to a broken shoulder blade. He had no choice other than to live with it.

There was little else of note. The knuckles on his right hand were grazed and the nail from the little finger on the same hand had gone walkabouts. Both irritatingly sore, but hardly life threatening. His worst fear was the possibility of internal injury but, had there been, he would surely have had some signs by now. He also viewed it a miracle that, with the possible exception of his shoulder, nothing appeared to be broken.

All in all he seemed to have got away with it a lot lighter than he could have reasonably expected. The wound in his leg could prove a major handicap, but at least there were things he could do to minimise that possibility. Assuming there was a first aid kit on board, he'd be able to make a more thorough job of it later. Other than pray it wouldn't be too much of a handicap, there was nothing to be done about his shoulder. After all he'd been through it was a miracle he was still alive, and to end up so relatively unscathed...weird to the point of uncanny. The more he thought about it the more uncanny it appeared. Perhaps Membril had been right all along. The idea was laughable, but perhaps he *was* protected in some way. He certainly seemed to have had more than his fair share of good fortune just lately. And this latest slice was the icing on the cake.

A search of his pockets produced two unused handkerchiefs and, thanking his lucky stars he carried it everywhere with him, his Swiss army knife. It was a start, but it would need more than a couple of handkerchiefs to cover the nine-inch gash close to the top of his thigh. Discarding the bloodstained area, he cut the rest of the torn trouser leg into strips. Not hygienic in the true sense of the word but, in his situation, beggars had not the option of becoming choosers.

Knotting the two handkerchiefs together, he draped them over the wound; pulling the makeshift bandage tight, gritting his teeth in response to the pain that was beginning to build. Fumbling behind his leg to tie the free ends, he did what he could to reinforce the newly blood-soaked white squares of cloth with layers of material taken from the redundant trouser leg. It was rough, it was amateurish, but it gave promise. To make sure, he sat still for several minutes. Utilising the time to gauge the distance separating him from the forlorn fuselage and to balance that against the useful time at his disposal. Fearing to delay longer than necessary, he brought the sabbatical to an end. It was encouraging. There was no sign of blood seeping through the crude dressing.

The time had come, the now-or-never moment that would decide his future. Having no ready way of knowing how far the day had progressed, a wicked red weal on his left wrist a reminder he once owned a watch, he sought guidance from the Sun. High in the heavens, it bore the message that there remained sufficient daylight at his disposal...providing he got a move on. About to stir, his eye was caught by a black blob in the otherwise untarnished snow.

Although only a few yards away, he was made to stare at it for some time before recognition stirred. It was nothing more exciting than the carcase of a lonely shoe. He looked down at his feet. His left foot sported a soggy woollen sock and nothing else. Cursing the time wasted, he decided to leave the shoe where it was. An artefact to be found, and no doubt wondered at, by someone with more time and energy to spare than he had. His foot was already sopping wet and icy cold, and retrieval of the errant shoe would entail having to walk that much further. In any case, it's loss was immaterial. There was more than one spare pair ensconced in his luggage...providing it was still accessible and in one piece. For all he knew it could have been spattered across the Andes when the plane hit the ground.

Short though it was the walk to the plane was fraught with difficulty. Every step exhausted the meagre supply of oxygen absorbed in the previous, gasping intake of the rarefied gas, every movement caused his chest to ache with the effort of inhaling the precious element, every step erupted crippling bursts of pain from leg and shoulder and, worryingly, every step marred the virginal snow with crimson blotches. It would have been so easy to sink to the ground, to await the coming of death and the blessed relief that would tag along. And many was the time the thought occurred. In the end, it was nothing more than sheer bloody mindedness that stopped him taking the easy way out.

He worried about his feet, in particular the unprotected left foot. He couldn't feel any of his toes and feared frostbite could already be wielding its fatal axe. To a lesser extent his fingers were another cause for concern. In common with his toes, and despite the warmer confines of the pockets in which they were incarcerated, they too lacked sensitivity. He tried to ignore the near inevitability of untreated frostbite turning to gangrene, but it was a deep-rooted fear that continued to dominate his mind throughout the arduous journey.

In a walking stupor and near to the end of his tether, he at last reached the harbour of promised salvation. Granting consent to pass through its portal, the open passenger door beckoned him into the slightly warmer, but substantially more comfortable, interior. He'd made it. A journey that seemed to have lasted a lifetime, had in fact taken less than half an hour.

Leaning against the fuselage for support, he utilised the time to restore breathing and replenish depleted energy banks. Gearing himself for one last effort, that of climbing into the welcoming arms of his potential harbour. The mini-break served a second purpose: the opportunity to piece together the jigsaw of events. How he had come to be deposited in the snow, instead of interred within what should have been his coffin. The centrifugal force, developed by the spinning aircraft when the wing collided with the unrelenting ground, would have been considerable; more than sufficient to hurl him across the cabin. He dimly recalled standing behind Kyle just before the crash, and that would make sense. Had he been seated it would never have happened. As it transpired he must have hit the door with enough impact to force the lock...hence the pain in his shoulder. When under attack by flesh and bone, metal doors are inclined to be somewhat unforgiving.

A touch revived and loath to waste more time than necessary, he threw the upper part of his body across the bottom rail of the doorframe. The exertion inducing yet another bout of breathlessness, he was forced to rest for a minute-or-two before crawling into the bowels of the cabin. He knew what he would find, there was not the remotest chance of it not being so, but it wasn't in him to reject the forlorn hope that burned inside. "Oh please, God...let me be wrong."

He wasn't wrong. The explicit scenario that greeted his eyes rendered confirmation redundant. Chest impaled on the control column and head little more than an emaciated pulp buried in the dashboard, Kyle Steinbeck was, most definitely, dead.

It may have been the sight of his friend's horrendous injuries, perhaps altitude sickness. Whatever the cause he barely made it to the doorway in time before vomiting into the snow. More probably Kyle's death, added to the unrelenting trauma of recent weeks, was one shock too many. The instant retaliation of a nervous system of which too much had been demanded.

The effort of emptying his stomach left his breathing in a parlous state, and it was with considerable relief that he collapsed into the passenger seat to recover. But needs must when the devil drives, and his needs were substantial. Feet and hands first. Chances were it was already too late. If not, then it soon would be. The tear in his thigh was similarly pressing. The crude dressing had helped, but not to any great extent. He'd lost a lot of blood on the way and that couldn't be allowed to continue. He was weak enough as it was.

Removing the waterlogged sock wasn't an easy task. However, although the bulk of his flying jacket made it difficult to reach his feet, the effort required generated aid in other areas. Manipulation becoming markedly easier, the fingers on both hands were beginning to tingle. Early signs of circulation being restored. His feet were a different proposition. When the sock finally admitted defeat, it parted company from a foot that showed no sign of life. Opalescent skin covering flesh pitted with white patches of dead or dying tissue and toes the colour of over-ripe plums, his worst fears were in danger of coming to fruition. Bating his breath, he wasted no time baring the other foot. Better...but nothing to get excited about. The skin was more opaque and, although bloodless, there was no discolouration.

Refusing to accede to the onset of despondency, he steadfastly denied permission to the lack of will to carry on. Turned deaf ears to the whispers of an obstinate voice insisting he give up, that it was all utterly pointless. He could see no valid reason to enthuse over the outcome, but having got this far he wasn't going to surrender that easily. He looked around, searching for...he knew not what. If there was a chance to be had, it had to be taken... and quickly. He had to think, and think fast.

When inspiration strikes, it is instant. There is no warning, no expectancy...it just happens. There, right in front of him. Staring at him. Ridiculing his stupidity. Seat covers and, hiding beneath the covers, material used to stuff the cushions. Frantically ripping open one of the rear passenger seats, he found what he was looking for. A virtual Aladdin's cave packed full of massed synthetic fibre.

It was a long wait, or so it seemed to he who waited. For nearly thirty minutes nothing changed. Buried deep within the fibrous material his feet were invisible but, worryingly, they continued to lack sensitivity. Fearing the worst and on the verge of accepting the inevitable, he was jolted by a trifling infusion of pins-and-needles. Just one foot to begin with, the other not far behind. The euphoria was fleeting, the agony prolonged. In desperation he rubbed his feet and lower legs, a seemingly futile attempt to hasten the process. Whether or not it helped he couldn't be sure, but at long last the pain began to ease. Tentatively removing the wrappings, he burst into a fit of violent sobbing. But the tears shed were not those of sorrow, they were those of blessed relief.

In better spirit he moved from feet to thigh. The crude bandaging had served the purpose for which it was designed, but would be nothing like man enough for the trek ahead. It had to be somewhere in the cabin. Kyle was too organised to have secreted such a potentially vital piece of equipment in the hold...but where? Having spent so much time in the aircraft over the past few weeks, it was a mystery he hadn't come across it before now. Even the smallest of first-aid outfits require a fair sized box to keep it all together, so it should be easy enough to spot. Casting his eyes around, he searched the cockpit for what seemed like the hundredth time. But there was nothing new, nothing he hadn't already investigated. Every nook, cranny and compartment was boringly familiar...with the exception of unexplored caverns beneath the seats.

Sinking to his knees he peered into the darkened cavity below where he sat. Attention taken by an item of greater interest he initially failed to spot the glistening, white-painted box emblazoned with a red cross hanging from the underside of the upholstery. Secured to the floor by a stout leather strap, an oxygen cylinder complete with regulator and mask. Mentally he kicked himself. He should have remembered. It was when he'd expressed a fear of flying over the top of the mountains. To reassure him, Kyle had said there was plenty of oxygen on board should it become necessary.

The effect was near to immediate. Within minutes of clapping mask over mouth and nose his head cleared, the ache subsided and he was able to view his position with greater clarity. The oxygen cylinder was of the type and size used by scuba divers, and capacity was therefore limited. Plenty on board there may be, but that didn't give carte-blanche approval to get carried away. For one thing he couldn't be sure if there were any more cylinders to be had. Assuming they were in the hold at the time of the crash, they could now be anywhere.

Feeling as close to human as he was likely to be for some time, he levered the medical kit into a convenient position on the arm of the seat alongside. Cleansing the wound with a handful of snow he plastered it with an antiseptic ointment prior to adding several layers of bandaging. Engrossed in treating the injury, he came to appreciate just how lucky he'd been. An inch to the left and the femoral artery would have been severed. Striking him as a classical understatement, putting spanners in works sprang to mind. He wouldn't be worried about spanners in works...or anything else for that matter.

Light beginning to fade, he progressed to the next items on the list. Extra clothing, food if there was any...anything that might come in useful. In the hope it was still there and not too badly damaged, he would find all he wanted in amongst either his or Kyle's luggage. Shoulder giving him a deal of gyp, he unearthed a packet of Ibuprofen. They would take time to work, but with any luck will have dulled the pain by the time he'd finished doing what had to be done. Deciding it would be unwise to put them at further risk he re-wrapped his feet. It would make walking difficult but dry socks and sturdy shoes beckoned...perhaps: maybe not. He would soon find out.

Balancing pros and cons, he decided to do without the oxygen temporarily. Transferring his needs back to the cabin was not going to be easy, and dragging the bulky cylinder along could be more of a hindrance than a help.

Making his way into the hold posed further problems. The floor of the fuselage immediately aft of the rear seats had sheared in several places, leaving the torn metal wickedly deformed: crested with vicious edges and lethal spikes. Walking across the damaged area would have been difficult under normal circumstances, with his mummified feet it would be nigh on impossible. Bearing that in mind he chose crawling on all fours as the sensible option. Standing tall would be courting disaster. It was slow progress but in the end worth the effort as his eyes rested on four suitcases and one briefcase, firmly anchored to the sidewall of the tapering tunnel.

Light fading and warm clothing essential before the icy fingers of nightfall made their presence felt, he didn't need telling where to start. The larger of his two suitcases would satisfy both criteria. A zipped compartment inside the lid produced a torch and a pair of woollen gloves in which cold hands were instantly and gratefully buried. Testing the torch, he breathed a sigh of relief. The battery was not the dead beast he half expected. Several pairs of socks, warm corduroy trousers and three thick sweaters followed in quick succession. The latter bringing a smile to his face as he recalled his mother's insistence. 'Don't care where you're going love, never know when you might need a nice warm jumper'. Dear old Mum. Right as usual. Adding a spare flying jacket and a pair of sturdy walking boots to the pile, he turned his attention to Kyle's luggage. If there was food to be had, that's where it would be. The recollection of his friend's passion for midnight feasting triggering a sad smile.

The larder was there sure enough but, apart from an opened packet of biscuits, one-and-a-bit bars of chocolate and a few boiled sweets, it was empty. Sufficient perhaps to keep him going for a couple of days but that would be about it. It was small compensation, but the meagre fare at least gave him a time-bracket. If he didn't find help within that time bracket?... nothing to be gained thinking along those lines. At least thirst wouldn't pose a problem, which was something in his favour. Melted snow was pretty tasteless stuff, but he wouldn't suffer from dehydration.

Wrapped in tissue paper and tucked away in a corner it could have been easily missed. Much as he hated the damned thing and the trouble it had caused, he couldn't leave it behind. It was Kyle's wish that the matter be seen through to the bitter end, and it was incumbent on him to carry out his friends wishes to the best of his ability. What difference did it make anyway? Even if he got out of this present mess, Membril would turn up sooner-or-later. And he wouldn't give a toss. One way or the other the statue would end up in his hands. He'd make damn sure of that. But there was something else. Something he couldn't explain, but it was definitely there. A voice inside his head telling him it was important he take the effigy with him. That he had to keep it secure...whatever the cost. He shivered. Aware of the hairs on the back of his neck standing to attention. Perhaps it was the altitude, the thin air and the bitter cold. Whatever, it was an eerie sensation.

In the process of gathering his hoard together, he was in danger of falling over a coil of rope. Not easily seen in the subdued light, he nearly missed it. Following his disappointment at the meagre rations available, the find was a huge boost. Apart from coming in handy for ideas that were beginning to fester, it could also prove advantageous in other areas. He knew nothing about mountaineering, but he could well imagine the benefit of having a substantial length of rope to hand. Adding it to the pile, he set off in search of the oxygen cylinders. Having as yet seen no sign of them, he wondered if he'd misinterpreted what Kyle had said. He might have been referring to the quantity in a single cylinder, not to the number of cylinders available.

Having to stoop ever lower, he ventured further along the fuselage. Guided by the disc of light, a legacy of the departed tail-plane, he didn't have far to go. Comfortably snuggled behind a secreting bulwark, six off-white containers glimmered in the gloom. Offering a prayer of thanks to whichever providence was responsible, he began transferring his accumulation to the cabin. A task sooner said than done. By the time he'd completed the several trips necessary, it was fully dark. Temperature dropping rapidly, he wasted no time throwing on the thick corduroy trousers, two pairs of equally thick woollen socks, boots and a couple of sweaters. Managing to squeeze the flying jacket over the bulk, he rummaged around for the oxygen apparatus. Denied its use for more than an hour

16

of frenetic activity, his head was reeling and his breathing had gone completely haywire. Clapping the mask in place, he inhaled deeply. Gratefully absorbing several lungs-full of the life-saving gas.

Tears misting his eyes and in a voice cracked with emotion, he turned to his one-time friend and ally.

"I'm going to have to leave you in the morning, Kyle, but, if I'm able and God is willing, I'll be back. Take you home, put you to rest and find sanctuary for your soul. I still fail to understand why it was you and not me, but it'll no doubt be my turn next...Membril won't hang around more than he has to and, if worse does come to worst, all we can hope is that providence will provide protection for what ever follows our mortality."

Covering the American's head with a plain white shirt retrieved for the purpose, he gazed for a while through the cabin window. Creeping over the horizon, a near-to-full moon was about to shed its golden glow across the stark landscape. As he turned to move away his eyes were drawn to the altimeter. He had no reason to doubt the accuracy of the reading. A touch over twenty-one thousand, nine-hundred and forty feet seemed about right. Not that the knowledge did much for him.

He slept soundly that night...so soundly he was unaware it was a night filled with restless uncertainty. Plagued by a blend of nightmarish dreams and tender emotions, he would on occasion shatter the tomb-like silence. Fearful screams would accompany visions of Kyle sitting up in his seat, rivulets of blood streaming down his emaciated face, staring at him...accusing him. Or it would be shrieks of terror in response to Membril mocking him, forcing him into a repeat of his confrontation with the Angel of Death.

Mercifully shielded from the horrors of those hours of darkness, it was in gradual awareness of the sun peeping into the eastern sky that he awoke. Rubbing sleep from out of focus eyes, he groped for the oxygen mask. The decision not to use it while he slept had seemed the sensible thing to do. Wasn't as though he'd any intention of dancing the night away, or any other energy-sapping silliness. Apart from feeling strangely drunk, which he seemed to recollect he'd read somewhere was a common side effect of oxygen deprivation, he appeared to be none the worse for the experience.

The rising sun adding a semblance of warmth to the air, he shed a few garments before making plans for the day ahead. Breakfasting while he worked, he managed to raise a bleak smile. A few soggy biscuits, two squares of chocolate and a swig of melted snow. No different from last nights supper...some novelty. First things first: make a sling. He'd use one of the seat harnesses for that. Ignorant of what lay in store he thought it would be wise to keep both hands free, which meant the oxygen bottle had to be carried on his back.

He was pleased with his handiwork. Crude but effective, he was satisfied it would do what was asked of it...as long as he kept the heavy metal cylinder clear of his dodgy shoulder. One job out of the way, he turned his talents to building a sledge to carry his essentials. He had a plan, he had the materials...but the marriage of theory and practice can be a devious relationship for the unwary.

Four cases lashed together with rope, willpower and tongue in cheek it wasn't pretty. If he was brutally honest the contraption looked ready to fall apart, but looks can be deceiving...or so he persuaded himself. It seemed solid enough when kicked. If that was anything to go by.

He was ready to start. Pawing the snow and straining at the leash, the sledge snorted its impatience. Irritated at the lethargy of the man in control, fuming at the delay. Nothing wrong with a bit of fantasy thinking...there was no one around to see or hear him making a fool of himself, and it was the only bit of fun he was likely to have for a while.

He didn't exactly relish the coming descent. His acrophobia was a lopsided struggle at the best of times. Simple things, like no higher than three rungs up a ladder. He was happy with that. But in his present situation there was no ladder, and a lot more than three rungs to cope with; stuck with feelings of sheer horror at the thought of what might be, he shivered in anticipation. Huascaran had no intention of staying the same as it was now, gentle slopes giving promise of an easy stroll all the way down to its massive foundations. It would soon reveal another side of its nature. When it did, how would he deal with it? A question he was powerless to answer.

It wasn't just the climb down the mountain it was the other, in a way greater, ordeal that worried him more. Kyle's family. Josh, Martha, his two brothers, Julie...most of all, Julie - she and Kyle seemed to share a special bond - they had to be told of his death. If it should turn out they already knew, then so be it. But it would make no difference. They would want to know the circumstances of his demise. More than that, theirs' was the right to know and it would be his duty to tell them exactly what happened, the full works unabridged: that was assuming he was still around to tell them. And what could he say that they would find believable? Julie was the only one who might. She had the advantage of having been given an insight into the world in which he'd once become entangled. As for the rest of the family? They'd have him carted off to the nearest asylum. He was looking too far ahead. There were more than a few obstacles to overcome before that dilemma had to be faced. Membril being by no means the least of them.

Ignited by an infusion of nostalgia, sadness swept over him. How could things have gone so horribly wrong? He had been in such great spirits when Kyle met him at the airport, but in just a few short weeks everything changed. The planned holiday of a lifetime, butchered into extinction by events beyond their control. A fleeting hallucination, driven into the mist by terror and despair.

Wiping moist eyes on the cuff of his coat, he grasped the tug-rope...

CHAPTER ONE

The Steinbecks' were rich...very rich.

Old man, Jeremiah, had struck lucky when prospecting for silver in the Sierra Nevada towards the end of the nineteenth century: capitalising on his hard-earned gains by investing in a small oil exploration outfit; one that was destined to grow into a mammoth organisation. He would insist, whenever the question was asked, that it was all down to luck. He just happened to be in the right place at the right time. In his eyes it would have been an irrelevance to include an account of the hard graft, the sweat, the tears and the many trials he faced before success was assured. He would not have reckoned his listener to be interested in the harsh realities of the life he was forced to endure for many a long year, before he was able sit back and reflect on the results of his labours.

Who the devil would want to listen, he would ask, to me rambling on about the perils of slaving away deep underground on my own? Who would be interested in me griping at having to work in temperatures hitting both extremes? Who would want to know that I was never sure of the purity of the air I breathed, or that there was more than a remote chance the undertaker would miss out on his burial fees if the roof collapsed? No one, according to the philosophy of old Jeremiah, would be remotely interested.

It is true, because of the nature of his work and his dedication to that work, that Jeremiah was a loner. He had no wish to be. On the contrary. By nature, he was an affable and friendly man blessed with an outgoing personality which ensured he mixed well with his peers. Sadly, however, this was not always the case. As in all walks of life there were those who determined to hold envy in their hearts, and they constituted a far greater threat than those faced in the pursuit of his work. The American West was a lawless country in the days leading up to the end of the century, and on more than one occasion Jeremiah was called upon to defend himself.

Unlikely as it might seem considering his lonely existence, Jeremiah met a young girl, Harriet, a milkmaid on the farm where he eked out a living as a labourer during the early days. Love at first sight for both, they were married within a few months of their first meeting. Rapidly acclimatising to the new way of life, Harriet encouraged Jeremiah in everything he did. Praising him when things went right, providing comfort and solace when they didn't. There was never a complaint from her during the years they lived in squalid conditions, never a recrimination at the lack of food on the table, never a word to condemn him for the hours, often running into days, she was left on her own.

The time Jeremiah and Harriet spent together was too good to last and, almost inevitably it seemed, the bliss they shared was brought to a premature end. Harriet died giving birth to their only child. Passing away before the birth was complete, she never saw the baby but lived long enough to wring a promise from her husband. Her dying wish, that if the child was a boy he would be named after his father. A lasting tribute to the only man she had ever loved.

Understandably, Jeremiah was devastated. The wife he adored cruelly taken from him, he laid the blame on his son. Had it not been for him, his beloved Harriet would be with him still. Unable to tolerate the child anywhere near and in danger of harming him during one of his many rages at the unfairness of his loss, he took the only sensible option. Fostering him to a middle-aged couple living nearby, gave him the opportunity to come to terms with his deep sadness. With the passing of time the pain eased and he came to realise that his rejection of

Jeremiah junior was not only callous, but contrary to what would have been the wishes of his wife. Hiring a live-in housekeeper to take care of his daily needs, he pushed aside his uncharacteristic selfishness and took the boy back under his wing.

Jeremiah never re-married. Harriet had been his only love and always would be. But, as grief subsided, the characteristics that marked him for the man he once was re-emerged. On his death in nineteen-seventeen, and in company of an accumulated fortune, those same characteristics were passed on to his son. And the trend was to continue. More than a hundred and thirty years down the line, the same attributes re-emerged in his great, great grandson, Kyle, who, in appearance, attitude and outlook on life, was the doppelganger of old Jeremiah.

The march of time however is not constrained, and although the two men were similar in appearance and demeanour their way of life was markedly different. Money was not the same scarcity as in Jeremiah's early days, and the demands on the younger man were thus different to those laid at the feet of his twice-great grandfather. Kyle's ambitions also trod a different path to those of his ancestor. He could raise no interest in the family business, nor indeed in commercial enterprise of any kind. But he was no shirker, far from it. He applied as much energy to the pursuit of knowledge, as had his ancestor to a more physical activity. Devoting the same time and passion to his ambition, as had his forbear to the trials of a more arduous existence. Whereas Jeremiah was made to knuckle down to the hard mill of life, his modern-day descendents were cushioned from having to do the same. The family fortune had been made, and was continuing to be made, by the multinational company in the hands of the present generation. And so Jeremiah's legacy lived on and, had he been alive to witness it, he would have been a proud and satisfied man.

As for Kyle, it was a fortunate twist that, for as far back as anyone could remember, the current family was not restricted to a single child. In addition to a younger sister there were two older brothers actively involved in the family business, each eager to ensure its continued success when their father, Josh, decided he'd had enough. He therefore had no compunction shedding what some might consider his duty, a commitment to a world that was anathema to him. Gifted the freedom to fuel his obsession with archaeology, he had grasped the opportunity with both hands.

Aware early on that commerce had no place in the make-up of their youngest son, his parents openly encouraged the pursuit of his passion; first at Stanford University then at Cambridge. Now, at the age of twenty-eight, Kyle Steinbeck was blessed with everything most young men could only dream of. A fine sportsman, tall, good looking in a rugged sort of way, and blessed with an easy, outgoing personality, the world was literally his oyster.

Most people he came up against accepted him for what he was; a guy who had struck lucky, a man to be envied but not to be decried because of his good fortune. Inevitably there were also resentful eyes that labelled him the typical spoilt brat, but it was water off a ducks back. As far as he was concerned everyone had the right to express an opinion, even one born of jealousy. In a way he felt sorry for them. They would never understand the bond of true friendship. A camaraderie based on trust and loyalty, where people mattered more than possessions. Few of his acquaintances fell into that category, but there was one who more than filled the role. He who had kept him waiting for more than five hours at San Francisco airport.

Kyle first met Jack Sibley some five years ago, when he'd responded to an advertisement to share a flat in Cambridge and the expenses that went with it. The two hit it off straight away. A host of common interests and a similar sense of humour laying the foundation for a solid friendship. At the invitation of the Steinbecks' he was now on his way to spending a couple of months in America, before having to knuckle down to the onerous necessity of having to earn a living.

Making the most of the chance to stretch his legs, Jack made his way to where his luggage was expected to arrive. Despite the excitement of what lay ahead, eleven hours of cramped conditions in economy class had not proved to be one of his more pleasurable experiences. But with that over and done with, he could now look forward to a nice long holiday...not to mention meeting up with Kyle again.

Resigned to a lengthy wait, he whiled away the time wallowing in nostalgia. He hadn't seen Kyle for something like eighteen months, when he'd driven him to Heathrow for his flight back home. They'd kept in contact, but e-mails and the occasional telephone call have their limitations. Neither fully substitute for a face-to-face chinwag.

Because of their differing backgrounds, he found it a mystery how their relationship had become so firmly entrenched. Kyle was loaded and, from what he'd been told, lived in a damn great house set in a ranch of God-knew how many thousands of acres. His fortune on the other hand was plastered in red and he lived with his working-to-middle class parents in a cosy three-up, two-down semi in London's southern suburbia. But was that in itself not the definition of true friendship? Apart from the wide financial divide, sport was also an area in which a notable departure might have generated animosity in many another relationship. He enjoyed active participation as much as his friend, but that was where the similarity ended. Whereas he had to strive for a modicum of success, Kyle was imbued with a natural talent that seemed to spread across the entire sporting arena. Rubbing it in by scoring eighty odd runs the very first time he played cricket.

With no sign of his luggage appearing, he switched his mind to taking stock of his surroundings. The noisy atmosphere was thick with general hubbub and no one, especially those awaiting the arrival of their belongings, seemed content to stand still. It was as if the entire populace of the United States had gathered in one place, all demanding the immediate return of their bags and baggage. That none were content to be idle in the meantime, in a way helped counteract his own irritation. With so many customers sharing a common pursuit, he had to accept the operation was going to take some time. Even so, it was a bit much. What with the two-hour delay at Heathrow...now this! True the pilot had put his foot down and made up some of the lost time, but he was still short of an hour-and-a-half of his holiday.

At last! All things come to he who waits - there was something in that quotation which caused him to wonder if its creator was a regular air traveller - first one case, the second not far behind. Now they'd turned up it didn't seem to matter they'd taken so long, Kyle would still be there to meet him. Or he hoped he was. The thought put him on edge. What would he do if he wasn't?

Customs first: another time wasting exercise. At least it was for him. The locals seemed to pass through without the hassle he was made to suffer. Didn't think he looked like a petulant junkie or a hot-headed terrorist but the interrogating officer seemed to have doubts. Immigration next...and relief. He could see Kyle waving to him on the far side of the barrier. Treating him to a smile that hadn't changed. He didn't need to speak, the sheer warmth in his expression conveyed more than words. It was as if time had stood still and it was only yesterday that they'd chatted away in a carefree world.

"About time! More'n five bloody hours I've been stuck here waiting for you to turn up." He grinned. "I know! Not your fault...these damned airlines. The age-old excuse. Caught an early flight to make sure I got here on time, and this is the thanks I get. Was reckoning on the eleven-ten back to Reno but we've had that." Glancing at his watch he mumbled. "Left twenty minutes ago. More'n an hour to the next one, so suggest we make the best of it and grab some lunch." Punching him on the arm he added, "Only kidding, you know that. Great to see you again, Jack, really is. Been a long time."

"Don't know what you've got to complain about. I'm the one who, having been commanded to arrive three hours before takeoff, had to spend goodness knows how long kicking his heels while they sorted themselves out. Organisation seems to be a dirty word in the annals of airline goings-on." It was his turn to grin. "But having got here at last I don't give a damn. The sight of your ugly mug puts everything else in the shade. Anyway, did I hear you mention food? If I did, it's only right you should know my stomach was listening and is in full agreement. The in-flight fodder was edible – need I say more?"

"Preaching to the converted, Jack. But don't you worry: retribution is on the way. I'm going to introduce you to the best seafood on the planet, and that's no exaggeration...believe me."

"Mmm 'tis good." Mumbling through a mouthful of brown bread, fresh crab and cress, "And, against my better judgement, I do believe you. And that's a first." Washing the last bite down with a swig of root beer, he changed the subject. "Reno? How long?"

"An hour, give-or-take. Then a four-hour drive to Tonopah."

"Have you always lived in Tonopah? By you, I mean your family. Might've told me, if you did...I've forgotten "

"Since time immemorial, in the words of that age-old expression. My great, great grandfather, Jeremiah, did the groundwork. Started off with a wooden shack back in the eighteen-seventies. Once he got the money ball rolling he began work on the spread we've got today."

"Where'd that come from?" Shaking his head in disbelief. "Must've been some ancestry site to dig up that much information about a long-dead relative."

"Didn't need none of that nonsense, Jack. Our old barn is littered with family history: portraits, artefacts, personal and company documents and the rest; dating all the way back to when our forebears first arrived in this country. Whatever we need to know, the answer's there; ready and waiting."

"Wish I could say the same. None of my lot knows what happened the day before yesterday, let alone a hundred-odd years ago. But never mind that, on a different subject...this aeroplane? Know the one I mean? The one you told me about in your last e-mail, and the one before that ...and the one before that. Not to mention the one before that!"

He chuckled, palm raised in token apology. "No excuses, Jack, the novelty ain't worn off yet. Nothing for you to worry about though. You'll get to see plenty of her before this vacation's over."

"By that, I suppose it's incumbent on me to say I look forward to the experience. But if you expect me to get carried away? forget it. Such trite admission would entail me lying through my teeth. In a word, aeroplanes fail to excite me anywhere near as much as they do you. Don't take it too much to heart though, Kyle. I promise to treat your new toy with due deference when we're introduced."

"Toy? How could you? A bolt straight to my heart." Clutching his chest, grimacing in mock pain. "My pride and joy...to be treated with such callous disdain."

"You'll get over it. But while convalescing you can explain to me why aeroplanes – ships as well for that matter - are referred to in the female sense. They're lifeless bits of machinery for heavens sake; not animated flesh and blood."

"It's like this, Jack. An airplane is, in reality, a broad in disguise. Just like any woman you've ever come across, it needs a man to keep her on the straight and level. Both are inclined to wander round in circles if left unattended, and neither can be brought down to earth without a flap."

"Ask a stupid question!" Eyes demanding attention, he leaned across the table. "What exactly were you getting at when you said I'd be getting to know your aeroplane? I presume it's got nothing at all to do with that rubbish you posted on facebook. You know what I'm on about. Spaghetti plantations in Idaho, centrally heated igloos in Alaska...and all that other nonsense. And you can wipe that silly grin off your face for a start."

"Oh, I've given up on all that. It was beginning to get too complicated. That then posed a problem. What the heck do I do with this pal of mine when he comes over? The only worthwhile place I could think of was South America. Not a lot going for it other than sun, sea, sand, historical interest and, arguably, the most beautiful girls on the planet. But there you are, it was all I could come up with on the spur of the moment. So what do you think...it's your holiday."

"You sneaky sod! You had this planned all along, just couldn't wait to wind me up." Aiming a soft punch at his friend's jaw, he shrank back in his chair. Face alive with delight. "I can't believe it...South America!"

"Do I take that as a nod of approval?" Ruefully rubbing the stricken chin, "Good...that's settled then. South America it is. Just think, Jack. All those lovely, dusky women fighting to lay hands on the Sibley-Steinbeck combo. I can see it now."

"Ever the optimist. If they've any sense, they'll shut themselves behind closed doors until we disappear over the horizon. And let's face it, if they're that gorgeous they're not likely to be desperate...not even with you around. On a more pertinent note, have you made your mind up exactly where? South America's a big place. I presume you don't intend to see all of it in one go."

"Mexico to start with. Loaded with Aztec and Maya history to keep us out of mischief, before we invade Acapulco and get into as much mischief as we can. When, if ever, we've had enough of Acapulco, then wherever our fancy takes us. Cuba, Aruba, Ecuador, Brazil...can't miss out on Rio. Lots of fun, interest and Latin beauties in abundance, that's what we want and if that's how it pans out I'll be more'n satisfied." He sighed; a long, low, drawn out sigh. "Now ain't that enough to send a guy's libido into orbit? You're looking doubtful, Jack. Haven't put you off? Something I said?"

"No...no way. It's a dream of an idea, and I can't wait. Just a few qualms about the cost, that's all. It'll sort itself out."

"Listen to me, Jack. No good beating about the bush, so I'll get straight to the point. I know your circumstances and you know mine. Luck of the draw, roll of the dice...whatever. This vacation was my idea, and it don't include you getting hamstrung with a string of expenses I know you can't afford. It was meant to be on the house right from the start, and that's how it's gonna be. No arguments. You'd do the same for me if it was the other way round."

"This gets more embarrassing by the minute. Believe me Kyle, I wasn't angling for a handout." Face reddening, he forced himself to look into the other's eyes. "What can I say?"

"Nothing. It's settled. Let's go catch that plane."

In a little under an hour the seat belt signs made their inevitable appearance, and the aircraft began to carve its habitual path through the mountains bordering Reno airport. A host of snow capped giants, creating a scene of such magnificence it took Jack's breath away.

"Wonderful landscape…just hope the pilot knows what he's doing." His phobia making its presence felt as it always did given the opportunity. "Those mountains look pretty damn close."

"Not heard of a plane running into one, Jack. Could be a boss-eyed driver of course. Always a first time." Appreciative of his friend's mindset, he tried to lighten the situation. "Sure is a nice sight. Not too often appreciated I guess."

"Middle of summer and there's still snow on the peaks. Must be awesome in winter."

"Treat those mountains with contempt and you're asking for trouble, that's for sure. You're looking at one of the more forbidding places on the planet: the Sierra Nevada doesn't tolerate disrespect."

"One of the more forbidding...in this day and age? Didn't know America had such things."

"Right in a way, I guess. Modern technology has made a big, big difference. No getting away from it. As long as you can lay a hand to it that is. Get stuck up there at the wrong time of year with a flat battery or no signal and you've got problems. And that's now. Imagine what it was like when communication systems were damn near prehistoric. Back in the so called good old days of the wild west, when immigrants were arriving in masses from all over Europe, droves of wagon trains crossed the Sierra from the east carrying folks intent on finding a new and settled life in California. In eighteen forty-six one such attempt was made by a group of immigrants from Illinois. That outfit, known as the Donner Party after the man who led the train, got into terrible difficulties. Although, to be fair, the difficulties were to some extent of their own making."

"How come?"

"Having settled on their route, they were fooled into changing it by a guy who claimed to know an easier and quicker way. You have to appreciate that, back in those days, the country was largely uncharted and the wagon trains were often led by men with little or no experience, either of the terrain or the difficulties it presented. So if someone said they could get you there faster, you listened. Sadly for the Donner party the man they put their trust in didn't know his ass from his elbows. Following his advice the train didn't arrive at the base of the high peaks until the last day of October, instead of the end of September as would have been the case had they stuck to their original route. Normally that wouldn't have been a problem, but in the year of eighteen forty-six the snows arrived earlier than usual and were frighteningly heavy, heavier than anyone could remember. Cutting a long story short, they were trapped. Stuck in drifts up to seventy feet deep. It wasn't until the following spring that the first of several rescue parties was able to reach them, and by then more'n half the group had perished. Those that survived did so at a price. Food supplies exhausted they were forced to sacrifice their livestock; mules, oxen and the like. When that source dried up, cannibalism was the only other option."

"Ugh! God, that's awful..." not knowing quite what to add, his voice tailed off.

"Hobson's choice, Jack. The folks were dead anyway and for those who were still clinging to that remote chance of survival, well...what would you have done?"

"See the point. Different circumstances cough up different reactions but me, in that situation? No way. I'd sooner be one of the unfortunates on the dinner table." He shuddered, "let's move on."

"Apart from the possibility that three of my ancestors were in that party and, if they were, that at least one of them must have survived, there's nothing more to add."

"Go on."

"I said the old homestead was choc-a-bloc with family history if you remember." Continuing in response to the nod. "The downside is that the records at that time were written in either Austrian or German - nobody in our family can speak either of those – and, rubbing it in, it's early nineteenth century text. As you can guess, translation wasn't easy. Finding someone to help took a time but it was worth it in the end. We were able to trace our ancestry all the way back to, Helmut and Anna Steinbeck who left Austria in eighteen forty-two. We know they settled in Boston for a year-or-two before deciding to join the crowd and make the trek to California, but from then on it becomes a bit hazy. The only things we're sure about, is that Anna gave birth to a boy in eighteen forty-five…and that they called him Jeremiah."

"Your great, great, grandfather?"

"The very same. But that's another story. The more interesting anecdote, is when Anna and Helmut took it in their heads to move to California they signed up with the Donner party and their names were on the original roll call…after that though, nothing. That they signed up there is no doubt, but we can't say for certain if they followed it through. Intuition tells me they did, and I'll tell you why. Whether or not his parents survived we'll never know but, Jeremiah, the guy who bankrolled us Steinbecks' further down the line, obviously did. Interestingly he mined his hoards of silver in the mountains of Nevada, the next-door state to California. The way I see it, Helmut and Anna, or whoever fostered the baby if they didn't make it, decided to backtrack to Nevada instead of continuing on to California."

"Could be Jeremiah relocated when he was old enough to make his own mind up. Joined the silver-rush when the news swept down the grapevine."

"True, but I got reservations on that. Nevada was Indian territory back then and folk went there at their peril. As a baby he wouldn't have had the choice, it would have been up to whoever looked after him to make the decision. Oh well, no good banging on about it. Don't suppose we'll ever know the full story."

"Don't want to worry you," Jack broke in, "but there's a stewardess up by the exit: if the look is anything to go by, she can't wait to get rid of us."

Themselves and the apparently patient stewardess apart, the interior of the plane was empty. Engrossed in the comings and goings of Kyle's long-dead relatives, the disappearance of the rest of the passengers had passed them by.

"Reckon she's got good cause," he grimaced. "Come on. Let's go make amends."

CHAPTER TWO

"Live and learn eh, Kyle? There was me thinking the U.S. was all burger bars and skyscrapers and you spring this on me." He squinted against the glare. The judiciously placed hand providing miniscule protection against the blinding rays, he searched for a break in the limitless vista of red sand bordering Highway Ninety Five. Two hours into the drive to Tonopah and there was little change in the landscape to alleviate the monotony of the Nevada wilderness. Dancing heat waves forming pseudo pools of water on the road ahead, he could imagine how a fraudulent oasis would appear before desperate eyes adrift in a sea of sand.

"Not a lot else other than desert in the mid-west, Jack. Desert and mountains."

"And is it always hot like this?"

"Too damn right this time of year. Hottest place in the country's not too far from where we are now...Death Valley, a macabre name but an apt one. Summer temperatures can hit a hundred and thirty on a bad day. Highest temperature recorded was in a part of the valley known as Furnace Creek. Not sure how high it got, but it was bloody hot. Different as a bloke from a broad in winter. Temperatures more often than not below freezing when the weather sets in."

"Here we go." Turning off the main highway onto a sand-covered track to follow a neon sign bearing the news that, 'Arnie's Place' was two miles further on. "Bit out of the way for a bar, eh Jack? But tell you this much. Good old Arnie gets plenty of custom from the regulars on this highway. Folks have tried more respectable looking dives, but they all end up reckoning Arnie's to be the best pit stop this side of Vegas."

Half an hour later, refreshed by ice-cold lemonade and a slice of the best cheesecake Jack Sibley had ever tasted, they reunited their acquaintance with the panorama of lurid red sand. "Soon be there, Jack. Hour at most."

As good as his word, he drove through the entrance to the Steinbeck estate well within his estimate: that it took ten minutes of fast driving before a large, single-storey building came into view seemed neither here nor there.

An attractive, middle-aged woman came running down a flight of wooden steps as Kyle screeched to a grinding halt on the sun-baked gravel. An energetic smile delivering two unmistakeable messages, one of greeting the other warning them she had no intention of letting them escape before she got to them. "What happened to you Kyle, for goodness sake? You've had me so worried. We were expecting you hours since."

"Yeah, sorry, Mom. Should've phoned. Didn't think...you know me. Jack's plane was late arriving and it kind of snowballed from there. Trouble with these Brits', they need lessons in punctuality from us deserving Americans'. By the way Mom, in case you were wondering, this is Jack Sibley. Jack, meet my mother. The best I ever did have. Adding, with a hand to his mouth, "That'll get her off my back. Tell you what I really think when she's not in earshot."

"Take no notice, Jack. He's full of baloney, just like his father. Been a long time coming, but nice to get to meet you at last. I take no truck with Kyle putting the blame on you. Wasn't your fault the plane was late, and don't excuse him not phoning. He'll try all ways to pin the blame on someone else." Leaning forward, she grabbed him by the shoulders and kissed him on the cheek. "More friendly that way. More fun too. Don't get much chance to kiss a handsome young man these days." Without so much as a pause for breath she changed the subject.

"Now you come on in and meet the rest of the folks. Joshua, my husband, and Ben and Luke our other two sons; they've just got back from the office. Then there's Julie - our daughter - she can't wait to meet you. Only finished college at the end of last month and since then she's been under my feet the whole time."

Smiling warmly, she led the way into the house.

It was as if he entered one of the grander, English stately homes. Palatial didn't come into it, and he was only in the entrance hall. Doing his best to quell mounting envy, he was compelled to stand and stare. So this was it. This really was how the other half lived. The height of luxury affordable only on a limitless income.

Granted permission to absorb the elegance, his eyes swept the room. Piercing the shadows through two roof-mounted skylights, the rays of the setting sun synthesised dancing patterns of coloured light on the polished- wood floor. A massive crystal chandelier, surrounded by oak-panelled walls adorned with ancestral portraits, trophies and obtuse relics of a bygone era, jostled with antique furniture to create an elegant yet cosy environment. It was as if the room had been designed for, and subsequently filched from, the set of one of the more lavish American soaps.

Mrs. Steinbeck urging them to move on, his intoxication was brought to an abrupt end. "We've all looked forward so much to meeting you, Jack. Kyle's told us that much about you it's almost as if we know you already. Never stops reminding us about how you took him under your wing, making him feel at home in your country. Not to mention tales of what the two of you got up to." Eyes twinkling she chuckled, "Mind you, guess we were only told as much as he wanted us to hear. There were some things he would've kept quiet about that's for sure."

"It wasn't all one-sided Mrs. Steinbeck. Kyle helped me out often enough, I don't mind telling you."

"That's a nice thing to say, but not sure he deserves it after trying to pass the buck like he did. And it's, Martha, if it pleases you, Jack. Don't contend with a young man calling me Mrs. all along. Makes me feel a durn sight older than I know I am."

Taking him by the arm, she propelled him along what seemed to be an endless corridor. Passing several closed doors along the way before ushering him into a vast expanse at the far end.

"Here we are. Come and say hello to the family."

Josh Steinbeck, in every respect an older edition of Kyle was the first to be introduced. Well over six feet tall, he was blessed with the same aquiline nose, an identical mop of jet-black hair - albeit greying around the ears - and the same, humour-laden eyes that were part and parcel of his offspring. "Hi Jack," he bellowed, pre-empting what his wife was about to say. "I'm Josh and everyone calls me as such. Apart from them as calls me other things when they think I'm not listening." Mauling his hand between two of his own as he spoke. "You're more welcome than I can lay claim to, and while here this home is as much your home as it is ours'. As for this lot," waving an arm to identify the lot he referred to, "they're chomping at the bit to meet you." Catching the icy glare spelling out, 'oh don't mind me but you're in dead trouble when I get you on your own', he was quick to make amends. "Gee, sorry Martha, got carried away there. Durned rude of me. Sure not my intent taking it from your hands like that. You carry on with Jack and take my apology as coming from an ignorant old sourpuss."

"No, it's alright Josh. You've made your amends and it's under the bridge." Her peeved expression replaced by the delightful smile that preceded it. "You'll get used to my husband, Jack. He's a lovely man, but impetuous to a fault. How d'you reckon then, Josh? Is that me being fair to you, you daft old codger?" Her other half nodding in sheepish agreement, the smile broadened into a mischievous grin.

"Take no notice of us, Jack. Me and Martha been together so long we sometimes forget the other one's there. Ain't no animosity intended, mark you. Just our funny way of showing how much we care. Anyways, this is Ben and his wife, Emily. This here other reprobate is our middle son, Luke."

"Rebecca - my wife - was hoping to be here to meet you, Jack, but we had an unexpected diversion. Deciding she wasn't going to wait any longer, Becky took to delivering a baby boy instead. Baffles me why women get so impatient. Weren't due for another three weeks yet. Had to promise I'd drag you along to meet the perisher sometime tomorrow. Say hello to the little guy too while you're at it."

"Well I, er…many congratulations." Caught unawares, he struggled for the right thing to say. Why the heck didn't Kyle warn him? At least he wouldn't have been caught on the hop like this. In an attempt to turn the conversation he homed in on Luke's light-hearted opening. "I'd like that, and I promise to try and keep quiet about what you said. You never know, she might get ideas and think you meant it." Joining in the laughter, he asked, "This your first? And does he have a name?"

"Don't know so much about first, could be the last if you don't keep your mouth shut. But as to the name? There you've got me nailed up against the wall. Right now it's a taboo subject, not to be mentioned until...well, let's just say there's a touch of husband - wife contention on that score. Know what I mean? Rebecca'll get her way in the end of course. It's what women do. But I'll grin and bear it, just like us husbands have always done since marriage became popular. It's a wicked spell they weave. Make you think their idea is the one you came up with in the first place. We men fall for it every time."

"Where's Julie?" Martha intervened, "She was hopping around earlier waiting for Kyle to come back. Now she's disappeared."

"Here Mom," the reply coming from a door on the far side of the room. "I was in the bathroom. Didn't know Kyle was back yet."

Turning towards the voice, he caught his breath. The girl who stood smiling in the doorway was stunning. More than that...she was beautiful. He knew Kyle had a younger sister, he'd shown him a photograph. Back then it was the picture of a young girl with close-cropped hair, refusing to smile and wearing a typical school gymslip. What a difference a few years can make.

He watched her as she walked across the room. Five-feet seven-or-so, slim, lissom, hips swaying gently as she moved towards him. Neatly turned-up nose balanced precariously above slightly sensuous lips, raven black hair hanging to her shoulders...she was gorgeous. It was in the eyes however that lay her true beauty. Of a deep, sparkling blue they radiated humour with a hint of mockery. Not a cynical or vindictive mockery, a warm and playful mockery. He was smitten. If the sight of Julie didn't exactly cause his heart to stop beating, it was responsible for many a tingling sensation in other parts of his body.

She didn't wait to be introduced. In her eyes it would be a complete waste of time. She knew who he was. There was no chance of him being anybody else. So why bother with the formalities?

"Hello Jack. I'm Julie, and to say I'm very pleased to meet you doesn't come anywhere near. Kyle keeps trying to convince me you're quite some guy, and I'm looking forward to finding out if he's been telling me straight." Adding with a teasing lilt as she held out her hand, "Don't believe everything he tells me, but got the feeling he might have got it right this time."

The softness of her touch sending messages up his arm, he replied in a voice that sounded as though it wanted nothing at all to do with him. "Wouldn't bank on it if I were you. Kyle's propensity for exaggeration knows no bounds. Kept you under wraps though. Didn't let-on he had such a lovely sister." Mentally, he kicked himself. What a stupid thing to say. Should've stuck with 'pleased to meet you'. Prudent...safer.

"Oh boy! Keep saying things like that and I can see you and me getting along real swell." Eyes inviting him to languish in their depths, she grinned wickedly. "Although reckon it might not be a bad idea to get your sight tested."

"Break it up Julie." Kyle interrupted. "Put Jack down and let the poor guy sort himself out. Nattie's joining us for dinner and I'm hamstrung with picking her up."

"Who's Nutty?"

"Nattie, Jack. Not Nutty. Oh that's priceless. Nutty," she couldn't stop laughing, "I'll have to tell her, she'll love it…she really will. Nattie, Jack, short for Natalie. Mind you, she must be nutty to be dating Kyle. Nattie, Nutty, whatever you like to call her, is his latest forever love. At least she is this week. Maybe next week. Who knows? Up till a short while ago it was Sue, before that it was Joanna and the …" breaking off as Kyle grabbed her round the neck.

"Listen, younger than me sister, it's a guy's duty to keep as many women as he can contented: on the grounds that it's better to keep as many as possible happy rather than make one miserable. And anyway, finding Miss Right ain't easy…a fellah has to be sure. Come on Jack," he stuttered, releasing Julie from his grip, "let's go get you settled."

He couldn't help but notice the cloud that dimmed his friend's eyes when Julie was going through his list of girlfriends, past and present. It was momentary and he dismissed it as imagination. It had been a long day. That probably had something to do with it.

Kyle leading the way, they ploughed their way back along the central passageway towards the front of the bungalow. Throwing a door open at about the halfway mark, he held it wide for his friend to enter.

"Here we are, Jack. Hope you approve."

"This the best you can do? He answered. Eyes sweeping the room as he spoke. Doing his damnedest to take it all in: king-size double bed, two enormous wardrobes, writing desk, bookcase filled with books…it had everything. "Puts my exotic twelve-by-twelve back home somewhat in the shade, but supposed I'll get used to it. Shame about that bloody great window with the panoramic view though, and that door…bathroom? I don't know, Kyle…I really don't know!"

"Do I gather you like it?"

"Yes, you could say that. But it would be one hell of an under-statement."

"Best room in the house in my opinion. I'm very fond of the old homestead but it can be a bit dark and gloomy in parts, most parts to tell the truth; you will have seen that for yourself. Keep on at Pop about fitting more picture windows like this one, but got nowhere as yet. Understand why of course. There's a strong possibility that the family history tied up in this place will be lost forever if we take it too far." Changing the subject he mused, "You and Julie seemed to hit it off ok."

"Hope so. She took me by surprise if I'm honest enough to admit it, but she soon put me at my ease. Might've have warned me though, you bastard. Said you had a sister, but didn't tell me she was absolutely gorgeous."

"Why would I? Guy's don't look at their sisters the same way other men do. Besides, she'd have been what? Fifteen...going on sixteen? Nothing but pigtails, braces and schoolbooks back then. Doubt you would've been much interested."

"Mm! I'll give you the benefit of the doubt. As long you don't have any more surprises to throw at me."

"Who knows? Haven't got any more sisters if that's what you're thinking, but can't guarantee nothing else will surface from the depths of my fallible memory. Sounds like you could be keen on Sis. Want me to put in a word?"

"Not on your life and, before you get any more carried away, I am not keen on your sister." He paused for a moment, shrugging his shoulders before admitting, "But I could get to be given the tuniopperty."

"Ah, the sweet smell of romance. I love it. Anyway," shooting a quick glance at his watch, "time I made a move. Running late as it is and don't want Natalie thinking I've dumped her. You get on with your unpacking, give you a shout when I get back."

Weary from travelling, he spent more time in the shower than intended and was still dressing when, following a peremptory knock, Kyle thrust his way into the room.

"All set, Jack? Chow's ready."

On the way through to the dining room, he thought it was time he showed an interest in Kyle's two brothers. Since meeting Julie, he had somewhat ignored the rest of the family.

"Ben and Luke, they live here?"

"Jeeze, no. The place is big enough but don't reckon the womenfolk would appreciate having their in-laws' breathing down their necks day in, day out. Both got their own places on the edge of town. Ah here she is. Natalie…feast your lovely eyes on Jack. One of my more dubious acquaintances."

"Pleased to meet you, Jack," struggling to keep a straight face, she failed miserably. "Julie, tells me you think I'm nuts. Well I'm gonna let you in on a little secret I don't share with everyone...you're right. Nutty as a fruit cake...don't deny it. But you might've at least have waited till you got to know me before spreading the word." Sensing his embarrassment, she was quick to make amends. "Joking, Jack...honest. You want to call me Nutty then you go right ahead. I won't mind a bit. It's a lot nicer than some other names I've been called."

"Here you are, Jack," Martha said, grabbing him by the arm, "I've put you between Em and Julie. It's not my intent for Kyle to have you all to himself, and there'd be something the matter if you didn't sooner sit between two pretty young ladies."

On the receiving end of a big, broad wink accompanied by an equally big, broad and stupid grin he couldn't help wondering. Was it all Martha's idea, or did Kyle have something to do with the seating arrangements? He wouldn't rule it out.

Towards the end of the meal Julie leaned close, asking, "You going to see Becky and the baby tomorrow, Jack?"

"Think so, but know if anything's been arranged."

"Well, Em and me are planning to visit tomorrow afternoon. Why not come along with us?"

"If it's no trouble and you can put up with me, then thank you very much. Kyle hasn't said anything but I suppose I'd better make sure first... apart from that, you're on."

A long and exhausting day continuing well past midnight, sleep turned out to be a tardy companion. The interest and excitement of the past twenty-four hours intent on ensuring that his mind stayed alert, it came as no surprise. The family as a whole; the way they'd bent over backwards to make him feel at home. Everyone. Martha, Josh, the two brothers, Julie...especially Julie. She was great, and not just to look at. Bright, intelligent and with a warm outlook on life in general, she was uncannily like her youngest brother. There was no doubting that the family as a whole were close knit but those two seemed to share a special bond. His mind moved on, wanting to embrace more of the fun and laughter of an evening spent in aimless chitchat but his body had other ideas. In unwilling surrender to the inevitable his eyes closed but the smile on his face stayed where it was.

At her invitation, they lunched with Emily before setting off for the hospital the next day. For him it was a new experience. He'd never been much into babies, but he need not have worried. Rebecca went out of her way to make sure he didn't feel out of it, even cajoling him into holding the baby for a few minutes. Saying it might give him the yen for some of his own one day. Partly to his horror, but mostly to his pleasure, he was forced to admit she had a point.

"Any idea when you and Kyle are heading off, Jack?" Having dropped Emily off, they were on their way back from the hospital.

"Wednesday, last I heard. But you know what Kyle is like for changing his mind."

"That's ok then. How d'you feel about a trip to Las Vegas on Monday? Less than two-hours by train, so hardly a distance."

"You serious? Las Vegas? You mean...you and me?"

"Course I mean you and me," she said, laughing. "Wouldn't send you off on your own. We seem to get on all right, and it'll be down to us if we don't enjoy ourselves. Been there once, a long time ago when I was in first grade. Too young to take it all in then, so it'd be good to go back again. See what it's like now I'm old enough to appreciate it. I'll check with Kyle...if you're game, that is?"

"Oh I'm game alright. I can't believe it. All of a sudden Monday seems a long way away."

By the time they returned to the ranch, there was just enough time for a hasty shower before dinner. Having barely settled in his seat, Josh called to him from the far end of the table.

"Tomorrow, being Sunday, Jack, it's usual for us to attend the eleven o'clock service. You'll know by now you'd be more'n welcome if you'd care to join us. But we all have our own ideas when it comes to religion, and no one here would hold it against you if attending church isn't in your way of things."

The question, to all but one of those seated at the table that night, was simple and straightforward. For Jack Sibley, it raised nightmare memories fuelled by a tortuous past. Mind in turmoil he sought an answer, but his brain had dropped into in limbo. Bloodless knuckles camouflaged against the pristine white cloth, ten strained fingers gripping the edge of the table for support and face blanched to a deathly pale, he strove to bring his emotions under control.

Aware of the entire table looking at him, he struggled to speak. He wanted to accept...no, it was more than that. He had to accept. It was the chance he craved for. An opportunity to lay his demons to rest for good and all...more than that: he wouldn't be asked to face them on his own. Words forming a battalion somewhere in the deep recesses at the back of his throat he opened his mouth to reply, the promised invasion halted by a mouth devoid of moisture and the tremor of parched lips.

Help arrived from an unexpected source...Julie. She didn't know why, that wasn't important. It was the state he'd got himself into that was concerning, an anxiety that threatened to boil over at any minute.

"It's ok Jack, calm down," covering his hand with one of her own. "Take your time. There's no rush if you've a problem with this."

Her touch and the whispered message delivering him from his stupor, he wiped the glistening beads of sweat from his forehead before bursting forth his reply.

"Thank you, Josh. Yes please. I'd like to join you...very much "

"Ok Jack, that's swell." In total disregard of his odd behaviour, he gave him an encouraging smile. "It'll be just fine having you along."

Flinging an arm round his shoulders, Kyle collared him as the party broke up. "Out with it! What in the name of all that's crazy was that about? Looked like you were on course for a heart attack, about to throw a fit and have a stroke: all together and at the same time."

"He's right, Jack. Kyle was facing you, so he would know more than me how upset you were...and I got enough of an idea." Julie butted in "You shaking all over like that...it was horrible. And it wasn't just us, everyone else were hit the same way." Raising a watery smile, it was more a demand than a request. "We want to know, Jack. What was it got at you?"

"A stupid over-reaction to something somebody once said, that's all it was. I behaved like an idiot, and I'm sorry. It won't happen again." Managing to return the smile he whispered, "Thanks, Julie. If it hadn't been for you your father would still be waiting for an answer."

Although whispered, the words failed to escape Kyle's ears, "Why, what did she…"

"Don't bother with it, Kyle. I had a quiet word; that's all there was to it." Turning to face Jack, she demanded. "But if you think you're going to get away telling us a whole heap of next to nothing, you can think again." Bolstered by an encouraging smile she implored, "Come on, Jack. You can't leave us high and dry like this."

"There's nothing more to add..." He paused, undecided if he should pursue what was going through his mind. Concluding the choice wasn't his to make, he carried on in muted tones. "I'm worried that there could be a follow-up in church tomorrow. Don't ask what or how, I've no idea...and please don't ask why. And, anyway, there's more than a good chance that nothing *will* happen. Without going into detail I got involved with the wrong crowd. When I came to my senses and decided to ditch them it was too late. The damage was done. My leaving their company upset a few nasty-minded people who weren't prepared to let matters lie without creating a stink. Words were said, dire retribution promised...the cause of my over-reaction. But that's all you're getting. For deep, personal reasons I can't tell you any more than that. Perhaps one day. But not now."

"What they get up to...this crowd?" Kyle asked.

"Oh it was nothing illegal, if that's what you're thinking. Not in the true sense of the word. Although some of their practices came pretty close. You'll no doubt have a good laugh at my expense, but your father's invitation reawakened dire memories; memories I hoped to one day deal with on my own: no one around to suffer the consequences of my indiscretion. Now, please, can we leave it at that? All I ask is you trust me, and understand my reticence is not without good cause."

"But I don't get it!" Kyle blustered, "What the heck has going to church got to do with anything? You can tell us that much."

"If I do, I want your promise there'll be no more bullying. No more trying to squeeze anything else out of me. Understood?"

On the receiving end of a reluctant nod from Julie, his reply was equally reluctant. "Don't go much on what you're saying, but if it's what you want? Ok. You have our word."

"It was while we were at Cambridge. You were in training for the university boat race and I was going through a rough time. Remember?"

"As if I could forget. Kept asking what was wrong, but you wouldn't say. All I ever got was, 'give it a couple of days'. Your couple of days went on for weeks."

"What else could I say? There was nothing physically wrong with me. It was all in the mind. Mentally persecuted by sinister threats and, what I believed at the time, the inevitability of those threats coming to fruition."

"But that was a long time ago...good couple of years. Don't mean to tell me you've been going through it all that time."

"Time doesn't come into it. It's a life sentence. Threatened on the one hand, cursed on the other. Both promising vengeance should I ever again enter a house of God."

"Oh do me a favour, Jack. Tell me you don't believe in all that rubbish. It's fairybook stuff. The sort of thing kids are frightened by. Not educated grown-ups."

"If you knew why and by whom the curse was laid you might think differently, and If things go pear-shaped tomorrow? I may well take you up on that."

CHAPTER THREE

Reluctantly dragging himself back to the land of the living he lay dormant for some time. Plagued by uncertainty, morbidity and a mind running the tortuous mill of imagination, the hours of darkness were spent in semi-stupor. But now, the long night over, dawn promised blessed relief. The day ahead would have a massive impact on his life: confirming or refuting his anxieties. Whatever the outcome he wasn't sure he cared. At least he would know.

As Kyle had pointed out, it was something like two years and, self-satisfaction apart, what would be the point after all this time? The manic vicar and his puerile threats didn't worry him unduly, but the other lot were a different kettle of fish. He knew from first-hand experience what they were capable of. He was also aware that the hierarchy had long memories and his salvation, if it should come to that, hinged on whether or not they could be bothered. At the time he would have been considered small fry in their eyes but vengeance is paramount when damaged egos are on the line, and if vanity was to be preserved? He was cognisant of the risk in calling their bluff but he had no choice. It had to be faced sooner or later. For personal satisfaction if nothing else. He had bowed to their persecution long enough, now was the time for him to have his say. The prospects might be less than fifty-fifty but he wasn't going to let that interfere with his determination. As he had told the others' the previous evening, a curse isn't rendered impotent by the passage of time. What he didn't add, was that it could be lifted if the perpetrator had a mind to...that would have been tempting providence beyond realistic boundaries. Until yesterday evening he'd been content to let matters ride. He wasn't an avid churchgoer so why take the risk? But for all his dithering he knew it couldn't be allowed to carry on ad-infinitum. There would come the day when he would be forced to challenge the restrictions placed upon him, and Josh's invitation had heralded the dawning of that day. It was the incentive he craved, the chance to lay his gremlins to rest for good and all. Although not religious in the accepted sense of the word he did believe in God, and, as a consequence, the effect of the ban on his future life was a constant worry. A church marriage would be out of the question, as would be the christening of any subsequent offspring. In the final reckoning, a funeral in accordance with his faith would be forfeited.

Having ditched the Satanists', he had sought the aid of an Anglican vicar. To seek forgiveness for his sins, to request sanctuary should it be necessary. He couldn't have made a worse move. Instead of the expected compassion, he was ravaged with cold and invidious threats. Warning him that, if he ever again entered a Christian church he would incur the full wrath of God. In hindsight he should have sought a second opinion. At the time he became so depressed he lost the will to try.

If the effect on his morale was devastating, there was worse still to come. The visit of Willoughby Trench, the high almighty of the group with whom he had become entangled. An evil omnipotent who used his considerable power for the furtherance of his own ends. Anyone who crossed swords with Willoughby Trench, intentionally or otherwise, would live to rue the day. Nothing had ever been laid at his door, but rumours of his involvement in one or two unexplained 'accidents' were rife. Rendering the old adage that smoke cannot exist without fire never closer to the truth.

Sneering as he laid the curse, Trench had added the words that would remain with him until his dying day. "It is sad you felt it necessary to depart our circle. Our lord and master does not accept rejection, and he will neither condone nor forget your abandonment. I have ruined your life by forbidding further association with the religion of your choice, an apt penalty to recom-pense those of our leaning for your disloyalty. But be not complacent, Sibley. You may consider you are being let off lightly, my leniency to be an indication of weakness." At this point Willoughby Trench had smiled, a smile beyond endurance. A sickeningly grotesque, evil parting of the lips as he informed him that a more awesome vengeance may yet be his lot.

For many weeks following Trench's visit he suffered trauma beyond measure. An unexpected sound, sinister shadow or sudden movement would cause him to shake uncontrollably, especially when out at night and the path poorly lit. A passing stranger, a vehicle moving slowly along the road he trod, a cloud temporarily blotting out the moon: the most innocent of events were imagined harbingers of evil. Terrifying nightmares were a constant companion and of such realism that fearful screams would disturb his flatmate, who would put a temporary end to his misery by shaking him into wakefulness. Not that Kyle ever complained, there was never so much as a hint that he objected to doing what he considered to be his duty. He knew - thought he knew - the dreams would come to an end eventually but, as time passed and the nightmares continued, he came to appreciate the flaw in his supposition. There was no hint of his friend's troubles ending and, worryingly, it was becoming more and more apparent that his physical state was going downhill at a rate of knots. In training for the annual university boat race, Kyle was caught between the two demands. Having to spend a considerable time at the sculls, wanting to spend more time attending his friend's needs.

Unbeknown to the American, his concerns were reciprocated. He appreciated Kyle had problems of his own, and he had no wish to burden him with his problems. It was his responsibility to sort himself out. It would be unfair to expect others' to do it for him…even if they were able to. He'd spent many a solemn hour racking his brains, trying to come to terms with his suffering, seeking escape from the imprisoned fear. He knew what had to be done, it was the only credible solution. In reality he'd known it from the very first moment Willoughby Trench entered his room, but reconciliation had been a long time coming. Now, having suppressed for too long the only available avenue of escape, he took the proverbial bull by the horns. Trench and his crowd were not going to go away, so he'd put himself where they couldn't reach him.

Thankfully the presumed necessity was rendered null and void by help from an unexpected source. It arrived in the form of, Angela Lomas, whom he had known since they'd lived in the same street and attended the same school. Now studying medicine at a London college, and by coincidence attending a seminar in Cambridge, she made use of the opportunity to unearth her lifelong friend. Her reaction, at the sight of the pathetic creature who opened the door, was that to be expected by someone who had known him as a fun loving young man full of life and dismissive of its trials and vicissitudes.

Her compassion at the sight of the dismal shadow of the Jack Sibley she had known and admired for most of her life instigated a complete breakdown. Sobbing his heart out, he related in full the causes of his parlous condition. An arm about his shoulder, Angela listened in silence until he'd finished.

It being obvious that her friend and former playmate was desperately in need of expertise beyond her ability, she contacted a Professor Lumberge: the chair of psychiatry and psychoanalysis at her university. She could not have taken a more effective measure. Within an unbelievably short passage of time, and without charging a penny for his services, the professor achieved a near complete cure of his patient. When the subject of a fee was brought up, the professor claimed his terms were met by the opportunity to research a unique case. Deep down he'd nursed his own ideas. Despite her strenuous denials, he was convinced Angela had made known his financial limitations to the professor. He'd never know for sure, but he hoped Lumberge had been honest with his assessment.

That was in the past, relegated to the archives of his mind. Left to gather dust in the vaults of lost memories...until yesterday. Now was the time of reckoning. Professor Lumberge had stressed that a curse, any curse, relied on autosuggestion and the fallibility of the human function for success. A self-imposed fantasy designed to wreak fear and subjugation within a fragile neurological system. Back then, presumably because he desperately wanted to believe, he'd gone along with him. Now the time had come to put his theories to the test, however, it was a different matter. He'd seen for himself the awesome power people of Willoughby Trench's calibre had at their disposal. They hadn't the need for autosuggestion and their damaging of peoples lives was no fantasy...it happened. The bottom line was that the curse could still be very much alive. But would the curse of a Satanist hold sway in God's abode? That was a new twist. One he hadn't thought of before.

A loud hammering bringing his musing to a halt, he grabbed his dressing gown and flung the door open.

"Morning Jack." The greeting sounding more cheerful than their expressions implied.

"You ok?" Kyle asked, voice tentative. "You know. After last night."

"Fine thanks. But please, can we forget last night? Its bad enough thinking about it, without having it constantly rammed down my throat. I lost control. No big deal. It happens…Ok?"

"Yeah, well! You weren't looking at you. We were."

"That was last night. This morning I'm a changed man, so please stop reading more into what happened than it merits. But that's not why you're here, is it? Have I changed my mind about going to church? That's what you're wanting to know, and my answer is the same now as it was then. You don't get rid of me that easily."

"That's good, Jack," Julie observed, "but whatever you say, it won't put an end to our reservations."

"We walk there as a rule, Jack," Josh informed him as they left the house. "About a mile-and-a-half across the fields. You ok with that?"

"Fine. Can do with the exercise, and it's a lovely morning for it."

Electing to sit near the back he felt rather like the filling in a well stocked sandwich might feel as his two companions sat, one on either side. Inwardly he smiled. Their fussing making it patently obvious it was prearranged. That they were leaving nothing to chance.

The service started with a hymn, 'Rock of Ages'. One of his favourites, he was happy with that. So far so good. He'd made it over the threshold, which was encouraging. If it was going to happen, it would have happened the moment he entered the building...the only way it would make sense. But then again the bastards could drag it out, drive him insane with worry and indecision.

Joining in the Lord's Prayer, he muttered the familiar words in subdued tones. That was odd. It was the line about forgiving his trespasses, a slight tremor sent shivers up his spine. It was cool in the church...that had to be it.

Growing optimism encouraged relaxation. The vicar was about to read his sermon, a sure sign the end of the service wasn't too far off. For a change he found what the vicar had to say interesting. Based on the values of family life and well delivered, it carried a wealth of meaning and understanding. For those few short minutes he was in a world of his own. Embraced by a sweeping euphoria, long-standing fears fast slipping away.

Sermon over, the vicar invited the congregation to pray for their loved ones', for those who suffered and to seek forgiveness for their sins. Before sinking to his knees, he took a quick peek at the order of service. One more hymn...that was it: the end of his jitters. The curse was nothing more than a spiteful con, and to have let it get under his skin like that...how could he have been so gullible? Professor Lumberge had been right all along. He'd invited it in. The fear was all in his mind.

Not long into the prayer he knew something was wrong. His voice blurred and his head started to throb. It was as if a soft-note guitar string was being plucked somewhere inside. He was cold, an icy clamminess that had nothing to do with the ambient temperature. Ugly doubts ringing alarm bells, he tried to will his mind to concentrate on what he wanted to say. To convey meaning to his words as he openly admitted his association with the Devil. It was only by making such admission that he could expect forgiveness.

It was mild curiosity that first drew their attention, to the twitching fingers drumming on the wooden backboard of the pew in front. An odd mannerism; nothing to worry about. That was the opening thought to cross the minds of his fostered guardians'. But all was to change. Frenetic glances across the back of the man kneeling between them signalled spiralling concern. Accompanied by a simpering, gasping moan, the irritable fingers metamorphosed into balled fists that threatened to split asunder the timber they assaulted. A prelude to his body convulsing in violent spasm, the low-pitched sounds were brutally nullified by piercing screams of agony.

To them, and to those members of the congregation who turned their heads in response to the commotion, he was throwing a massive fit. Delivered from a mouth foaming at the lips, heartrending cries echoed through the church; a plea for mercy from a soul in torment. In a vain attempt to rise to his feet, he was made to collapse in a heap by legs that refused to comply. Head clamped within shaking hands he lay writhing on the cold, unforgiving stone floor as he strove to exorcise the demons that embattled his lacerated mind. Oblivious of his friends and their attempts to comfort him, his condition deteriorated at an alarming rate. Impassioned sounds climaxing in a crescendo of verbal agony, he flayed his body in the confined space between the pews. A final, searing shriek of anguish...hushed into deathly silence. His suffering brought to an end in the welcoming arms of a deep coma.

"Give me a hand, Julie," Kyle barked, ignoring the intrusive stares flung in their direction, "let's get him outside." Struggling to lift the dead weight of Jack's prone body over his shoulder as he spoke. "Yeah, thanks, Pop," the rest of the family arriving en-masse to lend assistance. Mumbling a muted apology, they carried the comatose man out into the fresh air.

"Do what you can for him, Julie. I'll phone Dr. Krantz."

As the girl struggled to pull his dead-weight into the recovery position, Jack stirred. Eyelids partly raised, he lifted his head a few inches. Blinking in the strong sunlight, the tremor in his voice conveying confusion he whispered. "What's going on? Where am I?"

"It's ok, Jack. You had a nasty turn. Kyle's getting a doctor."

"Nothing a doctor can do." Memories flooding back, his muffled tones were barely audible. "Give me a few minutes, I'll be fine."

"If you're gonna say something, then say something sensible," she bent over him, her face a mixture of concern and relief. "otherwise you can keep quiet. You can't see yourself which is just as well, take my word for it...it's not a pretty sight. Death warmed up would have more life in it. And that don't include you shaking like a dervish, and your face all puffy from the punishment you gave it. We're not taking anything for granted, Jack." Leaning forward, she kissed him on the forehead. "Like it or not, you're going to have the doc give you the once-over." Voice softening, she added, "Haven't known you long, and I'd like the chance to get to know you better."

"My Dad used to say women will always have the last word, and seems he was right." His voice carrying more weight, the convulsions showing signs of easing off. "And I had nothing to do with my looks, they were part of the package when I was born."

"Cut the wise cracks, and behave yourself until Dr. Krantz has given you the once-over…and I'm *not* joking." Trying hard to constrain the smile hovering on her lips. Whatever else, the guy had guts.

"Aw come on, Julie. At least let me have a go at getting to my feet. This ground's hard enough to crack eggs, and it could be ages before your medicine man gets here."

"Medicine woman, Jack." Kyle corrected, giving him a helping hand. "Great lady. You'll like her. Knows her stuff and easy to talk to."

"What you said last night…was this it?"

"If it wasn't, then God knows…" He broke off. The priest nearby talking to Martha giving food for thought. "Excuse me, Julie. I'd like a quick word with your vicar before he disappears."

"Sorry to intrude." Shooting Martha an apologetic look, "But can I have a word with you, Father, not now…later. When you're free. There's a doctor on the way to check me out, but when she's finished?" Aware his voice was quaking, he coughed into his hand before continuing. "If you can spare the time."

"It'll be my pleasure...Jack, isn't it? I'm not going anywhere" He turned his head, glancing over his shoulder at the sound of a car engine. "Looks like your doctor's arrived. Come searching for me when you're ready. I won't be far away."

"Isobel!" Josh greeted the portly, grey-haired woman who stepped from the car. "You got a move on."

"Didn't dare not to, Josh. Kyle gave strict instructions, I wasn't to hang around. It was desperate he said, so did as I was told and got here as fast as I could."

"And it's appreciated. It was urgent at the time but things have calmed down to some extent. Anyway here he is, the one who caused all the trouble." Accompanying his words with the wave of a hand in the culprit's direction. "Took real bad and got us worried; had us thinking all sorts of things. Isobel Krantz, Jack. If anyone can sort you out, she's the lady to do it."

"Kyle was in a right panic on the phone, Jack. According to him you were on the way out. Yet here you are, on your feet and looking not so bad. Pale and some nasty-looking bruises, but nothing like he led me to believe. Best to make sure of course...goes without saying. Never know what's round the corner." A serious expression lightened by sparkling eyes, she proposed, "Let's go sit on that wall over there, away from the crowd so we can chat in peace. Give me a rundown and see if we can make sense of what happened."

"You've got me puzzled young man, and that's a fact." packing her stethoscope back in its case, peering at her patient beneath raised eyebrows. "I'll give you something for the headache, but I want you to promise to call me should you start vomiting, come over feeling dizzy or react to bright lights. Any of those could be a sign of something bad going on." Shaking her head from side to side she pierced him with startlingly blue eyes. "I would also suggest you refrain from using your cranium to batter holes in blocks of wood and stone in future, it wasn't designed for such practices. That apart I can find nothing wrong. Heart's beating like a good-un, blood pressure's up but not surprising in the circumstances. Pulse not much above normal, breathing up to scratch, and you can see straight. Could take blood and urine tests, but doubt they'd tell me anything we don't know already." She looked at him, suspicion reflected in her eyes. "You've told me everything, Jack? Known Kyle long enough to know he's not prone to panic, yet according to him you were at deaths door. Now here we are, less than an hour on, and you're as fit as the proverbial fiddle. And that includes the strings." She hesitated, eyeing him through the thick lenses of her spectacles. "Things don't come and go like that. Not in my experience. Only right and proper you tell me all. So come clean, Jack. Is there any little snippet you forgot to mention or maybe didn't think it was worth bringing up. Something," her eyes twinkled "you might have omitted because you, oh I don't know, find it embarrassing, hard to accept or makes you feel awkward for some reason. It's important I know the full works, Jack."

He had no choice, economical with the truth or the psychiatrists couch. Didn't really matter either way, nothing he said would help her diagnosis…not in the medical sense. "Not as far as I know. Felt fine when I got up this morning. Had breakfast, pleasant walk to the church. No problem with any of that. It wasn't until towards the end of the service that everything started to go haywire. Head started buzzing and I came over feeling dizzy...the rest you know."

"Mm," making it obvious she was far from convinced she said, "if you're sure. Don't like leaving things half-done, but not much else I can do. You see, Jack, I do worry there could be a recurrence and next time deaths door might be left on the jar. So I want you to promise me, should your memory improve and you are reminded of something you should have added you will let me know." Her mouth creased warmly, matching the twinkle in her eyes. "Now I think it's time the folks' were told of your miraculous recovery."

Refusing to listen to Jack's assurances, that he was capable of walking back, Kyle was adamant. It wasn't worth the risk. He'd jog back to the house and fetch a car. "Won't take ten minutes. Julie's going to look after you while I'm gone," a wide grin assisting the dangled the carrot, "and if the look on your face is anything to go by you're not gonna argue!"

"If you're still with Father O'haloran when Kyle gets back I'll head off home, Jack. No, it's ok," shaking her head, "I can guess what it's about and won't press. I made you a promise, and I don't break promises." An impish expression highlighting the twinkle in her eyes she purred, "Not if I can help it."

The priest listened to him intently, and with a compassion sadly missing on his previous encounter with a minister of the church. Had it been this man instead of the self-righteous bigot of his first approach, he wouldn't be in the state he was in now. Pent up emotions released by an understanding ear, the words tumbled from his quivering lips in torrents. A sense of freedom welling up inside him, he held nothing back. His involvement with the Satanists, the horror of the black mass, the ongoing trauma of the aftermath. Nothing was omitted.

"Your honesty does you credit, Jack...what you went through! I find it quite frightening. To be told that our fellow man is capable of sinking to such depths, to tolerate such blasphemy, is beyond belief. A credulity that has been shattered by your own, fearful testimony. But such fortitude...to cope in the face of the terrible events you've described? For that alone you deserve all the help of which I'm capable." Taking hold of one of his hands he stressed. "I have however to be honest with you. Having never yet come into direct contact with the occult, I admit to being somewhat out of my depth. That said, I'm ready and willing to do what I can to help. You ok with that? Or would you rather not pin your trust in a bungling amateur?"

"Sooner a willing amateur than a half-hearted professional." he replied. "I said how much I owe to Angela and Professor Lumberge. Had it not been for them I wouldn't be here now. But, as in all walks of life, they were limited by the bounds of their expertise. They could cure me mentally, but that was as far as it went. Neither could bring themselves to accept the reality of my condition, both convinced that my problems were all in the mind. A compilation of imagination induced by integrated fear. They were insistent to the point that I began to have doubts myself. I started to question the validity of what I'd experienced, what I'd seen with my own eyes...or thought I had. What if it had been nothing but imagination, the recollection of bad dreams...nothing more sinister than that? Any lingering doubts I might have had were removed by this mornings shenanigans. They were not imagined, I didn't dream what happened to me; it was no inexplicable, uninvited fantasy...you saw that for yourself." He broke off, a moments hesitation to gather his thoughts. "Although it was meant with the best will in the world, Angela and the Professor did their utmost to persuade me that I suffered delusions. I don't hold that against them...no way. They did what they were capable of, and I can't thank them enough. They did a tremendous job putting me back on the right track, and for that I'll always be thankful. That neither could bring themselves to admit the underlying cause of my condition was hardly to be wondered at. It isn't every day of the week that one comes up against occult forces. You, on the other hand, have not dismissed what I've said as the ravings of a lunatic, and I can't tell you how much that means. It has given me hope, a tool to shed the despair of isolation: the loneliness that has been a constant companion. Does that make sense?"

"Absolute sense. We all, each and every one of us, depend on the assistance of others in our passage through life but, sadly, such help is often in short supply. Fortunately for you, that was not the case with your friend and the psychiatrist. They did what they could to the best of their ability, which, with the help of the almighty, is all I can do."

"I don't want to put you to a lot of trouble."

"No trouble Jack. Good for the soul to try something different, and this is as different as it's likely to get. Never had the opportunity to take on the Devil and his works until now, and I can't wait to get going. But apart from that, my job description includes making myself available to a repenting soul in distress, and after thirty-two years in the business this is the first time that part has become relevant."

Returning Sibley's laugh with a wide grin he leaned forward, piercing him with darkly penetrating eyes. "Answer me this young man. What makes you believe it was the wrath of God that caused your suffering?"

"I didn't. Not at first. But had it been the curse it would surely have triggered the instant I entered the church, not waited until almost the final whistle. And besides that, am I wrong in believing that the work of a disciple of the Devil wouldn't hold sway within a Christian sanctury?"

"No, you're not wrong. But let me tell you what I think. To start with, let us take a look at the vicar of your previous acquaintance. A minister of the church unfit for purpose, a man reliant on fear to gain respect. Do you honestly think the Holy Father would listen to the ravings of such a tyrant? Our God is not a vengeful God, quite the contrary. He would never have condoned such infamy. On the other hand, although you are right in thinking that the work of a Satanist cannot penetrate a holy sanctum, it can be invited in by an unfortunate carrier."

The words took a while to sink in. When they did, his reaction was in accord with expectation. "You mean, me," he whispered. I carried the curse into the church." The pent-up expression exposing his inner anguish, he blurted. "Oh God! What have I done?"

"Take it easy, Jack. You weren't to know, and there's no harm done. It was you the curse was primed to affect, not the sanctity of this church."

"Something to be thankful for I suppose. But it's not going to stop, is it? Every time I enter a church it's going to happen all over again. It's as Trench said it would be. Barred forever from the faith of my choice."

"Not if I have any say in the matter, and let's look on the bright side. Don't know if you've noticed, but you happen to be inside a church right now. Not conclusive of course. You were participating in a service at the time the curse hit you, which may or may not be significant. So what do we do? Well I'll tell you what we're not going to do. We're not going to give-up without a fight. You ready for this, bearing in mind you could get hurt again?" On the end of an emphatic nod, he carried on with an enthusiasm that rubbed off on his listener. "Good stuff. First thing, first: exorcise the demons fuelling the curse. Then the acid test...has it worked? That's the awkward part. The only solution I can come up with is to hold our own mini service...a repeat of this mornings workout. Hopefully there will be no repercussions. If there are? Well...we'll have to think again."

"Before you go," everything having gone according to plan, Jack was about to take his leave. "this could turn out to be of use if you run into any more trouble. I pray such an occasion will not arise, but one can never be sure of what lies ahead." He scribbled a few words on a page torn from a notebook unearthed from somewhere deep within his robes. "I'm given to understand that, verbally delivered and backed by a crucifix, this phrase is a mighty potent weapon against evil in all its forms. Especially when the soul itself is under threat. In Latin I'm afraid, but that's apparently the only language the Devil and his fraternity understands. What bothers me - and don't ask me to explain, because I can't - I have the strangest feeling it will one day save your life. A silly thing to say, but it sometimes pays not to fully discard such premonitions. So, young man, to satisfy me if for no other reason, arm yourself with a crucifix and learn this off by heart."

"Well hi there Jack," sarcasm drooling in droves he was milking the situation for all it was worth, "beginning to wonder if I was ever gonna see my old buddy again. But here you are, large as life and twice as ugly. What kept you? The two of you have a party, or you thinking of taking the cloth?"

"Sorry, Kyle. I had no idea it would take so long," looking at his watch. "You shouldn't have waited. I know the way back."

"State you were in? no chance! Take no notice of me moaning, Jack; but just you wait till I owe you a favour. Boy-oh-boy; will I get my own back." Facial expression transformed from light-hearted to serious, he asked. "Work out ok? your talk with Father O'haloran. Guess it had something to do with what happened in there."

"Had everything to do with it. I needed to talk to someone, someone remote. Someone who didn't know me from Adam who would listen and understand. Your vicar did that and more. He accepted what I had to say with neither query nor disbelief, before going on to exorcise the curse that plagued me…giving me the confidence to forget the past."

"Suppose he was told a lot more than we were."

"Told him all...had to. He wouldn't have been able to help me otherwise." About to end it there, he changed his mind. It was only fair to justify what he'd said. "You see, and this is what makes it so lamentable, I brought it all on myself. That the outcome was to some extent inadvertent is a poor excuse, it doesn't detract from the reality: a bloody fool who got what he deserved. The events of this morning brought it home without compromise: I needed help, the help of an expert. Father O'haloran had the necessary credentials, and he was available. It was a circumstance I had to make the most of."

"No need explain, Jack. Known you long enough to know I'm not being taken for a ride. But what the hell? You need to confide or make use of me in any way, just let me know. Same goes for the rest of the family."

As the car swung round the front of the house, Julie ran down the steps of the veranda to meet them. Flinging her arms round his neck, she looked him straight in the eye. "Where you been, Jack? We've been worried sick home here. You ok? She glared at her brother. "Would've been helpful if a certain party answered his phone."

"He's fine, ain't you, Jack?" Kyle butted in. "And we can do without the histrionics. Reason I didn't answer the phone, it was in the car and I wasn't. And anyway, how was I supposed to know you'd be checking up on us all the time." Appreciating he was out of order, he sought humble pie. "Sorry, Julie. Didn't mean that. Of course you were worried, you and everyone else. Guess I'm still a bit on-edge myself. The gist is, Jack was stuck with Father O'haloran longer than he expected...leave him to fill in the details. And you've every right to be angry. Should've thought, and stuck the phone in my pocket. Only natural you'd be concerned."

"You're not the only one worked up, Kyle, and it don't excuse you flying off the handle. But ok. I'm sorry too. About tomorrow, Jack?" turning to face him. "Best call it off d'you think. Go for it when you get back perhaps, if we get the chance."

"Not likely. We both need cheering up after what happened today. I'm fine apart from a few bruises…ask Dr. Krantz, if you don't believe me. Las Vegas will put both of us back on an even keel."

"Vegas? When did that happen?" Kyle interjected. "First I've heard. Not that anybody ever tells me anything."

"Was going to tell you," Julie answered, "but events drove it out of my mind, and I reckoned the whole thing would be off…hardly surprising considering the circumstances. Didn't intend to keep you in the dark."

"Well how about…to make amends you understand," face creased in handcuffed amusement, "I string along? The three of us together? We'll have the whale of a time. Ok, get the message," in response to the, 'not on your life' glare from his sister. "three's a crowd. No need to rub it in."

Jack's prophecy was spot on: Las Vegas providing the tonic they sorely needed. A welcome sedative to banish harsh memories, a balm to repair shattered nerves. The vibrancy and exoticism of the massed casinos lining 'The Strip' replacing dark reminiscences with light-hearted banter and child-like mirth. But such emotions were not confined. Every now and again Julie would grab his hand, or he would throw an arm about her waist or shoulder. Part of the fun and all perfectly innocent, neither thought too much about it…not to begin with. Nothing was said, but as time passed both became aware of their feelings taking a different vein. Fine in normal circumstances, but for them it raised complications. The holiday over, he'd be one side of the world she the other. The answer was simple. Keep libidos under control. That was the sensible thing to do…but when did sensible ever enter the equation?

"If we don't find somewhere to eat soon, we'll miss the last train."

"Eat on the train, Jack, why don't we? No idea what the food's like, but can't be that bad."

Returning the empty wine glass to the table, he mused. "That was a great day, Julie, really was. All thanks to you." He sat back, stretched arms raised over his head. "My last day coming up, so how about we make the most of what's left. Will you let me take *you* out tomorrow night? There must be a decent restaurant in Tonopah...perhaps one that offers entertainment; dancing, cabaret perhaps? You'll know better than me." He shouldn't be doing this. It wasn't part of the 'sensible' process.

"Thought you'd never ask," she said, having to compete with the harsh blare of the horn as the train entered a tunnel. Beaming her acceptance she purred, "The perfect end to a perfect day." Sensible had left her way behind.

CHAPTER FOUR

"Thank you for a lovely evening, Jack...Kyle too. He said this was the place to go for a night out, and he wasn't wrong. It had everything." Straightening her dress as she settled in the cab. "Best night ever, and I mean that."

"Even with my two left feet?"

"That's what made it special...the bruises will be a lasting testimony." Smirking wickedly, she chuckled, "You're ok with the steps, it's just you don't necessarily get 'em in the right order. But I must be a glutton for punishment, because I want you to make me a promise."

"To take dancing lessons?"

"It's a thought, but not what I had in mind. I'm ignoring that," in response to the audible sigh of relief. "It'll depend what colour my toes are in the morning. No, what I'm trying to say if you let me finish, is you can take me there again when you and Kyle get back."

"You won't have to twist my arm. I'm going to miss you while we're away. I know I am, so might as well admit it...but at least I've now got something to look forward to." His words generated a silence that lasted for the rest of the journey back to the ranch.

"You in a rush to get to bed, Jack? Early start tomorrow," peering at her watch, finding it difficult to see in the starlight as they climbed the steps to the veranda," Nearly two...selfish of me, but I don't care. We need to talk."

"I'm intrigued. But ok, if that's what you want. Doubt I'll sleep much anyway. Has it got anything to do with me opening my big mouth about missing you? If it has…"

"That's got nothing to do with it," she interrupted. "leastwise, not directly. We have..." The catch in her voice giving vent to her feelings, she abandoned the pretence. "Oh hell, I'm going to miss you too you big ass. Been trying to convince myself I wouldn't, but you must've had the same thoughts and don't need me to spell it out. When the fantasy ends and you go back home? Won't see much of each other after that." She gripped his hand, pent-up emotions tightening her fingers. "Best change the subject. Don't want to ruin a lovely evening by looking at make believe."

"Tell me something I don't know. I've thought of nothing else since we got back from Vegas…almost from the moment we first met if I'm honest. Practicality will have the final say: fantasy won't make it out of the starting blocks." Adding with a half-hearted smile. "But that's not what you want to talk about."

"Because of what happened yesterday it does have something to do with it, but it isn't the main reason. We might both know there's nothing to be gained by letting our feelings run away with us, but that doesn't mean we can put a stop to them at the drop of a hat. I know I can get over-emotional at times. Can't help it. It's the way I am. What happened in the church keeps coming back at me, and I can't get rid of the thought it could happen again. No, Jack, let me finish." Countering his interruption with one of her own. "You might have convinced yourself there won't be a repeat, but you've done nothing to convince me."

"What more can I say? You know about the curse and my misgivings; not sure whether or not anything was likely to come of it…you saw for yourself what happened, so you need no enlightenment there. Finally, I've given you the gist of my meeting with Father O'haloran: you know the outcome, and you know he did the business. There's nothing more I can add that you don't already know." Unable to escape the look of disagreement flung in his direction, he tried a different tack. "Ok I'll go through it all over again if that'll help; but that's all I can do…there won't be anything you haven't heard already." Putting his arm round the girl's shoulders, he led her to a swing seat at the far end of the veranda. "Let's talk out here. It's a lovely night, be a shame to let it go to waste."

"It's not just what happened on Sunday," she said, snuggling into the arm he was in no rush to remove, "it's what Sunday was all about: the ins and outs, the whys and wherefores, the curse…what led up to it, the reason behind it. In other words, the full works. All Kyle and I have had so far is the abridged version which tells us nothing. Not good enough, Jack. I want to know everything, from the very beginning right through to the very end. No…that's not quite true. It's not so much that I *want* to know, I *need* to know. I need you to tell me about yourself; what got Kyle so worried when the two of you shared the apartment. Yes," reacting to the startled look, "I quizzed Kyle after we left you on Saturday night. He told me all about the state you got yourself in, how it affected you both mentally and physically. You admitted you got in with the wrong crowd, and I want to know exactly what that had to do with anything." No, Jack," halting another interjection, "let me finish. Put yourself in my shoes. How you would feel if it was the other way round? Wouldn't you worry the whole damn time I was away? Because that's how it'll be with me." She sighed, a gentle breath of air exhaled though trembling lips. "I was close to tears in church, and didn't know you then like I do now. Me and Kyle both thought you were about to die on us. And we weren't the only ones. How do you think it'll be if the same thing happens when you're all those miles away?"

"It's difficult, Julie. I'm not sure…"

"I know what you said," he could feel her heart pounding against his chest as she wriggled closer, "and I know me and Kyle agreed we wouldn't push. But if only for the sake of a friendship instead of what might have been, give me something to hang on to." Seeking a lifeline she clutched his free hand, "I need reassurance, and the only way I'm going to get that is by you being properly open with me. Won't stop me worrying, but it might help."

"It's the value I put on our friendship that makes it difficult. If I do as you ask there's a strong possibility you and your brother will never speak to me again. I'd rather face what happened on Sunday every day of the week than have that happen."

"You think I'm that shallow…Kyle too? You messed up big time, and you're ashamed because of it: we know all that. So what's the problem. We all make mistakes some time or other," the shy but purposeful smile hard to see in the subdued light, "even me on rare occasions. But joking apart, Jack, I mightn't have known you long but the same don't apply to Kyle. He knows you for the man you are, and he won't hear a word said against you. Nothing you have to say is going to change that."

"What about worshipping the Devil? You won't find that on my CV." He couldn't stop the outburst. A mixture of pent up anger and remorse seething to boiling point.

"You telling me this is what it's all about? You worship the Devil? Don't believe you. You wouldn't have come to chur…" the words died on her. A Satanist in a House of God? It would explain everything. His reluctance in accepting the invitation in the first place, the funny turn…his reticence in coming forward.

"Thankfully it didn't get that far. But that's beside the point. It doesn't detract from my stupidity in getting involved with a group of Satanists in the first place. That it was inadvertent is neither here nor there. It was only by an unexpected stroke of good fortune that I was spared from becoming a fully paid up member."

"You had me worried," the sigh this time one of relief. "but I don't understand. Inadvertent or not, don't see how anyone could end up in a mess of that magnitude without having made a conscious effort. The reproach soft, hinting at underlying compassion. "How'd it come about? That's what I want to know. And this bit of luck you said you had? You can't stop now...it can't get any worse."

"Wouldn't bet on that but you're right, I've said too much to leave it there. Ok, but be warned, it's a long, painful and not very nice story. Repulsive, frightening...totally unbelievable. Tell me when you've had enough."

"The longer the better," nudging his chest with her shoulder, "I'm comfy enough for a while yet."

"It was some three-and-a-half years ago it all started. Enjoying a quiet drink in a country pub, I slid off my stool to search my pockets: hoping to find sufficient loose change for another pint. Not looking what I was doing or where I was going, I knocked against the man standing next to me. Just a gentle nudge, but it was enough to send his beer flying."

"He had a go at you?"

"If only he had. But no, he laughed it off. Assuring me it could happen to anyone. But I couldn't leave it there. Accident or not, it was incumbent on me to get him another drink. Embarrassed as hell, I counted out what money I had - my worldly wealth in small change - enough to salve my conscience but it was goodbye to my second pint."

"Apart from missing out on your drink it doesn't sound much to get excited about."

"So you'd think, but it didn't end there. Having to check my finances in full view made it pretty obvious I was skint."

"What's skint?"

"Thought you American's spoke English," he chided. "Skint...a priceless cockney word for broke - no money."

"I'll add that to my vocabulary," manufacturing a haughty air, teeth sparkling in the starlight. "Just you carry on mate,"

"The Pearly Queen's got nothing on you. No," he hastened to add in response to her wanting to know who the hell the Pearly Queen was, "you won't want to go there." Comforted by her closeness, he tightened the grip on her shoulder. "You can probably guess what's coming. If I were to confide my financial problems, they could be in a position to help. Like a fool, I listened."

"They offered to lend you money?"

"Nothing that simple. A broken leg or two if I didn't cough up would have been preferable to the alternative. So no, that wasn't it. But what they did say sounded promising to a bloke who's finances, already in a dire state, were getting steadily worse: rendering me vulnerable to whatever was on offer. Looking back on it now I can't believe I was gullible enough to be taken in, but they new what they were doing, and they made sure I was in no mood to argue. Plying me with, as I believed at the time, sufficient booze to render me two sheets to the wind before letting me in on their secret. Surprising what's believable when you're sloshed. It was all very subtle, very professional, but they were experts in what they did."

"And what was that?"

"Manipulation, coercion, persuasion...call it what you will, I was on the way to being hooked. Although, to be fair, when I awoke the next morning I was beginning to have second thoughts. In hindsight that didn't surprise me. What did was I had no hangover which, considering the amount of alcohol I'd tucked away, didn't add up. Even more obtuse I could remember everything with remarkable clarity...some novelty in view of many past experiences. I shrugged it of. I shouldn't have. It was only later I came to realise that a more potent administration than booze was responsible. It also ensured my continued interest in matters that, had I been thinking straight, I would have laughed at. That's what I meant when I said these men were experts. Hypnosis, drugs, a spell...whatever it was, I was cornered. Happy to go along with anything they proposed."

"Don't fool with me, Jack. Drugs I can go along with, it can happen; but hypnotism? What they do, sit you on a stool in the middle of a crowded bar and demand you look in their eyes? And a spell? What d'you take me for? one of those silly wretches you read about in magazines for the unintelligent.

That's nonsense, and you know it. You're treating me like a five-year old, and if this is what…"

"How the hell do you think I was cursed," dragging his arm away and facing her, "if magic wasn't involved?" Red faced, his interruption angry. "I would never dream of fooling you, and I find it sad you should think me capable of doing so. But if you insist on having the complete picture, then you have to accept that every word I say is true. Most of it you will find unbelievable, I accept that…I'd be surprised if you didn't. But that's beside the point. It happened. None of it made-up, all very real. See it as bunkum if you like, that is your prerogative and I can understand why you would. But whatever you choose to believe, know this. I would never lie to you, and I wouldn't dream of making fun of you."

"I'm sorry for having to say it, but not for what I said. Your way of looking at things are different to mine, and you can't blame me for being sceptical."

"Of course not. I didn't believe any of it either. Not to begin with, and it was some considerable time before my eyes were opened. By the time they were it was too late." He shuddered, a reaction to the revival of memories he wished had stayed dormant. "Anyway, I had agreed to meet the men again the next evening. When I got there - same pub as before - they were there already; awaiting my arrival with some impatience. I was only a few minutes late but they seemed to be worried that I wasn't going to turn up. Whatever was going through their minds, I was greeted like someone they'd known for years instead of a mere twenty-four hours. It was all so cosy. Three fellahs' engaged in useless drivel while downing a pint-or-two, but it wasn't long before it was suggested we move on. It was important, so I was persuaded, for me to meet the people who would put my finances back on track. They understood my concerns, and the sooner they were sorted the better. I remember laughing, asking which bank they planned to rob. It was meant as a joke but the humour was lost on them. I was informed that the power of the occult rendered such crudity unnecessary. I saw it as an attempt to turn the tables with a joke of their own. Not for one moment did I think they were serious. I couldn't have been more gullible."

"Sounds to me like they were the gullible ones," pulling away so she could face him. "or you telling me different?"

"You'll find out soon enough. I was taken to a large house on the outskirts of Cambridge." He paused, shaking his head slowly from side to side. "I should have seen that first meeting as a warning. That I didn't was the first mistake among many. You will no doubt laugh, but that was when I discovered magic wasn't the childhood fantasy I thought it to be, and that it continues to flourish in the adult world of today."

"I'm not laughing, Jack."

"Well you should be. But if you don't see the funny side, you will admit to being dubious."

"Oh I'm dubious alright, and I find it rather worrying that you should consider it remotely humorous. How you could allow yourself be duped into believing such utter crap is beyond me."

"If that is to be your response to everything I say we might as well give up here and now." his anger again rising. "If you're not prepared to listen before making judgement, then there's little point in me carrying on."

"No need to get nasty, Jack. Because I say what I think doesn't mean I'm not interested, that I don't want to know...that I don't care. Of course it doesn't. I'm doing my best to keep an open mind, but what you're telling me is hard to swallow. None of that changes anything. I still want to know what happened. The cause of your attack in church." She turned to look him in the eye. "I'm sorry. It wasn't very nice to say what I did."

"I'm sorry too. But I was there. A victim of my own stupidity. The reason why I find it hard to accept the disbelief of others, why I'm reluctant to talk about it. When accosted, I tend to vent my anger on the sceptic." Tightening the handheld grip he cautioned, "Carry on like we are and we'll end up having a blazing row. Neither of us would want that."

"At least that's something we can agree on. Ok, I'll try to be more accommodating, more understanding; but you can still expect the odd comment." Smiling at him, returning the pressure on her hand. "I'm a woman, remember? And it's as you're Dad said. We'll always have the last word. But I promise to try to phrase my remarks more delicately in future."

"Mm, we'll see." returning her smile. "On entering the house, I was ushered into a room crowded with people of both sexes, all ages and from all walks of life. Even caught a glimpse of one of the Don's at the university. For a while it was boringly disappointing. What you would expect from any nice and cosy, conventional gathering. You know what I mean...all and sundry standing around, glass in hand intent on trying to make intelligent conversation. That said, it was all perfectly friendly and there was no faulting the hospitality. Buffet food in abundance, an unending supply of drink to wash it down."

"No music? No dancing girls?"

"You must be joking. Forget about music and dancing girls, there wasn't so much as a titter of laughter. Dull as dishwater puts it into perspective."

"You telling me it stayed like that the whole time? Must have livened up sometime surely?"

"Around midnight, and by then I was on the verge of packing it in and going home. The prospect of a long walk striking me as preferable to being bored to death. The turning point was a group of magicians, as fed-up as me no doubt, deciding to demonstrate their quite considerable skills. It made the evening and helped atone for the earlier lack of activity. But that was before I discovered black magic is indelibly handcuffed to Devil worship."

"Yeah, ok. I can imagine you took it for real at the time, but you must have realised afterwards it was a set-up. For chrissakes, Jack, I've seen 'em. These stage magicians can work wonders. As long as you don't probe too deep."

"Give me some credit. I may be dumb but I'm not that stupid I can't tell the difference."

"Ok, so convince me. But I'm warning you, I'll take a lot of convincing."

"Why doesn't that surprise me? But you'll see things in a different light when you hear what they did. "Taking a pause to collect his thoughts, he carried on from where he'd left off. "I wasn't the only newcomer that night, there were three-or-four others watching with mouths agape. Thinking about it some months later, I came to realise it was all part of the grand plan. A ruse to reassure us innocents, convince us there was nothing untoward. That it was nothing more than good, harmless fun. Hitting us with the sucker punch when we were fully enmeshed."

"What do you mean by that?"

"Well, to begin with I'd no idea what I was letting myself in for and I'd be surprised if any of the other newcomers did either. For instance, I didn't know that magic has a good and a bad side. That evening it was white magic on display, the darker aspect kept firmly under wraps. But I wasn't to know that. At the time I was unsure, caught between two minds. Wanting to believe my eyes but sceptical of the message they conveyed. Bathed in ignorance, I was comfortable with what was taking place."

"I can see that, but it still doesn't explain what you said."

"I'm coming to that. Without question, the entertainment at that first meeting was eye opening and, I have to admit, exciting. At the time it didn't register, but looking back a few months later it struck me it was designed to fool us greenhorns into believing that what they got up to was good, clean, honest fun: nothing dodgy, nothing to get alarmed over. To give you an idea, one of the first-timers was a middle-aged man who had either lost or mislaid a precious gift: an engraved wristwatch given to him by his wife shortly before her death from a long-term illness. Following weeks of fruitless searching, the poor guy was distraught. You can imagine his delight, when the missing watch was placed in his hand...by a warlock who never so much as left the room. Tell me how that was done, if magic wasn't the motivator?"

"Easy. The two were in cahoots. Surprised you didn't work that out for yourself."

"You're wrong, Julie. Take my word for it, if the expression on that man's face was contrived then he was a bloody good actor." Venting a hard done-by sigh he complained, "I can see this is going to be one of those nights. But ok! Argue your way out of this. Over in one corner of the room four people, two men, two women, were having one helluva ding-dong. No idea what the rumpus was about, but they were going at it hammer and tongs. Raised voices, blood vessels about to burst, fists clenched and ready for action...brought to a sudden halt by a witch with a wicked sense of humour. Switching the voices and mannerisms of the two sexes, she brought the entire room into uproar. Including those with the grudge to bear."

"Have to think that one over...but I'll get there. When I do, you'll be the first to know."

"Oh I don't doubt that! But, as I said, that first evening was nothing but charm and goodwill; but it wasn't to last. I won't bore you with the details, but subsequent meetings were neither as friendly nor as informal."

"You haven't said if they did anything for you. Why you joined up in the first place."

"That's the one thing I will say for them; they kept their promise, and very cleverly done it was too." Shifting in his seat, struggling with his conscience, he didn't answer straight away. When he did it was obvious that it was with considerable effort. "It was random but frequent. On the one hand a debit would go unrecorded, on the other an extra nought would be added to a credit. When queried, the bank would assure me they had double checked and all was as it should be. No errors, no mistakes; every entry was bona fide. It was wrong, of course it was. I wasn't blind. But what could I do? The bank would've had me carted off in a little yellow van if I'd let on they'd been got at by a practitioner of the dark arts. As a result my balance shifted steadily in the right direction and my continued interest was assured. As I said; it was cleverly done."

"But it couldn't go on like that. Whatever you thought, you must have known it wasn't magic. Those guilty of perpetrating the fraud had the screws on some bank clerk, short of a few bucks and out of his depth. Wouldn't have been long before someone noticed there was a strong smell of something fishy, and you can bet your bottom dollar the poor wretch would've ended up in the cooler."

"You're looking at the real world, and this is a long way from the real world. This is the realm of the supernatural; the paranormal...a parallel universe where normality ceases to exist. No one would have suffered financially. No one would have ended up doing porridge. Look on it as two accounts. The real one operated by the bank, a virtual one in the hands of scrupulous occultists."

"Not the point. Someone, somewhere along the line, was being duped. Whatever you say, it wasn't right and I can't believe you let it go on. Should've left it there before it got too far. Never having had money problems I suppose that's easy for me to say, but you know what I'm getting at. Leave it for now. Let's move on."

"Sure you want to? You sound tired"

"If you're looking for a way out, forget it." Stifling the yawn that prompted the question. "Course I'm tired. What d'you expect at nearly three in the morning,? I could do with a coffee though, that might help. And you?"

"Oh yes please. My throat feels like it's full of sand. All that booze and too much talking. Come on, I'll give you a hand."

"Mm, I needed that." Deciding to stay indoors as it was beginning to get chilly outside, he returned their empty cups to the kitchen before carrying on from where he'd left off.

"I mentioned the change in atmosphere, but that wasn't as worrying as the shift from white to black. The seemingly innocent, humane magic of that first meeting was shoved behind the curtains, the darker side taking centre stage with horrific effect. Bright sunshine transformed into a raging storm, day to night, bystanders humiliated just for the fun of it. They were the cosier activities. Once they got going it was different again. Sex changes, sex gratification, animals killed - resurrected - killed again. Unexplained 'accidents' to those they didn't like. And that's just the half of it."

"Illusions, Jack. Mass hypnosis, hysteria...something along those lines. Things like that don't happen. Can't happen. In the movies perhaps, but not in real life."

"You're doing it again. These are not the frivolous antics of a conjurer prancing around in the spotlight in full view of a paying audience. The morons I'm talking about didn't give a damn what they did, where they did it or who witnessed the outcome. The perpetrator was safe whatever he or she did; there were no fingers to point at them, no chance of anyone knowing who was responsible. After all, what would be the point of making someone look or act silly if there wasn't a crowd around to join in the fun?" Beseeching her with a pleading look he sought common ground. "Try to see both sides. I know it's difficult and I respect that. But please, Julie, reserve judgement until you've heard the full story. I promise you, there are things to come that even you will find hard to dispute."

"In other words, keep my trap shut till I've heard it all and can make a useful contribution. Ok! Makes sense, criticism accepted. From now on I'll keep any suspicions under my hat...my imaginary hat, not my witches hat!" Adding with a mischievous grin. "Then I'll pull it apart by the seams."

"Mm, yeah, well we'll see. You could be in for a surprise. Jumping forward some six months-or-so, I gradually became aware of changing attitudes towards me. The undivided attention of a senior member readily available if I ran into difficulties, a sympathetic ear and a plausible explanation if there was anything I either didn't understand or found repulsive...and there was plenty that fell into that latter category.

And all the time the substance of the rituals became darker, increasingly sinister."

"So why go on? By that time you must have had some idea of where it was going."

"I was torn between gullibility and curiosity, that's what it boils down to. But I *was* beginning to have second thoughts. Doubts that solidified when I was forced to witness a scene of such nauseating horror that I had a job not to throw up on the spot. I tried everything in my power to restrict my vision; masking hands over eyes, closed lids...every move thwarted. My preferences overruled by the obscene menace that threatened my sanity, or by the hierarchy for reasons they were unwilling to communicate. That horrific scene was one of my worst ever experiences, and should've tipped the balance. The next meeting I determined would be my last. I'd give vent to my feelings, hand in my resignation and bid good riddance to the lot of them."

"But you didn't."

"Curiosity winning and gullibility not far behind, I was persuaded to think the matter over before committing myself to an act I might regret. Having given due consideration - their words, not mine - to my reasons for leaving, the committee were of the opinion that I acted rashly. They under-stood my concerns, and considered it only natural that I should nurse them. But, by the same token, as a novice of limited experience it was not my place to condemn their practices out of hand. Also, as they were quick to point out, my wanting to leave was spurred by a one-off situation; so why jeopardise a promising future on a spur-of-the-moment decision? In short, I was persuaded to delay my departure until after the grand Sabbat, scheduled to coincide with the summer solstice in three weeks time. I would then see things in a different light. Doubts dispelled, faith and interest restored."

"Didn't take much to get you to change your mind. I'm not being nasty, Jack, but were you really that blind? That stupid?"

"Yep, they don't come anymore stupid but, hopefully, that's in the past...the look on your face tells me you're not so sure, but I'm ignoring it." The exchanged smiles going someway to lightening the tension between them. "Difficult to put into words, but when in their company it was always the same. Resolute in my approach I was adamant...until the next meeting. That was when my resolve would drain away and I would see things in a different light. It was as if they had some kind of hold over me. As if the moment I walked through the door I was under their influence. Even the invitation to attend the Sabbat had a strong smell about it. As far as I could gather all of the invites were posted...all except mine that is. It seemed I was a *special* case," his words shrouded in tones of deep sarcasm, "the postal service considered not good enough, my invitation was delivered by hand: a home visit by a man from the upper echelons of the hierarchy. More a demand than a request, I was told the agenda would include the cure of a woman with a terminal disease. If that was the carrot to make sure I stayed put, it was one hundred percent successful. I was also informed it was to be the occasion of my initiation. An addendum which, at the time, sailed way over my head."

"So, here we have a bunch of weirdo's claiming they're better equipped than qualified medics. What planet were you on, Jack?"

"If I remember rightly, you promised to keep all comments to yourself until you'd heard everything." Determined not to lose his rag again, he took a deep breath.

"Sorry, Jack...and you're right. I did promise. It's just...you know; what you're saying, I find it quite disturbing." An apologetic smile going some way to calming his temper.

"You'll be even more disturbed when you hear how and why the woman was cured; and, before you ask, no, there was no doubt she was ill. Desperately so."

Failing to find a suitable retort, she shook her head. Fidgeting with her fingers, keeping her own counsel. Content to await his next words in silence.

"The site for the Sabbat was a large mansion on the outskirts of a town called Saffron Walden. The property of a titled big-wig, it put all previous venues in the shade."

"Lords and Ladies too, Jack Sibley! You sure know how to tempt a girl."

"You don't know the half of it. There must've been close on a hundred people there, of which a good majority were from the upper classes...I was one of the peasants; part of the riff-raff to be treated with suitable disdain. Well, that's the impression I got. Having to suffer the indignity of public transport, I was one of the last to arrive but, right from the off, I wished I'd never gone near the place. Before I go on...gets a bit embarrassing in parts."

"Oh don't mind me. Having asked for the full works, I don't expect   to be fobbed off with an abridged version of what these people got up to."

"On your head be it, and you cant say I didn't warn you. It was weird. The instant I crossed the threshold I was filled with foreboding. Sounds ridiculous talking about it now, but it was as though a disembodied voice was warning me that I entered a den of iniquity, a place of evil. It was all around me. As if there to witness my humiliation. My destruction."

"Is the presence of evil that noticeable? Sure it wasn't a fantasy built on recollection? Know what I mean? Events are often exaggerated in the cold light of day."

"I tell you, Julie, that building exuded devilry from every brick, tile and stone. Apart from those who wallow in repugnance, I'm sure any innocent who entered would have been affected in the same way. And believe me, I'm not being melodramatic."

"Ok, but one thing I still find hard to get. If the place hit you like you said, why the heck did you stay? Should've thought getting the hell out of it was the thing to do...not park your butt and take the consequences. Keep asking the same old question, but all I get in return is constant shimmy-shamming ."

"I intended to, oh yes…I'd had enough; I was off through that door as fast as my little legs would carry me…after I'd witnessed the woman and her cure. It was grasping at straws, but I couldn't help thinking that perhaps this lot might not be quite so bad after all. Ridding someone of a terminal disease was surely a kindness, not a cruelty. So were they really as terrible as I was making them out to be? Anyway, that's how it was. I chose to stay around, make my mind up after this so-called miracle had taken place. It was a sad mistake! Had I run from that house there and then - which the saner me demanded - I wouldn't have been locked in a spell that prevented me from obeying my instincts."

"Guess we're all guilty of trying to find a trace of humanity in the undeserving at times, that I can understand. But there you go again, Jack - a spell…" Cringing at the anger beginning to erupt in his expression, she was quick to apologise. "Yeah, ok. Know what I said…sorry. Again!"

"Had I not been a first order idiot, you wouldn't be sitting there having to hold your tongue for fear of upsetting me. The crux of the matter is, I should have known better. Even now, after all this time, I find it hard to conceive I could have been so idiotic…so blind. The set-up itself should have been sufficient to start alarm bells ringing but I was too thick to notice. One end of a massive hall was dominated by a stone altar hung with red and gold tapestries, behind which was placed a huge throne: the head of a goat emblazoned on the backrest. An inverted wooden cross hung from a hook in the ceiling, flaring black candles burned at all four corners of the altar." Staring vacantly at her, he voiced the self-accusation that continued to plague him. "A crucifix, upside down! The height of blasphemy and I missed the implication…what clarification did I need?"

"Other things on your mind perhaps? The situation you were in? Excuses, poor excuses, but given the opportunity they can play havoc with the grey matter. That's beside the point and I'll say it again. When you eventually realised the significance of what you saw, why didn't you make a move?"

"It was too late." He shuffled in his seat, striving to push the terror of past recollections aside. "It took long enough, but I at last made up my mind. I was on my way out...that was when Willoughby Trench turned up."

"Not a name to argue with. Who's he?"

"Top man of the group I was with. A powerful magician and egotist of the first order yet, from the way he spoke, I got the impression that even he considered himself small fry in the present company. Making it clear he'd read my mind, I was informed a premature departure or similar abuse of the hospitality afforded me would reflect on him personally. As it was he who had recommend my initiation, it would be he who would be held accountable."

He paused to reflect. The passage of time failing to dispel the horrors of what could have been.

"I should've known. I'd seen him do it often enough. I turned to face him."

Head bowed he, as he had so many times in the past, cursed the lack of foresight that could have destroyed him as a human being. Julie allowing him sufficient pause, cognisant of the unspoken wish he be allowed to contemplate in loneliness. Pushing her natural curiosity to one side until she felt the time was ripe.

"Don't have to go on if you don't want to Jack. I understand."

"No it's ok. It's an awareness of the consequences that would have been my lot had not dame fortune intervened that bugs me. I was guilty of a cardinal error; a lack of concentration that could have sealed my undoing. I looked into his eyes. The briefest of instants, but that was all it took. From that moment on I was putty in his hands."

"You really believe this, Jack? No hypnotist I've come across could put someone under that quick."

"To an adept of the left-hand path the eyes are the windows of the brain, a direct route for the interconnection of two minds. A mere fraction of a second is all it takes." Biting hard on his lower lip, he spread his hands. "I was done for. Willoughby Trench controlled my every move."

"If what you're telling me is gospel, then perhaps it's time I shed my scepticism. Hate to admit it - and you can wipe that smug look off your face Jack Sibley - but if this guy can see what you're thinking...take you over in the blink of an eye just like that? Perhaps I was too quick thinking you'd gone quirky on me: convinced you were the victim of your own imagination I let you ramble on without believing a word. I'm sorry, Jack, it was wrong of me. Unfeeling. But I couldn't help myself. I'm going to ask you one last time, and I promise it will be the last...this is the solid truth you're giving me; not just some of it...all of it? No exaggeration, no twisting, no fooling?"

"I've already said I wouldn't lie to you and nothing's happened, or will ever happen, to change that. But I'll have you know the look on my face wasn't me being smug...it was relief. Your more positive approach will make it that much easier for both of us." Leaning close he kissed her on the cheek, adding as he moved away, "At least our verbal scraps had something in their favour, they helped to stop us nodding off."

"Anyway, back to Willoughby Trench. Bizarrely him butting in like that, unplanned and unannounced, did me a good turn...if good turn is the right expression. It stirred my reluctant brain into long delayed activity. The altar, the inverted crucifix, the black candles. This was no run-of-the-mill get-together. This was a Black Mass and, misguided fool that I was, it had been cunningly planned to make sure I was included in the proceedings. The supposed cure of the afflicted woman wasn't to be the only star attraction: my initiation was also on the bill. For me this was the point of no return, my initiation an integral part of the proceedings. There would be no argument, no defence. Against my will, contrary to my beliefs and dreams of the future, I was destined to become a novitiate disciple of the Devil."

"Black Mass? Some sort of thought-up argument to the Christian version?"

"In a nutshell. But what would you expect? Everything connected with Satanism is in direct contradiction to the Christian faith. Upside down crucifix, black candles; altar cloth of red, black and gold in violent contrast to the more muted coverings to be found in a house of God. To go through the entire spectrum would be pointless. Suffice to say the overall effect was one of complete contrast. Looked at logically it makes sense. There are no two opposites further apart than good and evil." Shifting in his seat he put his arm back round her shoulder, pulling her close. "Made to wear a hooded white robe - and you can take that silly grin off your face - I had no choice but to follow the crowd; act the part and do what they did." He coughed, a false and unnecessary clearing of his vocal chords. "Not quite everything thank, God…it tends to get raunchy in parts."

"Raunchy's ok. My over-vivid imagination will compensate for the bits you leave out." She chuckled. "So you'd better watch yourself. Give me too much to think about…who knows!"

"Don't tempt me," raised eyebrows accentuating an accusing grin, "but as for Trench, he had no intention of running the risk of me putting one over on him. Not content with the hold he had on me, I was appointed two minders to make doubly sure."

Removing his arm he stood, facing her. All she'd heard so far was second drawer stuff, now it was crunch time…the horrific events leading to the finale, and he was anxious to judge her reaction.

"It being a warm evening, the patio doors were opened onto a garden arrayed with tables loaded with obscene quantities of food and drink..." His voice stumbled, words drying up before leaving his lips.

She didn't need to be told his struggle continued. The evidence was there in the sweat glistening on his forehead, the faraway look in his eyes. Her heart went out to him. Wanting to help. Knowing there was nothing she could do.

"Sorry for that. It's just, how can I put it...credibility can be an awkward beast, so if I'm finding it difficult what chance do you stand? All I can say, is a lot of it is revolting, most of it frightening, all of it debase in the extreme. The one common thread: the abstract line that separates normality from believability. For any of it to make sense all inhibitions have to be discarded, previously conceived ideas abandoned. It's the occult we are dealing with, the abode of devilry...a world not of our conception. Implausible though you are going to find it, it is all terribly true. Nothing imagined. Nothing embellished."

"I know, Jack," her smile reassuring, "don't have to persuade me anymore."

"Ok, well, for the first hour-or-so it was everyone standing around talking, nothing more energetic than that, but at a given signal the floodgates were opened and all hell was let loose; the whole crowd embarking on a campaign of utter gluttony. Unimaginable amounts of food thrust through ever-open gullets, washed down by copious quantities of the hard stuff. But if that was nauseating, it was nothing compared to what followed. Young and old alike throwing off their robes, the prequel to indulging in scenes of obscene sexual depravity. Mind you there was a funny side to the shenanigans, most of those prancing around in the nuddy would have done better to have kept their clothes on."

"You'll never guess what was going through my mind," she laughed. "But, Jack, you're not telling me you didn't join in? They must've thought you a right party pooper!"

"Sorry to disappoint, but I was spared that ignominy. My two minders in bored attendance, I was made to stand and watch. Mind you, had Trench decreed otherwise, I would have been powerless to resist. But there was never any danger of that happening. Uninitiated low-life is barred from participating in activities of that kind. Such delights are confined to the fully-fledged. And, as I'm sure you won't need telling, the whole charade was nothing more than a subtle warm-up for the main event. A juicy carrot to get the masses in the right mood. The exploitation of mans' weakness on a human plane, founding the inexorable quest for power on a plane that is anything but human."

"Didn't understand a word."

"Don't worry about it," he said, sensing her bemusement. "you'll get the drift as we go along. Essentially when you hear how the lady with acromegaly was cured...by a creature from the depths of hell."

"Acromegaly? What's that? Never heard of it."

"Nor had I till I took the trouble to look it up . An incurable disease by all accounts. And a not very nice one at that. The symptoms are varied but nasty. Bones of head, feet and hands enlarge to grotesque proportions and side effects play havoc with soft tissue."

"Ugh! Sounds dreadful but must be rare."

"Very. Thank God."

"But this poor woman? You say her illness was incurable, then tell me she was made better anyway?"

Returning to the settee he found a loose hand to grab hold of. He would need comfort and persuasion if he was going to get through this. "Incurable as we know it, but this lady's treatment wasn't confined to general practice, it was way beyond such amateurish procedure! She paid the price though. By God she did. And I'll tell you this, Julie; I wish to heaven I'd surrendered my resolve to witness what turned out to be the most dire experience of my life. I go through hell every time I think about it, and you'll have to bear with me if I lose the plot along the way."

"Understood."

"A Black Mass - as with all major Satanic ceremonies - is conducted by an Ipsissimus. He, no reason why it shouldn't be a 'she' but I've not heard of one, is the equivalent of an Archbishop in Christian circles. The rank of Ipsissimus is restricted to followers of the left hand path who are at the very top of their game. Powerful magicians prepared to use their power for the furtherance of Lucifer. I didn't know the man who filled the role that night but he definitely complied with the job description. A frightening individual, he radiated a despotic authority: every movement, every word, leaving no one in any doubt who was boss."

"Not the man to meet on a dark night."

"Or any kind of night! Bringing the fun and games to an end by the simple expedient of raising a solitary arm, the cavorting mob was stilled into instant silence."

"Do I gather this high and mighty guy didn't take part in the goings on?"

"Not on your life. He and the rest of the bigwigs maintained a discrete distance. The enraptured congregation having been brought to order, the Ipsissimus then spent several minutes haranguing them for lack of dedication before turning his attention to the throne. The lights in the hall, together with the decorative lanterns in the garden, dimmed to extinction; the sixteen black candles providing the only source of illumination. Inadequate lighting, a silence deafening in its intensity, a room drained of air…the essential ingredients of fear, despondency and foreboding."

He sat with eyes closed for some time. Tautening nerves, quelling the terror raging inside. Voice not much above a whisper when he continued.

"A pale blue vapour began to enshroud the throne. Shimmering in the darkness, an ethereal-like glow emanated from the mist to envelop the altar...the cue for the priests to set up a weird chant, the fawning nonentities to prostrate themselves in supplication. Trench making sure I followed suit."

"You ok, Jack?" Her anxiety prompted by another lapse into silence."

"Yeah, I'm alright; take no notice. It just…well, it gets at me sometimes. What happened that night, the terror that held me in its dreadful grip....even after all this time." Adding with a half-laugh. "You insist on knowing everything, I'm going to milk it for all it's worth." Shifting in his seat, a ploy to hide his discomfort, he carried on with a degree of hesitancy. "Having been moved to the front for convenience, I was in prime position to see what was going on. Sprawled face down on a wooden floor may not have been the most comfortable position to be in but, with a bit of judicious wriggling, I at least had the advantage of an uninterrupted view of what was going on....what I saw made my blood run cold."

Tugging a handkerchief from a pocket he wiped his eyes, the prequel to a manufactured and unrealistic fit of coughing that did nothing to hide his emotions. She'd seen the moisture that dampened his lower lids.

"The mist thickened, taking on a defined shape. Tenuous to start with – somewhat reminiscent of a genie escaping from a bottle in an 'Arabian Nights' tale - I put it down to imagination. But this was no fairy tale, this was real and it was happening in front of me. Hirsute shoulders of immense strength were first to manifest, head and torso next; followed by the rest of the anatomy. The altar screened the lower legs from view but it didn't matter. I knew what it was long before I was allowed to get to my feet and see the thing in all its fearful glory."

"I'm surprised you hadn't seen enough already."

"More than enough. I tried shutting my eyes, but even that small mercy was denied me. Mind you, even if I'd had the choice I doubt it would have made any difference. It was one of those hypnotic scenarios...know what I mean? One of those sights you dare not miss but one you wished you'd never clapped eyes on?"

"Mm, yeah…I see what you're getting at. But what was this thing like? Describe it for me. Paint me a picture."

"A red-eyed, horned abomination. Head and upper body of a goat, hairless white legs of a human. A naked male fully twelve feet tall and of unimaginable strength. I knew what it was alright. I'd seen too many sketches. Read too many descriptions. The horror of all horrors…the Goat of Mendes."

"Sorry, Jack, didn't mean to be rude," she apologised, struggling to contain her laughter. "With a name like that? This

Mendes guy! Can't see him being thrilled to have a billygoat named after him."

"All I can tell you is that it's origin dates back to the time of the Egyptian pharaohs, when it was known as Baphomet, and that the Satanist movement adopted it as their mentor near the end of the eighteenth century. No idea why or when the name was changed."

"Guess it wasn't there for the booze."

"Nothing so mundane. Its role was to preside over matters of greater importance. Rid the poor woman of her affliction, welcome newcomers into the fold. Me, in other words. Not that I appreciated it at the time."

"You didn't know? No one told you."

"Not in so many words although, to be fair, I did dimly recall being informed that it was to be the occasion of my initiation when I received the invitation. But, as I said earlier and if you remember, I didn't take it in back then. But for all that it was becoming painfully obvious that the brute on the throne was going to have something to do with it. Otherwise, why make sure I was in the front row? As for the ceremony itself, I was completely in the dark. There was no prior instruction. No one thought to tell me what I had to do. My one and only wish was it didn't include close contact with that filthy malignancy."

"Heaven help us Jack! You must have been driven nearly out of your mind."

"Wasn't far off that's for sure. I remember shaking like mad, nausea filling my gut and head spinning." He wriggled in his seat, managing a wan smile as he searched the girls eyes for clues. "At least my worst fear didn't arise, which was something to cling on to. For some reason I was convinced I was to be first up, but that wasn't the case. It was the poor woman with acromegaly who had the number one spot. Arms spread wide in greeting, the Ipsissimus proffered a humble welcome to the Goat of Mendes, prior to pleading that it ease the suffering of a loyal subject in distress. The beast's response was to tap the arm of the throne with one of its massive hooves, the cue for the horribly disfigured patient to be led to the altar. With two priests to guide her movements, she knelt with head bowed before her master."

"You alright, Jack?" Her expression highlighting her concern.

"Could do with a beer? Throat feels like the inside of a hot-air balloon."

"Having never been inside a hot-air balloon," she laughed, "I'll take your word for it. You stay put. I'll go raid the fridge."

Bolstered by a few noisy sips of the amber liquid, he carried on from where he'd left off.

"All that was required was a straight 'yes-or-no' answer. Put to the woman in succinct tones, I could hear every word...it was a two-edged sword. For my own peace of mind I would have preferred to remain in blissful ignorance. The woman was asked if she was ready to commit her soul to the Lord Satan, as just reward for the curing of her ills."

"A big asking price. But she agreed?"

"There was no hesitation. But in her condition I suppose any one of us might be tempted to grasp the one straw on offer. Consent given, there was no hanging around. Assaulted by her minders, she was disrobed and deposited prostrate on the altar. Legs brutally pulled apart and shackled to iron rings sunk into the stonework, arms similarly immobilised."

Taking a deep breath he tightened the grip on the hand in his, seeking he knew not quite what.

"Why go to all that bother if she'd given her ok?" Julie asked. "Doesn't make sense."

"To ensure that nothing went wrong with what was to follow, as you'll come to appreciate. In a grotesque display of evil intent the monstrosity rose from its throne, wallowing in the glorification of the congregation...a sight too terrible for words to describe. It wasn't just the size, or the odious goat-man combination. It was the way it stood. The way it moved. The unholy stare from its red, passionless eyes. It was all those things rolled up in one."

"Jack? You're crying." The tears running down his cheeks a bit of a giveaway.

"Sorry. Can't help myself. It's the wimp in me coming out."

"You're no wimp Jack. You wouldn't be telling me all this if you were."

He squeezed her hand. Grateful for the encouragement. A sorely needed boost."

"This foul malevolence from the depths of Hades climbed on top of the manacled woman. Julie…it raped her." Vocal chords stuttering, bubbling emotions rising dangerously close to the surface, he compromised. "Rape is stretching it a bit I suppose. She must've had some idea of what would happen to her. But whatever her presentiments, I doubt she would have had any inkling of the ordeal she was to face. I said the beast was huge, and the poor wretch suffered untold agony as a result. Not that her protestations had any impact on the fiend. It was too busy enjoying itself."

Releasing her hand he buried his face in his own. Overcoming stressed nerves he raised his head. Looking at her through tear stained eyes.

"She was cured. The gross mutant who had associated with the fiend on the altar, instantly transformed into an attractive young woman no more than twenty-five years of age. Now it was my turn."

"Dragged along by the elbows with an escort on either side, I tried my utmost to fight the hold Trench had over me. But it was no use. The spell too powerful, my minders too strong. Saliva dribbling from its foetid mouth, the obscene being harpooned me with fire-drenched eyes. Forbidding me to avert my gaze, tearing all hope from my terrified mind…the cavities left behind filled by death and destruction. Icy fear plucked at taut nerve-ends, unfettered mania threatened my senses. I began to blubber, to pray that death would come to rid me of my torment...my despair. The monster was so close I could feel its hot, stinking breath on my face. I wanted to run, to put myself out of reach of this anti-Christ. But I was helpless."

"Jack!" Unable to add to that one word, strained features telling the world she relived his ordeal. Imagining how she would have felt had it been her instead of him.

He squeezed her hand painfully, an escape route from the menace of recollection.

"I stopped struggling. There was no way out of the situation I was in, so I might as well resign myself to the inevitable. Curiously, the acceptance of my fate seemed to calm my nerves; rendering me impatient to get it over and done with. Reconciled to the outcome, prepared for whatever lay in store. It was my own fault, and therefore up to me to deal with the consequences of my recklessness."

Pulling Julie close, he stopped talking. Holding her tight. Treating her to the most relaxed smile she'd seen since their return to the ranch.

"As if in slow motion, a slight eddy whirling around the garden expanded into a breeze that drifted lazily through the still-open patio doors...a mild disturbance that was destined not to last. Sending the crowd into hysterics, the breeze became a gale-force wind. The Goat of Mendes, who just moments before was tearing my mentality to shreds, became hazy, translucent...disappearing into the mist of its arrival. Lights returning to full brightness heralded the onset of unfettered panic. Dozens of frantic bodies searching for discarded robes in places they couldn't remember."

"I can imagine. Should think most of 'em looked a darn sight better in the gloom than they did with the lights on."

"You bet. But I didn't give a damn. Didn't know why, didn't care. I had been spared the disaster that would have brought me to ruin. Trench no longer had control over me, my minders had lost interest and I was given the opportunity to ditch this motley lot for good and all."

"But what happened? Nothing going your way one minute, everything in your favour the next. Did you find out?"

"Eventually. When I finally managed to shake off my euphoria, I bumped into someone I knew. The rumour going around was an elderly witch had suffered a massive heart attack and died on the spot."

"Surprised a little thing like someone dying would put an end to their fun and games."

"The decision wasn't theirs' to make. A coven of thirteen warlocks, witches, or mixture of both, is mandatory for the convening of a Black Mass. The woman who died was one of the thirteen. That was it. They were unable to carry on. Unfortunate though it was for her, that witches death was my salvation."

"And the signal for you to scarper?"

"Not right away. I thought it wise to wait until there was a general exodus…on the off-chance that I might be being watched. My absence from future meetings should be enough to tell them what I thought."

"But things didn't go according to plan. Is that what you're saying?"

"I was so naïve. Kidded myself no one would be bothered if I didn't turn up. Why should they?"

He went on to relate the visit of Willoughby Trench and the months of mental anguish that followed. Concluding with the help and support given to him by Angela and Professor Lumberge.

"This Professor, Jack? Some kind of shrink?"

"Not sure he'd appreciate the terminology but, yes, he's a psychiatrist. A very eminent one."

"But he didn't finish the job. If he had, you wouldn't have needed Father O'haloran's help."

"He cured me mentally, put my mind to rest, but that was the limit of his expertise. His qualification didn't extend to the removal of the curse: which is where your priest came in. And that, Julie, is that. Sorry it took so long...but I did warn you!"

"Oh it was worth it, Jack. Believe me, it was worth it. What happened to you on Sunday affected me more than you'll ever know, and I needed the assurance only you could give. You've done that and it's taken a big weight off my mind." She looked at her watch. "I've been twice selfish. There's you with an early start, and it's twenty-past four already. Reckon you'll be glad to see the back of me."

Flinging her arms round his neck, she hid her head in his shoulder. "God bless you, Jack, and keep you safe."

Moisture laying heavily on her cheeks, she ran from the room.

CHAPTER FIVE

The intrusive rattle of the alarm jerking him awake, Jack rolled out of bed. Quarter-past six. He was supposed to join Kyle for breakfast at seven so he couldn't afford to hang around. Surprisingly he felt wide awake which, following a mere two hours in the land of nod, was unexpected to say the least. It wouldn't last. Once the adrenalin build-up of the past few hours was exhausted, sleep would demand a replay.

The breakfast room was deserted when he got there, but he hadn't long to wait before the sound of approaching footsteps could be heard in the hall. Pausing in the act of filling his bowl with cornflakes he looked to the door. Half grin at the ready, he was made to swallow the prepared banter. It was Julie, not Kyle, who walked through the door. No make up, eyes heavy with sleep, hair tousled and wearing a hastily flung on, tied-round-the-middle dressing gown…still managing to look gorgeous.

"Nice surprise. Couldn't you sleep either?"

"Odd cat-nap that was about all." giving him a sleepy smile. "Sorry for the mess I must look but wanted to see you before you left. Didn't properly say goodbye last night and, well, I was awake anyway, so thought it'd be nice to come and see you on your way. Also want to apologise for running off like that. Wasn't meaning to be rude. It was, well, you know...we were both a touch vulnerable. If you get my meaning."

Before he had a chance to reply, Kyle blustered into the room. Incredulity masking his features he blurted, "Jeeze sis, what you doing up? The two of you were putting the world to rights when I got in, and that was late enough. Didn't like to intrude, but would've loved to have been be a fly on the wall. The two of you all alone, whispering sweet nothings...very cosy."

"All you ever think about," pink in the face, struggling to keep her tone light-hearted. "You'll find it hard to believe but it is possible for two people of the opposite sex to indulge in something other than the kind of thing you expect them to indulge in."

"If you say so, sis. I consider myself duly chastised."

"Anyway big brother," pushing him hard in the chest as she spoke, "out of the goodness of my heart I dragged myself from a warm and comfortable bed to wish you and Jack, 'bon voyage'. So," standing on tip-toe to kiss him on the cheek, "bye Kyle...have a great time. Phone me, Jack," she mouthed. Adding in tones loud enough for Kyle to hear "keep safe, and don't let him bully you." Hugging him tight, she kissed him quickly on the mouth. Rounding on her sibling, stopping him in his tracks. "Forget it, Kyle...no wisecracks."

"Only wondered why I didn't get a hug; but then I'm your brother, not your..."

The edge to her voice left him in no doubt. It was a command straight from the heart. "Shut it, Kyle. I'm tired, and I'm not in the mood for your pathetic humour. Clear enough, or do I have to spell it out?"

"As crystal. Sorry, Julie. Didn't mean no harm."

"It's ok, Kyle. I'm sorry too, but you push your luck sometimes. Anyway I'm back to bed. Enjoy yourselves, make the most of your holiday and come back in one piece."

"You and Julie have a good time last night?" Kyle asked as they settled in the Jeep.

"Couldn't have been better. That place you suggested was the tops - I owe you one for that – food superb, music great, and a good atmosphere. All in all it was an evening neither of us will forget in a hurry."

"Good, I'm pleased." Spinning off the drive to career across grass-covered fields. "No business of mine, but wondered if it didn't go so well. To say Julie was a bit scratchy is putting it mildly. She had a real go at me...you heard her. Not like her at all. Got the feeling you two might've had a bit of a tiff, and that's what put her in a bad mood. Couldn't miss the raised voices when I got back at some unearthly hour. And, well...like I said; got me wondering."

"Don't deny we had the odd disagreement, but nothing to sweat over. Most of the time was spent amusing ourselves by going over our respective old times, and the occasional contentious opinion can be taken the wrong way as in any conversation. Misunderstandings that end in a trivial altercation...a few harsh words, but a happy ending." He broke off, studying the profile next to him, inwardly praying his friend wouldn't press the point. "Anyway, you got it all wrong. Julie wasn't winding you up intentionally. Tiredness, that's what it was all about. Neither of us got to bed until some God-forsaken hour. You got the brunt of her lack of sleep."

"Mm, if you say so. But I'm not convinced. That hug she gave you? Could've been an apology from where I was standing. Besides, I saw her lips move but no sound came out. Looked to me like she could've been saying sorry but was keeping it to yourselves. Anyway, none of my damn business if you two are having a fling."

"For the record, Julie and I are not having a fling. So you can put that idea out of your head. Neither of us would gain anything from a brief affair, which is all it ever could be."

"Ok, get the gist. Subject closed. Here we are, Jack. All change," he chimed, bringing the Jeep to a halt outside a massive, wooden structure. "Make yourself useful and give me a hand with these." The 'these' being heavy double doors opening onto what turned out to be a makeshift hangar.

"Well, what d'you think? Ain't she just the bees knees?"

"Why ask me? What I know about aeroplanes is nobody's business. Looks good, I'll even go as far as impressive...other than that I'll reserve my right to silence until I've tried it out. What is it? out of curiosity"

"Well blow me down, Jack...she's an airplane. And there was me thinking you were an educated man. Didn't think for one moment you'd need telling."

"You know damn well what I meant...what make is it?"

"She, not it, Jack, if you remember our conversation when you first arrived, is a Piper Mirage. One-or-two minor modifications from the basic. Passenger seats cut from five to three to give more storage space, blind flying instruments added to satisfy a whim. Well, not just a whim if I'm honest. Had night flying included in my training syllabus just in case. We live in a pretty remote spot as I expect you noticed, and you never know when it could come in useful!" Slapping the fuselage as though it were a pet dog, he demanded, "Now you can earn your fare by helping me push this lovely lady outside."

Adding his weight to one of the wings, he called across to the American similarly occupied on the other. "Downright rude to ask but sensitivity was never one of my strong points. What sort of money does it take to buy something like this?"

"Dollars, Jack. Good old American greenbacks. Ain't no other sort where I come from."

"Don't know what you had for breakfast but, whatever it was, wish I'd had the same. There was a time, Kyle, when I thought you might've made a better comedian than an archaeologist, but then I thought again. No archaeologist could be that bad." He sighed, a long drawn out exodus of exasperated gases. "The English language was so simple before you Yanks got hold of it so, in deference to your deficiencies in that department, I'll couch the question in simpler terms. How much did it cost?"

"Not sure such unwarranted sarcasm is deserving of an answer. I shall however swallow my pride and rise above it." Tilting his jaw in mock disdain. "Not much short of a million with the alterations. Didn't take too long for the old man to get over his choking fit when I broke the news, especially when I pointed out the benefits of having twenty-first century transport on tap. That'll do, we can take it from here." Drawing the back of his hand across a sweat soaked forehead, evidence of a rapidly climbing temperature despite the early hour. "Dump the Jeep inside, get the doors closed and off we go. Next stop, Chihuahua."

"Why Chihuahua?" Puffing as he fought against the weight of the heavy door. "Apart from having a dog named after it, what else is there?"

"A useful stopover, that's all. But you never know. Wherever you choose to drop anchor, there's bound to be something worth looking at." Relaxing against the fuselage, getting his breath back before continuing. "The range of this young lady is about thirteen-hundred miles on a full tank. Merida - where we're aiming for - is close on two thousand. Apart from the obvious, I'll be in need of a break by the time we get to Chihuahua. It's a five-hour flight as near as makes no difference and, if it's the bad news you're wanting," eager eyes awaiting Jack's reaction, "two-hours is as much as I've managed so far without a break."

"Oh don't you worry, pal. I'll make sure you stay awake. Wonder how many times you've been told that by one of the opposite sex."

"It'd be different," he chuckled, "usually the other way round. But what the hell am I thinking of," slapping his hand against the metalwork, "there doesn't have to be a problem...you can take over if I need a break. No good reason why you shouldn't. If my head was stuffed with brains instead of sawdust, I would've had dual controls fitted when they were making the other changes. I'll have that done ready for next time you come over...don't you worry about that."

"Oh yeah, sure, me who can't so much as fly a kite. Let me know if you have any more bright ideas."

"I'm serious, Jack. Flying straight and level over flat terrain on a nice, calm day? Easy as eating apple clam chowder. No different to driving a car on an empty highway. And who knows? Might give you the bug to learn to fly something more'n just a kite. How exciting is that?"

"Frankly, I can't think of anything I'd rather not do...but then again, that's me. The mere thought scares me to death. So if you don't mind, Kyle, leave me out of it. A reluctant passenger is what I am, and I'm content to let it stay that way." Grabbing hold of the framework, he hauled himself into the cabin. "Like the decor. Fitted carpets, plush seats...where's the maid? It - sorry, she - seems to have everything else."

"Now that *is* a good idea," Kyle enthused, buckling himself into his seat as he spoke, "a nice, sexy maid. A dishy broad with a titillating voice, always around when needed and lots of stopovers. Let the engine warm up for a couple of minutes, Jack, and we'll be on our way, but if you're hoping for a nice smooth take-off...forget it. The field's too bumpy for that kind of luxury. One of these days I'll get the OK from Pop to lay a proper runway".

Half an hour into the flight, Kyle pointed to a stretch of heat-baked landscape below.

"The Mojave Desert, Jack. Right now we're flying over Death Valley. Told you about it when you first arrived if you remember. State line between Nevada and California cuts across one end of the valley."

"See where it gets the name. You can almost sense the hostility from up here." Eyes resting on the altimeter he exclaimed, "Twelve thousand feet...high for a small plane isn't it?"

"This is the twenty-first century, Jack. The Wright brothers' pegged it years back. Stated ceiling for this airplane is twenty-five thousand feet, which could come in handy when we hit the high peaks."

"High peaks? Geography may not be one of my strong points, but I don't recall there being any mountains on this part of the planet. Or you going to tell me different?"

"Hang on in there fellah, you'll see a different picture if we get the feel for places further down the line. That's where the mountains start to rear their ugly heads. Don't you take to worrying though," his friend's expression telling all, "it's not likely we'll need to test the limit but we're well equipped if we do. In the meantime I'll make you a promise. If we do end up having an argument with a mountain, it won't be me that started it."

"Not bad. A touch over the five hours I reckoned on, but not too wild of the mark. Wouldn't have wanted it much longer...blast! Hang on, Jack," leaving him stranded on the tarmac, he climbed back into the plane. "Damn documents and bloody bureaucracy, don't you just love it? They'd bung me in the cooler like they would a lousy felon if I deprived 'em of their bits of paper."

"Belated lunch, then reckon it might be best to take it easy for what's left of the afternoon." Kyle proposed as they made their way from the airport. "You ok with that? Don't know about you but I'm bushwhacked."

"Not surprised. I get the impression flying straight and level isn't the piece of cake you say it is. I found it exhausting just watching you do all the work so, yes...I'm all for it. Bite to eat, quick shower, then sweet bugger-all. Shangri-la!"

The prospect of a cosy afternoon was however brought to a premature end as Kyle, a sharp rat-a-tat-tat announcing his arrival, burst into his friend's room.

"Get a move on, Jack. Time to go see what Chihuahua is all about"

"What happened to that afternoon of idleness you promised? A short time ago you were on your last legs, heading fast for the scrap heap."

"That was then, now I'm rejuvenated. Surprising what a quick catnap can do for the system."

"So it would seem," he replied, glaring at his friend. "Ok, see you downstairs in five."

"A Planetarium, but hardly worth the bother. Can see one of those any damn day of the week." Kyle complained, thumbing through a guide he'd picked up in the hotel. "The cathedral was ok I guess. Same with the museum, opened my eyes with the Mexican revolution; didn't know it had so much going for it. Anyway time's getting on, so suggest we call it a day."

Coming to the end of their meal, Kyle interrupted the silence of a relaxed atmosphere.
"How about we change plans for tomorrow, Jack? This place could be worth a look." pushing a leaflet across the table. "Do no harm to leave Merida for a day."
"Valley of the Caves? Ok! Yeah, why not?" he said, scanning the leaflet while adding his opinion. "Should be interesting, if this is anything to go by."
"Good-oh! You stay and finish your coffee. I'll see if the guy at the desk can fix us up with an auto."

Their fast start was destined not to continue. Smooth, tarmac-covered surfaces soon deteriorated into little more than sand-covered tracks: ancient byways ploughing their way through the Sierra Madre as they had done for thousands of years. Having never before driven outside England, Jack Sibley found the experience exhilarating. He didn't give a toss that the roadway was littered with the debris of countless mini-avalanches nor, surprisingly given his fear of heights, was he daunted by the precipitous cliffs on one side and a quick trip to oblivion on the other. Kyle however was far from amused, and by the time they reached their destination he was in a foul mood. And when the caves failed to live up to his expectation steam flared forth in clouds.
"Not the first time I've been bamboozled by the crap they put in tourist guides." Using his companion as an escape route for his irritation. "All that boloney! Archaeological evidence the caves were inhabited in five thousand BC. What evidence? Bollocks! Absolute bloody bollocks! Warped minds dreaming up what best they can stick in their damn literature. Good for the tourists, but for me…crap. And the journey don't help none.

Damn useless bloody roads. Wouldn't get away with it back home."

"Ease off, Kyle. You're beginning to sound more like seventy-eight than twenty-eight. And it wasn't a complete disaster. That enormous pot in the first cave was something of an eye-opener: made the trip worthwhile on its own in my view. And so what if the roads aren't exactly fast, at least they're different."

"Don't know so much about different, but boring? Yeah! Can go along with that. Too forgiving, that's your trouble. Still, spilt milk and all that. Let's make tracks out of this hellhole before I get any more carried away. Don't move soon we'll be stuck in these damn hills when it gets dark. Took long enough in ruddy daylight. Want an early start tomorrow and if it takes longer going down than it did coming up, I might just blow my top." Having the grace to grin sheepishly, he grunted, ok. I know. Don't have to spell it out."

"Another long flight tomorrow?"

"Nearer six hours this one. Makes my blood boil to think we could've been there by now. Shut up Steinbeck! Done more'n enough whining for one day." Clapping Jack on the shoulder he recalled his earlier comment. "Sure am gonna get you up and running with a bird...and I'm not meaning the Limey version."

"Jeeze, I'm knackered." Slumping into one of the spacious armchairs littering the hotel lounge he changed the subject. "Good meal that. Chef knows his stuff."

"Not surprised you're knackered. At the risk of inflating an already over-inflated ego, you have every right to be. The weather, that detour, the extra time and effort...you did brilliantly." Poking him in the chest with a rigid forefinger, he accused, "You didn't let-on we were getting low on fuel. But I'm not blind. I could see the gauges and the needles weren't far off zero by the time we landed."

"What would've been the point? You don't like flying at the best of times, I know that. So why worry you some more? But now it's over and we're sitting pretty, I'm gonna be honest with you. You weren't the only one with the heebie-jeebies. That weather front nearly did for us, don't mind saying. Down to the last gallon by the time we hit the tarmac." He dragged a dog-eared notebook from his breast pocket. "Expect you'll be pleased to know there's no more flying for a week-or-so. A lot of driving, but no flying."

"Good! Gives me the chance to do my share."

"Too damn right. Time you did something useful, instead of watching me do all the work. And" adding in tune to a wagging finger, "you can put that violin back in its case. Cuts no ice."

"Have you booked a car?"

"Need you ask? An SUV, delivered to the hotel by the time we get up tomorrow morning. Glue your eyes on this, Jack, and tell me what you think. It's all there: itinerary, map, what's to see...a tourist guide to what's what and how to get there. As it's the furthest, it would seem sensible to make Nakbe our first port of call. Which reminds me; don't forget your passport. Nakbe is in Guatemala, not Mexico, and it'd break my heart to have to leave you behind. Palenque next, then the big one...Chichen Itza. Back here for a breather before setting off to chase the floozies in Acapulco." He sighed: a deep whispering sigh. Whether at the thought of the Latin beauties or his friend's loss of memory he didn't let on. "Don't know why I waste my breath. Told you all this before we left home."

"Having fought hard to stay awake listening to you droning on-and-on about your favourite subject, how could I possibly forget?" Shielding a synthetic yawn behind a raised hand, he complained. "But you do me an injustice. You might have mentioned where we were going, but not how you planned to get us there."

"Well now you know, and before you find something else to whinge about I'll give you a rundown on the three sites we'll be visiting. Nakbe and Palenque are little more than ruins, but Chichen itza is different. A heck of a lot of World Heritage money has been spent in its restoration and, by all accounts, it's paid off. That said, it's not the state they're in that's important. What is, is the opportunity to visit what are reckoned to be the three definitive Maya sites. See how they lived, worked and played. Get an insight into the family unit, the art of the period, scientific know-how…the whole damn caboodle. Not to mention stark reminders of some weird and bloodthirsty religious practices." Ramming the notebook back into his pocket, he mused, "Acapulco next, and what's to say? Acapulco is Acapulco! You know as much as me. Now, and in keeping with us wanting an early start, I hear a whisper on the airwaves. Think it's a guy calling himself the Sandman, and, oh boy…do I hear what he's saying."

"Can't fault the service," Jack muttered through the folds of a napkin, "not a lot wrong with the food either."

"Glad you approve. This place was Ma's idea. She and the old man stayed here a couple of years ago. She'll be pleased to know you like it. Get breakfast out of the way and we'll go see what Merida has to show us."

"Busy enough," Jack remarked, crossing a Piazza jostling with erratic sightseers and bustling locals."

"Biggest town in the Yucatan, so to be expected I guess. One of the biggest in Mexico for all I know." Coming to a halt, he pointed to a magnificently fronted building on the far side of the square. "Has to be the cathedral."

"Hey, now take a look at this, Kyle." Transferring his attention from the plaque in which he was engrossed. "South America's very first cathedral. "Sixteenth century. Pretty ancient...nearly as old as you."

"Oh funny man! Listen, Sibley, I do the jokes...remember? But I'm surprised you regard a sixteenth century cathedral as ancient. By comparison with, say, the Parthenon, or the Pyramids, it must rate as modern."

"True." Looking about him. Absorbing the magnificence of a bygone age. "It's just I didn't expect to find a four-hundred year old building in a state-of-the-art Mexican city."

"You can thank the Spanish for that, Cortez and his cronies. They couldn't have been all bad, not if this is an example of what they got up to."

Towards the end of the afternoon, footsore and in need of a break, they came across a colourful, outdoor bar. Ice-cold lagers repairing some of the damage, Kyle suggested, "How about we eat out this evening? Hotel's ok but change, quoting that much used cliché, is as good as a rest...and a rest is something we could both do with."

"As long as it doesn't involve walking. Done enough of that for one day. You've got something up your sleeve. You going to tell me what it is?"

"A place called Progresso, a beach resort about thirty miles off. No, Jack," laughing at his expostulation that, 'he hoped he wasn't suggesting they walk there'. "Wouldn't dare; not after listening to you mumbling on about your constant ill-treatment. Another of Pop's suggestions. He reckoned it a 'must-go-to' place if we got the chance. A wonderful little hideaway; nice and secluded, sandy beach and a great seafood restaurant by all accounts." He glanced at his watch. "Touch after five! Too late for the beach, but time enough for a quick sluice before we set off."

"That was a good evening, Kyle. Remind me to thank your Dad when we get back." The two men were enjoying a last nightcap in the hotel bar before retiring for the night.

"Shame it wasn't a full moon. Could've made more of the beach if it had been. That's life I guess. Given the chance, we'll go there again on the way back...but this time while there's still enough daylight to make the most of the beach."

"A nice thought. But that's then...what about tomorrow? Another early start?"

"No reason to break our necks. Overnight in Chetumal, on to Nakbe the next day...five-hour drive, give-or-take. The roads are in good nick so I'm told. Tenish...there abouts. Should be early enough."

The next morning Kyle was made to rue his optimism. The day turning out to be one when everything that could go wrong, did go wrong. To set the ball rolling, their showers were delayed until well after mid-morning by a power cut in the hotel. Having had barely time to dress, Kyle found himself on the receiving end of a visit by customs officials. Not content with his explanation of their purpose in coming to Mexico, they insisted on searching his aeroplane.

Using Jack as a target for pent-up fury, he ranted away at the mindless bloody bureaucracy of civil servants with nothing better to do other than foul up honest folks lives. "Stupid, grinning critters. Would've made their darned day if they'd found what they expected to find. Drugs is all they ever think about. Do I look like a goddam junkie for chrissakes? Let's get the hell going before I blow a gasket."

Had it not been for Jack collapsing in hysterics when the hired car failed to start, it was more than probable he would have ended up with something more than a blown gasket.

"Sorry, Kyle...but you have to see the funny side. Better that than a heart attack. And think of the excitement we would've missed if we'd gone for an early start!".

"Yeah, guess you're right," managing a lopsided grin. "These things happen and I shouldn't let 'em get at me. Ok, I'll go make that call."

It being late afternoon before a replacement vehicle arrived, they decided to delay their departure until the next day. Yet further reason to add to Kyle's annoyance.

"No more pussyfooting. Tomorrow we're gonna leave early like normal. We have another day like today I'll welcome a bloody heart attack. Least that way I'd be put out of my misery. Any more hiccups, Jack...let me warn you not to point out that everything has its funny side."

"At last! Beginning to wonder if it was ever gonna happen," the words ejected with considerable force as they left the hotel car park behind. "Perhaps now we can get back to making something of this vacation."

And they did. The morning following the one-night stopover in Chetumal, they set off for Nakbe in good spirit. "Hope we're not in for another rude awakening, Jack. That farce with the caves still rankles. I was lured into coming here by what I read, and if that turns out to be a similar load of junk you'd better stay out of my way."

"Oh this is great, Jack...everything I could've wished for. The blurb didn't exaggerate one bit...restored my faith in human nature. This place wasn't known to exist until the nineteen thirties, and I find it hard to believe that so much has been done in such a short time. Excavation didn't begin until nineteen sixty-two, and to have unearthed all this, and in such detail? Not bad going you must admit."

"Seems a helluva long time to me. But what would I know?"

"Not a lot it would seem. Fifty years is little more than a blip in archaeological time." Wagging an admonitory finger in his friend's face. "Can't use a spade, let alone a bloody great bulldozer. Knife and fork technology, patience and understanding...the tools necessary for work of this delicacy. Anything else and you've a disaster on your hands."

"I'm not that ignorant..." He broke off, peering across the American's shoulder. "Probably nothing, but there's a man over by the car-park: eyeing us up...don't like the way he's staring at us. A bit of a tramp...oh, ok, he's moving on. Imagination? don't know...not sure. His body language worried me. Anyway there's an end of it...he's disappeared."

"Too many late nights and early mornings, gets us all in the end. Does no favours, Jack. Bad for the digestion, plays havoc with your sex life and creates hallucinations of dodgy characters peeping over your shoulder". Tucking his camera back into its case he climbed into the car. "Back again tomorrow. The museum," tapping his tourist guide, "dedicated solely to this site and guaranteed to provide a wealth of information."

"That was some day, Jack. Got carried away at times. Almost felt as if I was part and parcel of the Maya and their way of life. You won't see it the same as me, but these two days have given me a wonderful insight into the way they lived, worked and had fun...not to mention what they got up to on the religious front." Turning to face him, flailing hands emphasising his excitement. "And those miniatures? Won't ever see craftsmanship like that again, that's for sure. Palenque tomorrow, and if it comes anywhere close I'll be a much contented guy."

From an archaeological viewpoint Palenque matched Kyle's expectations, but the visit was marred to some extent by an energy-draining, hot and humid atmosphere. Trudging to where they had left the car at the end of a long and tiring day, Jack stopped.

"Well I'm buggered! The car park at Nakbe, I told you a man was eyeballing us. You took the piss...remember? Well he's here," in answer to the American's nod, "over there, by the Temple of Inscriptions. Giving us another once over. I'm going to have a word. Find out what his game is."

"Leave it, Jack." Grabbing his arm, "Look at him, poor old guy. He's as puzzled as we are. Weighing up the chances of a handout, that's about all he's likely to be guilty of...reckon he could do with one too, if appearance is anything to go by. Now you've done it," he roared, slapping his confederate hard on the back. "You've frightened him off. Couldn't abide your ugly face glaring at him."

"You're blinkered Kyle. It's no coincidence him turning up here. Going through the same motions as last time."

"You worry too much. Didn't get a look at him yesterday, so have to take your word it's the same guy. But what if it is?

You have to admit he doesn't pose much of a threat. Too far down the road to be a menace. Sixty plus if he's a day."

"Have it your own way, but something tells me we haven't seen the last of him."

CHAPTER SIX

"What in hell's name happened to the time, Jack?" Kyle complained, tossing his phone on the bed in exasperation. Text from the car hire people, telling me the lease expired yesterday…wanting to know what I intended to do about it. Can't believe a week's gone by…don't seem possible!"

"If you remember, and honest enough to admit it, I reminded you over dinner the night before last. Nice to know you listen to my words of wisdom." "Yeah, now you mention it. Trouble was, by the time I took it on board I couldn't remember what it was I was supposed to remember."

"You'd argue your way out of a brown paper bag if you thought you could get away with it. Small wonder there's a string of confused ladies hanging on your every whim." There it was again. The glazed expression he'd noticed the morning they left Tonopah. "What's up, Kyle? Something's bothering you...your eyes are a giveaway."

"Don't know where that's coming from. Right now Chichen Itza's the only thing on my mind. Not giving thought to anything else."

He knew it was a cover-up but he'd let it go for now. It wasn't the right time to bully him for an answer.

"Ok, right...so let's make a move," he stuttered, hiding exposed embarrassment behind an empty coffee cup. "Don't want to waste more of the day than necessary. I'll sort the car out. See you upstairs when you're ready."

On the way to his room he tried to link the two events, but there was nothing he could put his finger on. On both occasions it had been a reaction to something said, and there was no mistaking what he saw. He hadn't imagined the shadow that flickered across his friend's face. He'd put it to rest for the time being, but he had no intention of letting it go.

"Did it right, Jack. Nakbe and Palenque would have been something of an anti-climax after this."

"Took the words out of my mouth. The way everything's been put back how it was: the time...the patience! The money! Must've stretched the national budget to near breaking point."

"I told you, if you care to remember. Chichen-Itza is a UNESCO World Heritage Site. That's where most of the boodle came from. The downside - always a downside - is it's turned the place into a major tourist attraction, and the way I see it that's not such a good idea."

"But surely that's how it should be? Everyone should have the right to glimpse the past, tourists as well as academics. If you think about it, it's what holiday-makers pay their hard-earned money for. Giving his friend a good-humoured pat on the back he observed, "You're here to satisfy your professional instincts, but it doesn't alter the fact that we, in accordance with the definition of the word, are among the tourists you deem responsible for any misbehaviour."

"They could do with you on their tourism board. But don't get me wrong. To some extent I agree with you but, although I accept that the majority treat places like this with respect, there are others who don't...as simple as that. And they muck it up for everyone else."

"When we have the time, we'll find ourselves a nice secluded table in a cosy bar. Some place where we can sit and argue the pro's and con's for an hour or two...before concluding I was right anyway."

"Ok, Jack, gloat all you like. I got it wrong." Goading him as they were leaving the Ball Court, an arena for a Mesoamerican ball game with a grisly finale: the decapitation of the captain of the losing side. "No bad behaviour, no hooliganism. So, to all those unfairly accused, I apologise."

"Gloat! Me? How could you? The thought never entered my head...but that could change. Back here again tomorrow?"

"Not just tomorrow, we've only scratched the surface. Another couple of days at least. Maybe more."

Four exhausting days later, with both men agreeing that everything worth seeing had been seen, they walked to the car park for the last time. Engaged in earnest discussion of what they had learned from the visit, Kyle veered the conversation onto a different tack.

"Can I interest you in my latest theory? Which I am more than happy to expound, providing you keep all unruly comments to yourself."

"Do I have a choice?"

"Course not. My ears only hear what they want to hear. I was thinking. Those stepped pyramids - the El Castillo and the High Priest's tomb. Doesn't it strike you as odd that the same mode of construction was all the rage thousands of years earlier? Back in the days of the old Egyptian empire."

"Can't say I've lost too much sleep over it."

"Well you should have. Because you must admit it's a mighty big coincidence. Identical structures, designed and built by different races in two countries thousands of miles apart."

"Hardly identical. The Egyptian pyramids are smooth-sided, not stepped like those we've seen here."

"That's where you're wrong, Jack. Leastwise, you are if you go back far enough. The earliest Egyptian pyramid so far discovered was built for a guy called Zoser, and guess what? The sides are stepped. Same in every way, shape and form to those here and what's left of those in Nakbe and Palenque. Which brings us back to my original question. How come two civilisations separated by a bloody big ocean, dish up dead ringers for the incarceration of their dearly beloved?"

"Great minds think alike? Not sure where you're going with this, but corporate espionage can be ruled out. Intercontinental traffic wouldn't have been exactly all the rage back in those days."

"Ah, but supposing there was a gigantic stepping stone between Africa and the Americas'?"

"Oh no...no, not that. Please tell me you're not about to drive me mad with yet another dose of your Atlantis obsession. How could I have been so naïve?"

"You exaggerate, I hardly mentioned ..."

"'Scuse, señor's. I ver sorry, I int'rupt."

"That's ok bud, what can we do for you?" Smiling at the deeply lined face, conscious of the tremble on the man's lips. "No need look so worried. We don't bite."

"Oh yes we do! It's him Kyle. The guy who's followed us around for the past week. Nakbe, Palenque...now here. I said we hadn't seen the last of him."

"You sure? I didn't know. But makes no difference. The guy's got rights."

"Buggered if he has. All this 'now you see me now you don't' malarkey. What's he got to hide? That's what I want to know."

"Pleases, Señor...I go Maya places, 'ope see you. No want toorist. I 'ave t'ing for monees to good man...no toorist. Nakbe see. Palenque sees more. I goes 'ere and more sees some. Pascal no see toorist."

"What's he on about, Jack? He's lost me completely."

"Can't be sure, but I get the impression he has something to sell but fussy who he sells it to. For some reason he doesn't want whatever it is ending up in the hands of a common-or-garden tourist. Denies he was stalking us, just happened to be in the same place at the right time...don't believe that for one moment. And as for harmless? He's either an exceptionally clever conman, or a few pence short of a pound...take your pick.

114

His name's, Pascal, by the way. But you probably picked that much up yourself."

"We all have our little foibles, Jack, so let's try him out. Give him the benefit of the doubt." He turned to the intruder. "You...Pascal?"

"Si Señor. Pascal Montez."

"You have thing to sell?" Making sure the man understood, he kept it simple.

"Si Señor."

Unearthing a small bundle from somewhere deep within his shabby coat, he removed the scrap of grubby rag in which it was wrapped before handing over the content.

Kyle stared in silent disbelief, striving to come to terms with the object in the palm of his hand. This couldn't be true. He had to be seeing things. One of the great treasures of the world and it was within his grasp. Instinct refusing to judge the providence that had brought it his way, he gave no thought to how, when or why such a priceless effigy came to be in the hands of such an overtly poverty-stricken individual. None of that mattered. Even the idea that it could be a clever reproduction was dismissed before the possibility entered his head. Every whim encouraged the belief that it was a genuine, Mayan artefact; an undoubted relic from a bygone age. Eyes glistening, he passed it to Sibley.

"Tell me I'm not dreaming, Jack. You know what this is?"

"The plumed serpent. But why the excitement? It's a fake, has to be. A good one, but there's no way it can be genuine." Raising his eyes he couldn't miss the eager anticipation on his friends face. "Don't tell me you're thinking what I think you're thinking."

"You're right on one score, it's Quetzalcoatl alright. But I'm as certain as can be this is no forgery. And if it is the genuine article, then it has to be old. Very old. I'm willing to stake my dwindling reputation on it. Similar to those we saw at Nakbe, but goes back a lot further. What I find puzzling, is how it comes to be in this guy's pocket instead of in a museum. My last buck says that's where it came from."

"You think he nicked it?"

"Is the Pope a catholic? He didn't find this in the local antique store, that's for sure. Let's try him out, see what he's got to say for himself." Taking hold of the Mexican by the upper arm he spoke with care, a precaution against words lost in translation.

"Nakbe...museum. You steal."

Making no attempt to deny the charge, the strange man held out his hand. "Pascal not t'ief. Pleeses give."

"He said that with real feeling, Jack. Ok, Pascal, where," moving the statue out of his reach, "you get? Me...you tell, or no monies."

"Pascal dig cenote. I find...I 'ave no monies. Americano 'ave monies."

"Who's he kidding?" Jack intervened. "A cenote? One of those waterholes where the Maya deposited their valuables to keep the gods' happy?" Continuing on receiving a nod. "Lying through his teeth. Does he really think we're gullible enough to go along with such crap. Finding it at the bottom of a bloody deep well? He must see us as a right pair of idiots."

"That's not what he's getting at. What he's trying to say, is he dug it up near a cenote...not in the damn thing. Looked at it in perspective, it's not beyond the bounds of feasibility. There would have been more than a few artefacts dropped in the mud, left to lie unnoticed for hundreds - if not thousands - of years until someone like our friend here comes along with his bucket and spade. His only crime was to have a lucky break. Finding something no one knew was there in the first place."

"Still sounds far-fetched, and even if you're right it doesn't detract from it being illegal. Treasure trove regulations must apply here, same as everywhere else."

"Technically, yes. But they who are kept in the dark? As far as I'm concerned it can stay that way." Balancing the statue on the palm of his hand, chewing matters over before coming to a decision. "He'll have no difficulty finding another sucker," the words addressed aloud to no one in particular, "and the more I think about it? How much, Pascal?"

"T'irty t'ousan Americano dollar, Señor."

Kyle whistled. Sibley gulped.

"He's talking silly money …" changing tack in tune with the look shot at him he challenged, "you're not serious?"

"If this is kosher, then what he's asking is small beer. Let's see how he takes it." Hands spread wide in mock horror, he protested. "Thirty thousand greenbacks…too much. No can do."

"Dollar…Señor. Americano dollar."

"Greenbacks confused him," Jack chuckled, "Poor old bugger thinks you're trying to rip him off!"

"Oh yeah...course. Should've realised." Turning to Montez, he tried again. "Thirty-thousand dollars, Pascal…too much."

As before, the strange little man held out his hand. "T'irty t'ousan dollar, Señor. Lots peoples give Pascal Montez."

"Wait Pascal…I talk amigo."

"He don't intend to let it go on the cheap, made that plain enough. And can't say I blame him. But whatever, it's still a lot of money. That don't matter if it's the genuine article, but I've gotta be certain…as certain as I can be. The base metal is unalloyed gold; no doubt about that, and I'm pretty damn sure the adornments are made up of rubies and jade; but that's bye-the-bye. It's value lies in the Maya connection. If it's the real McCoy you couldn't put a price on it." He paused, lost in thought before committing himself. "I have an idea, let's see how he takes it."

"Pascal, you trust me. I take statue my hotel…thirty thousand dollar if good. I get money mañana." Handing him a business card, he added. "I stay Merida...Fiesta Americana Hotel. Eleven hours mañana, you come."

The reply, an almost inaudible "Si."

"Good. You have monies…or statue," patting the wallet in his hip pocket and the object in his hand. "Comprenda?"

Montez nodded. His reply hushed, nervous, "'Ow know Señor come not?"

He could understand the Mexican's reluctance. In his shoes he wouldn't have gone along with such a dodgy arrangement, so why should he?

"You have God, Pascal?"

"Si Señor, I 'ave God"

"Good." My God...your God. He knows I honest man. He say, Kyle Steinbeck," patting his chest, "honest for, Pascal Montez. Comprenda?"

"Pascal Montez belief Señor good mans. Pascal come 'otel 'ours 'lefen, mañana." With that, he turned and walked away.

"How's that fellah get about? Be surprised if he's got two pennies to rub together, yet somehow manages to turn up at three different places a lot more than just a few miles apart. Seems Merida doesn't pose a problem either."

"Good point, Jack." Hands forming a megaphone, he shouted after the retreating Mexican. "Pascal...wait."

"Motorbike, that's how. Says Merida's no trouble." Glad I ran after him," smiling at the recollection, "seemed real pleased I made the effort. Must've given his trusting nature a bit of a boost."

"Gonna be real unsociable tonight, Jack, so you'll have to forgive me." Back in the hotel, they were near the end of their meal. "Heck of a lot to get through before I can let my head hit the pillow, and the sooner I start the earlier I finish. That's the theory."

Left to his own devices, Jack spent the time ploughing through the buttons on the remote in a forlorn hope of finding a television programme of some interest in a language he could understand. Concluding several buttons later it was a waste of time, he decided to make the best of things and indulge the luxury of an early night...until Kyle burst through the door.

"For God's sake, you scared the bloody pants off me. Come on in why don't you."

"Knew I'd be welcome." Excitement written all over his face he straddled the doorway. "Come on! Get yourself off that damn bed. Won't find anything on the goggle box to top what I've got to show you."

"What the..." giving up as Kyle's back disappeared into the corridor. Muttering something along the lines of 'there being no peace for the wicked' he dutifully followed the American back to his room.

"Took your time, but never mind that. Tell me what you make of this," holding the statue for him to take. "Come on, get a move on." impatient at his friend's hesitation, "hurry up. Not sure it's gonna last."

"For God's sake stop talking in riddles. What 'it', aren't you sure about?"

"Don't want to plant ideas. What I do want is for you to tell me if you notice anything odd about the statue. Has to be a genuine response, don't want what I think prodding you into giving me a wrong answer." He thrust the statue at him. "See if it hits you the same as it does me."

"Ok, but can we turn the lights up? Damn near stygian in here...bloody cold too. You got the air conditioning working full blast, or what?"

"Forget all that. Just do as I ask. No...not like that. Don't grab it. Treat it like you would a woman. Caress it gently with a loving touch."

Holding the statue in one hand, he sensitively explored the contours of the effigy with the fingers of the other. Paying no heed to the constant cajoling of his friend, he took his time. In silence he ignored the mounting irritation of the other man. Refusing to respond until he was certain. Inwardly panicking, he sought to erode the scourge that threatened to tear his mind to shreds. The meagre light reflected in golden beams from the body of the statue mocked him, tinkering with his emotions, plucking at nerve ends. He tried to convince himself he had to be wrong. That it couldn't be happening all over again. That it was against all odds for lightning to strike twice in the same place, and in such a short space of time.

"Well?" Perturbation and expectancy embroidered in the one word.

"The vibration? No Kyle, you're not wrong. I only wish you were."

"What sort of answer is that? Here's me as excited as a bitch on heat and there's you doing your best to put the dampers on."

Ignoring the outburst, he asked. "What were you doing when you first noticed it? How long before it started?"

"A few minutes before I came to get you. I was trying to make head or tail of an inscription on the base. Using this," pointing to a magnifying glass lying on the table, "but getting nowhere. All of a sudden like, and without any rhyme or reason, my fingers started tingling. Before I knew what the heck was happening the darn thing started to shake, almost like it was trying to escape...that was the impression I got. Then it sort of settled down to what it's doing now."

"This inscription," turning the statue over to see for himself, "did you manage to make sense of it?"

"Nope! As I already said if you were listening. Damn thing started shaking, and then the lights went on the blink."

"So the..." the lights returning to full brilliance froze the words on his lips.

"About time. Perhaps now we can get somewhere...took long enough."

"So the lights were working normally before this thing started to act peculiarly?"

"Can't be sure but, yeah, suppose so. Wasn't much in it."

"Doesn't it strike you, that there could be a link between the two events."

"Course not, what d'you take me for? Pure coincidence the two things happening together like that. For a start it wouldn't have been only my room that was blacked out; other rooms, the entire hotel for all I know, would've been affected."

"So you didn't notice when you came crashing into my room - the room next to yours - that the lights were full-on. Nor that those in the corridor outside were burning brightly?" Brow furrowing deeper he added, "Here's something else for you to think about. Just before the lights returned to normal, I was about to remark that the vibration had stopped...another convenient coincidence I suppose. And I don't know if you've noticed, but it's a lot warmer in here since the lights came back on."

"The statue don't like the dark maybe. Gets all of a tremble when the lights go out." The impulse to laugh at his own joke died, strangled by the pallor of the face confronting him. "Hell, Jack...what's wrong?"

"I'm holding what's wrong. Get rid of it, Kyle. For both our sakes. You'll come to regret it if you don't. When Montez arrives tomorrow, tell him thanks but no thanks. If you don't, then we must both hope I've made a monumental mistake."

Taking the statue from Jack's hand, he held it up close. Peering intently, a mocking expression underlying his response. "I've given this fellah a good eyeballing Jack, but damned if I can see anything to take the colour off your face. And you're saying he and me should part company when we've only just begun to get acquainted? Ok, so put an ignorant guy out of his misery and give him some answers. Because as I see it right now, Montez is gonna go home a happy man tomorrow."

"I haven't any to give. My concerns are based on gut instinct fuelled by past experience. No, hear me out." His manner sharp, the attempted interruption rebuffed in tones that defied argument. "The lights, the icy cold that hit me the moment I walked into the room. It wasn't the statue on its own. It was all those things together. A combination that raised memories of a time I wish I could forget. I couldn't go through it again…I pray you will never have to." He shrugged his shoulders in an admission of defeat. "I can see you're not convinced. Which is sad. Because it's all I have to offer."

"I know you're meaning it for the best, Jack, and don't get me wrong; I appreciate what you're saying. But there's nothing tangible for me to get my teeth into. An Impression is all you're giving me, and that ain't sufficient. Unless you can give me something more concrete, and don't take this personally because it's sure not meant that way, I'm going to be guided by what I believe and not by your fantasy. How I see it, is this statue holds a lot of history, and whether you agree or disagree don't matter. I'm gonna unleash that past. Whatever it takes."

"The vibration was no impression. That was fact. And how do you explain the more violent shaking that preceded it?"

"I can't. The only argument I can come up with, is it could perhaps be an embedded message. The Maya were heavy on scientific know-how and, for all we know, they might have perfected the means to integrate a signal within a lump of metal. No, ok," in response to the slow shake of the head, "just a thought."

"As we both agree that possibility can be ruled out, can we not both agree there is another that can't? Apart from scientific prowess, the Maya were red-hot on magic. Your very words!"

"Thought my idea of a built-in signal was harebrained, but you're now telling me magic was involved?" The half laugh dying on his lips. "You're serious!"

"It was you who told me how adept the Maya were in that area."

"Oh yeah sure, but that was then. Back in times when folk were fooled easy. Don't mean I go along with it."

"So I got it wrong. I had the impression you believed what you were telling me. That's not important. What is, is you put aside your scepticism and hear me out. Because the only logical explanation for tonight's events, is they were orchestrated by supernatural forces."

"Sorry Jack," face red, he struggled to keep his laughter under wraps, "don't mean to be rude but you have to see the funny side. Or have I got the wrong end of the stick? I have, haven't I? You're having me on."

"I'm glad you find it funny," rising anger reflected in his eyes, "because I can see nothing to laugh about. But then I couldn't expect you to understand. You haven't come into contact with events that can destroy your life."

"Don't go all shirty on me, Jack. Sure didn't mean no harm. But you must admit, what you're saying...it's bollocks. You know it is. But...oh, hang on," eyes igniting as the penny dropped,   "of course; this tripe you're spouting. It's what happened in church. Your funny turn and the rest of it. What you told us...not to mention what you kept quiet about."

"Before we go any further, let's drop the animosity. It'll do neither of us any good, and won't solve anything. As for what happened in Tonopah? Yes, you're right; of course you are. Which is where I suggest we leave it for the time being. Nothing I say is going to change your mind, and it'll only make matters worse if we carry on the way we are. I hope my silly ideas are way off beam, and that in the end your laughter turns out to be merited. However, if it transpires I'm right? Well...you know where I am."

"Don't know so much about knowing where you are, just wish I knew what the hell you're on about. But thanks, Jack. Whatever it is, it's appreciated. That said and the threat of us getting at each other's throats blown away, cast your eyes on this inscription: see if you can make sense of it. Thought I'd seen it all, but this is a whole new alphabet."

Although somewhat thinned by the passage of time, the engraving was surprisingly legible. To make sure, he moved closer to the light from the table lamp. He was in no mood for mistakes. He'd already given his friend plenty to laugh about.

"Runes, Kyle. Cabbalistic symbols...the language of mystery. This innocent statuette was once, still is in my opinion, a talisman of evil. But that's as far as it goes. Unfortunately I don't have the know-how to decipher the content, and I doubt you'll find anything on Google either...although it could be worth a try. Only other option is to try the universities when we get back. There could be a hard-up Don somewhere, waiting for someone like you to test his expertise if the price is right."

"What you say makes sense, and it sure ties in with what we know about the Maya." Hands clasped together and eyes having reclaimed their usual sparkle, he put the disappointment aside. "Shame we can't finish the job, but we've done enough for one night. We'll find out what tomorrow has in store when it arrives."

Having suffered the hassle of transferring money in the past, Kyle was at the bank before it opened. He wasn't going to chance another long delay, and the precaution paid off. Alone in a world to which he was unaccustomed, unsure of what to do and where to go, Pascal Montez walked into the foyer just minutes after he arrived back at the hotel.

"Senor...t'ank you. You 'ere. Pascal Montez 'appy me see."

"Nice to see you too, Pascal. Good news," grabbing a free hand and shaking it energetically, "we have a deal."

"You 'ave monies for statue?"

"You bet I have! Thirty grand...thirty thousand dollars." Taking him by the arm, he propelled him towards the lounge. "We go count money. Make sure you happy."

"Qué?"

"You...count...comprenda?" pulling the folder from his pocket, rifling the notes with his forefinger, "Make sure."

"You 'onest man, Señor. Pascal know."

"Course I am...but want you to be sure. We have coffee...you count?" The grinning nod implying he at least understood what coffee was all about.

"Evidently I'm not the only one with misgivings, or didn't you take what he said on board?" The Mexican having departed, they were on their second cup of coffee.

"What misgivings?"

"You know damn well. What he said about taking care: you might like the statue…it might not like you. Not his words, but it's what he was trying to say."

"Don't drop the damn thing it might break? That's how I saw it. You know, the nice, uncomplicated advice freely given by one friendly soul to another. You should try keeping things simple, Jack. You used to. The fellah I knew back in Cambridge was simplicity itself. But that's gone by the board. You'd sooner plague me with the stuff you nearly drowned me with last night."

"Stay blinkered, scoff all you like; do what you damn well please...but it won't change what is staring you in the face. Montez might have put it differently, but it doesn't detract from the fact that he was warning you to watch your back. You won't listen to me and now you're tossing his words in the bin. For chrissakes, Kyle, open your eyes and see it for yourself. We can't both be wrong."

"Give it a rest, Jack...shall we,?" Shrugging his shoulders, beguiling him with a lopsided smile. "I know what you say is in my best interests, and don't think it's not appreciated...but be real. As it stands this statue is about as lethal as a cuddly teddy bear. I know what you're gonna say," aborting the attempted interruption, "what about the electrics in my room last night, and the rest of the odd-ball stuff? No, I don't have an answer. But neither do you. All you keep coming up with is guesswork based on dark experiences from your murky past...goings on you refuse to talk about, but what I need to know if you expect me to have half-a-chance of understanding what you're getting at. Last night for instance. Might have been a touch strange – inexplicable I agree - but no harm was done. You and me are still standing ain't we?" Plucking the statue from his pocket, he placed it in the middle of the table. "The only way I'm gonna find out if this guy is a goodie or a baddie, is give it time to show it's colours. In the meantime I'll make you a promise. Until I know which way it's going, I'll treat it like I would a primed grenade. As long the pin's in place, it's not gonna do any mischief. That good enough for you?"

"Just be careful the pin isn't removed when you're not looking. But ok. Unless, or until, that happens, I'll shut up." Brushing biscuit crumbs from his trousers as he got to his feet, he asked, "So what next?"

"Oaxaca for a few days...two-or-three at most. Capital of the Yucatan, so has to be worth a visit...and as we're in the area! After that, the créme-de-la-créme. Acapulco! Imagine, Jack. Dusky maidens in their hundreds, queuing up in breathless anticipation as they await the coming of the Sibley-Steinbeck combo. If that does nothing to set the testosterone a bubbling, I don't know what will."

"You could fantasise for America if the vacancy comes on the market." Trying to raise a level of enthusiasm he far from felt, he surmised, "If the dusky maidens of your imagination have any sense, they'll go running back to Ma and Pa as fast as their little legs will carry them."

"Ah! The optimism of you English...it doesn't change. No romance, no adventurism, forever simmering away in hope rather than expectation and without ever coming to the boil. But you hang on in there, Jack. I've been hit with inspiration. I'm Ok though, it didn't hurt" Face aglow he announced the content of his inspired thinking. "Progresso. Said we'd go back if we had the chance, and no time like the present. Plenty enough daylight left to make the most of the beach, so why don't we? Take a dip, polish up the tan and finish off in that gourmet restaurant."

"Your rare burst of inspiration worked for a change."

"Nice to know I'm appreciated, but it's my turn to do the honours. You and me had such good times in Cambridge, and back then it was you showing me the hot spots. Not to mention the fun we had when we took to London. Wouldn't have known where to start without you showing me the ropes. Often think about the time we had that few too many. D'you remember it as well as me, Jack? Pissed as the proverbial newts we were, as merry as a couple of cows in clover. Went to the theatre to see - what was it? Can't remember what it was called, but it was bloody funny. Yeah, that's it...'Run for your Wife'." he replied reacting to Jack's prompt. "Was when we came out of the theatre and found that pub things really got going. I'll never forget that night. Haven't had one like it since and don't suppose I ever will. Your memories Jack...as good as mine?"

"Oh sure! I was so ill, how could I forget? So were you if you care to remember. The entire next day was spent fighting for the one and only bathroom. That landlord feeling sorry for us, and those other guys who joined in...that was the crunch. If he hadn't opened up his back room we'd have been tucked up in our beds long before we got anywhere near the state we were in. Then those girls turned up - where from was anybody's guess - and that was it. Suppose I must have enjoyed it at the time, but regret soon took over if I did. And you were a fine help. With your eye on one of the lasses I was forgotten, left to ferment under the table where I somehow managed to get myself stuck. When you eventually decided to come to my rescue I was bundled into a taxi, the driver instructed to deliver me to our hotel by first-class mail. But I suppose you don't remember any of that."

"As if? But that poor landlord! We later heard he had his licence quashed for out of hours drinking. Bit unfair in my opinion. He was a sound bloke in my book."

"There's the rub, Kyle. The laws aren't written in your book, which is probably just as well. Dread to think what would happen if they were. While I think of it, do you have Julie's mobile number? Said I'd phone when I got the chance." Mentally bracing himself. He knew the way Kyle's mind worked..

The lumbering grin, the jubilation in the voice; it was all there. "Of course. Must keep Julie in the picture. Let her know what we're up to and if we're behaving ourselves. On second thoughts, why don't I call her? Save you struggling with the hotel phone." Unable to keep a straight face he passed his mobile across. "Sorry, Jack, that was rotten of me. But I couldn't resist it." You'll find her number on the list. I'll go make myself scarce."

"Go grab a table, Jack, won't be long. There's a news stand in the foyer, want to find out what American papers are available...if any. Anything you want while I'm at it? No...sure?" Replying to the shaking head. "Ok, right!"

It was their second day in Oaxaca, and the comfort of the hotel lounge was seen as the preferred alternative to the blistering heat of the mid-afternoon sun outside. While waiting for Kyle's return, Jack whiled away the time reflecting on a friendship that had continued to blossom over the years. It was an odd relationship in many ways, and he found it strange that it had ever got going in the first place. With his upbringing, and the wealth that accompanied that upbringing, Kyle was the epitome of all he had no right to be. Were their roles reversed, would he have been as generous, as forthright, as self-effacing? It was an interesting thought, albeit a random one.

Lunch lying heavily, he got up and walked across the lounge to gaze at the gardens through an open window: while absorbing the myriad of colours dancing on the sunlit patio his thoughts turned to the family. They all seemed to have the same outlook on life. There were none of the airs and graces he'd half expected. When Kyle had suggested he spend a holiday in the States before being tied down to a working life, he'd pondered long and hard. Apprehensive of being looked upon as a scrounger homing in on a freebee, he was in two minds. Wanting to accept while mindful that meeting his family might strain their relationship. He couldn't have been more wide of the mark, his fears evaporating the instant Martha met them on the steps of the veranda. From that moment on he was made to feel completely at home. All erstwhile concerns falling faster than a barometer with a hurricane brewing.

Then there was, Julie. Erasing any lingering doubts, she had gone out of her way to make him feel comfortable in an environment that was foreign to him. They'd hit it off the instant their eyes latched. But there was more to it than that...they were comfortable in each other's company. And that was what made it special. He'd had a few girlfriends in the past but had never felt completely at ease with any of them...which was where Julie was different. It wasn't just her physical attributes, it was her warmth, her vibrancy - he failed miserably to suppress the emotion - she was not only lovely, she was lovable. Like no other girl he had ever met, he knew he faced an uphill task trying to forget her when he returned home.

"Had to make do with a local rag, but at least it's in English." Kyle interrupted his daydream. "What you doing over here, anyway? Thought you were finding us somewhere to park."

"Apart from you and me the room's empty. Or did you not notice?"

"Oh I see...have-a-go at Kyle time. Ok, clever-dick," tossing the paper onto a nearby table, "You sit your ass anywhere you like, I'll get the coffee."

Browsing through the negligently flung paper while he waited, his eye was captured by a compressed article on one of the inside pages. It was the headline that aroused his curiosity...it was the content that sent a chill through his body.

Approaching the commandeered table, Kyle was made to pull up short. He didn't need to be told something was wrong. The pale, fraught expression that faced him spoke volumes.

"You're worried, Jack...what is it? Found something nasty under the chair, or you been propositioned by one of the waiters?"

He made no reply, pointing to the article that had caught his eye with a trembling forefinger.

MAN FOUND DEAD
Police are investigating the death of a man, killed yesterday in a motorcycle accident on the

outskirts of Merida in the Yucatan district. The deceased, believed to be in his sixties, was identified from his driving licence as Pascal Montez.

The man's death was initially thought to be a direct cause of the accident, but a detailed examination of the body raised doubts in the eyes of the local constabulary. Aside from a facial expression of abject horror - described by one officer as 'if he had seen a sight so terrible death was deemed to be the better option to staying alive' - there was no outward sign of physical injury.
The police are further puzzled by the large amount of money found on the body, given that from his attire the man appeared to be impoverished. This raises the assumption that the money, in new American Dollar notes, was stolen. In all probability from a visitor to the area. The police have issued an appeal for information to help establish the source of the money and for anyone who may have witnessed the accident to come forward. All contact will be treated as confidential.

"Poor old Pascal. Gets a few hard-earned bucks in his pocket, then blown away like that. Life is full of rough justice for some."

"What if he didn't come by the statue like he said? Suppose he stole it from someone who wants it back very badly...badly enough to kill?"

"You're not suggesting he was bumped off? For chrissakes, Jack, you read it yourself. There wasn't a mark on his body...tell me how that can happen if he was done in. Unless of course you're trying to tell me he was poisoned? Not easy to do that to a bloke riding a motorbike."

"And the look of horror? Tell me what that was all about."

"No, you can't," the resigned expression hard to miss, "but I can. He either saw or heard, death on its way."

"Oh God, how I am made to suffer! I know what's coming ...the statue. Got no arms and got no legs, but it don't matter none...it's number one suspect for doing the business on poor old Montez."

"Not the statue itself you idiot. That's not at all what I'm saying, and you know it. So get off your high horse and have the decency to hear me out. Supposing, just supposing, Montez stole it from someone who would go to any lengths to get it back. Someone who could kill without recourse to violence."

"Non-violent murder. Now that's a good-un. What fairy story that come..." His words brought to a sudden halt by the unexpected onslaught."

"Leave it Kyle. The last thing we want is for us to fall out. Hear what I have to say and, I promise, not another word. Whether or not you go along with how I see things is neither hear nor there. What is important, is that we don't allow a wedge to be driven between us. Because, if by chance I'm right, Pascal Montez might not be the only one to end up wearing a horrified expression."

"Listen to me, Jack. If I'm to understand any of this garbage, I need to be told a whole lot more than you've given me so far. You might see things in a different light, but to me it's nothing but hocus-pocus. I've no idea where you're coming from, and you've told me nothing to keep me on track. So give me the full works. Tell me in plain and simple English everything and anything, those intimate secrets you keep close to your chest. You bubble on about what's happened in the past, but it don't help none if you keep papering over the facts."

"Yes, you're right; I can't hang it out any longer. I've told Julie all there is to know, and there's nothing to be gained by keeping you in the dark." Guilt rising, he hastily averted his eyes. "Yes, I know what I said," blurting an apology, "but she gave me a very special reason. I planned to tell you when I plucked up enough courage but circumstances have changed. It has now become imperative that you *should* know...later could be too late. Having heard what I have to say might help you appreciate, that what you regard as the fantasy of today could well be the reality of tomorrow."

CHAPTER SEVEN

"That's about as much as I can say." leaning forward, his chair dextrously positioned so as to face the American who sat on the edge of his bed. "Sorry it took so long but I did warn you." Having got it off his chest, he aimed to finish on a lighter note...the smile hovering on his lips rendered immobile by the cruel response hurled in his direction.

"How in the name of all that's sensible," Kyle barked, climbing to his feet to add impetus, "were you taken in by such garbage? When'd it happen, before or after you got sectioned? You may be the nicest, most genuine guy I've ever had the pleasure to meet but I was wrong on one score...had you down as one of the more intelligent of my acquaintances. But that's been blown into kingdom-come. And If you expect me to fall for the nonsense you're peddling you must reckon me as much a goddamn lunatic as yourself. Don't reckon on being one of the brightest sparks on the planet, but I know first-degree crap when I come up against it. The whole darned business stinks of chicanery. Something a number one idiot would've picked up on right from the start. But you...you not only believed, you indulged. What's the matter with you, Jack? Born nuts, or did it take practice?"

Continuing without so much as a pause for breath, he returned to his seat. "Goat of Mendes...who the heck could come up with a name like that other'n a registered imbecile? And there's you taking it as gospel. You and the rest of the sad morons who joined in. Whole damn lot heading fast for the institution if you want my opinion...and that don't exclude you. Love to know what Julie had to say when you were out of earshot. She's too bright, too level headed to be taken in by the kind of rubbish you flayed her with. Can see her now...laughing her damn socks off. Wondering how her brother came to get himself tied up with such a brainless weirdo. Collapsing in hysterics as soon as she got you out the way, giggling fit to bust at the thought of the sad misfit that'd been thrust on her."

"Ok Kyle, you've had your say," voice trembling with heated anger at the verbal onslaught from a man he had thought to know so well, "now you can hear me out. Not that I can hope to compete with the spite of a pig-headed, righteous know-it-all. My God, you masked your true nature well during the three years we shared the flat. Now I see you for what you really are. Never easy to be wise after the event, but I should have known what your reaction would be. Exactly what I would have expected from a narrow-minded, conceited country bumpkin. A self-opinionated Yank, too cosseted by rich parents to appreciate the reality of what goes on in the outside world. No...let me finish!" Shouted at full volume, the command drowning the attempted interruption. "Who the blazes do you think you are, to have the temerity to cast your pathetic opinion on events that shattered my life? What you saw in the church at Tonopah was nothing compared to the hell I went through back then...yet you have the effrontery to tell me it was my mind playing tricks. About time you grow up and face facts: you know nothing, absolutely bloody nothing, beyond your nice cosy existence."

Anger vented, he continued in softer mode. "I don't deny Julie found it hard to go along with. Of course she did. But as usual the indefatigable Kyle Steinbeck gets it wrong...she listened intelligently and with compassion. That she queried plenty goes without saying, but there was no laughter, no mockery. Unlike her worldly-wise brother, she refused to allow scepticism to suppress the reality of my personal trauma. There was no assumption that, because she was so obviously right, I had to be wrong. Neither did she see me as teetering on the edge of insanity, heading fast towards inevitable incarceration in an appropriate institution. And it was just as well Angela and Professor Lumberge took me seriously. Had they not done so, I wouldn't be here now."

In an atmosphere thick enough to have been cut by only the sharpest of knives, the room fell silent. Each man reflecting on the nastier side that had surfaced in the other. Each in his own way desperately sad that the person they had known, - thought they had known - was capable of giving rein to such unbridled viciousness. Both finding it hard to accept that a long-term friendship could find its end in bitter acrimony.

Kyle was first to break the silence.

"Can't go on Jack, not if that's how you see me. I can go along with your disappointment, your frustration; but to come back at me like you did was beyond the pale. We've had the odd disagreement in the past; only natural. But whatever the argument we never sought refuge in vile abuse. Seems inviting you over was one big mistake. They say you should never go back, and seems they were too damned right. That way I'd still have fond memories. Now it's all gone. Every time I think of you in the future it'll bring back those names you reviled me with. Makes me sick to think you could do that, Jack. We'll head off back home tomorrow," glancing at his watch, "later today...rid ourselves of one another for good and all."

"What bloody nerve! Talk about the pot calling the kettle black. I wasn't the one..." He stifled what he was about to say, simmering anger crumbling in the shadow of doubt. "Before doing anything we might regret...no, Kyle, please listen. This is all wrong. It isn't us. Not the way we behave. We have our faults, but they don't include resorting to vile, verbal recrimination when we don't see eye-to-eye. So why the change? And it's not as if it was gradual. It was sudden. Two personalities altered in the blink of an eye. It doesn't make sense. Unless it's to someone's advantage that we fall out."

"Oh sure! Another of those odd-ball friends of yours!" He blustered, choking on a false laugh. "Not interested, Jack. Better admit you're a two-timing bastard, than keep pumping that rubbish you continue to swamp me with. Don't you ever give up?"

"No, not if there's a chance we can sort this mess out. I know how you feel and, if your slagging off of me is anything to go by, I can understand why you're so angry." Striving to keep his own temper under control he pleaded. "All I ask is you drop the antagonism until you've heard me out. I'm not asking you to agree with me, just listen before chucking my words on the garbage heap."

"If you insist, but it'd better be good. I'm not saying more'n that."

"That's all I want. Before we go any further, take a look at our relationship so far. You have to agree that, until tonight, we were as close as two friends could be." Acknowledging the tentative nod, he said. "So what happened? What changed? Something must've done, and unless we can iron out the cause, the reason, we'll get nowhere. For a start I have no recollection of what I was supposed to have said, so I'll have to rely on you to put me wise…what did I say to upset you."

"Don't come the bullshit with me, Jack. You know damn well what you said…what you called me. So cut the memory deficiency, I ain't buying it. Got my faults but I'm not the country bumpkin you reckon…nor none of those other things."

"Did I really call you a country bumpkin?" he chortled, trying to suppress his laughter. "I'm sorry," wiping away the smile, "it's not you I'm laughing at...it's what I said. Or what you think I said."

"Glad you see the funny side. But you still don't fool me Jack. You were over the top and it's too late for 'sorry'. Should never been said in the first place."

"Of course it shouldn't, and that's my whole point. I just wondered where I dragged bumpkin up from. Not a word that's bandied around too much these days. But you know me better than that, Kyle. Can you, in all honesty, imagine me referring to you in that way if I knew what I was doing? I know you for what you are. A highly intelligent, sincere and honest bloke. A guy it is my privilege to have known and to have been friend's with for a good long time. I've never, other than in jest, insulted you either to your face or behind your back in the past, so why would I do so now?" He shrugged. "I'm still the same bloke, nothing's changed. What else did I say?"

"For old times sake I'll humour you. But what you said, Jack. It hurt. You reckon on me being a self-opinionated, cosseted Yank. Self important and obsessed with my own magnanimity I don't give a toss, about anyone else. Actual words used might not be exact, but it amounts to the same thing."

"Ok, so you've every right to be angry. No argument. Now the other side of the coin. Do you remember what you said to me?"

"Every word. I was trying to make you see it for yourself. That what you were telling me was nothing but fake. What you said happened, the things you saw...none of it was real. Clever trickery, no more'n that. Difference was, I didn't get personal."

"Oh! So it wasn't you who called me a lunatic, a village idiot on his way to the funny farm. It wasn't you who reckoned your sister would have doubled-up with laughter when she disappeared into her room? And that's only the half of it. There was plenty more besides. But I guess that wasn't you either."

"Don't lie to me, Jack. You know damned well to say things like that ain't my way. You must see me as the idiot I was supposed to have called you if you think I'm falling for that baloney."

"Of course it's not your way, that's precisely what I'm getting at. And neither is what I said in character. That's why you have to try and understand what I'm trying to say. I couldn't make up what you called me...quite apart from not possessing that kind of imagination, why would I? Yet I heard everything loud and clear. I didn't dream what you said, Kyle, and neither am I exaggerating the content. It's the honest truth, and if we had a bible handy I would willingly use it to prove my point. I can't be sure, of course I can't, I can only guess but, as I see it, an outside influence must have taken control of our speech. Putting it simply: we were both guilty of saying what we did, but the words were not of our choosing. Does that make sense?"

"Of course it does...silly me. There was this guy with his hand up our backs, pulling strings to make our mouths work while he did the talking. Carry on like this it'll be me heading for the funny farm. We said it, but it wasn't our words! I've heard enough, Jack. Can't take any more of your weird ideas."

"Same old story. You promise to listen, but you've already made your mind up. So I suggest you go easy on the spite: it's neither justified nor pertinent. Just for once push your ingrained scepticism aside, hear what I have to say and put that thing between your ears to work..." Stopping in his tracks, seeking the expression on his friend's face, fearful he'd gone too far...relieved by a look of petulance but nothing stronger he carried on. "Do you remember what I said when we read of Montez's death, that it was important we didn't allow a wedge to be driven between us? That it was essential we stick together...irrespective of whatever or whoever?"

"As if I could forget. Didn't know what you were on about then and still no wiser."

"You're so bloody obstinate I could scream sometimes. But I'll find a way through that stubborn streak you call a skull if it kills me. No, sorry. I apologise," aware of rising anger contorting his friend's features, "but you just refuse to take what I say on board. Everything I propose is contradicted without reason and derided without thought. So please, Kyle, do me a favour. Chew it over before you spit it out. We won't get anywhere if you don't."

"Seems whatever I say makes no damn difference. Sorry fellah, but that's how it gets me."

"There's the trouble Kyle. It's as I said. Your mind is made up before I open my damn mouth. I can go along with sceptical but what I can't handle is your dismissal of everything I suggest without giving it at least some consideration. Keep on at this rate and we'll spend the rest of our days wondering what the hell went wrong. Is that what you want?"

"Now hey there, Jack, you know damn well that's not what I want. Not what I wanted when we started this carry-on. But that don't mean I have to see sense in your way-out ideas."

"Touché! Ok, but there has to be some common ground we can agree on. Where possible I'll add fact - proof if I can - to my, as you put it, way-out ideas. You on your part must analyse the substance of what I suggest before passing judgement. Take, for instance, my assertion that we were not responsible for what passed between us earlier on. Alright, so I put it badly. Try looking at it this way. Our vocal chords were infected by an outside influence, the infected routes commandeered by an alien source...does that make more sense?"

"I've come across some nutty suggestions in my time, but this takes the biscuit. Even supposing you're right, who the hell would want to do anything so damn ridiculous?"

"Whoever wants the statue."

"Must be a clever fellah. Not only knows we've got it, but knows where we hang out. I'd give up sex for his powers of perception."

"That'll be the day! But alright, answer this. How and why was Montez killed? What caused the statue to vibrate, and why the funny business with the lights and the air conditioning in the hotel? Then the crunch. Simultaneously, and without rhyme or reason, we go berserk and behave in a way totally foreign to both of us? Give me a straight answer to any of those questions, let alone the combination, and I'll concede defeat without batting an eyelid."

The flash of uncertainty in his eyes radiated the message, his reply giving tentative confirmation. "Don't fool with me Jack, I'm trusting you in this. Did I really say all those things? And do you honestly have no idea what you called me?"

"On my life, Kyle...the solid truth." Tone earnest, he gripped the American's arm. "Think about it. Can you, in all seriousness, see either of us resorting to verbal thuggery?" A relaxed smile registering relief he concluded, "Friends again?"

"Didn't want it any other way. It was just, you know...thought you meant what you said." Sounding more at ease than at any time since Jack's outburst he continued, "Ok, good! We weathered the storm and came out the other side still solid. But don't get carried away. Nothing's changed the way I see things, and still don't go along with all this magic baloney. And before you say it, yes, you're right. A large part of me doesn't want to be persuaded. And the only way you're gonna get over that hurdle, is show me something concrete. Come up with facts I can wrap my teeth around...and that's not gonna be easy. I'll listen, and I won't argue the point until I've heard your doubtful words of wisdom. But if - not if - when, I find answers of my own, you'll be the first to know."

"I hope you find those answers, Kyle, I really do. I'd far rather eat humble pie than face the alternative. Anyway, don't know about you but I've had enough for one night. Oh," pausing half-way through the door, "the Goat of Mendes? Any nasty dreams...you know where I am."

Sinking into the mattress he found solace gazing through the open shutters, a patient vigil while waiting for a dilatory sleep to make its presence known. His reward was the magnificent vista of a beautiful Mexican sky, a cosmic serenity that delivered calm and helped to relieve the tensions of the day...lulled into dormancy by a myriad of stars silhouetted against the deep blue velvet of the night. When he awoke, it was in response to Kyle banging on the door.

"Get a move on you lazy limey. Know what time it is?" tapping his watch, "Gone ten, which is a major a calamity. Means we've missed breakfast and I'm famished. See you in fifteen." Beating a retreat through the door, he didn't wait for a reply.

"That hit the spot, Jack." Swallowing the last of his coffee, rubbing his stomach in appreciation. "Reckon on seeing the rest of the day out now I've a good healthy breakfast doing it's stuff on my innards. What's the plan? Have a look at the Basillica de Nuestra Señora? Seems a good enough place to start. There's a museum attached to the church by all accounts...a bit different to the usual run-of-the-mill. Play out the rest of the day as we go along.

Nearing the end of their meal, having opted to dine in their hotel at the end of a long and tiring day, Kyle peered at his friend on the opposite side of the table. From his expression he could have been anywhere other than where he was. Nat King Cole's crooning of 'Unforgettable' on the piped music prompting him to ask, "Got a woman on your mind...Julie? Someone I don't know about? Where are you, Jack?"

"Eh? Sorry, I was miles away. What did you say?"

"I was querying the far-away look on your face."

"What far-away look?"

"The sort of look that tells the world a bloke is thinking about a dame."

"Yeah, you'll have to forgive me, but I'm not in a particularly sociable mood tonight I'm afraid. And you're right. I did have Julie on my mind. Looking at the future and not finding much encouragement. That's about the size of it."

"No need apologise when it's a woman hogging your thoughts. And when the woman's my sister and I approve of the guy doing the hogging? Nothing else left to say! But Julie,...she special to you, Jack?"

"You might say that."

"You in love with her?"

"Get straight to the point, why don't you?" Kyle's exuberance forcing a smile to his lips. "Put it this way. She's like no other girl I've ever met and I can't get her out of my mind. If they are the symptoms then, yes, I suppose I must be. But it doesn't makes sense. I've only known her for five minutes. Love at first sight might work for the Mills and Boon brigade, but it doesn't happen in real life."

"You've a lot to learn about women, Jack. Takes no time at all when the right one comes along."

"Oh boy, I can't wait to hear this. The guy who changes his girlfriends more often than he changes his socks, now claims to be an expert on relationships. That's a good-un" he laughed, making no attempt to hide his humour. "You've never treated a girl seriously in your life, so how would you know?."

There it was again...the glazed expression.

"Take the piss all you like, Jack, but there are certain things you don't know about me and one thing you don't know is, strange that you might find it, I was in love once. Still am, and always will be I guess. That's how I knew what was going through your mind. I wear the same look every time I think of her. And that's nearly always. Even when I'm with someone else. My dream ended before we met, and there was no point plaguing you with my sad memories. The subject was too painful to keep bringing up then, and ain't much different now. Her name was Sadie and we planned to wed soon as I finished my studies. A poor excuse, but it's how my obsession with women came about...forever trying to find another Sadie. Never will of course. I know that."

"I'm so sorry, Kyle, but why on earth keep it under your hat? A trouble shared and all that." So that was it. The lost expression: Sadie coming to the surface. Her memory haunting him as it always would. "Was it someone else?"

"She was killed, Jack. Her parents and brother too. Entire family wiped out by a drunk son-of-a-bitch driving a heavy truck. The car was demolished...and when I say demolished, I mean demolished. None of 'em stood a chance. The powers that be, in their wisdom, saw it as an unavoidable accident...the stupid, blind bastards. It was no bloody accident. Any damn fool would've rated it grade one homicide because of the state the lorry driver was in. But despite all the evidence against him, the dimwits in charge dismissed it as an unfortunate tragedy."

"I don't know what to say...you must have been devastated. But still don't understand why you never said anything. Keeping it to yourself wouldn't have done any favours. It's a wonder you didn't fall apart."

"Called grief, Jack. Different folks handle it different ways. My way was to keep the depression to myself. Not sure it did any good, but there you go...that's me. Long time ago now, and they say time heals…being a damn long time in my case. Anyway, enough of my problems," secret memories hidden behind the half smile, "yours can be dealt with. Mine can't."

"I wish. The cause of my dilemma is, thank God, nothing like as tragic as yours, but the happy ending is just as inaccessible. But hey...what makes you think I have a problem anyway?"

"Elementary my dear Sibley, coining the great detective's phrase. There's poor old Nat crying his heart out and all you can muster is a look that says, 'think I'll go drown myself'. You admit to having strong feelings for Julie and I'm sufficiently well acquainted with my sister to know it's not one sided. Ergo, you should be on cloud seven. But if the expression is anything to go by, you're looking at nothing less than everlasting misery. So tell me about it...then you can go jump in the lake."

"Letting our emotions run away with us is what it boils down to. Cloud seven is fine if there's a ladder long enough to reach it but there isn't, and Julie and I are left stuck on the ground floor. Put yourself in our shoes. 'How about dinner tonight, Julie?' 'Oh yes, Jack. I'd love that,'" making a complete hash of a mock girlie voice. "That's good. Hang on for fourteen hours-or-so while I grab a flight to San Francisco and hop on another to Reno. Tell you what, why don't you meet me at the airport? That would cut out the four-hour drive to Tonopah.' That's why, Kyle. Cloud seven is way out of reach."

"Seem to remember some old saying about faint heart never winning fair lady? Tell you this much, there's one fair lady hoping you don't have a dicky ticker…or I don't know my little sister. The way she's been behaving shouts it at me. She's as nuts about you, as you are about her. So you just listen to me, Jack. Instead of giving up and moping about your rotten luck, start thinking what you're gonna do about it. You'll spend the rest of your life regretting it if you don't. And you can't say I don't speak from experience."

"So what do you suggest...change the world's geography?"

"There's always answers, Jack. One of them is staring you in the face, and altering the globe don't come into it. Means I could end up with you for a brother-in-law but for the sake of true love it's a sacrifice I guess I'll have to make."

"Beam me up, Julie? Is that it? Another dose of your cockeyed humour?"

"Sarcasm is uncalled for. It is, as is quite rightly said, the nadir of wit and whoever said it knew what he or she was talking about. But I refuse to allow unkind words to hinder a humane desire to rescue two souls in distress." Hoisting upper body across the small table, he pierced him with his amber eyes. "Why not come over here; for good I mean. Leave the old country behind, join the throng and earn yourself a fortune in he process. Scientists of any ilk are in constant demand. Pop for instance. He's always on the lookout for guys of your calibre. And it'd make the family happy. Been trying to get Julie off their backs for ages." Unashamedly laughing at his own joke, he burbled, "Now you've come along it's their big chance. Seriously though, Jack. The family think you're the bees-knees. You'd have no argument from them, and I'm sure as can be they'd be delighted to help out."

"Although I appreciate what you're saying, aren't you missing the obvious? Quite apart from anything else, I can't see me getting a work permit. America must have more than enough indigenous physicists without me adding to the pile."

"That'd be the least of our worries. There's never a shortage of bent hierarchy around. You know the type. Willing and able to lend a hand if the price is right...know what I mean? Should do. There's enough corruption and open abuse of power where you come from, same as all over. Steinbeck Inc. is a massive outfit and, as such, carries lots of clout. Given the right encouragement: lining a salary pack with a little extra, a sleeping vice-presidency...whatever tickles the appropriate fancy. Tell you, Jack, they'll be queuing up. Dangle a juicy carrot in front of a receptive nose and all sorts of miracles are possible."

His unannounced presence brought their conversation to an abrupt end. Well over six feet in height and embarrassingly thin the man surveyed them with cold, humourless eyes. When he spoke, the voice matched the eyes.

"Dr. Steinbeck, Mr. Sibley? Good evening to you."

Rendered temporarily off balance by the interruption, their response was not readily forthcoming. When it did, it was Jack who answered.

"You seem to have us at a disadvantage,." looking at Kyle for confirmation. "We haven't met as far as I am aware." Feeling strangely uncomfortable, he forced his eyes from the hypnotic stare.

"In the context to which you refer, Mr. Sibley, I have not had the pleasure. But although we may not have met in human form, we are spiritually acquainted. To clarify that remark, let us say that I have formed a close familiarity with both you and your companion on the ethereal plane. You seem to regard my words as gibberish Dr. Steinbeck. To be expected in your case but you will be enlightened in the fullness of time." More a threat than a promise, the words were hissed through near non-existent lips that barely parted. "My name is Membril...Sir Charles Membril. I am a scholar in certain arts that remain a mystery to you, but not to your colleague. He is possessed of a quite considerable learning."

"You might know what the devil you're on about, but the same don't apply to me. You'd make more sense talking through your butt" Hackles rising, readily attained boiling point threatening to burst at the seams. "Don't go too much on your manners either. You bust in on us without apology, and bamboozle us with a load of bullshit worth about as much as a bent dime. So cut the crap and get to the point."

"Your opinions, Dr. Steinbeck, are irrelevant. As is your demand. I will nevertheless strain your patience no further. I have a proposition to put to you. One to which I would advise you give careful consideration."

"Don't believe I'm hearing this! Now you just listen to me..." temper snapping audibly, he made to move from his seat. "For hells sake, what's going on?" Invisibly shackled to the chair, his plea verged on hysteria. "I can't move...for chrissakes, Jack! I can't move."

"It's alright, Kyle. Calm down. You can't fight it." Pulsated by past memories his voice shook. "Don't need him to tell you, I know full well what he wants." Pushing fear aside, he rose to face the intruder. "The statue. That's what this is all about."

"Your acumen does you credit, Mr. Sibley. It is a pity you chose to follow the wrong path." Probing eyes registering contempt he simmered, "You are of course correct. The effigy of Quetzalcoatl, the plumed serpent god of the Maya: stolen from me by a common thief." Cod-like eyes turned on Kyle, he continued in lighter tones. "I am cognisant that the statue was purchased in good faith and that it was not for you to know from whom it was pilfered nor, indeed, that it was stolen in the first place. However, and despite your misguided animosity, I am minded to return the thirty thousand dollars you gave in exchange. Having released your bonds, you are at liberty to fetch the statue from your room. But before you do so, I would warn against any further display of violence."

Flexing his arms to make sure, Kyle rose to challenge his aggressor. Inwardly shaken, he chose his words carefully.

"What you did was mighty clever and don't claim to know how you did it. But there's one thing I am sure of. I would no sooner deal with you, than I would any other egotistical son-of-a-bitch. You want the statue? It's yours...over my dead body."

146

"A reckless choice of phrase if I may say so, Dr. Steinbeck; most reckless. Poor Montez. He was perhaps of a similar opinion as yourself. Such an unfortunate accident. One cannot help but wonder if it was in retribution for his way of life. Needless to say, I would not wish upon you a similar fate. But destiny is an arbitrary parameter, and who can tell what lies around the corner?" His next words were uttered with menace. "You should be aware, that although your co-operation would be agreeable it is far from being a necessity. I tell you that as a token of goodwill, because it would give me no pleasure should harm befall you. I also appreciate that your attitude arises from ignorance. That was made clear by your refusal to give credence to the reality of Mr. Sibley's narrative yesterday evening. Oh yes," responding to Kyle's look of incredulity, "I am fully aware of what passed between you. I in fact enjoyed it so much, I was obliged to add my own contribution. It was a pity my endeavours came to nought, but it was fun while it lasted." Nodding towards Sibley, his eyes conveyed a trace of humour, "But he will no doubt try again. When he does, I would advise you listen to what he has to say."

"Ok, so if you're so damned clever why don't you just take the statue and have done with it? From what you're saying I wouldn't be able to stop you. Or you all bluff and no substance?"

"I have never found the need to bluff, Dr. Steinbeck and, be assured, my level of substance surpasses your will to resist. That you will find out for yourself in due course. However, to answer your question, the route you suggest is barred to me. Should it be of sufficient interest, I am sure Mr. Sibley will enlarge on why that is so." Adopting a darker tone he added, "For your own sake, you should know that the statue will be returned to me…whatever it takes."

"I don't give a…"

"You don't give a damn, Dr. Steinbeck? Words said in haste are all too often regretted. In this instance, it could be for the rest of your mortal life and throughout the duration of your spiritual existence. However," his manner becoming polite, almost docile, "as I would prefer a more amicable arrangement I will give you time to reconsider. I would also suggest you take on board what your friend has to say. His counsel could be your saviour."

"And just how long do you intend to give us."

"You have until the next time we meet, Mr. Sibley. Other than to say my patience is not inexhaustible, that is all you need to know."

"That's you're idea of keeping me out of harms way, is it?"

"You doubt me, Dr. Steinbeck?" The tone oily, ingratiating, "In that case I must prove my goodwill. I will join you later tonight. Not as you see me now, but we will meet nevertheless. Look upon it as my contribution to your education in matters that are foreign to you. I am sure you will find it most informative."

Turning on his heel, he walked away.

The silence was oppressive. Neither man trusting himself to speak, each focussing on the effect on him as an individual. One stunned beyond despair, the other desperate to deny the possibility his friend had been right all along. It was as if time stood still and that Membril was nothing more than a figment of their respective imaginations.

Kyle's dilemma stemmed not so much from the exchange of words but from his brief loss of mobility. That it was Membril's doing he couldn't deny...but magic? The idea was absurd. Jack would see it differently of course, that was without question. But the way he saw things was nothing less than unmitigated nonsense. There had to be a more realistic, a more logical answer...if only he could lay a hand on it."

The more he thought about it, the more obvious it became. The episode with the chair, the conviction he couldn't move. He could have done if he'd tried. He remembered reading somewhere that hypnosis - had to be something along those lines, nothing else fitted the bill - could be over-ridden by positive thought. He had only himself to blame. He'd let the man convince him. That's all there was to it. If he could persuade Jack to see it in the same light. Make him understand that those weird happenings he prattled on about were all in the mind. Wouldn't say anything yet awhile though. Wouldn't want to upset him again. Done too much of that lately.

"You going to give it to him?"

"Eh...give who, what?"

"Membril...the statue of course? What do you think I meant?"

"Nah, he won't come back. You can bet your life on it. For a start he's not gonna know where to find us. The guy's all fig and bubble gum, talky-talky and plenty of bluster but precious little else. We're off to Acapulco in a day-or-two, and he's not gonna have a clue where to come looking. Surprised you didn't pick up on that." Gesturing to the bar, he rose to his feet. "Want a beer, Jack? That old fraud's given me one heck of a thirst. Not to mention a throat full of all the nasty words I should've used on him."

"So what makes you think he won't know where to find us when he comes looking?" Accosting Kyle on his return, armed with two brimming glasses.

"Stands to reason. Don't know ourselves where we're gonna end up till we get there. So how in the name of all that's sensible is he gonna know?"

"So how come he knew where to find us tonight?"

"Montez, of course. More-or-less admitted it was him who did for the poor bugger. Squeezed the info out of him before he snuffed it."

"So you not only told Montez we were going to Oaxaca, but threw in the name of the hotel - the one we don't yet know the name of - for good measure? That was clever."

Initially at a loss, he argued. "Wasn't necessarily me. Could've been either of us let the cat out of the bag. And alright, I couldn't have told him where we were staying...so what! No need to come the high and mighty on me."

"Acapulco's a big place and, I would imagine, plastered with hotels of all shapes and sizes. It'll be interesting to see your face when he comes knocking at our door - the one we don't yet know about. Perhaps then you'll understand what I've been trying to drive into you. As for me mentioning our next port of call to Montez? I didn't say a word to the man. You and he were too busy counting the money for me to get a word in." Parking himself on one end of the table, he looked his companion in the eye. "Membril won't need us to tell him where we are, he'll know almost before we do. So please, Kyle, face facts and stop this continual pooh-poohing of everything I come up with." Hands clasped he leaned forward, eyes riveted on those fixed on his, anxious to drive the message home. "Where Membril stood, the lights were behind him. Right?"

"Can't say I noticed. But yeah, alright. Suppose they must've been."

"So how come what should have been there wasn't?"

"Jack, listen to me. You may know where you're coming from, but give thought to the guy you reckon on being a country bumpkin. My poor, befuddled brain feels like it belongs to an Oozlum bird what's going round and round in ever decreasing circles before disappearing somewhere it shouldn't. You're now tearing my poor, overworked brain apart; telling me something should've been there but wasn't? You gonna let me in on what the hell you're on about, or leave me in confusion for the rest of my natural?"

"I was hoping you'd see it for yourself, then you wouldn't have to take my word for it. A bright light, a mere few feet away, yet he cast no shadow."

"So what are you saying," laughing at his own humour, " he did a Peter Pan? Left it in a drawer somewhere and Wendy wasn't around to stitch it back on for him."

Ignoring the jibe, Jack slid off the table to stand where Membril had stood earlier.

"Any more ha-ha comments, Dr. Steinbeck?" Pointing to the prominent shadow spread across the table. "And I'm nothing like as tall as he is."

"Then you must've got it wrong. But that's not gonna be the way you see it. I can tell by the look I'm getting."

"There was a time, Kyle, somewhere around a hundred years ago, or so it seems, when I was as blithely innocent as you. But remember the promise you made? You would do your best to keep an open mind? I don't want to come over as melodramatic, but it has reached the point where it is vital you keep that promise. Before going further I suggest we replenish our glasses, because we're going to need all the solace we can get. You stay put. My turn to be waiter."

His absence set Kyle thinking along different lines. For all his outward bravado and the continued search for a saner approach, he was conscious of doubt becoming an issue. Until Membril appeared on the scene there had been no contest, but his turning up like he did had changed everything. Reluctant as he was to admit it, his earlier convictions were beginning to crumble. Erstwhile transparency obliterated by an impenetrable opacity. Was it possible it was he who had got it wrong? That there was a degree of substance to Jack's beliefs?

"Here you go, wrap your lips round this. I'll talk…you listen. You can have your say afterwards."

"You said that like it makes a change. Reminds me of a woman once you get going…never know when to stop. But don't mind me. You just carry on. You'll get the message when I nod off."

"Next time you bombard me with one of your endless theories about nothing in particular, I'll remind you of that." He inwardly smiled. This was more like it, just like old times. The pretend spats neither of them took seriously. "Before we go any further, consider what's gone on since you first got hold of the statue. The odd happenings in your room, Montez's death: those events alone were enough to ring alarm bells. Then out of the blue Membril turns up. He admits to killing poor old Pablo who, so he claims, stole the statue from him. We've only his word for that of course, but my gut feeling is he was telling the truth. Going on to demand the return of his property, he puts a stop to you threatening to land one on him by locking you in your seat. He further rubs it in by letting us know it was he who supplied the voice-overs last night. Finally, he has the gall to walk away without giving us a glimpse of his shadow. An anomaly that puts the cap on any argument you can come up with."

"Wasn't an actual confession. Only hinted it was him who blew Montez's lights out. Didn't exactly hold his hand up."

"Couldn't have been much closer to a full confession, but that's beside the point. The intimation was there. Letting us know the lengths to which he was prepared to go. Warning us - you in particular - he wasn't prepared to take no for an answer. Give him what he wants, face the consequences if you don't."

Taking a long draught from the rapidly diminishing contents of his glass, he made use of the pause to repair frayed nerves.

"You don't have to accept what I say, Kyle. Take the plunge and try to see it for yourself; form your own ideas. What we are faced with is the daunting fact that normality and logical interpretation has gone by the board, a combination that has rendered us poles apart. We now have the added complexity of an occult presence...the lack of a shadow: irrefutable proof that Membril is both black magician and Satanist, and an adept of high order at that. An Ipsissimus, at the very least."

"I wish to hell I could prove you wrong. Solid reasoning tells me you have to be, but I don't know where I'm going anymore. None of the odd things you mentioned have an easy explanation and that worries me. Now this bloke Membril pokes his nose in, and...I don't know Jack, I just don't know. Is there a chance what you've been telling me isn't the garbage I want to believe it is? The rubbish common sense tells me it has to be? Part of my brain tells me there's no alternative, that there is substance in what you're saying. That's before the other part kicks in telling me it's bunkum. I'm that confused I don't know whether I'm on my ass or my elbows. But this guy, Membril, gives me the creeps. If you're right and he didn't get it from Montez, how'd he know our names? And even more crazy, how'd he know we had the statue and where to find us?"

"You saw what he was capable of in the short time we were made to suffer his presence. To locate the statues whereabouts would have been far from easy, and I don't pretend to know how he did it...but it could explain the happenings in your room. My guess is the violent shaking you mentioned at the start, was him trying to make contact; the more muted vibration an indication that a connection was established. The rest would have been easy. My persona would have identified me as a one-time member of his community, and he will have latched onto you while up to his fun and games last night. The link having been secured, the statue will let him know where we are at all times. Get used to it, Kyle. There's nowhere to hide."

"He said you'd explain why he just don't take the statue and have done with it."

"As you might think, followers of the left hand path are fettered by very few restrictions. In the general run of things they go their own way and do as they damn well please, not giving a toss as to who gets hurt in the process. However, there is an inviolable rule that forbids a practicing occultist from procuring an object without the holders consent...any such item must be transferred willingly and without sufferance." Look anxious, he stressed, "The rule is rendered null and void by the death of the owner. In that sorry circumstance it becomes a case of first come, first served. Which is why Montez had to be eliminated. But Membril was too late. By the time he got to him he had passed the statue on to you."

"Not making sense Jack. If Membril's telling it straight, Montez stole the statue. How'd he manage to do that if it was breaking the rules?"

"Montez, was neither magician nor Devil worshipper...the rule doesn't apply."

"Don't know that. He might have had a leaning that way."

"No chance. You asked him if he had God. Remember? And he was most emphatic with his answer."

"Yeah, suppose so. But what goes with your other supposition? Membril might be a magician, but don't necessarily follow he's a Satanist."

"Oh but it does. Devil worship and black magic go hand-in-hand. The one can't exist without the other. If there was ever any doubt, the lack of a shadow provides confirmation. But you don't have to take my word for it, tonight's outing will complete your education more than any words of mine."

"You think I'm taking him up on his invitation, you must be mad... I'm staying well away from him, tonight and every other damned night. As I said...he gives me the creeps."

"You won't have a say in the matter. He wants a get-together, he'll have one. But it won't be the conventional, sitting round a table having a chinwag and getting sloshed in the process...nothing so cosy. Your meeting will be on the astral plane, while you're asleep and dreaming. But they won't be pleasant dreams, and they won't stop when you awake."

"You and your fancy names? What's with this astral plane?"

"Most of us think of a dream as a string of disconnected events, visions assembled with no rhyme or reason. But there is more to it than that. In reality a dream is a record of events witnessed by the spirit along the path it takes while we sleep. That path, the degree of consciousness to which the spirit ascends, is known as the astral plane: a complex set-up with several levels of attainment. Mere mortals such as you and I are restricted to the lowest of those levels...next one up at a push. To achieve a higher status the spirit has to be well drilled. Tonight, however, you are in for a treat. You have been given a personal invite to accompany Membril on the most exalted of those grounds. The downside, is your dream will not be a collection of random occurrences. It will be focussed on a specific theme, and recall will be complete."

"It gets worse. Here's me doing my best to keep an open mind like you want, then you throw this crap at me. Your spirit might get up to all sorts of tricks at night, that I wouldn't know. But I can assure you mine stays firmly entrenched with me in my bed. Don't argue Membril's got things going for him I don't understand, but the idea of me cavorting with him in some place I've never heard of? Sorry, Jack. That's pushing me too far."

"Whether or not you go along with it is immaterial," rubbing a hand through his hair, massaging his scalp, seeking words of comfort. "It will be a grim affair, Kyle. One that will, as I've already said, continue to haunt you when you wake up. But remember. At the end of the day, it is only a dream. You will have suffered no physical harm. I can't give any assurances as to the effect on you mentally, that's a different matter. But you've a strong will and, hopefully, the aftermath won't last for long. All we can do is wait and see. Something for you to hang on to because, and make no mistake Kyle, it will not be a pleasant experience."

CHAPTER EIGHT

"You tired, Jack?"

"The way that was said, I get the impression I'm supposed to say no. So, ok…no. Not particularly."

"Know I scoffed, but this business with the astral plane...it's getting right under my skin. Tell the truth, I'm as scared as hell. But it's not only that, I hate the idea of him putting one over on me. So I'm gonna be awake long enough for him to get his balls in such a twist he won't know if it's doomsday or Christmas."

"Like the idea. The thought of, Membril crossing his legs with great delicacy conjures up some delightful pictures." Jack laughed, "But don't get too carried away. Staying awake won't do you any favours in the long run. Even if you do manage it tonight he'll still be there, waiting, ready to pounce tomorrow, the night after...whenever. He's in no rush and he'll get you in the end...don't kid yourself. But that's beside the point. Where does me being tired come in?"

"Help me stay awake of course - prolong the agony if you like - a nightclub loaded with loud music and plenty going on might be just the ticket, but not much fun on my own. Need you there to get under my feet. Tell you, Jack, I'm that on edge I'm like a woman what's forgotten to take her pill...say so if you'd rather not."

"Ok, I'm game. And we could both do with a bit of light relief." He glanced at his watch. "Not ten yet...anywhere in mind?"

"Not off hand. I'll pop down to reception, see if they can come up with something. Meantime you go get yourself ready, won't be any longer than I can help. Think I'll try my luck with the girl at the desk if it's the same one who was on earlier." Lips pursed in anticipation he added an afterthought. "Never know, might be nearing the end of her shift and on the lookout for an evening she'll never forget. Could perhaps have a mate to bring along...be a bit of fun, deciding which one's yours and which one's mine."

"Wouldn't dream of depriving you of first choice. But don't get too carried away. If it's the one I think you mean, she strikes me as having met your type before and knows only too well how to handle it."

"Ok, so you were right. But I ask you, Jack, how degrading can it be for a guy with my attributes to be told that, flattered though she was by the invitation, her boyfriend might not go too much on the idea? What she said hit me where it hurts most, and that's apart from decimating my already low esteem."

"You'll get over it, but it's not your hurt feelings that bother me. I'm more interested in knowing how you got on with what you went down there for in the first place?"

"Fat lot of sympathy. Thought you'd at least give me a shoulder to cry on." Drying crocodile tears on the back of balled fists, he abandoned further pretence. "All set, Jack. A nightclub called the Azuka. Five minutes walk away. Oaxaca isn't exactly a hotbed of nightlife by all accounts, but she tells me this place tops the best of the rest. All rock and salsa…just what we want."

"If we're not too late. Some clubs set a time limit."

"Checked that. No prob. Quick wash and brush up, then off for a night like we used to have."

"Live music eh, Jack. Don't get much of that these days. I'm gonna enjoy this." Shouting above the noise as they pushed their way through the mass of people thronging the bar. "This is going to be one great night. Can feel it in my bones."

"Mm, maybe. I'll reserve judgement. You get the drinks. I'll grab a table."

"Made it!" Depositing a largish tray near to overloaded with an ensemble of bottles and glasses on the table as he spoke. "Thought it best to stock up. Going back and forward all night otherwise. Had a good look round while waiting to get served and, I tell you Jack, this place is full of unattached females. One-or-two eyeing us up already if my eyes weren't deceiving me. Yep, this is gonna be good. Real good"

"How is it you manage to see things invisible to us mere mortals? That's what I'd like to know" Pointing at the tray with an accusing forefinger he changed the subject, "Sure you got enough? Any more, you'd need a licence."

"Better too much than not enough, that's my philosophy. But besides, I wouldn't want to keep trekking through that crowd hanging round the bar more'n necessary. There's a few didn't take too kindly to me barging my way through as it was. We came here to have a good time, not spend most of it waiting to get served."

The good time was assured. The music lively and enjoyable, the supply of partners inexhaustible and, much to Kyle's aggravation when he found out, waiters ready to attend their every whim.

"Great place, Jack. Have to thank that receptionist when I see her next. Even if she did turn me down."

"Suppose so...oh I'm enjoying it alright, don't get me wrong. It's just some of these girls. Not exactly slow in coming forward are they?"

"Just how it should be, Jack, but I'm not in the mood to tell the truth...and you can wipe that disbelieving look off your face. It's that bastard Membril. Can't get him out of my head. Not gonna let him get at me though." Scraping the remains from his plate with the last chunk of bread, "Buggered if I will. Every time I bring him to mind, my hackles rise and makes me more determined than ever."

"That's the spirit." He yawned, the sight of the little hand of his watch creeping towards two-thirty widening the yawn by a few more centimetres he sighed, "How you going, Kyle. Don't know about you but I'm on my last legs. Time to call it a night I reckon?"

"One last dance, Jack, then I'm with you all the way. That gorgeous chick, next-but-one table. Had my eye on her all night, but too many guys quicker'n me."

It was a salsa of the genuine Latin American variety and he made the most of it, holding the girl close as they gyrated around the limited space available on a packed dance floor. Over the moon to have at last got his wish, he pulled away from the girl to see if she was enjoying it as much as he was.

His heart leaped. He didn't know why or how, didn't care. Reason despatched beyond recall. This was no mirage. No trick of the light. The face that returned his gaze was indelibly stored in his mind. A vista destined to haunt him until his dying day. Her unsurpassed loveliness, a memory he would hold for all eternity. His head buzzed. The girl he danced with was no stranger…it was his beloved Sadie, unfettered love shining in her wonderful eyes. But she had died. That awful car crash. That dreadful night she was taken away from him. But it didn't matter any more. She'd come back. Must have known how much he missed her. Understood his loneliness without her.

She smiled up at him. "Hello, Kyle. I've been waiting for you to dance with me. It's been a long time, so long…too long. I love you so much. Don't ever leave me again. I hate it when you go away from me."

His Sadie! It was his Sadie! The phrase repeated over and over inside his head. He wanted to shout it out loud. To let everyone know it was his Sadie. It was her voice. Her face. Her body he held in his arms. He didn't give a damn, didn't know how or why…what the hell? His lovely Sadie had come back to him. She hadn't changed. Her beautiful grey-green eyes sparkled the same as ever. Her teasing smile sent shivers up his spine as it always did. And her wonderful hair. A golden sheen with a hint of red glistening in the half-light, teasing him as he ran his fingers through it. She hadn't died, couldn't have...wouldn't be here now. But he'd make sure she never left him again...but she said he'd left her. Why would she say that? He loved her far too much to ever leave her. But what did it matter who left who? They were back together again, and this time he would make sure it stayed that way."

With an ear-shattering whoop that echoed around the dance floor, he scooped the girl into his arms. Oblivious of her frantic attempts to break free he hugged her close, kissing her with a passion born of yearning.

He pulled away, to see again the face that was so dear to him. To feast his eyes once more on her shining loveliness. A reminder of how much he loved her. He lowered his eyes...

His piercing scream rent the heavy atmosphere, a shrieking plea for deliverance from the terror that held him in its violent grip. Heads turned to locate the source, ears covered to subdue the deafening sound burning into them. Panic stricken and out of control, his bemused and tearful partner left stranded in the middle of the dance floor, he thrust aside anyone foolish enough to get in his way. The face he adored, the picture of serene loveliness that haunted his every waking moment...transformed into a skull of deathly white. Glazed eyes staring listlessly from what should have been empty sockets. The once beautiful features mutated into those of an obscene phantom. A vision sent to drive him to the depths of despair.

By the time Jack caught up with him he was seated on a low wall shaking uncontrollably, a low moaning escaping from quivering lips; a disturbing glint of insanity in tear-filled eyes. Placing a comforting arm round his friend's shoulders, he stayed silent. Saying nothing until his agonies subsided.

It was Kyle who spoke first "It was Sadie Jack, I was dancing with Sadie. She told me she loved me, then...then she went away." Uninhibited tears running down his cheeks he sobbed, "Why, Jack...why did she leave me? She still loves me...she told me. Why would she do that?"

"It wasn't Sadie, Kyle," speaking gently with as much compassion as he could muster. "Sadie is dead, you went to her funeral. She can't come back. The girl you danced with was the one you asked to be your partner. Your vision of Sadie was just that...a vision. An illusion. Membril - it was him of course - making you suffer as only he knows how. A foul twist of the screw to make sure you do what he wants."

"No, Jack," he sobbed. "I couldn't mistake Sadie. Wasn't just her face, it was everything about her. Her voice, the way she moved...it was her, Jack. Like she always was. Like I'll always remember." Seeking assurance he grasped Sibley's arm, "Membril had nothing to do with it. He never knew her, never seen her, never talked with her...wouldn't have known she existed. He couldn't have matched her voice or copied the wonderful softness of her body. Wouldn't have known how her lovely eyes shone when she smiled. It was my Sadie. I know it was."

"He wouldn't have had to know Sadie in the material sense, he was introduced when eavesdropping in on our conversation. We were talking about her just before he turned up, if you remember. From then on it was a piece of cake. Your fond memories were all he needed."

"No, that can't be," still sobbing, "he was nowhere near close enough. And anyway. He didn't turn up till after we stopped talking about her."

"It wasn't eavesdropping in the sense of the word. He will have used his skills to penetrate the innermost recesses of your mind. Learned of your suffering. Uncovered the tragic circumstances of her death. All he had to do was implant the idea it was Sadie you danced with, twisting your mind into believing what you wanted to believe. It wasn't Sadie you held close, it was her memory. The recollection of your lost love...the perfect catalyst for his evil."

"But her face, Jack. Right before me. It was obscene. A skull with ghastly eyes. Sadie's eyes...but different. They stared at me. It was horrible. To turn her into a lifeless, loathsome creature: a living, dead thing? How could he - how could anyone - do that?"

"Membril and his ilk prey on the despair and torment of others. It's how they exist. There's no compassion, no penitence. They don't give a damn or a thought to the damage they cause. What you described, what he turned Sadie into…it's what they do. Sadism, debasement, debauchery. Without those obscenities they would cease to survive. By transforming a live and vibrant Sadie into her long-dead counterpart, he planned to drive you to the brink. By the time this night is over, he will expect you to have tumbled over the edge."

"You must think me a goddamn fool," the tears stopped, his voice marginally steadier, "I know she died. I went to her funeral…like you said. But I wanted so much for it to be real. Wanted so much to believe Sadie had come back to me. You said the proof was there, but I was too dense to see it. I've been an idiot, Jack, and you've shown me a whole load of patience. A lot more'n I deserve."

"I'm just sorry you had to learn the way you did."

"But how could I have been so blind? You had to remind me I'd seen Sadie in her grave for chrissakes. Godammit, Jack, I said goodbye to her in her coffin. Saw her lying there, cold and lifeless. Her beauty untarnished by death adding to my distress…my heartache. Membril, the shit-laden creep! He knew it. Knew what I would give for the chance to lay eyes on her again. Sussed I yearn for her more'n anything else in this whole damn world. Played on my vulnerability and like a fool I fell for it."

"Always easy to be wise after the event. I'm the living proof of that." He looked the American in the eye, "You'll let him have it? The statue. Sticks in my gut to say it, but he'll get his own way in the end. And if you don't do as you're told? He couldn't have put it more clearly."

The response was not immediately forthcoming, but he was content to wait. He could advise…Kyle had to make the decision.

"Membril did for me tonight," he said, peering at him through the darkness, "abusing Sadie was one big mistake." Turning his head to one side, he rose to his feet. "He's gonna pay for besmirching her the only way I know how. Told him he'd have the statue over my dead body and that's gonna be the way of it. Appreciate what you say, Jack, but makes no difference. Having fouled my precious memories of the girl I'd hoped to spend the rest of my life with, he'll be doing me a favour." Determination in every line of his expression, he returned his gaze to look at Jack full on. "You're out of this, fellah. Not gonna have you put in danger on my account. I'll book a London flight first thing."

"Applaud the motive, but think about it before you do something you might regret. Your family for a start. What about their feelings? Don't they count? Their youngest son, murdered out of sheer bloody mindedness...is that what you want? This isn't a game you can quit when the going gets tough, it has to be played through to the bitter end. And as for getting rid of me! You really think I'm going to bugger off and leave you to face that maniac on your own? Not on your bloody life. It'd be a passport to suicide and you damn well know it. So cut the crap and let's talk this through sensibly."

"Yeah but…"

"No buts. All along I've stressed the importance of staying close, no matter what. There lies our one and only strength, and Membril knows it. Why else do you suppose he rigged that battle of words the other evening? Say what you like, I'm staying put. It's what friendship is all about."

"All very well to say but this is different, and even friendship has its limits. It's me laying myself on the line. Deliberately and with eyes wide open. It's neither right nor fair for you to get involved in a mess of my making. Particularly when it could end up a life-threatening one."

"In case you've forgotten, I happen to be more aware of what I'm letting myself in for than you are. I know what he's capable of, and I'm not blind to the fact that he'll stop at nothing when it comes to getting what he wants. But I'll be damned if I let you go it alone. For better or worse, you're lumbered. But it's not all doom and gloom. Might not happen often, but the guy holding the trumps sometimes cocks it up and lays the wrong card. A belief in his own infallibility could turn out to be Membril's comeuppance. Play our cards right...who knows? Convinced he can't possibly be wrong, he might be tempted into a dodgy move. It's said that fortune favours the brave, whether or not that includes a couple of raving lunatics? That's another matter."

"The key to Pandora's box might help, but not much chance of that happening. If tonight was anything to go by, he'll have us for breakfast."

"Even scum like Membril have their weak spots and, ok; not much to go on, but his rampant hubris could work in our favour. Letting you in on his plans for tonight for instance. That gives a clue to the way his mind works. He gets his kicks by letting his adversaries know what's in store in advance. What he doesn't seem to take on board, is that a forewarning can also be a forearming."

"And if his rotten scheme goes haywire he does away with the two of us, and a fat lot of good that'll do. What's the point both of us ending up in the morgue?"

"The price one has to pay for humouring a stubborn American." The grin pulled apart by a more sombre expression, he continued in darker tone. "Haven't mentioned this before but there's something you should know before it's too late to change your mind. Our mortality may be at risk...our souls face the graver threat."

"Suppose you're gonna tell me they'll end up in Hell. Paying homage to the Devil."

"Something like that."

"You know, Jack, when I want cheering up you're definitely the bloke to do it. Look! I know you mean it for the best, but nothing of what you've said changes anything. Don't need you to tell me I'm stubborn, I know I am. But only when there's a special reason. And they don't come any more special than this. It's down to me. My responsibility. A personal vendetta if you like. If it goes wrong, then it's my problem. So please, Jack, don't shove yourself in the mire because of my stupid obstinacy."

"Obstinacy isn't your sole prerogative, I have the odd spasm-or-two myself. And I'm telling you straight, Kyle: you're not going to shift me. I never knew Sadie, but that doesn't mean I wasn't as sickened as you by what he did. No," pre-empting the protest, "save your breath, I'm not listening. Ok? Good," in response to the hesitant nod. "Now I don't know about you. But I'm knackered and it's long past my bedtime."

He'd get into bed, but that didn't mean he was gonna capitulate. He'd put a spoke in Membril's plan alright, and that'd do for the bugger. Cut out the shuteye, cut out the dreams...put his nose firmly out of joint without having to raise a sweat. With any luck he'll spend all night waiting for him to turn up. What he wouldn't admit was, it wasn't just bloody mindedness; fear was the secreted, the unspoken motive. Mentally it was the hero making the decision, deep-down it was the coward.

He glanced at the clock on the bedside cabinet...nearly four. Another couple of hours and the sun would be up. He wouldn't be able to get at him after that. Ghouls like Membril were only happy during the hours of darkness. He'd get what sleep he could when daylight came.

The bedside lamp flickered, flickered again: light growing dimmer. Bulb on the way out. Damn nuisance. Still, nothing he could do about it. Have to wait till morning to get it sorted. It was no good. His idea had been to pass the time sorting out his notes, but that idea had gone out the window. Couldn't see a damn thing. He shivered. It was cold. Freezing more like. So much for the tropics. He pulled the duvet up under his chin.

He was sleepy, so very weary. Until just a short while ago he'd been wide-awake. He'd close his eyes for a bit; not for long, just enough to give his eyes a rest. A few minutes, no more. The cold was getting at him. Made no sense sitting up. He'd be much cosier snuggled under the inviting duvet. Mustn't get too comfortable, he'd be in danger of nodding off if he wasn't careful...but why shouldn't he? He was allowed to...it was the middle of the bloody night for chrissakes. But the voice inside his head was insistent...he had to stay awake.

Seduction complete, the lower reaches of the bed gathered him to its bosom.

The speed at which he moved was astonishing...frightening. The mountains, seen on the far horizon at the start of his journey, were upon him in a matter of moments. He began to climb. He knew where he had to go, knew how to get there; didn't know how or why...didn't care. Didn't matter a damn, as long as he got where he was going...that was all he had to worry about. The gently rising foothills he encountered at the start were becoming steadily steeper. The earlier, by comparison comfortable, walk across convivial grassland about to be replaced by a difficult climb across a rock-strewn terrain. But the added hazards failed to slow him down...this wild, frenetic journey was programmed to continue at a pace that was more exhilarating than dangerous.

Cresting the top of a boulder-strewn mound he paused, peering over his shoulder at the ground far below. He had climbed several thousand feet in the blink of an eye. Not bad for someone who had never before scaled a mountain of any sort. There was a man waving to him in the mid-distance. That would be Membril...they'd arranged to meet. Absorbed in the climb, he'd almost forgotten.

"Dr. Steinbeck...thank you for coming. You might see this wilderness as an unlikely place to meet, but the reason will become plain in due course." His smile encouraging, he patted him on the shoulder. "Follow me. There's not much further to go."

Pursued at the same unending velocity, their path followed narrow tracks across a widely varying landscape. Without so much as a pause they dealt with precipitous scree-strewn slopes, fast running streams and the icy surfaces of one-or-two glaciers before eventually coming to a halt on a snow covered ridge. Taking his arm, Membril pointed to a small town many thousands of feet below.

"What you see is all that remains of an ancient civilisation. A once proud community, reduced to the verge of extinction by the interference of unwelcome intruders. And this is where you come in Dr. Steinbeck. With your co-operation, I aim to restore the race to its former glory. You have in your possession an object that, though of minimal value in the material sense, is of inestimable value if I am to succeed in that objective." Talking as they walked, he ventured to the periphery of the cliff. "It is decreed that certain earthly memories are forbidden to ordinary mortals on the astral plane, so you will be ignorant of the item to which I refer. It is a small statue, an effigy of the one god with the power to save that sorry populace from inevitable demise. On your return you will recognise it as the familiar of Quetzalcoatl, the Plumed Serpent. You will also come to appreciate the necessity of acceding to my demand."

He spoke with such a head of steam that he wondered why he found no difficulty keeping up. Did nothing conform to reality in this weird environment? He'd got it wrong though. What he'd said about being unable to remember things. Wasn't much, but his head was invaded by a constant string of messages. Nothing particularly meaningful, but Membril was constantly in the fore. There was something about that demand of his. He'd said it was important, but the voice inside his head was adamant: it was imperative he ignored what Membril was saying; dismiss that and all other demands he might make. Another message stressed the urgency of keeping what he was told to himself. The tone harsh, authoritative, more a command than a message. Suddenly it all changed. This time it was words of tenderness spoken in compassionate tones. Membril had hurt someone he loved and must be made to regret it.

"We shall see, Dr. Steinbeck...we shall see." A sickly smirk openly mocking him. "I confess to being at a loss to explain the origin of your thoughts, but it is of little or no consequence. I can read your mind as easily as I can the printed pages of a book. I would however advise you of the danger you encourage should you refuse my request. Believe me, Dr. Steinbeck, that is no idle threat...it is a promise. I nevertheless harbour the hope that there will be a change of heart, when you see for yourself how these people are made to suffer."

"And what's in it for you?" He couldn't resist asking. "Don't come over as the type to do something for nothing."

"I will tell you," the voice quieter, less menacing, "yes, I will tell you. It will perhaps convince you that any attempt to thwart me will end in tears. Your tears, Dr. Steinbeck, not mine. You wish to know what is in it for me? My very being...that is to be my reward." Eyes momentarily glinting red, he sneered. "You apparently see my demise as of little consequence. You will however forgive me if I cannot share that view. The stakes are high Dr. Steinbeck, and I have no intention of prolonging longer than necessary. Time is an important commodity, and as I don't have a lot of it to play with I would advise you take note. The choice is yours. Return my statue the easy, the sensible, way...or face the darker alternative."

He paused, brow creased in thought, eyes penetrating...gauging his reaction. "I am about to show you sights that will worry your conscience. Perhaps arouse sympathy for your fellow man. We shall see. Later on you will be entertained by the re-enactment of a ritual that has not been performed for many hundreds of years. In view of your profession, I would expect you to find the ceremony of especial interest. More so, as you will be both witness and collaborator."

Face creased with hidden humour, he turned on his heel to follow the downward gradient...a near vertical slope: dispatched with the same consummate ease as every other obstacle had been.

Upon reaching ground level they walked along a man-made path bordered by farmland, but it wasn't the scenery that dominated; it was the workers in the fields. There was no discrimination between male and female, all were clad in the same depressing attire. Baggy trousers, hooded knee-length coats fashioned from a course, hessian-like material, feet encased in what appeared to be wooden clogs. But it was neither dress nor occupation that caught his attention…it was the expression of sadness – no, it was more than that, hopelessness was the nearest he could come up with - on the face of every individual. A deep despair that neither hoods nor downcast eyes could hide. There was not the glimmer of a smile in the misery-filled eyes. Not a hint of curiosity at the sight of strangers in their midst.

The absence of bird-life also struck him as odd. They walked through fields laden with crops, an avian paradise in which he would expect to find hundreds scavenging away to their beaks content. But it wasn't the case. Birds were as non-existent as laughter on the faces of the workers in the fields. His unsavoury companion had a point when he spoke of sympathy and compassion. Such emotions would be difficult to subdue in the hardest of hearts, but the suffering of these people had nothing to do with a defunct deity well past its best before date. These poor souls were the downtrodden victims of a vile and ruthless regime. Their misery broadcast loudly enough for all to hear who were willing to listen.

Leaving the farmland behind, they continued in silence until arriving at what he assumed was the town centre. A spacious piazza towered over by a huge cathedral-like structure, bustling with people who all seemed to be going nowhere in particular.

The bastard had read his mind again. Letting him know that nothing was sacred, his eyes gloated. "As you have observed Dr. Steinbeck, fun and laughter is denied to the populace; such emotions are as foreign to them as are my practices to you. That you choose to disagree as to the cause of their depression is immaterial. All you need know is that my mission will be fulfilled and that any attempt to defy me will be ground into the dust." He stopped, turning to face Kyle full on; beseeching him with a look verging on compassion he warned, "Should you continue your obstinacy, Dr. Steinbeck, you will not be around to verify that prediction. And that would be most unfortunate. I would rather you were given the opportunity to witness for yourself the effect of Quetzalcoatl's return upon the masses. But as I have said, it is down to you. Your decision. Your prerogative."

"Here we are." He said. Ushering him through a massive teak door.

In contrast to the warm sunlight outside, the interior was dark and chillingly cold. No windows interfered with the monotony of the stonework, the sole source of light many yards away at the far end of the building. Difficult in the semi-gloom, he tried to make out his surroundings. The walls were draped with tapestries that conveyed the same, never-ending theme. The glorification of mass slaughter pursued in the presence of cavorting gods: deities comprising a sickening collection of horns, cloven hooves and half man-half beast conglomerations. The human element was confined to the sorry victims of slaughter. He shivered. It was all very weird...very frightening.

He supposed it to be an altar. It had the general appearance of one, but it was nothing like any altar of his previous experience. Red and gold drapes blazed a violent contrast to the eight black candles which, apart from the smattering of light from the half-open door, provided the sole source of illumination. An inverted crucifix hung from a bracket on the wall behind the altar...the height of blasphemy. Someone should get a rocket for that. Inwardly he gloated. Something else he could remember...which way up a crucifix should be. Another one in the eye for, Membril.

Clad in hooded robes of white and gold, four figures stood at the altar. Priests, he supposed. The garb was a bit of a give-away. They were looking at him: horrible, piercing stares.

Almost like he was expected. As if they were awaiting his arrival. Sinister in its intensity, the engulfing silence wove into his senses. Realisation belatedly dawning as the onset of fear nurtured by imagination took hold. This was no cathedral...no house of God. This was a place of the Devil. It was Satan who ruled in this abomination of a church.

Two chickens, one black, one white, were plucked from a basket by one of the priests. Wings flapping in violent unison, the frantic birds were held above a metal dish. A second priest stepped from the shadows, the raised knife glistening in the yellowish light. The thrashing necks offered no resistance to the flashing blade. Oh God! It was obscene. He tried to avert his eyes, but a mind more powerful than his made sure he saw what he was meant to see.

Each priest in turn filled a silver goblet from the collecting vessel, the noxious contents consumed in a single swallow. Purpose fulfilled, the empty flasks were reverently placed at the head of the altar. He wanted to be sick, the bile rising in his throat. He willed his eyes to close...but such luxury was barred. In growing horror he was forced to absorb the revolting theatrics.

Pointing to a gigantic sculptured snake that towered on the wall facing them, Membril spoke in hushed tones. "Quetzalcoatl, Dr. Steinbeck. A larger version of the statue temporarily in your possession and the reason for your presence here...to experience at first hand the inevitable outcome should you continue your reckless crusade."

He nodded to the priests who, without preamble, dragged him to the altar. In blind panic and near to losing control, he screamed at his tormentor to intervene. Pleading with him, seeking compassion. But there was no response.

Thrown face upwards onto the cold, stone slab, immobilised by iron shackles securing wrists, ankles and neck, he lay alone and afraid. His sole companion the dread of a fate unknown. Membril's face appeared above him. Eyes cold, merciless. "I should have mentioned, Dr. Steinbeck. As an alternative to the statue...a human sacrifice."

Mesmerised he watched the knife, blade darkened by the blood of the fowls, raised high above him...prior to the downward thrust into his unprotected chest.

Curiously he felt no pain. Unbelievably, he still lived. Not that he knew what death was like, but surely he would be aware of it when it happened. The unholy creature with the knife was hell-bent on finishing the job. He could feel the blade ripping his chest open, ribs cracking, muscles tearing. He must be dead. The pain would be unbearable if he wasn't.

Plunging a hand deep into the prepared cavity, the priest held his trophy on high. Continuing to beat, the still living heart dripped blood onto the shackled figure below.

He screamed...

He carried on screaming. The sound threatening to drown the intrusive, rhythmic thumping that was tearing his head apart. They were shouting at him, words he couldn't understand. They'd killed him for chrissakes. Were they too damn stupid to know you can't hear anything when you're dead? But he could hear. That was the funny thing. The noise, the banging, all that shouting: wouldn't be driving him up the bloody wall if he couldn't. Death got more surprising by the minute. But they'd made sure alright, no doubt about that. Confirmation doesn't get any more definite than having your own heart dangled in front of your eyes. Perhaps they'd taken it away. Please God make them take it away.

In dread he opened his eyes...the prepared scream reaching no further than the back of his throat. His heart wasn't there. Oh, thank God! The priests too, they'd vanished. So who the hell was doing the shouting? He couldn't fathom where was it coming from, couldn't see where they were. They were hiding, that was it. Biding their time. Making him think they'd left him. They hadn't really...but he was wise to their game. Subconsciously he became aware of other changes. The vast, towering pillars, the arches, eerie shadows on the walls and roof...all gone. Nothing remained. The only sights within his vision were a white ceiling and a glowing light bulb inside a semi-opaque shade. Where all around had been dark and gloom, was now light and airy. So different...wonderfully different.

He ran fearful fingers over his chest. No blood, no sign of a wound. But this was crazy, it didn't add up. He didn't imagine the knife cutting him open, hadn't fantasised his heart spurting blood. Perhaps it was some kind of after life condition. That this was what dying was all about. Bodily damage repaired, trauma dispensed with. Seemed like death wasn't such a bad idea after all.

If only that damned row would stop...it was doing his head in. Given some peace and quiet, he might be able to think. He sat up, anxious for a wider view. The room was small, a wooden door set in the wall opposite. That was where the noise was coming from. The shouting...it was a man's voice. Now his head wasn't buried in the pillow he could make out the words. His name, bellowed at the top of the voice doing the calling.

"Kyle...for God's sake! Open the bloody door."

The voice sounded urgent but he wasn't stupid, no way was he going to open that door. It would be one of those priests come back to torment him. The voice was demanding to know if he was ok. What a damn silly question...of course he wasn't. What the hell did they expect after what they'd done? But there was something strange about the voice. It was one he recognised. But how could that be? None of the priests had said a word?

Flinging the door open, he fell into Jack's arms.

CHAPTER NINE

"You said it'd be bad, but when it got down to my own heart playing a tune I didn't much go for...that was it. Tell you, Jack, I couldn't have taken any more. But it carried on even when I was wide-awake and with you banging on the door...not that I knew it was you. Not to start with. Up till then I was a gonna. All I had to look forward to was for some angel to turn up with a harp."

"It's the risk you face when you run off with someone you hardly know in the middle of the bloody night? Sorry," he apologised, aware of Kyle's eyes burning into his, "not the time for stupid remarks. Must learn to keep my big mouth shut. But what he did comes as no surprise." Carrying on talking, he made his way across the room to the window on the far side. The spectacular gardens helping him to find the right words. "You won't agree, I wouldn't expect you to, but something good has come out of all this. We now know for certain that Membril is an expert in what he does. We were apprised of that already, but it's good to have it confirmed. We also know that, as far as you are concerned, he's in deadly earnest. His antics on the astral lane provide crushing proof. Last night was carefully planned to achieve maximum effect. And it did that alright."

"Maybe. But if he thinks he's got me by the short and curlies, he can go boil his head. I'm not caving in. And if he don't go much on the idea, he knows what he can do."

"Mm...if only! At least it's handy to know why he's so desperate to get his hands on the statue. Doubt it'll help us much, but a little knowledge isn't always dangerous."

"What would I know? But give it a rest, eh, Jack?" Standing to flex his legs, "Let's take a walk. Blow the cobwebs away. Get in the mood for Acapulco."

"Leaving my long johns behind wasn't such a bad move after all." Lowering himself to the tarmac as he spoke. "It's hotter than a Turkish bath out here."

"Jack…what the heck were you playing at? The floozies are gonna go mad when they find out. The most sort-after hunk in Acapulco, and he forgets to pack his erotic underwear. Think of the uproar that's gonna cause when the word gets around. But I'll hang on to that," he beamed as his feet joined Jack's on the tarmac. "something to cheer me up next time I suffer a major stroke of depression. What you complaining about anyway? Of course it's hot. What else would you expect in Mexico's number one 'get away from it all' spots?"

"Doctor Steinbeck?" The receptionist asked as they approached the desk.

"Yep. That's me, and this likewise unattached good-for-nothing is Mr. Sibley. But to you sweetheart, I'm Kyle, this here English guy is called Jack. That's on a good day…won't let on what folks call him when the mood takes." His smile sending the girl into fantasyland.

"A gentleman was here earlier today, sir," informing him it was against hotel regulations to drop the formalities. "He wishes to tender his apologies for having not contacted you before, but that you are not to worry. He will be in touch shortly. He declined to leave his name. Said you would know who he was."

"This man…very tall, bald, dark eyes, yellowish skin?"

"That's him. You know the gentleman, Mr. Sibley?"

"Should he call back," Kyle interjected, "his name is, Membril. Sir Charles Membril. But there's one thing you should know…he's no damned gentleman and the 'sir' don't fit. Not that you'd know it. He can switch the charm on when it suits."

175

"Still don't get it, Jack. We didn't book this hotel till last night. How the hell did he find out almost before we did?"

"You can work that out for yourself, don't need me to tell you. The business with Sadie, the way he read your thoughts on the astral plane? That's how. He sees your mind, mine as well I expect, as an informant: a cheap source of up-to-date information. Whatever we plan, whatever we decide, he will know. He'll not miss a thing."

"That's not good."

"Let's say it's something we could do without."

"Must be some way we can get the better of him? Stop thinking about what we're gonna do for instance. Might work if we try hard enough. Concentrate on things that don't matter, instead of the stuff that's relevant."

"Be real, Kyle. Thoughts aren't planned, they arrive in our heads unannounced and uninvited. We have no more control over them than we have over tomorrow's weather. Like it or not we are Membril's personal enigma machine, and he'll be tuned in twenty-four-seven with both ears flapping. There is an upside though. Call him what you like...he won't miss a thing."

"Don't need to tell him what I think, reckon he knows already. But what the hell we gonna do, Jack? If what you say is right, an iceberg stuck in the middle of the Sahara desert's got more chance of staying afloat than we have."

"That's about the size of it. Nothing's changed. It's what we already knew. As things stand our survival, or not if that's the case, is in his hands. All we can hope for is that he slips up, and we are in a position to make the most of it if and when he does."

"Don't see that happening, not after last night. He was too precise." He concluded while licking lips in anticipation. "Could murder a coffee. Got a throat like a cactus in full bloom, and it might give me something other than him to think about."

"Some place, Kyle." Eyeing the assortment of pastries that joined the two brimming espressos. "The balconies look more like cottage gardens than lumps of concrete. All rooms the same? Or just those occupied by the privileged few?"

"How would I know? And right at this moment I couldn't care less. More interested in giving the pool a try. A quick splash while the sun's still up…what d'you reckon? Demolish this lot first of course."

The next three days they spent in idle indulgence, making the most of the wide range of activities available. Tennis or golf, fishing from the shore or relaxing on sun drenched beaches dominated the daylight hours. But the nights were a different matter. The onset of darkness ignited inner demons. Lurking shadows turning heads in dire expectancy.

Neither Kyle nor Jack would openly admit to these misgivings. Both were weighed down by the fear that such confession would re-ignite grim memories in the other…each aware of the dormant terror awaiting the opportunity to erupt in his ally. There was neither sight nor sound of Membril during those three days, but the threat was always there. Hidden round every corner, jeopardising their every move. Awake or asleep made no difference…during those hours of darkness he never left them.

It was Jack who bore the weight of responsibility, the burden of the guilt of his deception. He tried to make light of it, but deep down knew he raised false hope in creating the myth of Membril making a mistake. That was not going to happen. He'd shown what he could do and his actions had so far been little more than token gestures. As for his next move? He shuddered. God only knew what was waiting up his sleeve, but unforced errors would not be part of what he had hidden away. That was concrete. He was too focussed. Too precise.

Kyle on the other hand suffered no such similar conflict of emotions. His difficulty was in trying to come to terms with reality. He still found it hard to accept that his erstwhile, uncomplicated ideas of life had been scattered into the emptiness of space. Confused and impatient at the lack of activity, he was inclined to bask in dangerous optimism.

"What's he doing of, Jack?" Seated at a table in a dark corner of the disco bar, sipping drinks while watching carefree couples swan around the floor. "Three days we've been here...and sweet nothing is all we get. Turns up at the hotel before we'd even arrived, then sods us about not knowing what the goddamn hell he's up to. Way I see it, he's having us on. Leave us sweating buckets while he shoots off back where he came from."

"You're blinkered, Kyle. He'll turn up when he's ready and not before. He's no intention of giving up. Made that clear when you were with him on the astral plane. But you're not on your own, this waiting is driving me up the wall too you know." Glasses empty, he caught the eye of a passing waitress before carrying on. "What worries me, is he decides to take the next step without a pre-warning; deny us the chance to defend ourselves. In a real bad mood he could even go for broke. Not that we'd know much about it if he did."

"Put us under the daisies? No ceremony. No second chance? That what you're saying?"

"It's a possibility that can't be ruled out although, to be honest, I think it unlikely he'll go that far unless he's forced to. But you'd better believe it, Kyle. He won't need telling if you have a change of heart. He'll get the message almost before you do. Meanwhile he's content to play the waiting game. Soften us up, lower our resistance to the level where we decide to take the easy way out. Unless there's something he's not letting on."

"Such as?"

Reluctant to admit to a more recent fear, he took his time. It had been nothing more than a random thought to start with, intuition absorbed with no evidence to breed confirmation. But the lingering doubt continued to bug him...should he keep it to himself, or let Kyle know what it was that worried him? Common decency said his friend had to know. Whatever the effect on his state of mind, he had to be told.

"What was Membril trying to prove? putting you through hell like he did. None of it adds up...unless, of course, it was to prepare you for a fate he chooses to keep under his hat. I've more than likely got it completely wrong, but I can't help wondering. Was he telling you straight? or is a human sacrifice essential. Not the alternative he wants you to think it is."

"No, got that wrong, Jack. He said it loud and clear. If I don't give him the statue, I end up as dead meat on the altar. The choice was all mine. The motive was to scare the living daylights out of me, and the son-of-a-bitch did that alright."

"Doctor Steinbeck, Mister Sibley. Good afternoon."

His silent approach did not go unnoticed by the flies engaged in disposing of the remains on otherwise empty plates. Concluding they were insufficiently qualified to compete with the newly arrived putrescence, their activities were abandoned. The frivolous insects were not alone. Similarly taken by surprise the two men were caught napping: portcullises raised, defences down. A noonday visit was one they hadn't expected. Membril was a creature of the night. He was designed that way. Werewolves, vampires, black magicians...one of a kind. Nocturnal creatures with an abhorrence of daylight hours. A dark omen contaminating all that was bright and cheerful. Sunlight their anathema, a crucible of death in which they ceased to exist.

Ignoring the lack of invite, he commandeered a chair from a nearby table.

"Having no wish to be regarded as an irksome intruder, I must apologise for disturbing your leisure. But the passage of time, and all that...I am sure you understand." The contemptuous look portraying his delight at catching them on the hop.

"Having you turn up any time is irksome. Not that you need me to remind you."

"You disappoint me, Dr. Steinbeck. Moving on from our camaraderie of a few nights ago I had hoped my presence would be welcome." His expression cold, humourless, "However, on a different note, I find it sad you did not find comfort in your reunion the other evening. Such a lovely girl..."

"Leave it!" Flinging his hand across the table, Jack grasped the raised arm. "Don't even think about it. He wants you to respond. It'd make his day."

Satisfied his warning had struck home, he released his grip before rounding on Membril. "You bastard. You sick, bastard."

"I most probably am, Mr. Sibley. But despite your opinion, I must say you acted wisely. I'm impressed."

"You'll never come anywhere near knowing what I really think, but how about an abhorrent apology for humanity to be going on with? That should give you the general idea. Identifies you for what you are: a festering carbuncle blighting the lives of all decent-minded people. So why don't you do that eminent majority a favour and crawl back into the cesspit of your conception, where you can revel in the salaciousness of your vile following."

A flash of scarlet highlighting smouldering eyes, he thundered "You will live to rue those remarks, Sibley, as will your companion." He swung round to face Kyle, the secondary victim of his verbal blitz. "I gather your position is unaltered, Dr. Steinbeck. Unfortunate, but it matters little...and enough is enough. I made you a fair offer for the statue, and I have stressed the alternative should you not accept that offer. You have made your decision, now hear mine. You have debated between you what my next move will be, and the possibility that I might possess a weakness from which you might benefit. A wise move, and one not to be decried. So, to prove I am not an unreasonable man, I will provide you with the opportunity to discover my Achilles heel; assuming I have one. Having borne witness to events that can drive a man insane, Mr Sibley, I plan to reward you with an encore." A low chuckle rose in his throat, a half-laugh as the humour struck him. "I will put you to the test. You shall have an opportunity to prove yourself in direct conflict. I would however advise you take heed. You regard arrogance - which I am forced to agree is one of my attributes - as a potential weakness. But beware. It could be one of many strengths."

The gauntlet thrown he sneered, "I will grant you sufficient leeway, to consider your options and engage your preparations." The tone darkened, his voice the rumble of distant thunder in the delivery of his parting thrust. "That is all you will have. There will be no prior warning. You will not know when I will strike. When I do...one of you will cease to be a problem."

Turning on his heel, he walked away.

"Boy! Am I glad to see the back of him. Come as no surprise if he weren't Lucifer himself." Pent up anger, frustration and fear surfacing in the tone of his voice. "But I tell you this much. It knocked him sideways when you told him a few home truths. Thought for one moment he was gonna take your advice. Didn't like what he said though. That bit about one of us ending up not being a problem. Didn't at all like the sound of that. So help me out here, Jack. All very well me having principles, but tell me what you think. Am I being stupid just for the hell of it? Is it about time I face facts, give him what he wants and have done with it? Beginning to hit home just how far out of our depth we've got ourselves into...I've got us into."

"Point of no return, Kyle. He no longer gives a toss whether or not you part up with the statue. He made that abundantly clear. Then, as you say, his parting shot. One of us is seen as a thorn in his arse...an irritation to be got rid of at the earliest. You or me? Your guess is as good as mine, but I get the feeling that I'm the fly in the ointment. Makes sense if you think about it. Goes back to what I was saying earlier: the business with the altar. He has plans for you...I'm no use to him and his foul scheme." Shrugging an apology he concluded, "Sorry for having to play Devil's Advocate, but we might as well face the facts."

"You know, Jack, I sometimes wonder if you're my best friend or my worst enemy. But ok! So what are we going to do about it? All that stuff: getting ourselves ready and prepared? You got any idea what he was on about?"

"The clues were there...good, solid clues at that. But I can't be sure." He paused, chewing over what he'd said before speculating further. "He didn't mess about, there was no hesitation, no double innuendo but I wonder, was it all a blind. Know what I mean? Put an idea in their heads, fool 'em by doing something completely different. Knowing what we do about him I don't think it's likely, but I wouldn't put money on it. He's full of bullshit but I doubt his ego would allow him to lead us up the garden path. And that infuriating gesture...give us time to prepare. The threat, the mocking eyes; the twitching lips covering what he saw as the funny side...it was all there. He was taking the piss, putting us - me in particular - in our place. Then there was the rest of the kerfuffle: direct conflict, not knowing when he would strike and all that codswallop. He knew damn well I'd cotton-on to the game he wants to play...inwardly gloating at the predestined outcome. That remark about one of us being done away with for instance. He could do it the easy way but he would forfeit his orgasm if he kept it too simple. Keep us squirming on that wretched hook of uncertainty, bring the game to an end when he gets fed-up playing it...his rules, not ours." Slumped in his chair he changed tack. "I wonder what changed his mind. Made it clear he still wants the statue but it's no longer top priority."

"No, you got that wrong, Jack. Wouldn't keep bugging me if it was any different."

"But the urgency's no longer there. I've been driving myself mad these last few days, trying to find logical answers to illogical questions and failing miserably. One left to pose a problem? Why just one when he could have both of us at no extra cost? If the statue is his sole interest, why not take the easy route...the safer route? And that funny business on the astral plane. Why only you when he could have had me accompany the pair of you? What was he trying to prove? Unless of course there is another, a more pertinent, motive? The one that's been nagging at me ever since you told me how you were made to suffer on the altar." He paused for a moment, seeking a reaction that didn't materialise. "You're staying quiet, Kyle, but don't you see the implications? I'm a fly on the wall, a pain in the arse to be dispensed with. But he wants to hang on to you. That sordid melodrama the other night. It wasn't a threat…it was a preview of your designated fate."

"Don't know that for sure." He responded, face pale.

"No, you're right. It's me doing what I do best. Shooting my mouth off without knowing all the facts. One thing I am pretty sure of though, is that his next move will answer a lot of questions. Whether the freshly acquired knowledge will do us any good is neither here nor there. But that's for another day. Deciding what we do about this latest threat is our number one priority."

"You're quiet, Jack, and when you're quiet there's usually a problem. Can I help?"

"If only! Lack of inspiration, devoid of ideas…call it what you like. I know what he's got planned - or I'm pretty damn sure I do - but even if I'm right there's bugger-all we can do about it. Not quite true. If circumstances were different we might stand a chance but there's no consolation in knowing what to do, if the doing isn't possible. It's where we are. The situation we're in. He damn well knew it when he said he'd give us time to prepare. He's knows that, when the time comes, we'll be virtually defenceless. Crucifixes will help, but even they won't be sufficient when the going gets tough."

"Might help if you tell me what you think he's up to."

"You heard him: 'time to plan our defences'. That tells us all we need to know. Unless of course? No…forget it. We'll get nowhere by looking at random possibilities. It's not time we need, Kyle, it's space. And he damn well knows it. Given the right environment we might stand a chance. But he wouldn't want that. For all his fine talk he doesn't intend to run the risk of us putting one over on him."

"Yeah, ok. So what you say is all very well, but it still don't tell me what you think he's gonna do."

"He will plan to damage us mentally by exposing us to foul entities from the abyss...offensive sub-beings sent to destroy our sanities. The end will be my coupe-de-grace and your submission. Guesswork, but it won't be far off he mark. And our hands are tied...we won't be able to do a damn thing to stop him. Membril knew it when he issued the challenge. He languishes in the knowledge, that the one and only defence is out of our reach."

"Explain, Jack. If there's any sort chance of we've gotta go for it. Don't matter what it takes or what it costs. It's our lives at stake for chrissakes."

"It's not money, certainly not incentive...it's lack of space. Stuck in this hotel...any hotel. That's our nemesis." He walked across the room, gazing at the lush gardens through the window. "The only effective defence against an occult attack is the pentagram. Given the protection that can offer, the odds would be something like fifty-fifty. Without it, we're done for. It's as simple as that."

"What's a pentagram?"

"The prime ingredient of a battle between occult forces differs little from those fought in the natural arena. In other words, and stating the bleeding obvious, if one side heavily outweighs the other you would expect a walk-over. You wouldn't, for example, rate the chances of a cavalry unit pitted against a tank regiment. The situation we're in is no different. A paranormal attack can only be repelled by a paranormal defence, and this is where the pentagram comes into its own. It provides a nigh-on impenetrable barrier against all forms of supernatural activity."

"So what's the problem? Why don't we stop messing about and get ourselves one of these contraptions. Yeah, ok," replying to the contemptuous look aimed in his direction, "I was taking the piss. But what the hell d'you expect? Keeping on-and-on about this damn pentagram, telling me what it does but not how it does it. Like, f'rinstance, it not being much use in a hotel. What's that got to do with anything."

"For a start you don't get it, you draw it. Construct it might be nearer the mark. Here…I'll show you." Sketching on a blank sheet of hotel notepaper as he spoke. "The pentagram is a five-pointed star within two concentric circles, as I've sketched here. The inner circle circumscribes the valleys, the outer the peaks. A container filled with holy water at each of the valleys, a sprig of garlic at the peaks. Add a surrounding border, inscribe certain commands in the space between the two outer circles and there you have it…the answer to every maiden's prayer. That's the easy bit. Where to put it is another matter. Which is why being stuck in a hotel doesn't help."

"None the wiser, Jack. Ok! So you've told me what it is and what it looks like. What you haven't said, is what we'd do with it if we had one. And another thing. You might think you've explained why being in a hotel makes it awkward, but if you did I missed it."

"Fair enough," he conceded, "but I haven't finished yet." Pointing to his drawing he went on to explain. "For our purposes, the pentagram has to be drawn on the floor of an empty room and be big enough to sleep in. So we're looking at an outer diameter of something approaching fifteen-or-sixteen feet minimum. This room? What d'you reckon? Twelve by twelve, thereabouts. Your room is no different. Apart from the lack of size, both rooms are carpeted and cluttered with furniture." Explanation over, he sought Kyle's reaction.

"See where you're coming from. But the hell, Jack. Even if we were somewhere more convenient the bastard wouldn't give us time to work it out. Let alone put the damn thing together."

"Oh but he would…believe me, he would. When he said he'd give us time, he meant it. He'll have us sweating buckets before pressing the button. Keep us hanging on tenterhooks for as long as he jolly well can. Softly, softly, catchy monkey...that's his *modus operandi*. It's pie in the sky anyway. There'll be no pentagram. Nothing for him to wet his pants over."

"You said something about sleeping in the pentagram - if we had one that is - but what about other times? Daytime f'instance. What would we do then? Couldn't spend twenty-four hours sitting on bloody floorboards. Membril wouldn't need to worry about driving us bonkers. We'd do it for him."

"You should know by now that his hands are tied while the Sun's up, and even more so with what he has in mind. He'll be relying on the creatures of darkness to do his dirty work, elementals with an abhorrence of light...that's when we need to beware. Between dawn and dusk we're safe. It's at night we're vulnerable."

"Who needs Membril to give me the creeps, when I've got you around?"

"Better to know than to live in blissful ignorance." Sensing increased doubt in restless eyes he decided further explanation was necessary if he was to ease his friend's fears.

"Nothing's changed, Kyle. Over the centuries, from almost the very origins of man, it has always been the same. Black magic is, and always has been, at its most powerful during the hours of darkness. It's the time when we're at our lowest ebb. The reason why children – and not only children - have a morbid fear of the night. It stems from ages past. An hereditary trait given birth at a time when dark forces ruled men's lives."

"OK, you've said enough. So what do we do, arm ourselves with a crucifix each and pray for our salvation? That seems to be the sum total of our hopes and aspirations."

"Unless you can come up with something I've missed."

"Even if I could, there wouldn't be much point. You just reminded me he sees everything that goes on inside our nuts. Might as well face it, Jack. A hosepipe would stand more chance of quenching all the fires in Hades, than us coming out of this in one piece."

"Back to square one. Hang on tight to a golden cross and pray like we've never prayed before. Guaranteed to keep him at bay for at least two minutes."

"It's so damn frustrating, if only we…" Interrupting himself in mid-sentence, he came near to shattering the light bulb hugging the ceiling in his enthusiasm. "Hang on in there, Jack. I am yet again blessed with inspiration. Might not come to anything, but better than sitting on our asses doing sweet nothing. Cling on to your hat and don't hold your breath!" Leaving a highly bemused Sibley in his wake…to return nearly an hour later.

"Seem to recall you saying bucks ain't the answer, so how does this grab you? Empty room: twenty-six feet one way, twenty-two the other. Ours from mid-day tomorrow for as long as we pay the rent. Carpet done away with, furniture disposed of. Don't come too heavy with the plaudits."

"Oh yeah…another laugh at Sibley's expense. Try another one."

"Listen to me, fellah. There's a time and a place for joking, and neither of those fit." A raised hand telling his friend to keep his trap shut he squatted down on his haunches; a sure sign that he didn't want to be interrupted. "I had a word with the manager. Seeking his help for a bit of fun I had in mind. When I told him what I wanted and what was in it for him, the guy couldn't believe his luck." Unable to contain himself he laughed aloud, his listener having to stay patient while he got his act together. "I've booked the Bridal Suite. So hope you're not gonna turn me down, 'cos I reckon we'll make a lovely couple. Will it last though? That's what I keep having to ask myself."

"About five seconds if you don't wipe that stupid look off your face and tell me what this is all about."

"Spilled the news to the big white chief - big brown chief to be politically correct - friends of ours were getting spliced. Didn't know exactly when the happy event was gonna take place, but knew it was imminent and wanted to make sure we didn't miss out. Said our wedding present was for them to spend their honeymoon in this hotel. Had to be the bridal suite of course, else no dice. Should've seen him, Jack. His eyes popped and he couldn't stop rubbing his hands in anticipation of what he was gonna make out of it. Specially when I told him what else we had planned." Again giving way to laughter. Shoulders heaving, tears running down his face before he was able to continue.

"This newly married couple," wiping moist globules from his eyes, struggling to find words between the laughter, "we're gonna play a trick on 'em. Instead of the fully furnished suite complete with shrouded four-poster they'll expect, all they're gonna find is an empty room. Not so much as a carpet to muffle their little tootsies. Not completely empty. Had to give 'em something to sleep on - was their honeymoon after all said and done - so told him a couple of single mattresses might add that touch of romance not often found in hotel rooms. After all, wouldn't be right to have 'em sleeping on bare boards. That would soon put a stop to their nuptials. Tried to get the manager to see the funny side, but he was too busy adding up what he was gonna get out of the deal. He was that mesmerised, his eyeballs lit up with dollar signs."

"If I ever get married remind me not to have you look after the wedding arrangements," Jack responded, unable to avoid joining in the laughter. "So what happened next? This manager. He must have had some doubts. Can't be too often he's confronted by a crazy yank full of daft ideas."

"Honest, Jack, he couldn't have given a pea in a pod. He was too occupied drooling over the couple of grand sweetener I put on the table…up and over the room rent of course. Lining his own pockets was his one and only interest. And when I said there could be more if the room was cleaned till it was spotless, I thought he was in for a heart attack. Did right, did I? You wanting the room all spick-and-span like? Mom was always telling me dirt and the Devil go hand-in-hand when I was a kid."

"I'm impressed. You not only listened to your mother, you took it on board! What is the world coming to? But yes, you're right, a pentagram on an unclean surface would be about as useful as a monk in a nunnery." Something in Kyle's expression prompted him to say, "You seem to have got a taste for this."

"Don't be fooled by the outward expression, Jack. It's one big cover-up. Beneath this calm exterior there lies a gibbering coward. Oh...nearly forgot," he tossed two small, leather-bound boxes on the table. "These any good?"

"You're joking!" Dangling one of two shining gold crosses from outstretched fingers. "These hidden talents of yours never cease to amaze me. How did you fit it all in? You weren't gone an hour."

"Easy, Jack. Didn't have to so much as leave the hotel. Those shops in the foyer: know the ones I'm talking about? That's good." In answer to the nod. "One happens to be a jewellers." Returning the crucifix to it's box with a wry smile on his face, he mused, "Make a nice present for Julie and...whoever, when this is all over, and we've finished with 'em." He didn't add, 'if we're still around', but it was there in his eyes.

"Purely as a matter of interest, what excuse are you going to come up with when this money-obsessed manager wants to know why this blissfully married couple fail to materialise?"

"As long as he gets his precious boodle, can't see he'll be much bothered. If he should get curious, however, I've got the answer ready and waiting. There will have been a disaster on the romance front. It was one of those togetherness things you hear so much about. On the verge of saying they did, both parties decided they didn't. By the time they got to 'till death they did part', they were at full-scale loggerheads."

"As if..." what he was about to say cut short by the shrill demand from Kyle's mobile.

"Hi, Pop...nice surprise. Unexpected but welcome." A brief pause as he listened to the voice at the other end of the line.

"Nothing serious I hope." A longer delay this time.

"Nonsense, Pop. Kidding you. No way. Having you on. Julie's far too sensible to land up in that kind of mess."

"Well if you say so, then I suppose it has to be. But, Sis? Can't believe it. Not her way. Not her way at all. So how the hell did she end up in that condition for chrissakes? Silly question. As if you'd know. As if anyone would know"

"Oh I see. Well to tell the truth, I don't see. Not like Julie to get in that state. But yeah, ok Pop. We'll talk it over when I get there. I'll explain to Jack and make a move. Get back soon as I can. Sometime tomorrow. Barring the unexpected."

Turning to face his friend, he was spared having to find the right words.

"It's alright, Kyle. I got the gist from your side of the conversation. But why didn't she say anything?" the words whispered, almost as if he was asking the question of himself. "She knew how I felt. How I thought she felt. If she'd just said. It would've been that much easier to come to terms."

"Waiting confirmation? In denial? Praying it was a false alarm? Who knows? Trouble is the folks want me back home, seem to think I can help in some way. God only knows how. Everyone upset and not thinking straight if you ask me. Just because the two of us are close knit, they've got it into their noddles I might help calm the waters - which are pretty rough at the moment apparently. Don't know how I'm supposed to do that, but there you are...it's what Pop thinks, and I can't let him down. Also, Jack: bit awkward...ok with you if I go on my own? Folks' apparently know about you and Julie...she must've told 'em I guess. Anyway, they seem to think it best if you're not around. Reckon it could make things more difficult than they are already. You ok with that? Get back as soon as I can. Won't hang around more'n necessary."

"Don't worry, I understand. The last thing anyone would want is me putting my oar in. Julie wouldn't appreciate having me around either. But what I don't understand is, she must've been going steady with someone. Did she never mention she had a boyfriend?"

"That's the bit that makes even less sense. One night stand at a party apparently. Had a drop too much and the rest, as they say, is history. But, Jack...Julie's not the sort to do things like that. The complete opposite of the sister I know and love. Apart from being a number one romantic she's a very pious girl. One area where she don't take after me. No sex before marriage has always been *her* motto. Having one too many ain't her style either. Must've seen that for yourself." He shrugged, "Oh well, find out more when I get there. Get going straight away; sooner I leave, quicker I'll be back".

In the process of lifting a suitcase from the top of a wardrobe, he stopped in midstream. "Membril! Holy shit, I'm sorry mate. Didn't give him a thought. That settles it. They'll have to do without me. Not leaving you on your own. Not with that bastard up to whatever he intends getting up to. Might not be much use with the practicalities but, it's like you said, we need each other."

"No, Kyle, you've got to go...no argument. The thought's appreciated, but your family comes first. Don't worry about me. I'll be ok. Putting the pentagram together will help pass the time, and you'll be back before you know it." Should have..." He paused. What his friend said hadn't registered at the time, but the words now came back to haunt him. "Kyle. What you said about Julie's behaviour. How it was so unlike her. Doesn't it strike you as all too familiar? The way you and I changed the other night when we had that God-almighty bust-up? How neither of us could credit the altered personality of the other? This time it's Julie ditching her normal behaviour pattern. Succumbing to a moments madness that belied her scruples." Hand in readiness, it was more an order than a request. "Give me your phone, Kyle."

"Him! Membril! It was your mother I spoke to, and she gave us all the proof we need. Your Dad is attending a meeting in Houston apparently, and isn't expected back before the end of the week. As he can't be in two places at once it obviously wasn't him on the phone. Julie's fine by all accounts, and is spending a busy few days helping Rebecca with the new arrival. Your Mum said she'd let her know I called. Oh…she sends her love by the way. Hopes we're enjoying ourselves."

"How's he do it for chrissakes? Not only mimics Pop's voice to perfection, but fixes it so our home number is displayed on my cell phone. Fooled me completely, don't mind saying. Hadn't been for you I'd be making my way back by now. Wondering what the hell I was gonna do when I got there."

"Food and drink to him. But look on the bright side. You can put that case back where it came from. You're not going anywhere."

"Yeah, but this is getting too much, Jack. First he violates my memories of Sadie, now he's done his best to drag my sister's name through the dirt. The filthy critter don't give a toss whose life he messes up."

"We believed what he wanted us to believe. Had it not been for your ties with Julie…doesn't bear thinking about. Still, the experience won't have done us any harm and hopefully it's a lesson learned. From now on we treat every sight, sound, touch, taste or smell with deep suspicion."

CHAPTER TEN

"This is something else," Jack enthused, eyes sweeping the room for the first time. "You said it was big, but I didn't think it was this big...it's enormous. And spotless. Not a trace of dirt anywhere. Mattresses though? Not to sure. Clean enough, but look as if they've been through the mill a few times...or am I being pernickety?"

"Be as pernickety as you damn well please, you know more about this malarkey than me. And one thing's for sure, we can't afford to take chances." Lifting a corner of one of the mattresses, he raised his eyebrows. "And if this one's anything to go by? Ok! Forget mattresses, we'll go for camp-beds instead. Not as comfortable but we can get 'em brand new and unsullied. Airbeds are another option."

"No, I draw the line at airbeds! Had my fill camping with my parents. Lost count of the number of times I had to get up in the middle of the night to put more air in. Can't say I've had the pleasure of camp beds, but they can't be any worse than ruddy airbeds. So what do we do with the mattresses? Can't have them cluttering the place up, especially if we have to spend too many nights cooped up in the pentagram."

"I'll grab a hold of the room maid - not literally, though have to admit she's got certain qualities - she'll get rid of 'em for us if I butter her up. Told her about our bit of fun; gave her a good laugh. If she wants to know why we're not happy with the mattresses, I'll tell her I've heard that camp beds are better passion-killers…and them on their honeymoon! She curled up!"

"One of your many female conquests doesn't happen to be proficient in putting pentagrams together by any chance?" He queried, the question accompanied by a half-hearted grin. "I could do with some help in that direction I don't mind admitting. It's not the layout, that's plain enough: it's the level of precision required that is frightening…every detail has to be spot on, or as near spot on as possible. Anything other than a slight inaccuracy and you might as well not have bothered. Even if we had the right tools it wouldn't be easy, without them it'll be damn near impossible."

"I've got this worrying feeling that tells me you haven't done this before."

"The need to construct a pentagram doesn't arise every day of the week so no, I haven't had the pleasure…we'll just have to learn as we go along. If all goes well we could perhaps start our own business. Call ourselves 'Trial and Error – Pentagram Putters Together By Appointment'. How's that sound? Could be fun,.."

"I've had more fun cutting myself shaving. But ok, that's enough of that. Come on Jack, let's get a move on. We could sit here all day discussing the why's and wherefores but it won't get us anywhere."

"Yeah, you're right. Bemoaning our fate won't get us very far. A list of the necessities would be a good place to start, so grab yourself a pen and paper and make a list while I try to think what we're likely to need." Using his sketch as a reminder he began, "Chalk, tape measure…how the hell do we draw circles that big? Any ideas?"

"Depends. Impossibilities come quick, miracles take a bit longer." Sinking his chin into the angle formed by thumb and forefinger, he sat lost in thought for some time before leaping to his feet." Beaming with delight, he shouted the content of his inspired thinking. "Got it! Could be tricky but it should work. Godammit…it will work. What we need is one of those plunger things plumbers keep in their tool-bags. Know the sort of thing I mean? Ok," acknowledging the dubious nod, "so here's what we do. Press the plunger to the floor where we want the centre of the circle to be. With me so far? Good!" In response to further nodding. "Fix a stick of chalk to something suitable: piece of wood, something along those lines. Tie onc end of a piece of string to the handle of the plunger, the other end to whatever's keeping the chalk in place and that's it! We have ourselves one giant compass. Adjust the string to the required radius, keep it taut, make sure it slides nice and easy round the handle...and bingo! What d'you reckon?"

"I reckon you're a bloody genius...even if it does stick in the gullet to say so."

"Wondered when you'd notice. Took long enough."

"Don't press your luck, it doesn't surface all that often. Ok, so what else? Protractor: big and heavy would be useful. The kind used by civil engineers if we're lucky enough to find one. They tend to stay put until persuaded otherwise. Five small glass containers: jars, vases, anything along those lines. A few sprigs of garlic. That's it. Don't think I've missed anything. Apart from the holy water of course. But we won't find that in a shop!"

"I can think of a few things you've overlooked. Buckets for instance. Stuck all night in the pentagram...don't have to spell it out do I? Radio. Something to read. Pack of cards might be useful. We'll need something to keep us occupied when we can't sleep, which is likely to be most nights. Camp beds. Mustn't forget them" He broke off, a puzzled expression crossing his features. "Understand the holy water, but what's with the garlic? Where's that come in?"

"Holy water guards the valleys of the star, garlic the peaks. Don't mean to tell me you haven't read Bram Stoker's classic? Strange as it may seem he got it right. But the literary count and his cronies are not on their own. All things evil are repulsed by garlic. Makes you wonder. Was it just imagination...or did Stoker learn from experience?"

"At least the lucky bugger didn't have you around to cheer him up. So what's the plan? Downtown? Get the shopping over and done with?"

"Lunch first." He glanced at his watch, "Nearly one, so it's about time and we need to eat well. Knowing the regard you have for your stomach, I didn't dare mention it before. Dinner is off the menu. No, listen," wincing at the 'what!' shouted with some vigour, "it's for our own safety. Food is a point of nucleation for evil in all it's forms, and for that reason it's imperative we adopt a starvation diet during the hours of darkness. From now until whenever - or whatever - we fast between midday and breakfast."

"That was a good lunch, most enjoyable. More so, seeing as how there's bugger-all else to look forward to. You're sure about this? Not another bean till breakfast! By the time that comes around I'll be heading full tilt towards malnutrition. And will anyone care? Not on your life."

"You can save the histrionics for later...they cut no ice. Once the pentagram's up and running you can moan away to your hearts content. Come on…can't hang around here all day!" He said, banging a fist on the table to emphasize. "There's a lot to be done, and time's getting on."

"That was a lot easier than I expected," shopping completed, they were back in the hotel.

"Haven't got the holy water yet."

"No, haven't forgotten." Jack responded. "I'll shoot off to find an obliging priest and leave you make a start on the pentagram. You happy with that?"

"Yeah. Fine by me. Can't wait to see if my idea for drawing circles works. Theories don't always come good in practice. What about size? Big as practical?"

"Bigger the better, by and large. As a rough guide, the inner circle should be about half-to-two-thirds the diameter of the outer. Just make sure you leave enough space between the outside border and the walls for us to walk relatively unhampered. Other than that it's down to you." Tucking a street map of Acapulco into a convenient pocket as he spoke he added "I'll take your mobile with me if that's ok…in case I need to get in touch. Oh" he continued as the thought struck. "The keys to the car. Won't get far without those."

He was made to visit six churches before finding a sympathetic ear. Two showed no signs of life, and at three others he was greeted with overt suspicion; 'holy water' having hardly left his mouth before being sent on his way. Near to despair and on the verge of giving it up as a bad job, he stumbled across 'La Iglesia del Sacramento Santo'; a tiny Catholic church set away from the city outskirts and presided over by a priest who was only too happy to welcome him into his sanctuary. An outgoing and friendly man, he imbued him with the confidence to relate all: his entanglement with Satanism and the horrors of the aftermath. That Father Osvaldo Martinez, the newly acquainted vicar, having lived in England for a number of years, spoke English fluently was an added bonus."

Listening intently through to the finish, the priest took him by the shoulders. Looking him in the eye, he chose the moment to render a confession of his own. "During the short time I have been privileged to serve my profession, I have counselled many people with difficulties that affected their daily lives. Problems with their work, in their marriage: life in general. On occasion it would be that they were plagued without reason…but the cause mattered not. I had the remedy…I was the man in charge. The man to put an end to their troubles. Whatever the situation, I could handle it. But I now find myself at a loss. For the first time I suffer a sense of helplessness. I am unsure whether you are very brave or terribly foolish, there is perhaps nothing but a small margin separating the two. Yet somehow I envy you, and that I find disturbing. I am a devoted man of God and it would be my humble wish to conduct myself with your endeavour should I be asked to face that with which you are confronted.

There lies my guilt, my insecurity. To my shame, I harbour doubts that my faith would last the course…that cowardice would overshadow my beliefs. That raises the question I find impossible to answer: would I surrender the conviction that my God will protect me? I pray those fears will never be put to the test but that, if they are, the Holy Father will forgive me should my courage fail."

"We all suffer human frailties, Father. None of us know how we would behave in a crisis. But at the end of the day we usually make the right decision."

"I'm sure that is so." He smiled gently. "Anyway, enough of my preamble. As to your request, I am only too pleased to be of service. On one condition."

"Which is?" The thought crossing his mind that he might have known there was a catch, rapidly replaced by guilt at the priest's reply.

"Should you survive your perilous path, you will let me know. I will give you one year. If at the end of that time I have not heard from you, I will accept the ending was not, as I am sure, God would have wished. In such sad circumstances, I will kneel before the altar and pray for the sanctity of your soul and for that of your friend."

Privileged to have met such an honest, open and friendly man he made his way back to the hotel…to find Kyle lounging on a camp bed in the middle of, to all intents and purposes, a completed pentagram.

"Beginning to worry about you Jack, but then thought…what the hell? Should've known you wouldn't come back till the hard graft was done with. So instead of wasting time with excuses I won't believe, tell me what you think. Super, fantastic? Could stomach miraculous if that's what takes your fancy. Don't fret over sparing my blushes. I can live with it."

"As a sop to your rampant ego, I'll go as far as workmanlike. But that's all you're getting." Walking a full circuit of the pentagram for the third time, he relented in face of the hurt expression. "I'd never hear the last of it if I admitted you've done a good job but I'll have to risk it, because you have. Can't find a single fault, and I tried hard enough. So what's with all that balls about me being away so long? If I'd got back any earlier I'd have only got in the way, which would've given you something else to moan about. But in case you're interested, I wasn't fart-arsing around doing nothing. It took me ages to find a priest who would so much as listen, let alone come up with the goods."

"Yeah, ok! I'll believe you but thousands wouldn't. To tell the truth, putting this lot together was a whole lot easier than I thought it was gonna be. Once I'd got the angles right it was a breeze. Leave you to put the holy water and the garlic in place…and oh, you said something about an inscription. That's all yours too." Patting Jack on the shoulder he ran his tongue between his lips. "Don't know about you, but I'm famished. If you'd been much longer I was on my way to the dining room."

"Didn't take you long to forget...or were you hoping I'd be the one with the memory deficiency? No dinner, not so much as a taster. Tonight and every night for the foreseeable?"

"Well…it was worth a try. But you one-hundred percent sure about this? Wasn't kidding when I said I was famished...bloody starving would be nearer the mark. But ok, you know best. We'll go on the razzle instead. A belly-full of booze might help me forget I'm hungry."

"Not sure how to put this without giving you a massive heart attack, but it has to be done. It isn't just dinner…" Looking the American in the eye and crossing his fingers. "Alcohol is another no-no. Fruit juice, tea, coffee? as much as you like...booze is out. I'm sorry, Kyle, I really am," struggling not to laugh at the suicidal expression on his friend's face. "Don't blame me, I don't make the rules."

"Can't believe I'm hearing this. First you tell me there's no grub, now you torture me some more by removing the one thing that could make the lack of it tolerable. What else you gonna throw at me, Jack? Work my guts out and what do I get? No chow, no booze. All that's on offer is a bloody fruit juice. Hara-kiri has gotta be a damn sight less painful than what you're giving me." Hands clasped in prayer, he lifted his eyes heavenwards. "Dear Lord, give me strength. Release me from my misery and protect me from further deprivation. OK! So bang goes my street cred. Let's go get that orange juice...I'll never live it down if it ever gets out."

The night passed, a long night in which sleep was at a premium...a night of frustration, a night of innocuous inactivity. A night inwardly cursed by both men as they reflected on the needless fast, the unwarranted abstinence and the far from comfortable sleeping arrangements.

"Gee, Jack, what a wonderful night that was. I've always said there's nothing to beat spending eight hours on a lousy, rotten bed; hungry, thirsty and bored to kingdom come and gone." Pulling on his dressing gown, he grabbed a towel. "I'm in for a shower. A damn quick one, no need worry about that. Breakfast's calling loud enough to bust my eardrums. And I'll tell you this much: they'd better make sure there's plenty on offer. My needs are gonna take a lot of satisfying."

"Take it easy today, eh Jack?" Kyle mumbled, returning his empty cup to the saucer in waiting. "That breakfast might have put me in better mood, but can't say I'm up for anything more energetic than a day on the beach. Take a dip if and when we feel like it...anything that don't involve too much exertion. The only worthwhile effort will be making sure we have a damn good lunch. Get ourselves prepared for the next episode of bloody Ramadan. But bugger today. Got an idea for tomorrow. Deep-sea fishing? What do you reckon? There's a boat leaves at seven every morning. Saw the add down on the quayside. Fully equipped for chasing all the big 'uns: tuna, swordfish: whatever's going. I'll book us in if you're up for it. See how we feel in the morning. If we don't turn up...we don't turn up."

Interrupted by an occasional dip in the comfortingly warm sea and an occasional stroll along the beach, they spent the day relaxing in the shadow of cliffs bordering the golden sands. Unfortunately the night that followed their enjoyable day was as per expectation. Taking turn and turn about, one would stay awake while the other slept. But the revised plan did little to overcome their insomnia, and it was with reluctance that they roused themselves in time for the deep-sea fishing experience.

"Lucky for them they start breakfast good and early Jack. Wouldn't hold myself responsible otherwise. What with having no dinner last night, a boat trip on an empty stomach wouldn't hold too much appeal " Stretching one arm above his head, rubbing his lower torso in rapt appreciation with the other, "Time to make a move," he stressed, glancing at his watch, "Kyle Steinbeck is raring to go, and those denizens of the deep better watch out. Mood I'm in they don't stand a chance."

"Yeah, quite. What a pity Jack Sibley isn't relishing his night of rest with the same gusto. I know we had to get up early…but five o'clock? Was that really necessary? Especially after all the sleep we didn't have."

"You'll stop complaining when you get that sea air into your lungs. Nothing like a salt breeze to blow the cobwebs away. And anyway, stands to reason we want to get there nice and early. Make sure we get the pick of the gear before the mob arrive. Don't want to get lumbered with the rubbish left at the end."

The day was one to make the most of. Weather sublime, the sport exhilarating. All on board friendly and willing to pass their skills on to the two novices. That was how it was to begin with but, following nearly three hours of excellent fishing, the area began to show signs of depletion…hence the decision to relocate.

"Ere we ees Señors'. Thees where we ees a stopping." Decision made, the ship's captain gave the command to lower the anchor. Well versed in the drill, two men stepped forward to dispatch the heavy metal object to the seabed. Sweat-covered bodies and bulging muscles evidence that turning the winch was no easy task. Rapidly accelerating from a slow beginning, the anchor hit the sea with a loud splash. The creak of the capstan and the vocalised grunts of the two men the only sounds to break an otherwise all- consuming silence.

It was strange that, when later questioned, no one, passenger or crew, could describe the sequence of events. It had happened too quickly and everything was going too smoothly. The sea was calm, no clouds marred a clear blue sky, surfacing dorsal fins were in abundance. Now several feet below the surface, the anchor continued its steady progress. Probing the underwater environment, anxious to reach it's final resting place. Oblivious to the sights and sounds from above.

The noise boomed through the small ship.

Snarling its gratitude the ruptured rope snaked from the winch which, exulting in its new-found freedom, rapidly increased the speed of its revolutions...brought to an abrupt halt by the forearm of one of the men. The force of the impact was such as to take no prisoners, and with his arm smashed beyond repair the victim's screams refuted any argument.

Despite the severity of the injury, the poor man was not to receive the attention his plight deserved. There was another shout. One of greater urgency. An anguished cry that ricocheted throughout the becalmed vessel. Attached to the heavy metal anchor in free-fall, the flailing end of the rope ensnared Jack's body. Intent on devouring its prey the constrictor bound its coils ever tighter, crushing the weak flesh into uncontested submission. But the serpent was to be denied its anticipated reward. A more powerful, more avaricious monster lay in waiting. The mouth into which he was fed was the wide-open aperture of the mighty Pacific. Mercifully for Jack Sibley, he knew nothing of the drama and the ensuing chaos...he was out of it. Pulled viciously across the rails guarding the perimeter, his head struck a stanchion. By the time his body hit the water he was unconscious.

Kyle's reaction was instant. Jerking his head round to meet the cry, he was just in time to see his friend disappearing over the side. Kicking off his plimsolls, in keeping with everyone else on board his only apparel apart from a pair of shorts, he unthinkingly vaulted the rail. It was a meaningless gesture. There was no hope of saving his friend and ally, he knew that; but he had to do something. Had to try. Strong swimmer he might be, but the huge mass of an anchor propelled by the constant force of gravity would render his efforts puny by comparison. That, and the near impossibility of finding Jack in this inhospitable wilderness...what chance was there? None, none at all; not if he gave common-sense half a chance. But he wasn't listening. They were wasted words. The vacuous propaganda of a feeble intellect. He couldn't let him go...not just like that. He would do his damnedest.

Sheer bloody mindedness generated the adrenalin to keep him going, but it couldn't last. His lungs were fast mounting a protest, torn between two time factors. One dictating how long he could stay submerged, the other specifying how long his friend could survive. Both were academic. He had no say in the matter. If by some miracle Jack was found quickly there might be the ghost of a chance. If he wasn't? He didn't want to go there. It was too painful to contemplate. But whatever the odds he wasn't going to give up. He'd carry on searching until all hope was gone. In the meantime he had to keep going...keep believing. Deeper and deeper, eyes probing the clear water: hoping against hope...knowing there was none.

He couldn't delay any longer. Lungs near to bursting point he had to get to the surface...and fast. The increased pressure at this depth was becoming noticeable, and his pulmonary organs were letting him know.

There was a body away to his right. Despite the clarity of the water it was hard to judge, but he guessed the distance separating them to be no more than about thirty-or-so yards. He tried to change course but his arms and legs were leaden...a combined refusal to obey all commands however insistent. Depleted lungs demanding instant replenishment, lest more than one corpse was destined to take residence in this watery graveyard.

Oh thank God! Help was at hand. Incredibly he wasn't alone in this silent and vindictive environment. An unknown, unlikely and unexpected accomplice was fast making ground towards the inert submariner. The stranger spotted him, signalling that he could handle it. Rocketing upwards towards his own salvation, he prayed as never before. 'Please...please! Let it not be too late'.

Inhaling greedily he clung to the side of the boat. Allowing an all too-brief time for his body to respond, he wallowed in near ecstasy as great swathes of air swelled oxygen-starved organs. Calmed by the precious gas, the pounding in his ears quietened. He pushed away from the hull, impatient to lend assistance to the unknown swimmer and his precious load...he didn't have to. The stranger and his precious cargo broke the surface not many yards away. The supported body was limp, hanging motionless; dire confirmation that they were too late. It was a lifeless body the man held in his arms. The pitiful victim of an unmerciful ocean.

A stretcher was thrown over the side. From the captain down, this crew could not be faulted. They knew what had to be done and they got on and did it, quickly and without fuss. The instant Jack was manhandled onto the stretcher there was no delay. Watching eyes from above sending the signal for the contrivance to be raised the moment the body made contact with the canvas. A rope ladder was lowered for the benefit of the two men left behind, comforting hands ready to help them across the rails when they reached the top. Resuscitation already under way by the time their feet touched the deck. Draped face down over a barrel, the inert body was being rolled to-and-fro...seawater gushing from nose and mouth.

The comatose body convulsed, shaking shoulders heaving in response to abused stomach and lungs venting unwelcome contents. The agonised sounds of violent retching impinged on Kyle's ears as a symphony, a celebration that Jack Sibley lived. Within minutes the wracking spasms subsided, breathing retuned to gurgling normality, flesh assumed something like it's rightful colour and his worst fears laid to rest.

Striving to master emotions demanding an audition, he sought seclusion from the anxious crowd. He'd prepared himself for the worst. Convinced himself there could be no happy ending. The man he had known for so long. Their treasured friendship over…finished. Blown away in a microcosm of time. Having given his friend up for lost, the reaction was understandable. But the anticipated tears of anguish were replaced by those of gratitude and relief.

Emotions attended to, he made his way to the front of the milling throng gathered round his friend. Jack was sitting up and a liquid, which he rightly assumed to be brandy, was being forced between reluctant lips. He moved closer, his pose that of a frustrated father figure bent on berating his errant charge.

"Next time you decide to take a dip, let me know goddammit. Prancing off with never a hint of where you're going. Do that to me again fellah and you're on your own. Be damned if I'm gonna ruin another perfectly good pair of shorts for your benefit."

The voice weak, the reply quick and argumentative: a sure sign that he was on the mend. "Now I know where I stand. Next time I need rescuing I'll grab someone who won't be bothered about getting their bloody shorts wet." Managing a watery smile he asked. "What do you say to someone who's just saved your life? 'Thanks', doesn't seem enough. But it's all I can come up with." Wincing as cream was applied to the abrasions on his legs, stomach and torso: injuries left behind by the whipping rope on its malicious trajectory.

"Not me you have to thank. The Aussie over there. The guy in the blue shorts talking to the captain? He was the one pulled you out. Hadn't been for him you'd have had it. His name's Frank, but he ain't the only one you owe your life to. These guys..." indicating the deckhands crowding round, "bloody marvels. Absolute bloody marvels. Worked their socks off making sure his efforts didn't end up on the scrap heap. Get you sorted, we'll decide what we're gonna do by way of showing our appreciation." First aid coming to an end, he changed the subject. "Those wounds, Jack. They look real bad."

"Blooming sore, but I'll survive." Wincing as he leant forward. "Those are the worst," indicating several deep lacerations blighting his lower abdomen, "legs aren't so bad. Doubt I'll get much sleep tonight though...Membril or no Membril. But I tell you what, Kyle; I might not relish reuniting with those camp beds, but it's nice to know I'm still around to wallow in their discomfort."

"You can forget the idea of camp beds, and all the other stuff. The minute this boat docks you're off to hospital for a check up. And you're gonna stay there overnight...just in case. No arguments," stagnating the attempted interruption, "I'm not taking any chances. Don't know what kind of reaction's gonna set in after what you've been through."

"No, Kyle, honest: it's not necessary. I appreciate the thought but it'd be a waste. I know you mean well but the worst is over, soreness apart I'm as right as rain. Time and a fistful of painkillers will sort me out. Nothing a hospital can do I can't do myself."

"Cuts no ice, Jack. Never know what's hiding round the corner. You didn't breathe for about ten minutes for chrissakes, and you're trying to tell me that ain't done some damage? So no dice fellah, I'm not hearing you. Like it or not, you're gonna do as your damn well told for a change."

"And what about Membril? Forgotten him? Oh sure! He'd love to have you all to himself." Not wanting to admit his wounds were giving him hell, he eased his body into a more comfortable position. "It'd make his day, and you know it."

"Ok, so we compromise. Get the medics' check you out, see what they have to say. They say stay then that's what we do, and I'll stay with you. Drop a hint there's a healthy donation to the fund for wayward nurses in the pipeline and they'll find me a bed alright. And I promise, hand on heart and all that, they say you can go...then we go. You happy with that?"

"Still think it's unnecessary...but ok. I'll go by what they say. If that's what you want."

He didn't gloat, didn't say he'd told him so, but fate was to decree his concerns were justified. Before the boat reached its moorings, Jack began to sweat and his temperature rocketed; the preliminary signs of a severe fever. For four nights and three full days he lay in a restless coma, it being not until the morning of the fourth day that his delirium finally showed signs of abating.

"Good timing," poking his head gingerly round the door "told you were on the mend, but didn't want to wake you if you were still asleep. This'll cheer you up more'n any medicine." Thrusting his mobile into Jack's hand he chuckled. "Give her my best."

Kyle's prediction was spot on, all carried over symptoms dropping away in droves at the sound of her voice. Knowing it was only fair she was kept informed, Kyle had phoned Julie on a regular basis. Now Jack could speak for himself she was going to make the most of it...and she did."

"Well? What did I tell you? Bet that did more good than a packet of paracetamol." He beamed, following Jack's breakfast into the side ward. "You've been well out of it, but I've been driven mad. On the bleeper three, four times a day. Got to the point where she was threatening to fly out so she could see for herself you were being properly looked after. Don't for the life of me understand why she would. Poor girl must have it real bad. Gotta be nuts in my opinion. But that's love, and who am I to knock it?"

"Suppose it was for the best, putting her in the picture I mean. But had it been me making the decision I'm not so sure.

One of those either-or situations. Worry without cause, or leave none the wiser?" Pausing to take a bite from his toast and marmalade, he disregarded etiquette and chewed as he mumbled. "But you had no option, I see that. I was on a knife-edge for a while apparently, and, well...who knows? Still, all's well that ends well, as in the words of that well worn cliché. And I have to say you got one thing right...your sister was a lot more effective than any of the medicines they've shoved down me." Her parting words he kept to himself. Said in a whisper as she put the phone down he wasn't a hundred percent...but he didn't think he'd misheard.

"What happened?" Jack, asked. "I'm completely in the dark," peering at Kyle over the top of his cup. "The only thing I remember was being hit bloody hard from behind. From then on it's a blank."

"Don't rightly know to tell the truth...not the full facts. These two guys were busy lowering the anchor when there was an almighty bang and the rope broke. In the midst of all the chaos and confusion I heard you yell. How in God's name it happened still bugs me, but you somehow managed to get yourself tangled up in the rope. The weight of the anchor was enough to pull you over the rails, and that was it. Everything else went by the board. But you weren't alone on the disaster front. One of the winch-men got his arm busted so bad they had to amputate."

"Odd, wasn't it...the rope breaking like that? Did they find out why?"

"Nope. Not a clue. The rope was new at the start of the season which rules out wear and tear, and the safety experts - they had to get involved of course - could find nothing wrong with it. The fibre was top quality; there was no sign of any damage. No indication it'd been tampered with. Whole thing was a complete mystery. There's no way that rope should've snapped, but it did...facts speak for themselves."

"Another inexplicable accident the newspapers love to get their hands on."

"Sure thing. But it don't end there. The rope breaks and a guy loses an arm. Unfortunate, but it happens...but you? you have to be different. How in God's name, does the rope manage to wrap itself round your body so dam tight you end up in the drink? You're the one with the physics, Jack. What kind of mechanism can work a trick like that? But then it gets even more bizarre. Having got you trussed up like a goddamn chicken ready for the roasting, it lets you off the hook. You were dead to the world and there was no one else around to give a hand. Thank God that was the way it happened, but I can't for the life of me see how or why it did. The entire scenario is utterly without logic. You were on your way to Davy Jones' locker for good and all, and there was bugger all anyone could do to stop it. Weird ain't the word. Beyond speculation."

"Anything from our friend? Silly question. You would have said if there was." Back at the hotel, the two men were relaxing in the lounge.

"Not a whisper. He'll know what's gone on of course. His inbuilt radar would see to that. Surprised he didn't put in an appearance though. What with you out cold and helpless like you were. Doesn't seem so sure of himself when you're around. On the other hand, maybe the hospital's a bit too public for his liking. Who knows? But can't say I was disappointed. Life's more fun without him breathing down our necks

"And the Bridal Suite? Is that ok?"

"You've gotta be kidding. Gave it the once over at least twice a day while you were banged up. Wasn't gonna leave anything to chance. Rubbed it into the staff they weren't to so much as open the door unless I was there, and it seems to have paid off. Come and see for yourself if you're up to it."

"Vases need topping up, otherwise..." Coughing into his hand, he complained. "This is damn silly, I'm so weak and wobbly I feel like an old man...bloody nuisance! Thought I'd be better than this by now."

"Don't come as no surprise to me after the beating you had. I'll see to the vases, you go and have a lie down. Look in on you later."

Whatever his needs, they were put on hold. His sought for respite sidelined by the room telephone demanding attention. He didn't need the girl to tell him who it was, he knew only too well who it would be before he lifted the receiver.

"Mr. Sibley?" Her voice sparkled, which was more than he could say for his spirits. "I have Sir Charles Membril at the desk. If it is convenient, he would like you and Dr. Steinbeck to join him in the main lounge."

As if they had a choice? "Ok, thanks," he'd love to say no, tell him to bugger off, but it wouldn't solve anything, "we'll be down in ten minutes." No, it's alright," in answer to her query, "I'll let Dr. Steinbeck know."

He was in a foul mood, making it painfully clear he didn't like to be kept waiting. "You told the girl ten minutes...not twenty-five, Mr. Sibley. If you were delayed you might at least have had the decency to let me know."

He didn't feel up to arguing but his mumbled apology was slammed down. Kyle wasn't in the right frame of mind for humility.

"Now there's a thing, Membril. I wouldn't have thought you'd be bothered by such trivialities. Judging by the way you've treated us I'm surprised you know the meaning of the word, decency. You seem to think we exist for your purpose and everyone else can go to blazes. Turn up whenever you like, and there we'll be. At your beck and call whatever time of day or night suits your miserable self. Well have I got news for you. You want our company...make an appointment, or go take a hike. Take your pick."

"If that is meant to put me in my place, Dr. Steinbeck, I must disappoint you." Anger evaporated by Kyle's outburst, the smile was cynical. Anger they could tolerate, amusement carried sinister under-tones. "I do however bow to your courage. So very brave…stupid would perhaps be a more meaningful adjective. Some, I am sure, would argue that placing yourself in peril for the sake of a friend is to be admired. Personally I tend to regard such thankless motives as idiotic…but there you are. We cannot all think the same way. Were that the case life would become intolerable." He laughed, a burbling sound from deep down in his throat that failed to mask the underlying evil. "A regrettable accident Mr. Sibley." The smile vanished, the voice hardened. "You should be dead…why aren't you?"

"Oh shit! You…" Turning to face Kyle who looked equally thunderstruck. "We didn't give this bastard a thought." He blustered as if Membril wasn't there. "How could we have been so thick?"

"All too frantic I guess. Too much to think about. Too much to worry over." Tearing his gaze away from Jack, he directed his venom at the gloating magician. "I know you can get the better of me right now but one of these days things are gonna change, and when they do you'd better watch your ass…because if I get the ghost of a chance you're a dead man, Membril. And I don't make promises I can't keep."

"And you, Dr. Steinbeck, amuse me with your pathetic threats," he answered with a guttural cackle. "Should your promise ever reach fruition, I will welcome the challenge." Humour exhausted, his manner changed. "I asked you a question, Sibley."

"How the bloody hell should I know…?" He stopped, the dubious expression mirrored in the eyes that bore into his he found puzzling. It reflected doubt, wariness and…fear. "What's worrying you, Membril? Could it perhaps be that, in spite your conviction to the contrary, you are, after all, prone to error. So come on...spit it out. What happened to that grand opinion of yours? A somewhat idle boast it would seem in view of what you're now telling me. Your surprise at my continued existence has however gone someway to confirming my suspicions. I now have proof positive that it's me you want out of the way." He paused, taking stock before continuing. "I've answered your question, now it's your turn. Why have the goal posts been moved? The statue that you were so anxious to have returned to your safe keeping seems to have slipped down your list of priorities. Why? What's changed?"

It was the *way* it was said rather than *what* was said that aroused their interest. "My preferences are of no concern, as you will do well to take note." They couldn't miss the shaky delivery, it was all too apparent. Reaching fever pitch in his dismissal of Jack's earlier attempt to wind him up, he shrieked "How many times must I keep telling you? My status renders me incapable of error. Are you so dim that you cannot understand what I say, or do I have to spell it out in words of one syllable. Mock all you will," he simmered, glowering at the 'oh yeah' sneer on the face of his tormentor. "I stick to facts. Whether or not you choose to believe me? that is your prerogative. A stroke of good fortune can be ruled out - no one, not even you, could be that lucky - which leaves just one alternative...an alien entity. Admit it, Sibley. The facts are irrefutable."

It hit both of them the same; his manner exuded doubt and confusion. His attempted nonchalance failed to hide the tremors bubbling beneath the surface. He was a troubled man, and it wasn't anger that caused his voice to shake...it was fear.

"Oh come off it, Membril, I'm not that gullible. You don't really think I'd be daft enough to let you in on our little secrets. Have we chummed up with someone? Now that's interesting. Possibly. On the other hand possibly not. Perhaps you'll find out one day. Either way, I would suggest you take nothing for granted."

"Good-day Mr. Sibley, Dr Steinbeck...I look forward to our next meeting. As I trust you do."

"What was all that about, for chrissakes?"

"Same old story...his ego not allowing him to absorb the facts. Rather than admit he cocked it up - which he obviously must've done - he convinces himself another power has entered the scene. More gratifying for him to wallow in the belief that there is someone looking after my interests than admit he got it wrong in the first place. By doing so his self-inflicted infallibility remains intact. The idea of me having a minder might get under his skin, but he views that possibility as preferable to the alternative."

"Yeah, I know all that. But it raises the question. Why'd he need confirmation? Surprised you didn't notice. If he can read your mind like he can mine, he wouldn't need to be told. One peep inside your head he'd know damn well you don't have a hood working on your behalf. Now that's gotta be good news. He won't know if he's coming, going, been or gone if you are able to keep everything under wraps."

CHAPTER ELEVEN

"Fed up, Jack. Fed up to the bloody eyeballs. Four nights of cramp, starvation, no booze and bugger all else on the horizon to save my sanity. I know. No good making a fuss, 'cos it's not gonna change anything. Don't have to remind me." Thumping the canvass mattress in frustration. "Ok, I admit it. I'm a right pain in the butt...it's me, the way I am. But you one hundred percent sure he's not playacting? Riding some sick scheme. Kidding us into doing what he wants without putting the effort in? No more magic in him than a few tricks he picked up in a conjuring set he got for Christmas?"

"You're right, Kyle. What an utter fool I am! Your vision of Sadie, my two-and-eight with the anchor, Julie's phantom pregnancy and your fun and games on the astral plane. Straight out of a cardboard box, and I didn't cotton-on."

"Ok! I know, so no need to come heavy with the comments. Having to put up with everlasting boredom and sleepless nights on top of what I've already mentioned, what do you expect? I'm one of those blokes who like things kept nice and simple. Had some good, solid chow those few days when you were banged up in hospital and I got to like it. And why's he taking so long for chrissakes? All this waiting, it's enough to drive a saint up the bloody wall. And believe me, I ain't no saint. He don't come shy letting-on he wants you out the way and got plans for me...but he don't do nothing And that's what gets up my nose."

"Letting off steam might give you a coronary but it won't change the rules, and we'd be better employed trying to think of ways and means to bend those rules instead of sitting on our backsides bemoaning our lot. He'll know all about the pentagram of course. It might come as a surprise, but he won't be overly bothered. He'll see it more as a challenge than an obstacle. Something solid to get his teeth into. Gives him the chance to prove that, even on a level playing field, we still won't be able to compete. He'll find it difficult, he knows that and he won't need reminding; but, unless we are blessed with a considerable amount of luck, he'll have his way in the end."

"Thought you said the pentagram was nigh-on impenetrable," Kyle butted in. "Now you're telling me we don't stand a monkey's. So why go to all this bother? Might as well give up here and now."

"The pentagram will protect us against all outside physical forces of psychic origin, but it draws the line when asked to mollycoddling it's inmates. It has no say in what we do. If one of us loses the plot the blame stays with the perpetrator. In other words, the only way Membril can get at us while we have the protection of the pentagram is if one of us cracks. He can't get at us physically but he can mentally. We must be constantly aware of that and be on our toes at all times. Somewhat similar in a way to those unfortunate soldiers stuck in the trenches during the First World War. How they must have felt in those last few minutes before the balloon went up. They'd no idea what was in store, neither do we."

"And I'm showing him his ideas are going to plan. That what you're saying?"

"He'll be rubbing his hands," topping up the vases with holy water as he spoke, "but you're not the only one to be driven to drink - forgive the oxymoron - not by a long chalk." a wan smile making a brief appearance he carried on in philosophical mode. "I know I keep on, but I've never been more serious. Our one and only chance we have of coming through this in one piece, is to cling tight to our marbles. The last thing we want is for one of us to put the ball into our own net."

"And I'm the one who's likely to be the fall guy. Ok, point taken. I'll try to keep my feelings under wraps in future. Make no promises though. My natural self kind of takes me over when I'm down in the dumps. Oh by the way," belated memory striking a chord, "Membril keeps getting up my nose, so thought I'd get up his for a change. It was while you were in hospital; thought it'd be a good idea if I got rid of the statue. Might not do much, but if it upsets his little scheme it'll be well worth it."

"You what? For God's sake, what were you thinking of? You couldn't have made a worse, a more dangerous move. He'll do for us like he did Montez." His face bloodless, panic rising to the surface. "Why the hell didn't you check with me first? It won't stop him. With us out of the way, the poor sod you lumbered it with will be left to face the music."

"Calm down and untwist those knickers you've just ruined. Haven't lumbered anybody. I'm not that stupid. Though according to you I must be the biggest idiot on the planet. Shipped it to my bank in Tonopah. Told 'em to keep it locked away till I tell 'em different. Nothing more deadly than that. Can you imagine the tantrum when he finds out it's not where he thinks it is? Especially if that don't happen till he's got me tied down on that foul altar he's got waiting for me. I'll be laughing so much I'll forget to be scared...as if!"

"Phew, don't do this to me, Kyle. I've got enough on my plate without having you scare the pants off me. But you're missing the obvious? You should know by now you can't hide anything from him. The statue won't get as far the bank. It'll be returned to sender before it hits the mailbag. That's how I see it, and you'd better hope I'm right."

"Yeah, suppose. Didn't think...me all over. But this latest turn up of his: you got someone in your corner. The mere idea frightens the living crap out of him. He made that pretty damned obvious. Ain't there a chance it'll stop him making our lives as miserable as his?"

"You know what he said would be his reward if he doesn't come up trumps...there's your answer."

"Yeah I know. His master would make sure he got his."

"Precisely. He has to finish what he's started. There's no other way out."

"That's it, there you go again...blowing all my hopes to smithereens as per usual. And for that you can treat me to the sinful delight of a glass or two of orange juice...straight from the bottle, nothing added." Disgust ingrained in every line of his features, he growled, "Mood I'm in, I might be rash enough to go for more than just a couple. So you'd better make sure your pockets are well filled!"

"Tell me, Jack," he asked, peering at his friend across the table, "why don't we just pack it all in and head back home?" Glaring at the unappetising glass in his hand, thumping it on the table to express his irritation. "We'd have more'n enough help; Pop, Luke, Ben...that bunch of heavyweights! Membril might not fancy his chances with that lot breathing down his neck."

"And put your entire family in peril? Is that what you would want? Your own somewhat limited experience should leave you in no doubt that he can't be stopped that way. Remember what happened when you lost your rag the first time he appeared out of nowhere? You were made to sit in the chair like a spoilt brat until you learned how to behave." Bringing the conversation to a close, he yawned heavily. "Come on. Time we tucked ourselves up in those delightfully comfortable camp beds."

Something woke him. A sound, a movement...he wasn't sure. A shadow flitting across half-closed eyes, he rolled onto his side. Kyle was on the move.

"You alright, Kyle?" He glanced at his watch. Nearly one.

"Sorry, mate. Didn't want to disturb you. Going for a sweater. Bloody cold...woke me up"

He was right. It was cold, icy cold. "You can get one for me while you're at it..."

Through the numbness of a semi-conscious brain somnolent thought patterns began to stir, assembling into worrisome groups as they gathered impetus. Belatedly, and barely in time, the penny dropped...the instant Kyle's foot was about to cross the threshold.

"No Kyle," he shrieked, "for God's sake don't move." The frantically delivered outburst having the desired effect, he lowered his voice; relaying his inner thoughts in more subdued tones. "As your life's worth, put your foot down behind the line and stay just where you are."

A small voice inside his head telling him his companion was deadly serious, Kyle returned his half-raised foot to the floor. "What the heck? Only be gone a couple of jiffs for chrissakes. Be back quicker'n a roadrunner with a rocket up its ass."

"You're going nowhere. Look at the lights."

Further explanation was unnecessary. The four wall-mounted lamps, permanently on during their occupation of the pentagram, were noticeably dimmer...growing dimmer as he watched.

Voice quavering, he shot a nervous glance at Jack.

"This it? Oh Christ..." Ducking as a telephone, deposited on a window ledge in the absence of any furniture, hurtled towards him: brought to an abrupt halt as it ran out of wire. Its flight-path blocked by an unseen obstacle, the directory that followed fluttered to the floor in resignation.

"That's good. If we needed proof the pentagram is doing its job, we have it. That directory had you well and truly in its sights."

"So pleased, I really am. Here's me thinking I was about to have my bloody block knocked off and all you harp on about is your precious pentagram. Good to know you get your priorities right."

"Whinge all you..." Suffering the same fate as the directory, a solitary shoe aimed in his direction stifled what he was about to say. "The point I'm trying to make, Kyle, if you

218

can get your brain in order; is that nothing is crossing the boundary. Any weak spot, we'd both be nursing sore heads."

"So that's supposed to help me rest easy?" making no attempt to hide his inner feelings, "But if that's it, why go to all this trouble? A few bruises here and there don't seem much justification. Or you telling me there's more to it."

"Don't kid yourself, this is only a warm-up. Nothing like a petulant poltergeist to get the party going. Make the most of it Kyle. From now on it won't be quite so friendly."

"I remember reading about poltergeists in my boys book of fairytales. But everything was nice and simple back in those days. Then you come along and my whole world changes."

The lights went out.

No lead-up, no warning. The precious remnants of a meagre effulgent replaced by stygian blackness. An all-engulfing silence eating into their consciences, fear taking reign. Eyes struggling to pierce the impenetrable darkness, ears straining to catch the slightest sound. Nerves taut as guitar strings striking sinister notes in terrorised minds. The dread increasing with the waiting…that went on…and on…and on.

"What's he doing?" Kyle whispered, a whimper impinging on fraught ears.

"No need to whisper," the words belied by his own attenuated response. "This is only the opening chapter: his way of building the drama to heighten the expectancy. Do nothing. Keep them guessing. Hold hard until they're on the brink. That's the premise. The epilogue is in our court...not his."

In the darkness it was an unseen and wasted grimace, in reality it provided a platform for further observation. "Whatever he gets up to, Kyle, it will not be pleasant…and that's putting it mildly. But as long as we stay calm, keep our cool and resist intimidation nothing of his volition will harm us. It won't be easy, but as long as we hang on to those golden rules we'll be ok. It might sound like a walk in the park, but don't be fooled. He'll try every trick in the book to make one of us crack. What we see, what we hear, what we smell or feel…whatever form it takes we have to stand firm. The aim will be to drive us over the edge; using fear, revulsion and, arguably the most difficult of all, temptation. Whatever the carrot, it's up to us to refuse it; content in the knowledge that our undoing will not be of his choosing but by one of us making a terrible mistake."

"You sure know how to make a bloke rest easy. Next time I want a confidence boost I'll get me a guy suffering a nervous break-down." He swallowed hard, "Pass the water, Jack. Got one helluva thirst."

"Holy cow! What the hell you put in there?" Punctuated by an eruption of violent coughing, he ejected the offending liquid through screwed-up lips. "Tastes like horse shit and monkey droppings mixed with castor oil that's seen better days." Shoving the flask across the floor to within his friend's reach, he blustered, "Here, you filled the bloody bottle…grab a taste of your own medicine."

"Nothing wrong with it." No pun intended, but this is a taste of what's to come." Replacing the cap he pushed the container back to Kyle. "I said temptation would be the most difficult, and this is as good as it gets. He was hoping you'd end the game early by rushing off to the nearest tap. Game over almost before it started. Try it now. I think you'll find it ok."

"So much for the pentagram." Nodding his agreement that the water was more to his taste. You said nothing could get past it, but he got that message across alright."

"It's as I've already said, the role of a pentagram is to provide defence against all forms of psychically generated physical onslaught: telepathy doesn't fall into that category. It's up to us to deal with it, and it is within our power to do so. Keep the must-do's in mind. Stay alert, and don't let the bastard grind you down." Taking time to refresh his thoughts, he carried on in different vein. "He did us a favour if you think about it. We now have proof he can't enter my mind as he can yours. If he could you wouldn't have been the only one to be hit with a raging thirst and we'd both be fighting to get to the bathroom."

For some time they were made to suffer the trauma of uncertainty, as all went quiet and activity stalled. Time that seemed to stand still for the two individuals imprisoned within the pentagram. Dire imagination reigning supreme there was no attempt at conversation in the vast, anechoic chamber of their confinement: a sepulchre for the breeding of the persecution that was to follow. A low wail of paranormal origin, the only sound to break the cloying blackness, wound its mournful path through the ether. Seeming to emanate from the long lost beginning of time the barely audible, flat monotones slowly drove them into a frenzy of despair. Driving all passion, all desire from mouldering, lifeless bodies.

The change was as sudden as it was merciful. Sanities in disarray and in danger of caving in to the demonic rhythm, it came not a moment too soon for the two cowering victims. But the new arrival was a double-edged sword, the soulful sounds were replaced by an instrument of greater torment. A wild cacophony of evil strings plucked by a band of demons. A vile spectrum of discordant notes, impinging fear and confusion within morbidity ravaged minds. A choir of high, rasping voices creating a crescendo of noise sufficient to shake the walls joined in. It was more than they could take. Sweat embalmed hands clasped uselessly over embattled ears, they sank to their knees in disarray .

The torture continued. The succour to be found in uninhibited madness not yet theirs. But relief was at hand. The disjointed lyrics faded, a sinister libretto muting the lessening volume of the ragged orchestra took over. Difficult to discern, a multitudinous assembly of shapeless figures conjoined around the perimeter of the pentagram. Continuing to grow in number, the nefarious aggregation began to chant: a raucous cacophony of rasping sound. The diction perfect, each and every syllable projected with precision. Four immaculately articulated words thundering through the ether; 'Jack Sibley…Kyle Steinbeck…Jack Sibley…Kyle Steinbeck: a sibilant monotony vibrating through the opacity of their surroundings, the evil choir continued unabated...'Jack Sibley...Kyle Steinbeck...Jack Sibley'.

"For God's sake, Jack! Will it never stop?"

Remembering his own helpless state of mind on that awful night, the night he had so nearly become enmeshed in Satanism and it's blasphemous doctrine, he could understand what his friend was going through. Recalling the same feeling of terror and abandonment that now found their familiar in his friend's tremulous tones, he strove to give encouragement.

"It's only a noise, Kyle. Remember...it's up to us. It can hurt us only if we let it."

"Goddamn it Jack, easy enough to say." shouting to make himself heard above the din, "But can't take much more of this."

The tremor in his voice was noticeable...and worrying. He was on the edge. A more assertive, more demanding approach might have more success. "Ok Kyle. So what are you going to do? Give up? Say to hell with it, and kill us both in the process? For God's sake pull yourself together. Put yourself in the shoes of those poor sods in the trenches. Those lads never stood a chance when they went over the top, but they had no choice. They were under orders. You're master of your own decisions. Stay safe in your personal trench or put both of us in mortal danger by surrendering. It's your call." He paused. Fearful he might have gone too far; his worries dwindling with yet another change of scene.

"Oh, I like that...could doze off listening to that." If the reprimand had upset him, it was forgotten. "The accompaniments not bad either."

Above their heads the room scintillated with phosphorescent figures, a subtle blend of silver and purple artistry gyrating in time to delicate music. Lulling them into a state of euphoria. Banishing fear, replenishing frayed nerves.

It wasn't to last. The choir quietened, slowly merging with the ambient silence until the two amalgamated. Brutally pushed aside, the artistic combination was vanquished by a return of the hissing strings. Their all-too brief comfort zone banished, psychotic symphonies composed in the foetid vaults of Hades and strummed by dervishes took over. Similarly transformed the beautiful, harmonious visions of their earlier admiration were contorted into a disorganised mass of eerie, ghostly figures. Part human, part animal, they flirted with them. Leering mouths and threatening eyes mocking their refusal to respond. Growing in intensity the pale glow at their origin increased, granting the spell-bound men sufficient light to discern the expression on the face of the other. There was little difference. Both registered repugnance.

"Jack!" He screeched. Nose grasped between thumb and forefinger. "That stink. It's bloody awful. What the hell is it?"

"Over there. The corner by the door."

The sight that met his eyes was a throbbing mass of heaving, putrescent slime: choking the air with sulphurous gases exuded from puss-filled craters. In rising fear he watched the snarling apparitions take it in turn to slither into the avaricious mass, each addition celebrated by a further eruption of the poisonous fumes. A sepulchral glow of simmering yellow light illumined the desperate scene, allowing their vision to absorb the implication. This was the ultimate scenario. A final thrust aimed at their undoing.

The last of the phantoms reunited with the nauseas abomination of its birth, the throbbing mound subsided into silent expectation. The odorous emissions abated, the phosphorescence diminished. But the dormant state was a temporary respite. Slowly, imperceptibly, further change was taking place. In the glow of a pulsating miasma of green and purple candescence they waited. In rising trepidation they watched the craters in-filled, the eruptions fade to extinction...a prelude to the finale that would precede the fall of the final curtain.

Drained faces and erratic breathing registering their mounting horror, a human arm was ejected with great suddenness from the calmed malignancy; inadequate lighting failing to secrete the long slender fingers of a female hand.

Before the initial shock was given time to simmer, the appendage was met by the shoulder to which it was joined: a faceless head following close behind adding to their revulsion. Lush raven tresses brushing the silkily smooth flesh of a long, graceful neck removed all lingering doubt. The incarnated being was a young, sensual female. Fear can on occasion breed strange companions, and this was one such. Dire though the situation, both men floundered in conflicting emotions. Cowering terror on the one hand, testosterone fuelled anticipation on the other.

A tall, shapely, fully naked female form stepped from the foul mass of its birth. Lustful eyes entranced by the desirable body set masculine urges bubbling, rendering the possessors dangerously vulnerable. In awe they watched the featureless countenance change...to a loveliness with one aim. The total and final destruction of their karma."

"Julie!" Doubting the evidence of his own eyes, he took a step closer. "Heaven help us, Jack! It's Julie."

"Don't look at the eyes, Kyle...for God's sake, don't look at the eyes." Throwing an arm across the American's face to ram home the command. "It's not Julie, it's an abomination from the very depths: another of Membril's ghouls. Look into its eyes and you're done for...we're both done for."

He paused. It wasn't Julie, he knew damn well it wasn't but the knowledge was of little comfort. Striking him that this was how Kyle must have felt that night on the dance floor, he banished the illusion from his mind.

"The dance hall in Oaxaca, Kyle...remember?" Silly question, as if he was likely to forget! "Sadie was an implanted memory. That thing is a living corruption in Julie's likeness. But the motivation is the same...the presence of loved ones' is a potent weapon. If I'm right, then this has to be the last throw of the dice. Past the softening up stage he's going for the jugular, and it's going to be tough...but it's our call, so hang on to that. Win or lose...it's up to us. Keep our nerve. Refuse to be intimidated. Deny all enticements. And remember. As with

Perseus and the Gorgon, our immunity lies in the avoidance of eye contact."

"Got it, Jack. What the..." Choking on his words as the door into the corridor opened. A figure silhouetted against the backlight.

The outlined form was again that of a woman; that the face was indistinguishable in the darkness was irrelevant. Jack hadn't known Sadie, had never seen a photograph, but he knew without any doubt whatsoever that the newly arrived menace would be in her image.

Hand-in-hand, the two phantoms walked to the edge of the pentagram; the men shielding their eyes, seeking further insurance by turning their backs on the female monstrosities. Pointing to a mirror on the far wall, Jack said, "You can watch what they're up to, Kyle. A reflection doesn't carry the same threat as direct eye contact."

Inadequate lighting failing to mask the reflected images, the two men were hypnotised into watching the scene enacted for their entertainment. The two fiends were locked in a kiss. A kiss that hinted at a more intimate, a more personal relationship than a friendly welcome.

"You could do without this after the charade in Oaxaca." Jack whispered. I know it's not easy, just keep telling yourself it isn't, Sadie, it isn't, Julie. We won't have much more of this, so keep it going. Membril must be nearing the end of his tether by now, and he'll be feeling the strain. It's exhausting work going at the rate he has, and I doubt he'll be able to carry on much longer."

"No need worry on my account. I'm not gonna give...what the hell? God, no! Not that!"

The Sadie image, running tantalising hands over its bare breasts, leered in mockery at the two men reflected in the mirror before performing the same act on its more-than willing partner. Despite their inherent loathing, both men were mesmerized. The mirror their personal screen; spellbound by a portrayal that sickened them beyond measure.

Naked bodies glistening in the semi-gloom, the fiends danced in tight embrace. A slow, sensual swaying of hips and torsos; hands free to explore willing and receptive bodies. Erotic caresses bringing the creatures to the heights of arousal.

The debauched display was too much for Kyle. In stark danger of losing control he thrust a hand over his mouth, a flimsy barrier to the bile buffeting the back of his throat. Mind in turmoil, eyes exposed, discipline surrendered: defenceless...vulnerable.

"Don't be angry with me, Kyle." The words purred through the pouting lips of the Sadie abomination. "This is just a silly bit of fun to get you in the mood. Don't turn away from me my darling, I need you, want you. So badly it hurts. I love you so much, like I've always loved you...love you more than you'll ever understand. Come to me dear heart...love me like you used to."

For the briefest of instants it was no apparition that tortured his stressed mind, it was his precious Sadie. There was no mistaking her voice: the delicate, seductive lilt that thrilled him to distraction. Jack had got it wrong. Of course it's her...and why should he take notice of what he said anyway? Resistance torn to shreds, he quailed into submission. He would go to her, to love her. To look into her eyes...the blood-red eyes of the she-devil from hell.

"No, Kyle...no!"

The panic-stricken command falling on deaf ears, he strode unerringly towards the perimeter...in blind and total obedience to an order he was forced to obey.

In desperation Jack threw his arms about his friend's shoulders but it was a wasted effort. The American, bigger, stronger and aided by unseen forces, flung him to the floor in contempt. Falling foul to a descending foot, a shattered glass vase emptied its contents across the polished floor. A trivial incident unnoticed by the perpetrator, who proceeded along the pre-destined path beyond the limits of safety...into a cauldron of peril.

The pentagram was breached. The empty vase an open portal to the massed evil congregating at its borders.

It was over. The instant Kyle's eyes pierced those scarlet orbs he knew they were finished. They'd tried. They'd so nearly got there. But it wasn't to be. Membril had boasted of his power. Warned them of their inadequacies. That they'd given him a good run for his money was poor consolation. Eternal damnation was all that was on offer to the losers.

It was strange he felt no terror. Emotionally he was utterly flat: he hoped the end, when it came, would be clean and quick. But that didn't explain the lack of fear. There had to be a reason, not only to account but to make sense. Perhaps the brain shut down when faced with certain death instead of working overtime as he would have expected. Becoming a safe haven for the inevitable, rather than a host for despair.

Resigned to the fate that would soon be upon him, he watched the two temptresses wind tentacle-like arms about Kyle's waist and shoulders. It was out of his hands. There was nothing he could do.

It wasn't soon…it was immediate.

Manifesting close to where he lay sprawled on the floor, a massive cobra reared above him. Surveying its victim with dull, listless eyes. Loathsome body swaying from side to side. Flickering tongue preparing the fatal strike. But is that how it was meant to be? Serpents, of all species as far as he knew, tended to swallow their prey whole, and this beast was the size of a constrictor. 'Please, God! Please…let it be the venom'.

Mesmerised, he watched as the reptile faded into the ether: the scaled body undergoing embryonic change into an apparition that needed no introduction. The dread harbinger of death and destruction, summoned by Membril to carry out his execution: the cobra, an entity of minor proportion, pushed aside. Cringing in newfound fear he struggled to his feet, wanting to run from the foul presence. But there was no escape. No way out. Terrorised he shrank back, a puerile attempt to find seclusion within the now useless pentagram he stood quaking in the presence of the supreme evil.

A corpse...a living skeleton swathed in a cloak of flaming red and startling black: a Satanic curse risen from the bowels of the cosmos thundered into the pentagram. The talisman of catastrophe and depression, mounted on a stallion as black as the darkest night. Dead fish-eyes set in a skull barely visible beneath a hood laden with sinister shadow drenched him in a baleful stare. Paralysing him physically, creating havoc within an already blistered mind.

Foam exuding from its gargantuan mouth the stallion pawed the ground, impatience registered in clouds of steaming gases ejected through flared nostrils. The sound of its ferocious neighing echoing the mournful cries of dead and dying souls from around the galaxy, a vibrant dissonance primed to strike terror into the incumbent of its wrath. The mounted figure drew a curved sword from deep within its robes, brandishing it high. The horse reared on its massive hind legs, wickedly shod hooves poised to strike. First the blow from the thrashing hooves, then the finale...his head cleaved by the wielded blade in the skeletal hand.

Dimly, through the mishmash of a clouded brain, a voice spoke to him. A voice he remembered from long ago. Father O'haloran, giving instruction: beautifully intonated words ringing stridently in his ears, embellished by fiery letters that burned into his eyes. - 'used in conjunction with a crucifix, it is a highly potent weapon against all evil'.

Facing his antagonist, he stood tall and unafraid. Grasping the crucifix that dangled from his neck, he thrust it towards the ghostly equestrian. Demanding his deliverance in a voice loud and clear.

"Credo in deum patrem omnipotentum."

Hurled across the room by an unknown, unseen force he was flung against the far wall; cringing with fright as the room burst into chaos. Lightning flashed across the ceiling, thunder roared its mighty message. The compassion of an entity of unimaginable power had been sought and agreed. His plea had been answered. The Angel of Death denied its mortal purpose.

Semi comatose and initially indifferent to what had happened, he sat up and looked about him. Lights were back on, the spectral horseman had disappeared together with all traces of their earlier persecution. Not one shred of evidence, of a torment that had lasted for more than two hours, was to be seen...apart from a body lying prone upon the floor.

Trauma having taken its toll, the effort required to stagger to the comatose figure was considerable. Fearful that the Angel of Death had not after all come in vain, he squatted beside the seemingly lifeless figure. In dire anticipation he felt for a pulse. "Oh thank God!" The cry echoing round the empty room, he breathed a sigh of relief at the weak but rhythmic discovery.

Whether it was the warmth of his hand or nature making subtle intervention, he had no idea. Whatever the reason, the violence of his friend's reawakening shook him to the core. Head clasped between shaking hands, writhing in a demented torture of which only he knew the cause, he screamed in tear-strewn agony.

He was helpless. The screams were not of physical origin, they were the product of a pitiful distress for which he had no solution. Cries growing louder, violent convulsions wracked his friend's body...but that was nothing compared to the fearful punishment absorbed by his head beating a wild cacophony against the bare floorboards. He had to do something, and quickly. Lest the damage done was irreparable.

In desperate need of assistance and there being none to hand, he went for the only other option available. Praying as he had never prayed before, he again sought the help of a higher source. Whether it was his silent offering or a self-contrived inspiration that managed to pass him by didn't matter. He had the solution...it was up to him.

Forcing the crucifix into the reluctant hand of his friend he recited the words of the twenty-third psalm...the only one he knew.

"The Lord is my shepherd; I shall not want."

No change. If anything, the spasms were worsening.

"He maketh me to lie down in green pastures…"

Still no change.

"He restoreth my soul…"

Slight improvement perhaps, but he couldn't be sure.

"Yeah, though I walk through the valley of the shadow of death I will fear no evil, for thou art with me."

Screams shallower, not so drawn-out.

"Thou preparist a table before me in the presence of mine enemies."

Convulsions subsiding, head motionless, cries dwindling to a pitiful whimper.

Inwardly thanking whatever or whoever was responsible, he continued through to the end of the psalm.

"What the hell, Jack? Last thing I remember was those obnoxious women getting all randy like. Nothing more till I see your ugly mug looking down at me."

Knowing he would be devastated if he was to tell him the truth, he diplomatically laundered the reality. "My clumsiness. That's what happened. Walking backwards and not looking where I was going. Trod on one of the vases. That was it. The pentagram was breached. An invitation not be ignored, Membril wasn't going to hang around. He summoned the Angel of Death. A nice tidy way of removing the inconvenience of yours truly." He stopped to think, rubbing his chin in contemplation. In hindsight it became clear. "Must've been pretty sure of himself to summon a major deity...and it doesn't get any more major than the Angel of Death.

He of course had every reason to be confident. My negligence made it easy for him…as he would have reckoned at the time. We know different, but from his point of view it all went bottom-up. Which explains the state you were in when you returned to the land of the living. You were mirroring his agonies."

"What's that supposed to mean?" The voice still weak, uncertain.

"Calling up a superpower is fraught with danger. If everything goes pear-shaped whoever it was dialled its number substitutes for the intended victim. Your mental affinity with Membril explains why you were affected. You were reciprocating his torture, his pain and his spiritual torment. On a more cheerful note he'll still be suffering. You're over it."

"And can't say he don't deserve it. But if you're right and he's still going through it, why's it stopped for me?"

"Can't answer that, I'm afraid. It was weird. Almost as if matters were taken out of my hands. You were in a bad way and I was out of my depth. All I could do was pray for inspiration. I'm not saying that had anything to do with it, but it was only then that I hit on the solution. I had to put the crucifix in your hand and recite the twenty-third psalm. But you know, I can't be sure that anything was down to me. It seemed all along as if something was nudging my thoughts, steering them in the right direction. Probably my imagination doing somersaults...I just don't know. The thing is it worked."

"One more thing," he said, voice growing stronger. "Said you were as good as done for when the weirdo with the horse turned up. Something must've gone right, wouldn't be sitting here otherwise."

"Father O'halloran, remember? That Sunday in Tonopah…"

"As if I could forget!"

"Well if it wasn't for him, I wouldn't be sitting here nursing you I'd be dead. He gave me an inscription in Latin which translates as 'I Believe in God, the Father Almighty'. He advised me to remember the Latin version word for word. Said it could be useful if my soul was ever under threat. Thankfully I took his advice. Bellowing the words good and strong, I shoved the crucifix under the receptive nose of the Angel of Death...Father O'haloran saved my life."

"Took some nerve though, Jack. Doubt very much if I would've remembered the bloody words if I'd been in your shoes. Not with that apparition prancing around before my eyes."

"But that's just it, Kyle. I was on the verge of giving up - not true...I'd already given up - but then it all changed. I had the uncanny impression that someone took hold of my hand. Guiding me as to what I should say and do. But that wasn't the end of it. The words I had to say...out there, shining in front of me. Blazing like a damn great neon sign. There was no danger of me forgetting my lines. I'm not going to attempt to explain it...it was weird."

"Nothing surprises me any more. But think about it, Jack. This could be a blessing in disguise. Membril's already worried you have a minder working for you. Now he's gonna be convinced."

"If he's still around. There's every possibility he could be dead. It's as I said. If the Angel of Death misses out on its intended it diverts its attention to whoever summoned it. Exceptions can be made according to circumstances however, and Membril's pact with the Devil might fit that category."

"About time his luck ran out, but don't hold out much hope of that happening. Something else I'd like to know. Why wasn't the rest of the hotel woken by the din? All that screeching, the weird music and the rest of the caterwauling...enough to give the dead permanent insomnia."

"To the outside world this room didn't exist. What went on was for us and us alone. No one else would have had an inkling. But never mind that, there are other, better things to think about. Eat what we want when we want, sleep the night away in comfortable beds and down as much booze as we can stomach. If that doesn't put a smile on your face then I'm a monkey's uncle."

"Always did think there was something funny the way you swing your arms. But how come you're so sure? Said yourself he could still be alive, even if he ain't kicking. For all we know he's already plotting the next threat to our miserable existence. Chaffing at the bit, having been diddled out of what he'll reckon was his just deserts."

"If he's not dead, you can take it as read that he'll be in a bad, bad way. Tonight's escapade will have drained him both mentally and physically, and it'll take him some considerable time to get over it."

CHAPTER TWELVE

"Can I use your phone, Kyle? Time I gave Julie a call. Haven't spoken to her since leaving the hospital."

A further three days having elapsed, they were preparing to leave the disappointment of Acapulco behind. Plagued with disaster of one kind or another, their erstwhile enthusiasm had been dashed almost from the moment they arrived. Now, and despite his earlier assurances, Jack was unable to shed the nagging doubt that he might have got it wrong in thinking Membril could be dead, or that his recovery would take some time if he wasn't. Mostly for that reason his nights were spent in restless turmoil. Fighting a losing battle with the duvet when awake, submitting to dire recollections of their pentagram experience when he slept.

He mentioned none of this to Kyle but, unbeknown to him, the American had problems of his own. Plagued by a host of similar insecurities, he too found rest hard to come by. The difference was, whereas Jack's persecution was firmly rooted in the possibility that Membril could turn up prematurely, his confidence increased on a daily basis. As far as he was concerned, his non-appearance was a sign he might not have got away with it. That the arrangement with his master was no excuse.

Jack worried him though. It was he who bore the weight of responsibility. His lot to make the decisions. His to dictate what needed to be done. His to anticipate Membril's next move and how to deal with it. Unable to shoulder at least some of the burden, he suffered feelings of inadequacy and selfishness. Hence the reason for moving on...it was the one area where he felt in control.

"Thanks, Kyle."

That sounded a touch more cheerful than of late. But if talking to Julie didn't lift his spirits, what would? They sure seemed to have something going for them, those two. He hoped it would work out all right...if working out was to be given the opportunity.

"And how's my kid sister?"

"Fine. Sends her love and to tell you to take care."

He didn't let on that Julie repeated what she'd said last time, and that he'd given free rein to his own feelings. That information was classified and would remain so for the duration. But his elation at talking to the girl he was rapidly falling in love with, was marred to some extent by the delicate question raised near the end of their conversation.

"Apart from sisterly concern for your welfare, she wants to know when we're coming back. You told her six weeks and, as she rightly points out, the six weeks ran out ten days ago." Passing the buck in company of an apologetic shrug of the shoulders he added, "Told her it was up to you, but I'd find out and let her know. Apart from assuring her I couldn't get back quick enough, what else could I say?"

"Oh, bloody Norah! Didn't give that possibility a thought. Your damn fault. You hadn't got Julie so damned infatuated she wouldn't have cared less how long we stayed. Still, guess she's got a kind of vested interest? Apart from dropping me in it, what else did you talk about?"

"Said you were tied up with work, found something you could get your teeth into and was reluctant to let go. She didn't sound convinced, but it was all I could think of on the spur of the moment. Had to stop there before I dug a hole too deep to dig my way out of."

"Ok, I'll think of something. Cook up a list of reasons she won't believe. Not easily fooled, that's Julie's trouble. Too

darned bright and, like all women, got a suspicious nature."
Biting hard on his lower lip, eyes watering in protest.
"Problems...bloody problems. Don't they ever stop? And this is
one we could sure do without. Can't go back for the reasons
you said...ok, Jack. Leave it with me, I'll think up a good
excuse. Talk to her when I've thought it through."

"Why not give the statue the chance to earn its keep? Tell
her where and when you got it, get her interest. Prattle on about
the advantages to be gained in researching its history in the
country of origin. Don't like lying overmuch, but telling her the
real reason is out of the question. Sweeten it a bit. You know the
score. Get down on your knees. Apologise for failing to
appreciate the passage of time...plus any other codswallop you
can come up with. She might believe it coming from you.
You're a past master at the blarney."

"By blarney, I presume you refer to my irrepressible
charm and gentle powers of persuasion. I shall, however, ignore
the insult and give it some thought. Give it a go if I can't think
of anything else. Won't call her yet awhile though. Best leave it
till we get to Aruba. Do it too soon and she'll guess it's a tale
concocted by the two of us. And who's going to be brave
enough to tell her she's right?"

"But will she fall for it? whatever it is you decide to come
up with."

"Course not! She'll not give credence to one solitary
word. In her devious way of thinking she'll be convinced I've
hooked up with a dame I'm not yet ready to ditch. But that's not
my biggest concern. What really worries me, is she's hot headed
enough to come and join us. That'd put the fox among the
chickens."

"You know your sister better than I do, but surely she
wouldn't go that far."

"If the smug look when you came off the phone is
anything to go by I wouldn't take bets. You've a lot to learn
about my sister. Got a will of her own, and if she wants to do
something she'll damn well do it. Can't say for certain, but it's a

possibility to bear in mind. If worse comes to worse, we'll just have to think up a good reason to stop her before it's too late to do anything about it. But there again she could keep it to herself till she got here. Planning on making a grand entrance; catch us off guard...now that would be awkward." Grabbing hold of his cases he sighed, "Come on, Jack, let's get moving."

"Havana? A pit stop?"

"Yeah...just the one night. Which is a pity. Lots of fun to be had in Havana from what I've heard about the place. Not too sure it's fun we want right now though. One day perhaps. When we're tired of reminiscing over this wonderfully stress-free vacation."

On the morning following a comfortable night in Havana, they set off on the second leg of the journey. Cloudless blue skies giving promise of a smooth flight it was the time to relax. To put to one side the perils that continued to haunt them. That was how Kyle saw it, and that's how it was...to begin with.

"What's happened to the sun?" Wearing a puzzled frown, he spoke as if he couldn't believe his eyes. "Coming up misty...strange. Don't get that too often in this part of the world."

Jack peered out of the port window. Threatened with extinction by a mist that was rapidly becoming a dense fog, the skies had lost their charm. He cast his eyes downward, trying to gauge visibility but the ground was out of sight. Obscured by the creeping menace.

"You're not going to be able to land if it's like this in Aruba." He tried to stay calm. He wasn't happy flying at the best of times.

"No choice, Jack. Fuel enough to make Aruba, but that's about it. Won't be much left to play with. Maracaibo's the only other airport in range, but if it's foggy in Aruba it's not likely to be any different there. Caracas is too far...another couple of hundred miles or-so. Nowhere else near enough. Have to rely on the guys' in the control tower helping out if it don't shift. But don't you worry, Jack," patting his arm, "if they can't - or won't -

it'll be an opportunity to put my night-flying skills to the test. Let's see what they have to say."

"GAK 651 calling AUA control..." having to repeat several times before receiving an answer. "Sixty miles off shore, thick fog getting progressively worse. Advise landing conditions."

"Nah, all ok. Nothing to worry about. The fog must be localised. No sign of it in Aruba apparently. What don't make sense, is ours is the only report they've had of fog in this vicinity. All I can say is they must have a bloody short vicinity. That's beside the point. All I'm interested in, is what it's like on that lovely little island...and we don't have a care in the world."

"If it stays that way."

"They'd know if fog was likely to molest their airfield. Give 'em some credit."

"That's not what I meant. I'll explain when we get down." Inwardly thinking 'if we get down'. He bated his breath, nerves jingling in tune with the second request.

"AUA control. GAK 651 calling AUA control. Imperative you confirm approach conditions. Twenty miles off shore in thick fog, visibility less than two hundred yards."

The answer was the same as before. Expression impassive, he made no comment. Unwilling to admit he was thinking along the same lines as his companion. The idea hadn't occurred until that last report, which was when the meaning behind Jack's remark kicked in. The fog...natural, or manufactured? No, it was damn silly. He wouldn't choose this way. He'd said it plain and simple. He wanted him alive. If he messed up the landing it'd be a miracle if either of them made it. He'd try again. See if there was a chance they'd misread the conditions.

The reply this time was more definite. In the eyes of Aruba's air traffic control they did not exist. In their opinion his navigation was seriously at fault, and wherever he thought he was it wasn't in their airspace. Telling him in no uncertain terms to get his act together, they suggested he clarify his position and sort himself out. In response to his advice that they get their effin' eyes tested, he was curtly informed they no longer lived in the dark ages. They had this thing called radar. A wonderful contraption that made spectacles a touch redundant.

"Him again!" The comment causing Jack to mutter, 'better late than never' under his breath, "Well now he's gonna have me put a spoke in his damn works for once. I'll get this plane down if it kills me," the irony of what he said bringing a smile to his lips. "I'll drop us down a few feet, see if I can persuade Aruba to humour me by switching the runway lights on. Not that they will. Probably won't grant permission to land either. Seeing as how they don't think I'm anywhere near their stupid airport."

Levelling out at just above two hundred feet, he glanced at Jack.

"Is it me, or is it getting thinner?" Addressing the remark to no one in particular. "Well I'll be damned...it's gone! It's bloody gone. Oh hallelujah!"

The impenetrable curtain of dense fog had dissipated, replaced by an untarnished expanse of beautiful blue sky. Glistening white in the early afternoon sun the landing strip protruding into the sea no more than a mile-or-two ahead.

"Did him an injustice, Jack. Wasn't his doing after all," they were on the veranda of their hotel, sipping refreshingly cool pina-coladas. "But buggered if I'm gonna apologise to the bastard."

"And what makes you think it wasn't him?"

"Stands to reason! We were as good as finished, and can't imagine him pulling out with us at his mercy. Not his style. Would've had me pan-caking the plane from a hundred feet up and short of the runway...or worse. That way, he'd have got rid of the two of us in one foul swoop of his vindictive nature."

"Don't pretend to understand the motive but you're wrong. It was him as sure as chickens lay eggs. Fog that thick doesn't come and go in the blink of an eye, Kyle. And how come the guys in the control tower knew nothing about it?

Swearing we weren't so much as in the area, let alone within landing distance. It was Membril making a point, no doubt about that. It's the point he was trying to make that beats me." In danger of sending his cocktail flying, he smacked a hand on the table. "A message! What an idiot I am. A message, letting us know he's alive and with his hand on the rudder. Clear as daylight. Nothing's changed. He wants you in one piece. There was never any real danger of you having to land in that fog."

"Yeah, suppose. Had hoped. Still...weren't to be." He sighed. "Guess it won't be long before he's banging on our door, tongue wagging, hubris overflowing as per normal."

"Good afternoon, gentlemen. We meet again." he oozed, catching them on the hop as they entered the hotel foyer. "I'm so pleased you chose to visit Aruba. A charming little island. I in fact envy you your stay, and were life not so hectic I would be hard pressed not to join you. However time is of the essence and such diversion would be imprudent. As it is I must ask you to forgive me if I am brief."

"Oh don't mind us. Be as brief as you like. Piss off now and give us all a break. No need to apologise."

"You disappoint me, Sibley. I had envisioned that your latest experience would have brought you to your senses. Sadly, it would seem I was misled." His expression a mixture of confusion, disbelief and anger he blared, "Very few have come face to face with the Angel of Death, and survived." Voice in tatters, he stopped; fighting to regain control before continuing. When he did so it was through taut, stretched lips; a purple hued countenance projecting escalating fury. "I refuse to accept that a puerile inconsequence such as yourself commands either the power or the ability. So I ask again...who aids you?"

"Oh boy! Am I enjoying this? The puerile inconsequence you speak of seems to have got well and truly up your nose." He felt strangely calm. So the man was in total ignorance of how the Angel of Death was denied. That was good. Having once again got him on the back foot, he intended to make the most of it. "Your weakness, Membril, is you're so full of hot air you can't see the wood for the trees. No," he shouted, putting the boot in to counteract the manufactured laugh, "you'd be wise to take a moment-or-two to reflect. Almost without exception, your plans have come unstuck in the most mysterious of ways. The two attempts to kill me off have failed miserably, and I've lost count of the number of times you've tried to drive a wedge between Dr. Steinbeck and me without success. As for your puny efforts to push the pair of us off our trolleys...what is there to say? Yet for all that you refuse to put it into an open forum. And why I ask? Would it be that deep down you're a much troubled man...because I can assure you that's the message we're getting. But that said, I can understand why you would prefer not to have to run the risk of antagonising a power with the ability to put your gruesome executioner in its place."

"I would guard against complacency if I were you, Sibley," the words faltering, the presentation stumbling, tremulous, "next time your accomplice may not be to hand." Tone changing to a sorry attempt at light-hearted banter he stuttered, "As the main reason for this visit is to bid you both farewell, I would find it gratifying if we could part without acrimony. However, before I go, I trust you both enjoyed my little bit of fun yesterday. Fun however could be misleading. Prophecy would perhaps be more meaningful. Something for you to take note of, Sibley. Words that may come back to haunt you...as you see your death approaching,"

"Oh I don't now about that, seems to me you deceive yourself far more often than you do us. So here's something for *you* to think about. Dr. Steinbeck and I are two simple souls, more than ready to back down when the other fellah is right. We make no exception to that, not even for you. So you'll doubtless be pleased to know that your assumption is correct. I did need help to escape the Angel of Death, but that's all you're getting. All you need worry about, was it help from outside or due to another cock-up on your part? If the latter, then perhaps it is you who should take note. At the end of the day you can only mess-up so many times...next time could be one too many."

He'd hit him where it hurt. Unable to challenge the mocking eyes with the humorous undertones, he turned away. Seeking to escape the verbal arrows of his tormentor he rounded on, Kyle. In tones that hinted at battered self-esteem, he struggled to reassert a level of composure.

"For you Doctor Steinbeck it is merely adieu. We shall meet again. Oh I forgot," slapping an open palm against his forehead, "the statue of the serpent god. I took the liberty of returning it from whence it came. I tend to not trust banks, especially where the safe-keeping of precious objects is at stake."

"Stretching it a bit," Kyle muttered as Membril walked away. "what you said about having help. Did the business though. For a while he was in a right old mix up."

"Might not have been the kind of help he was expecting, but it doesn't detract from the fact that I had the support I was desperate for. When I said I wouldn't be here now if it hadn't been for Father O'halloran, I meant every word. By the same token we can't dismiss the possibility that he might have messed up as well. My only crime was to stick to the bare facts." He chuckled. "Not my fault if he put the wrong interpretation on what I said. Wonder how he'll take it, if he ever discovers that my powerful friend is a priest way back in Tonopah. The look on his face would be a treasure."

"Yeah but that apart, what was it with those threats? What was that all about?" Expression registering concern, accentuated by the doubt in his speech. "You seeing your death coming at you, and the other things he come up with? Scares me when he says things like that. And the melodrama when he walked off. You're gonna get yours, and I get the privilege of hanging around till he does the same with me. Like to read his thoughts on that one. And another thing, up to now he's always given us clues. This time there wasn't so much as a hint."

"Not quite true. The incident on the boat came out of the blue, as did that fiasco with the fog on the way here. Having made up his mind I have someone working on my behalf, he probably thinks it safer to keep mum. And can you blame him? In his position I'd be very wary of letting too many cats out of the bag. But I do wonder about yesterday. It was what he said about it being a prophecy. Was that a clue? Can't make my mind up on that one. But even if it was it doesn't help much. We're still in the dark: not sure if he's a past master at cocking things up or we just happen to be unbelievably lucky!."

"Most of what he says goes over my head, but it's not like you to strike a blank. Every damn time he's blown his own trumpet for the benefit of our suffering ears you've cottoned on: no messing. The pentagram for instance. You picked up on that straight away, just like he knew you would. So if the bit about the fog being a prophecy wasn't a tip-off...why'd he say it?"

"Toying with us? A fun deviation from the stark realities of his chosen profession? Has to be something like that. Unless of course I'm barking up the tree of negativity, that well-intentioned disposer of all dubious thought-up theories deemed unworthy of consideration. This time though he made it clear there'd be no hanging around. My escape from the Angel of Death must have shaken him more than he cares to admit. His paranoia at a possible recurrence putting him into full-steam ahead mode. He continues to pooh-pooh the possibility that he might be capable of dropping a cod but, although the idea that I have my own personal minder may boost that belief, the concept that one might exist worries him. Instils the fear that the longer he drags it out, the greater the chance of this unknown accomplice tripping him up. No doubt about it, Kyle. He's a troubled man. Make no mistake."

Retrieving sunglasses from a shirt pocket, Kyle stood facing the slowly sinking sun. "Let's take a walk, Jack. Every time that skunk makes an appearance he leaves a nasty smell behind."

"Won't get rid of the stench, but might help blow the cobwebs away. As far as I'm concerned he's already destroyed what's left of the day."

"You know. Didn't think I'd ever say this. But I'm scared, Jack. Terrified more like. For the first time I'm beginning to see things the way they are. Facing up to a tardy reality is one way of putting it. Up till now it's been in the distance, as if it was happening to someone else and not us. Like we were bystanders on the outside looking in. And I don't like it. Don't like it one bit. He might of made a bucketful of errors, that I wouldn't know...but he's gonna get it right sometime. And when he does we ain't gonna stand a snowballs." He sighed, a solemn exhalation of warm air to match his depression. "Take no notice. It's the mood I'm in."

"What's that old saying? Not over till the fat lady sings? She's been singing our song so far, so why would she stop now. For as long as we stay positive, she'll carry on crooning...that's the way I see it. Whenever I'm down in the dumps, I force myself to remember the last time I was in this kind of mess. Luck was on my side then, and who's to say it won't be again? That's what I keep telling myself. What I have to keep telling myself. After all said and done, you can't deny that we've had more than our fair share of good fortune so far...and long may it continue."

"Ever the optimist. Still, you're right. No good comes of being miserable and it don't help to let it get at me." He stood, shielding his eyes against the suns glare. "To hell with Membril, and sod the walk. A good energetic dose of the pool followed by a large intake of alcohol is what we need."

"He wasn't wrong, Jack. The statue's back where it was. Same case, same place." He paused for a brief moment, peering through the window at the myriad of lights dancing on the wave-rippled water. "But I'm learning. Ok! So it didn't make the bank. And tell you what? I don't give a damn."

"You've come a long way Kyle. There was no surprise in your voice when you said that."

"Nothing surprises me anymore, Jack. Way I look at it, the statue coming back home is small beer by comparison with what's gone before. But don't be fooled by my light-hearted acceptance. On the inside I'm a hundred years old."

"Philosophical tonight aren't we?"

"Don't know about philosophical. Bonkers? Yeah. Could go along with that. Phoned Julie this morning by the way...you were in the shower and I forgot by the time you came out. Told her it'd be at least three weeks before we could even contemplate going back home. Played the harp strings. Told her how desperately sorry I was but knew she would understand. Said we'd make it up to her as soon as we'd done here. All the things a lady likes to hear."

"And?"

"She was so sympathetic it brought tears to my eyes. For a full five minutes she went on about how privileged she was to have such a brother. How I was so utterly selfish, how I didn't give a toss about anyone other than myself, how I had to be the most insensitive beast in the entire history of the Steinbecks'. You can't imagine what you missed out on as a one and only child, Jack. The eloquent chitchat exchanged by adoring siblings is just one example of the numerous advantages. Reading between the lines, I think she was trying to tell me I was a complete asshole to keep you away from her for so long." Leaning across the table to thump his friend on the shoulder he said, "Watch yourself fellah, she can't wait to get her claws into you." Adding more solemnly, "If she gets the chance."

"At least you won't have to think up any more excuses. Poor consolation, but better than none at all. By the time the three weeks are up? if you see what I'm getting at."

The first few days following Membril's visit were mostly shared romping on sandy beaches and drowning their sorrows in one of the many companionable bars on the island. When the need for more strenuous activity made itself felt they sailed catamarans, snorkelled from tall ships or joined in games of beach volleyball with other holidaymakers. The time passed all too quickly until, with a shared reluctance, it was agreed the time had come to move on.

"Quito? Lima perhaps? After that? Depends how things go I guess. Didn't plan either of those places but keeping on the move is the only way I'm gonna stay sane. Not to mention that, with a handful of luck, it might also make things more complicated for 'you know who'" A spasm of despair flickered across his eyes. "Quito should be interesting. Built on top of an Inca metropolis, it's the worlds highest capital city. Then Peru...stronghold of the Incas', Machu Picchu, Lake Titicaca...I'm rambling. Sorry, Jack. Ignore me. Anything to stop my mind wandering where it's best it don't."

"Trying hard, Kyle, but you're not fooling me in the slightest. You've been a right miserable bugger all day. So tell me about it."

"Touch of the blues, that's all...I'll get over it. Membril keeps getting at me and I can't shake him off. Not much you can do about it, so thought it best to keep the depression to myself. Truth is, Jack, I'm frightened. And I don't know why. For some strange reason the thought of climbing back into my airplane terrifies me and I don't understand...haven't a clue. Flying's never bothered me up till now, just the opposite. I'm good at what I do. Know I can handle a bird with the best. But I've got this feeling."

"You think he's going to pull a similar trick to last time? Is that what's worrying you?"

"Could have something to do with it."

"Only in your mind, Kyle. We've been through it time and time again. There's no way he's going to put you at risk."

"So he says. But what's to stop him changing his mind? And that's the thought that keeps bugging me...every time I hear him saying it could be a prophecy."

"What can I say other than repeat what I keep trying to drill into you: it's not very likely...even less so at this late stage. Tell you what," hands spread in resignation, "we'll hop into a bar and discuss it over a glass-or-two. Nothing like a drop of the good stuff to improve clarity of mind."

"Not sure practice will prove the validity, but I'm sure willing to put it to the test."

Making the most of the warm air of early evening, they sat outside watching wishful pelicans on the quayside fluttering their wings in anticipation as they awaited the arrival of the fishing smacks.

"I thought the same as you at first," Jack said, starting the discussion, "that his comment about the fog being a prophecy was in some way related to his next move. But it didn't take me long to ditch the idea. Not his style for a start. We've only known him for a comparatively short time, but we've learned sufficient to appreciate that he doesn't try the same thing twice. That, though, and as you might guess, is not the number one reason for refuting the possibility. We've argued over this time and time again. He has too much at stake to risk an air 'accident'. If you want proof of that statement consider what he said would be my fate...I would see my death approaching. Not you, not us...me, just me. Then the clincher. For you it wasn't goodbye, it was merely adieu. He couldn't have put it any plainer."

"Oh he won't try the fog again, I know that. But I can't get rid of this premonition that keeps bugging me. He's gonna do what he has to do when we're up in the clouds...that's what I feel and no matter what you say I'm convinced that's the intention."

"Premonitions are premonitions, Kyle, nothing more, nothing less. Most of the time they come to nothing, and on the rare occasions that they do they co-join with coincidence. So ditch the demon inside your head and give logic a chance. Barring a miracle, if the plane crashes we both get killed. He leaned forward, forearms propped on his knees. "And as I've no intention of committing suicide, the possibility of me jumping out at ten-thousand feet isn't on the cards."

"What's to stop him putting the idea in your head. You know what he's capable of."

"He most probably would, if he could; but he can't. To him my mind is a blank ...or had you forgotten?"

"Yeah, I guess. But what's to stop him using me? Persuade me to bundle you out through the door."

"Come off it, Kyle! You might have more beef than me, but I wouldn't go down without a fight and who's going to fly the plane in the meantime. It's not on, a risk too far: one he's not prepared to take. He wants you alive...and he wants it to stay that way."

"Yeah, ok; you've made your point." Peering sadly at his empty glass, he cleared his throat, "Thanks, Jack. Not sure I feel any better for it, but you've given me something to think about."

He made no further mention of his misgivings, but the tremor in the hands gripping the controls was enough to tell him Kyle hadn't shed his fears completely. In the meantime he would keep his thoughts to himself. Nothing he could say would erase the doubts that plagued his friend's mind. He was the only one with the requisite qualification for that.

A calm, uneventful flight easing his depression, the American began to show signs of a return to his normal, extrovert self. By the time they arrived at Quito international airport, his demon had been put firmly in its place.

"You ok? Didn't say anything but you seemed a bit on edge."

"You noticed!" The tone implying he'd have been surprised if he hadn't. "The moment those wheels left the tarmac...don't mind telling you, Jack, I was damn near petrified. Didn't last, thank God, but for a while I was on a different planet. But that's all done and dusted as they say. Jitters dispersed, shakes redundant, no more whinging...not till I think of something else to whinge about. So, while waiting for that

that happy day to come about, let's go find out what makes Quito tick."

Slow to acclimatise to the altitude, the next few days were spent in lethargic exploration of a fascinating city; a city of two halves...the old and the new. The thriving modernity of the city centre a dramatic contrast to the more humble abodes in the outskirts, where the Ecuador of earlier years was to be found. A take it as you find it panorama of traditional clothing and alpaca powered carts.

"Listen to this, Jack." his voice bouncing off the pages of the museum guide in which his nose was immersed, "This place was a hospital a few years back. Common sense isn't dead after all...why knock it down if it can be used for something different?"

"Good to see you're back to normal, whatever normal is in your case. You've been a right pain in the arse for the past week or so."

"Ah but that's not all, so let not my erstwhile solemnity ruin the surprise I have in store. The lady I was talking to last night, the one waiting for her husband in the lounge bar? Well they're visiting the same as us, and, according to what she told me, there's a not-to-be-missed sight unique to this neck of the woods. Happens most nights and don't have to go a million miles to see it."

"Never seen anything to compare with this, Jack...breath-taking ain't the word for it." Viewing the slowly setting sun from their vantage point on a crowded hillside beyond the city boundary, they stood entranced by one of natures many wonders. "A symphony in colour. No other way to describe a scene like this...you can almost hear the music if you listen hard enough. Make the most of it, fellah; we're gonna remember this for as long as we live."

With neither man brave enough to voice the identical thought, that their time for such memories was on a knife-edge, his words provoked a silence that lasted for some minutes. The mute spell eventually broken by Kyle, asking." You ok with that, Jack? Make tracks for Lima tomorrow. Stay there till it's all over...whenever and whatever."

"Might as well. As good as anywhere. And we can only run so far."

"Scenery doesn't get much grander, Kyle," peering through the starboard canopy, eyes shaded against the glare of the morning sun reflected from the snow clad peaks. "But those mountains! You're not serious about going over the top?"

"Might look stupid but I'm not a complete idiot. These peaks are among the highest in the range. We'll be crossing further south where they're nothing like as high. That huge beast with its head in the clouds is a good example - fifty or sixty miles off at a guess. Nevado de Huascaran: twenty-two thousand feet, and then some. Highest in Peru...one of the giants of the Andes."

"Thought you'd never been to Peru. If this was a first-off, you wouldn't know one mountain from the rest of the bunch."

"Can't pull the wool over your eyes." Tossing his head at Jack, grinning broadly. "No...whenever I fly somewhere new I like to do my homework. No good taking chances, especially when the terrain can be a bit dodgy. Study the route, get to know the pitfalls," he turned his head to despatch a broad grin at his passenger, "learn the names of the more prominent mountains and where to find 'em."

"Yeah, whatever...you want to keep me happy then just make sure you keep well clear of those biggies. Me and flying do not constitute a good relationship...as I may have hinted on odd occasions."

"Twice a day, and that's on a good day. But who's counting?" Dropping the banter, his voice took on a more serious tone. "No need worry a while yet, Jack. There's still a long way to go, and I'll let you know when the time comes to get on your knees and start praying. Facing his companion to instil confidence, he finished by adding "No worries, Jack...not from natural causes."

"It won't happen, Kyle. We've been through it a hundredfold. He's not going to do anything to put your life in danger. Trust me. Having come this far he's not going to run the risk of throwing it all away."

"Might be how you see it, but it's not the same from where I'm sitting...he's got something brewing alright. Believe me. And what's to say he's not changed his mind? Concluding it might be a good idea to get both of us out of his hair in one mad swoop. An unexpected twist telling him he don't need me after all. Go on all you like, but I can't shake off what he said...he was giving us a clue. Can feel it in my bones. Like you once said: he gets a thrill showing off his plans...and he's done that nearly every time. So why not this time. Nothing is gonna get rid of this gremlin that keeps bugging me. Don't matter what you say."

"You're blinkered, Kyle. You and me are invited to different parties. He's stressed that all along, and nothing he's said since has changed anything."

"Yeah, well, we'll have to wait and see." He shivered, knuckles on the hand gripping the control column showing white. "God, Jack! Whatever way it goes, won't be sorry when it's over. Don't think either of us can take much more of this."

"Maybe but that doesn't mean I'm about to give up, and right at this moment my concern is limited to purely natural pursuits. Those mountains worry me. You sure there's no other way?"

"Only practical route without adding a few hundred miles to the trip. But never you mind, Jack. I'll make sure there's plenty enough room between us and what's underneath. If it's the altitude that's bugging you, forget it. There's more'n enough oxygen on board if we need it."

"It's not altitude, It's the thought that we could end up having one landing fewer than we have take-offs that worries me. Now that..." Unease creeping over him, he didn't finish the sentence. Stunned by the pallid complexion confronting him, he rounded on his companion. "You alright, Kyle?"

"Bit of a headache, that's all. Eyes watering...sort of misty like. Nothing to get wound up about."

"Where's the first-aid..." He broke off, alarm bells ringing in frantic disarray. "Kyle! What's wrong? For heaven's sake, what's the matter?"

"Oh, God!" The agonised screech bouncing back from the walls of the fuselage, volume at screaming pitch. "My eyes...I can't focus."

He had to be the one to remain calm, early signs of panic in his friend's voice making it clear it wasn't going to be him. Stretching across to where his friend sat he gripped his shoulder, a token effort to calm irascible nerves, quell mounting terror.

It was too little, too late.

Whipping his shoulder from Jack's hold, he grasped his head between gloved hands. "I can't see. Oh Jesus Christ, I can't see...I'm blind. Help me Jack. Oh God, please help me...I can't see!"

He was in turmoil. The urgency of the words hammered into his brain, driving constructive thought into the far-reaches of his sub-conscious. Not that it mattered. There was nothing he could do. Nothing either of them could do. Kyle had posted the warning and he had dismissed it. Refuting all that had gone before, Membril had changed his mind. Despite his continued insistence to the contrary, they were destined to die together.

The thought of him snug in his salacious abode, murderously orchestrating their deaths made him angry. Angrier than he had ever been. He might not be able to stop him, but he was buggered if he was going to sit and wait for it to happen. It wouldn't do any good, but it had to be preferable to doing sweet bugger all.

Unlatching his harness he grasped the abandoned controls in a shaking, sweat-soaked hand. Bringing the aircraft back to something near level flight, he strove to erase the vocal tremors in his appeal.

"It'll be alright, Kyle. Piece of cake, this flying lark That's what you told me...remember? Said you'd give me lessons, and there's no time like the present. You tell me what to do, I'll soon get the hang of it." In an attempt to exude a confidence he far from felt, he enthused, "I could be getting a taste for this, Kyle, and I'm doing ok...not bad for an amateur eh? So you just relax: take it easy and your eyesight will be back to normal before you know it."

"Relax? You joking? How the hell d'you expect me to relax? And what do you know about eyes anyway? Know you got high opinions of yourself, but didn't for one minute imagine you were stupid enough to think you know every damn thing there is to know. Now you're telling me you can fly this bloo..." A fit of impassioned sobbing brought the violent outburst to an end. "I'm sorry. Please, Jack...I'm so sorry. Didn't mean what I said."

"It's ok Kyle, I know you didn't. But you're right. I can't fly this plane...but you can."

"Oh yeah, sure." Co-ordinated thought struggling to the surface through the angry turbulence of despair. "I could fly the damn thing alright...if I could see where the hell I was going. Or did you miss that bit?"

"Of course I didn't, that's not what I'm getting at. What I'm saying, is I know damn well I can't fly this plane but I could be your eyes. Read the compass, make sure you stay on course, watch the weather...whatever you need to know. If it doesn't work? Well...we tried, and it can't make things any worse."

"Yeah...fine. And what about landing? That is if we find somewhere to put down in the first place. You gonna talk me in? You're speaking rubbish, Jack."

"Not necessarily. Your sight might come back before we have to face that problem. Temporary loss of vision isn't uncommon, and yours came on so suddenly...and without warning. It doesn't make sense. Blindness, permanent blindness, doesn't happen without good reason. So what do we do? Your call. Sit here feeling sorry for ourselves or give it a go." His sight wouldn't come back. He knew it. The chances were Kyle knew it too. But voicing his fears wouldn't help either of them."

"Oh I don't know, Jack. I just don't know. It's...I'm frightened. I don't know what's going on, what's happening to me." His voice quavered to a halt.

"Don't have to apologise, not your... " Breaking off in mid-sentence he shrieked. "What the...the steering. It's gone berserk." Fighting a losing battle to stay on his feet he grabbed his friend's hand, joining it with his own on the control column. "Tell me what to do, Kyle. I don't know what to do!"

"It's a wild thing. I can't, I don't know...don't know." Hysteria mounting he screamed at the top of his voice. "Jack...do something. Help me. Please, God! Let me see."

He didn't bother to respond. Guided by unseen hands the plane was in violent thrall, and there was nothing he could say or do that would be relevant. He had enough trouble trying to stay upright.

"All ok, Jack. Controls back to normal. On we go."

He wasn't wrong. The buffeting had stopped as suddenly as it started, but a more worrying aspect was beginning to emerge. The cowering individual of a few moments ago had become a man bursting with exuberance. Blindness no longer a handicap.

"I can handle her Jack. Can't read the compass, you'll have to do that for me. Know what to do. Someone's telling me what to do. Not you is it, Jack? Doesn't sound like you. Important you keep an eye on the compass. The voice is telling me to stay on two-twenty degrees. Got to be exact. You ok with that?"

"Kyle, don't listen to it. For God's sake...we're heading straight for the bloody mountains." He tried to stay calm, forcing himself to speak in more measured tones "Keep on this course and we'll crash. Listen to me...not the voice in your head. Turn to port. That's the safe way. Carry on the way we are we'll hit the mountain."

"Just as you say, old buddy."

Opening the throttle to its fullest extent, he pulled hard back on the control column. So this was it. He could talk till the cows came home, there was nothing he could say or do that would change anything. It was the phantom voice that held Kyle's unwavering attention.

In dread of the inevitable he began to shake. Beads of sweat sought shelter in his eyes, blood pounded in his ears. The high peaks were now no more than a few miles ahead: monstrous denizens of the skies, ready and waiting to pay homage to the humans invading their royal presence.

In a thankless bid to divert his friend's attention, he made a final plea. "Kyle, listen to me..."

"What's the compass say Jack? Are we there yet? Asked you to let me know when we hit two-twenty. Talk to me, Jack."

He didn't bother to look. The reading would be spot-on. The remote navigator would make sure they didn't deviate from the pre-arranged course.

He was suddenly calm. What was about to happen was out of his hands, there was nothing he could do to avoid their prepared fate. He stood behind the pilots seat, hands resting on his friends shoulders, viewing their appointed executioner through the forward cabin window. Mesmerised by the sight of Huascaran appearing to move towards them, instead of the other way round: the illusion bringing Membril's words back to haunt him...'when you see your death approaching'. But he didn't understand. The words appointed him the sole victim, a somewhat arbitrary proclamation considering there was nothing more certain than they were both about to be killed.

The aeroplane was now close enough for him to make out the fissures on the side of the mountain, every mound, every undulation in the snow. An awe inspiring panorama intent on their annihilation. At least the end, when it came, would be quick.

Clasping the shoulders of the man who had come to mean so much over the years, he prayed. The words sounded fatuous but he hoped they would ease the torment of a tortured mind.

"Soon be all over, Kyle. We'll make it just fine."

CHAPTER THIRTEEN

...He was to regret the time wasted. The makeshift sledge looked what he imagined a hastily put-together sledge should look like but performance destroyed the image. The harder he pulled on the rope handle, the deeper the square front ends of the two cases used as runners dug into the snow. Cursing lack of forethought, he leaned dejectedly against the side of the fuselage. So much work gone to pot. His own damn fault, should've tested it before loading it. It was a right bugger, and that was putting it mildly. 'Still, no good standing there moping.' He muttered inwardly. 'Feeling sorry for himself wasn't going to solve anything, and if he didn't get a move on he'd end up even deeper in the mire.' He was half-tempted to leave his belongings behind, concentrate instead on getting his body down the mountain. But it took less than no time to realise that could end in disaster. No oxygen, no extra clothing to add warmth at night and, meagre though it was, no food. He couldn't so much as trim the load without seriously diminishing his chances of survival. There was no knowing how long it would take to find help, and ditching the most trivial item could be catastrophic. No: that wasn't the way to go. Concentrate on the runners and how to get the best out of them, that was the sensible option..

He would take his time. Time he could justify, time he could ill afford...he couldn't run the risk of another balls-up. The cases he was stuck with, nothing else came close for the purpose he had in mind. But what if he changed things around? Instead of upright and side-by-side, flat and for-and-aft could be a better bet. The rounded edges would be less likely to dig into the snow and the area in contact with it considerably increased. Two significant advantages that he should have picked up on before he'd got carried away with his original plan. 'Still, better late than never; as the saying goes.'

More in hope than expectation he pulled on the rope handle, coming close to weeping with relief as the sledge glided smoothly across the packed snow. It had taken nearly two hours to get to this stage, and the sigh of satisfaction vented through the confines of his oxygen mask echoed the released anxiety. Encouraged by a sudden burst of euphoria, he tossed the rope over his shoulder and started on his way.

Every debilitating step was a recurring nightmare. Feet forever sinking into the icy softness of the cloying snow, the weight of the sledge and the bulk of the oxygen cylinder strapped to his back silent reminders of the pain in leg and shoulder. Pain he could do nothing about. Pain that had to be ignored. It was essential he kept going for as long as his bodily functions allowed. With nightfall not far away he'd soon be forced to take a rest, then would be the time to sit and worry about his mobility. That gave him something else to think about...the drop in temperature that would accompany the setting of the sun. He would need to find shelter well before then.

That was when fate took a hand. He'd heard of such geological anomalies but recall in the inexperienced is an unlikely attribute, and so it proved. The next step, another automatic swinging of one leg in front of the other, a repeat of the same monotonous movement that had been his lot for the past hour-or-so, met with nothing. The resilient snow crunched under his probing foot as usual but there was no support beneath.

Before he had time to realise what was happening he was dropping faster than a kestrel pursuing its prey, somehow managing to cling on to the rope as the sledge shuddered to a grinding halt. Swinging in space in the semi-gloom, he searched frantically for a foothold. A haven to ease the agony of a shoulder already stiff and sore from the effort of tugging the sledge, but there was not a kink in the black rock to relieve the strain that threatened to tear him apart. He couldn't hold on for much longer. God only knew where he'd end up when he was forced to let go of the rope.

He wasn't to find out. Too heavy for whatever had brought it to a halt in the first place, the sledge slipped its moorings: falling several feet before jamming up against another obstacle. Flung from side-to-side against the callous, unforgiving lining of his dungeon he bounced from the walls as if he was a rubber ball in a squash court. Bemused and in pain but still managing to hang on to the dubious security of the trailing rope, he initially failed to appreciate his changed fortune. He had ended up half laying, half sitting, on a narrow, ice-coated ledge. Not the most comfortable of platforms, but it went some way to easing the strain on his shoulder. It didn't alter the fact that he was stuck several feet below ground with no future to embrace, but perhaps this was how it was meant to be. His life destined to drift aimlessly away on a slab of unforgiving ice; the inevitability of a long-delayed funeral his only comfort. He had to smile at the black humour of the situation. When the end came he wouldn't have to go looking for a cemetery.

Accompanied by a thunderous noise and a shower of debris, the sledge slipped again. Echoing through the narrow tunnel, the vibration threw him from his precarious perch into the depths of nothingness. The rope snatched from his hand, he fell some distance before realisation kicked in. He wasn't falling…he was sliding. The traverse had changed from the perpendicular to a steep angle. A roller coaster which, at another time and in another place, would have been great fun. Although giving him sufficient pause to ponder his plight, the ride ended almost before it began. His dread while stuck on the ledge had been the thought of a slow death due to thirst, starvation...whatever. That thought was still with him but there was now an added fear. The near certainty of the sledge overtaking him. If worse were to come to worst, he could end up with an injury that would make death seem ever more remote.

In the event both potential catastrophes were avoided. Slowing his rate of decent to little more than a crawl, the slope eased to a sweeping concavity: terminating the ride on a snow-bound ledge in full sunlight. Before having time to appreciate his lucky escape, the sledge announced its arrival with a gentle nudge against the oxygen cylinder strapped to his back.

Finding it hard to come to terms with the providence that had come to his aid, he crawled up the slight incline towards the edge: a distance of about a hundred yards. It was tough going and by the time he arrived at his destination leg and shoulder were crying out for relief. He wasn't listening. He was itching to find out what lay beyond the boundary of this unplanned, but nonetheless welcome, sanctuary.

Laying facedown at full stretch, he peered tentatively over the edge. He should have known it wouldn't last. His luck had to run out some time. The sheer drop of four-or-five hundred feet sent his head spinning. His old enemy having yet another laugh, he was forced to turn away. Not content with adding to his despair, the sight churned his stomach and teased his nerves.

His back to the precipice, he sat with eyes closed. The comforting darkness a balm to ease disappointment, he stayed in that position for quite some while before persuading himself he had to make a move. Increasing languor threatening to take control, it needed all his willpower to force eyes open and gear limbs into action. The sun was beginning to dip over the horizon and there were things to do before darkness announced its inevitable arrival. To save time he chose to walk rather than crawl back to where he'd left the sledge. Staggering to his feet, he was greeted by a scene that put all else into stark perspective. From the mouth of the funnel to the edge of the cliff the snow was blotched with lurid red stains. A self-explanatory note of caution that the wound in his thigh was in dire need of attention. As with the rest of his body it had taken a pounding over the past few hours, and crawling across the snow had been the final straw.

Blood continuing to mar the white expanse he half hitched his trouser leg, pressing the loose fold hard against the wound as he walked. Although slowing his pace, the enforced stoop engendered by the crude tourniquet was justified by the absence of further blemishes in the snow. It was however patently clear that something more drastic than bandaging was necessary if he was to survive this manic journey. It didn't need much thought to appreciate that the 'something more drastic' meant stitching the damn thing. And how the hell was he to do that? No needle, no thread...no know-how! More to the point...no alternative. He couldn't carry on losing blood at this rate.

He cast his eyes upwards, searching for the plane: a guide to how far he'd come...wishing he hadn't. Reflected powerfully from the blue and white paintwork, the last of the Sun's rays picked out the wreckage in great clarity: six hundred feet? – seven at a push. And that could be optimism running wild. The effort, the mental stress, the physical strain...for what? A few measly feet. But he couldn't complain. It was his own damn fault. If he'd taken more care putting the sledge together the first time round? But he hadn't, and it was no good crying over spilt milk or obstinate runners. Looked at it in perspective however, he had to admit it wasn't necessarily all bad news. He wouldn't have to look far for shelter, it starred him in the face. Drag the sledge and its contents across the mouth of the funnel...that's all he need do. It would give him some defence against the icy cold and the strong wind that was beginning to make its presence felt.

It wasn't the Ritz - not that he'd ever sampled the privileges of that illustrious establishment - but it was cosier than he could have expected. So much so that he felt he could look forward to a night of comparative - comparative being the operative word - comfort in this hollowed-out ice cube that was to be his home for the night. For all he knew, and despite the antisocial environment, he might even be granted the luxury of a few hours sorely needed sleep. Assuming of course that such opulence could be purchased in near arctic conditions. The mental probing blurred. Gradually, and without his being aware, subtle changes were taking place. The blending of conscious thought and ethereal dreams within the diaphanous barrier that separated wakefulness and somnolence. The nagging ache of the wound in his thigh, the more acute agony of the pain in his shoulder were put on hold. Sleep became the priority, and so it stayed until the early morning Sun encroached on his unlikely abode.

Eyes loath to open and recollection of his whereabouts not readily forthcoming, he lay in a semi-comatose languor planning the day ahead. Shave, shower, breakfast...brain dropping belatedly into gear as realisation dawned. His leg! Fearful of what he would find, he pushed the coat that substituted for a duvet to one side. Inwardly breathing a heavy sigh of relief at the sight confronting him. Only a very small, red stain marked the sweater that had served as a mattress.

Chary of setting off further bleeding he gingerly removed his trousers. Covered in dried blood, he tossed them to one side. The second pair he'd ruined within the last twenty-four hours. Removing the bandages proved more difficult. The dried blood having glued them solidly to the wound, separation was both painful and delicate. His major concern was however ill-founded. Contrary to the inflicted punishment, the encrusted plasma was not going to be parted from the jagged wound that easily.

He'd eat first. Not that there was much to get his teeth into, but it was that or nothing. He would occupy the time eating doing what he should have done last night before sleep had interfered. He knew what he had to do...how to do it? That was the tricky bit. Then there was that other, arguably more pertinent doubt...was he man enough? He'd never attempted anything like it before, wasn't sure how far up the scale his pain threshold stood. But what purpose would knowing serve anyway? If he wasn't up to it, he might as well throw in the towel here and now. A bottle of single malt might help. On the other hand, perhaps that wasn't such a good idea. The warm, inner glow would be comforting but the swimming vision of a drunk in harness could be disastrous.

Whether the combination of soggy biscuits and dubious chocolate could claim responsibility he neither knew nor cared. He was just thankful that, by the time he'd finished eating, a plan of action was firmly entrenched. The theory was sound enough, it was the application that could be flawed. However he could sit there all day pondering the whys and wherefores, there was only one way to find out...put it to the test. Seated on a roughly scarred blister of rock not intended for the role, he spent a few moments in quiet contemplation. Willing himself mentally, preparing himself physically. Refusing to consider the consequences should he funk what he had to do.

Cutting several strands about twelve inches in length from the nylon rope, he laid them in a tidy row across the snow at his feet. Cleaning the prepared fibres and the scissor attachment of his Swiss army knife as best he could, he leaned back against the rock. Eyes closed. Breathing deeply. A brief pause to summon the courage and stamina to keep him going...for as long as it took.

Removing the dried blood with a handkerchief soaked in snow, he smeared the exposed flesh with an anti-sceptic cream found in the first-aid box. Not slow to accept the invitation, blood started to ooze from the disturbed wound; an initial trickle that rapidly became a steady flow. Unnerving, but not unexpected. Clutching a nylon strand in one hand, he gripped a single blade of the scissors between thumb and forefinger of the other. Hysteria threatening and running short of hands, he transferred the thread to his teeth: grasping the blood-soaked and slippery, ragged edge of the wound with the twitching fingers of the freed hand. Brushing away the sweat that, despite the cold had accumulated on his forehead, he stabbed the sharp point of the blade through skin and flesh.

It hurt! It hurt like hell...but he could live with it. As if he had a choice!

Leaving the blade in place to mark the spot, he carefully eased the filament through the hole to half its length. Pain increasing in step with the blood flow, he had to work fast. The agony he could tolerate, the bleeding he couldn't. Using the same technique to pierce the opposite side, he fed the fibrous strand through the hole in the plasma-drenched flesh and out through the skin. Pinching together the two halves he pulled the suture as tight as he dared, securing it with a simple knot before moving on to the next stage. Then it was that the real agony started. Intensifying with every touch. Fingers, scissors, thread, each adding their contribution to the excruciating pain. He dare not stop to rest, not even for a short, albeit well-earned, breather. This process had to be carried through uninterrupted to the bitter end and in double quick time.

Tears streaming down trembling cheeks, he screamed at the top of his voice with every pain-blighted action. That there were none to hear was irrelevant. It helped him bear the agony...a verbal balm to banish the torment of sadistic arrows intent on using his body for target practice. Tunnelling a way through his distress, the thought occurred that the noise he was making might trigger an avalanche. The cliff above held God knew how many tons of snow in a tenuous grip. He wasn't sure he cared. It would be a quick end to his misery.

Seventeen stitches and countless minutes later, the tortuous ritual at last came to an end. Sweating heavily, he reached for the painkillers. A hundred-and-twenty grams of codeine phosphate was way above the prescribed amount, but as long as it did the trick he didn't give a damn. The wound continuing its malicious throbbing, he waited with simmering impatience for the drug to do what it was meant to do. On the brighter side, it was good to sit and do nothing for a while.

Following a wait of some twenty minutes the pills finally kicked in, the pain dwindling to a dull ache. The soothing relief however was short-lived. As the agony subsided a creeping languor assaulted his body. Totally shattered he sat immobile; head in hands, desperately trying to summon the strength, the motivation, to get going. His body might have other ideas but he couldn't afford the time to listen, he had to make a move. Push himself to the limit and sod the outcome.

It looked a mess, but what did he expect? Makeshift tools, scrappy bits of nylon, and him - he who had never so much as sewed a button on a shirt cuff - in a blind panic to get the job over and done with. Ok, it wasn't pretty...so what. Bugger the appearance, performance was what mattered.

Tentatively getting to his feet he was made to sit down again quickly by the wave of dizziness that swept over him. Reaction, exhaustion, or too many pills? He tried again...taking it slowly this time. The light-headedness persisted but at least he managed to stay upright. That was encouraging. Allowing the giddiness a few minutes to sort itself out, he took a few steps across the slippery surface at the mouth of the cave. So-far, so-good, but a more robust test was necessary before it could be trusted.

For something like fifteen minutes he walked at varying speed across a selection of snow-covered surfaces. Intent on taking no chances he included skips, hops, jumps and one-or-two contrived falls in his attempt to replicate the forthcoming assault course. Satisfied he'd subjected his repair work to a realistic variety of mishaps, he sat breathless on a convenient outcrop. Unconvinced that his suturing efforts would have stood up to the hammering, he dropped his trousers...no sign of blood on either the protecting bandages or the bare skin below. Shouting his success at the mountains, he made himself a promise. That if by some miracle he survived this mess he'd treat his leg to some cosmetic surgery as soon as he got back to England.

On a high he made his way to the edge for another look. Hoping for confirmation that the drop he'd seen last night wasn't as bad as it had seemed. No such luck. No nice surprise awaited. There was no difference. No change. If anything the climb looked more sheer, more hostile, than before. His big fear was that his rampant acrophobia would ensure he wouldn't find a suitable spot anywhere. Facts had to be faced...had there been a ladder all the way to the ground floor he would baulk at putting his foot on the first rung.

Then there were his injuries to consider. His damaged shoulder concerned him most but, and although fairly confident his handiwork would hold out, he couldn't ignore the possibility of the wound in his thigh posing a problem. He was left in two minds. Take the gamble and risk it, or move on in the hope of finding somewhere more amenable.

A final glance convinced him there was no choice. It would be sheer madness to try. But that then raised another problem. Which way...east or west. Whichever way he chose it would be bound to follow that well-known, irrefutable law. The rule that gets on everyone's wick and has a jolly good laugh at their expense. He looked one way, then the other. Nothing positive, no beckoning finger...no bloody difference. The ledge was boringly similar in both directions. Ok, so it was stupid. But without a coin to toss he might as well dwell in the realms of stupidity. He recalled an old film he'd enjoyed many years ago when he was a young lad. Bob Hope - he remembered he was in it. Him and Jane Russell. There was a song about buttons and bows, with a line that went something like 'east is east and west is west' and, whoever it was, he or she chose the wrong way to go. He was pretty sure that way was west. Probably got it wrong but it was something to go on. Ok! He'd take the advice given in the song and head east...to hell with it and sod the consequences!

For the first half-mile or so there was little change. The ledge appeared to have narrowed slightly but he couldn't be sure... as to the rest? The same monotonous, dreary, barren wasteland that had been his companion all along. Equally unfriendly, the precipice remained as steep and as unhelpful as before. Unsure of what to do for the best, he gave thought to retracing his steps. He couldn't afford to waste any more time, on what was fast becoming a fools-errand. A couple of hundred yards ahead an enormous boulder encroached across almost the full width of the path. He'd make that his marker. If there was no improvement on the far side of that rock he'd turn round and try his luck the other way.

It wasn't a boulder in the sense of the word, it was a bulge in the cliff face…not that he was in a mood to be bothered. His depression at the scene that greeted him on the far side of the obstruction drove all such trivia into the dust. The width of path he hoped to pursue had dwindled to less than twenty feet…continuing to narrow before disappearing round a bend some fifty yards-or-so ahead. So this was it. The end of the line. The decision had been made for him. This route was going nowhere. It was turn round and try again time: and that was the problem. The mere mention of the word 'time' hit him with the force of a pile-driver. 'Time'…running away from him and he couldn't keep up. That was of far greater concern than the increased physical effort involved if he retraced his steps.

Had he harboured hopes that things could get no worse than they already were, the far side of the bend refuted such optimism. The width of the ice-coated track had further reduced and, more significantly, it dipped into a slight decline. If he needed confirmation, this was it. To carry on would be sheer madness. He'd get down alright, a bloody site quicker than bargained for.

Depressed and cursing the way things were going, he huddled against the rock wall. Leg throbbing and shoulder on fire. Both bellowing the same message, a note of warning not to be ignored. His body needed a break. He despised himself for surrendering to the strident demand, but found consolation in the thought that it wouldn't be time wasted. It was important he listened to his body.

Twenty minutes later and feeling slightly more human, he reflected on his position. He felt unsafe and far from comfortable as he sat in gloomy silence, shielding his eyes against the glare of the noonday sun high above the peaks. The combination of ice, snow and a walkway with a downward trend? He should be committed for even thinking about it but, in reality, did he have a choice? Time was a potent, ever-present enemy; a sadistic opponent who gave no quarter and asked for none. If the Sun was anything to go by it had taken him something like two hours to get this far. Time he couldn't afford to chuck away without due cause. A bulky spur almost within touching distance from where he sat set him thinking. If he could reach it – what he really meant was, if he had the guts to try to reach it – it might open up a whole new vista. It wouldn't be easy, but if he wasn't prepared to face the odd risk-or-two he might as well give up now.

Extending the rope handle to make recovery easier, he decided to leave the sledge where it was for the time being: he'd have enough trouble getting himself across. Though only a few feet away, he suffered many a heart-stopping moment before he reached the comparative safety of the narrow cleft that separated the outcrop from the cliff face. Taking a brief rest to recover his equilibrium, he spent several more minutes reassessing the situation. Four feet in height, a tapered apex…should be ok for what he had in mind. Rope himself to this obelisk - which could be done without having to get to his feet – and he should be safe enough. Then would come the crunch. The heart-stopping disappointment that he was sure would greet him when he plucked up the courage to peer over the edge. At least he was prepared, and whichever way it went made little difference. Decision made, he must stand by it.

Gauging the distance to the ledge from his anchorage point, he tied the required length of rope round his chest: looping the noosed, free end over the tapered spur; pulling it tight, taking in the slack. Breathless and shaking, the prequel to nervous exhaustion, he sat prone for some time in contemplation: mind and body given the opportunity to recuperate before having to face reality. Securely fastened to the spur he slid facedown across the snow towards the perimeter.

He couldn't believe the sight that greeted him. Until now everything in his favour seemed to be lined up against him, but the sight that met his anxious eyes changed all that. Clearing the watery mist that blurred his vision, he took another look. It would be tough but it was possible. That was all he could ask for.

Wary of making a rash commitment, he studied the descent in greater detail. He had to be one-hundred percent sure...once begun there was no going back. He estimated solid ground to be not much more than a hundred feet beneath where he lay. That was encouraging in itself but, even more so, the cliff-face was neither as sheer nor as stark as it was the last time he looked. Falling away at a slight angle and heavily scarred, it appeared to offer all the help he would need.

He double checked his arithmetic. Twenty-three coils, two-feet in diameter. Hundred and forty feet...give or take. More than enough rope to get him down to ground level. He was aware of the pitfalls but as long as he kept them in sight he'd be ok. If he didn't? Forget it. No good thinking along those lines. Ok, so vertigo and bodily damage would limit his mobility. So what? There was bugger-all he could do other than get on with it and forget about what *could* go wrong. He was looking too far ahead. The sledge had to go first, his turn would come when that was firmly on the ground. Bulky, heavy, and held together with bits of string, it would be a miracle if he got it down in one piece. He was deluding himself...living in fantasy land. Apart from anything else he wouldn't be able to handle the weight. The instant the sledge disappeared over the top, he'd be forcefully persuaded to let go of the rope.

Moving clear of the edge before plucking up the courage, he got to his feet. Engrossed in the tomb-like silence, he gazed across the empty expanse that lay beyond the escarpment. Earlier euphoria fast disappearing, ferocious talons of despair ripping his confidence to shreds. It was no use, the sledge would have to go. It was courting disaster but there was no other way. His energies would be better confined to getting himself down.

He came over dizzy. It was just for an instant, but in that short time he didn't know if he was coming or going. He shook his head to clear the mist...eyes widening in disbelief at the sight that commanded their attention. A large, curiously shaped horn of rock lurking against the backdrop. A cold shiver swept over him, the hairs on the back of his neck jingling in harmony. How could he have missed it? A thing that size? Because it wasn't there. That's how. A mere couple of yards away and he didn't notice? Come off it!

Somewhat shaken it took a while before he was able to pull himself together, concluding he was a complete ass when he finally got there. It was there all the time. Had to have been. Blooming great chunks of stone didn't suddenly materialise out of nothing. Other things on his mind, altitude playing havoc...tricks of nature? Membril, up to his funny business? That was a thought, but he didn't think it likely. Why would he bother after having tried to get rid of him on more than one occasion? There were plenty of answers but none of them sounded convincing. He shook his head, cursing his stupidity...but doubt had staked it's claim and had no intention of letting go.

On closer examination he was left even more mystified. Had he been able to design a regulator to take the weight off his hands and control the speed of descent it would have borne a close similarity to that rock. A single turn of rope, another round the outcrop tethering the load...it was ideal. The sledge would be coming with him after all.

Dragging the sledge to within kicking distance, he aimed a hefty blow with the foot at the far end of his sound leg. In slow motion it glided over the brim, to be brought to a halt by the tethering rope. It was crunch time. The now-or-never moment that would confirm if theory and practice were in a meaningful relationship. Ignoring the cries of protest he forced his legs hard up against the outcrop. Drawing the back of his hand across his forehead to disturb the gathering globules of sweat, he sawed away at the holding rope with his penknife.

In tune with the surrender of the last few fibres he whipped his right hand across to join the left, thus relieving some of the strain on his damaged shoulder. Heart poundng he watched the two loose folds of twisted nylon snake across the snow. The line held. Remained taut. Encouraging, but it wasn't the be-all and end-all. He had to make sure. Again squirming across the snow on his belly he peered over the edge in trepidation, but his fears were unfounded. Undamaged and still united with its load, the sledge hugged the cliff face in a cosy intimacy. But he couldn't get too excited yet, that was the easier part. It was what happened next that would decide which side of the amorphous barrier separating success and failure his future lay.

Barely daring to breath he moved the foremost hand aft of the other, allowing the rope freedom to move. It worked! Thank God, it worked! The strain on his arms was hardly noticeable, the rate of fall his to dictate. Denying complacency the opportunity to rear its ugly head, he took it slowly. Tacitly refusing the demands of the dangling load that it be given more freedom, that it be allowed to descend at the speed it wanted to.

The rope slackened. He released a few more inches. The inert line an indication of one of three possibilities. The rope had snapped, the sledge had snagged against a projection or it had reached ground level. Using his tried and tested technique he inched across the snow to take another look. Mixed feelings giving way to yelps of jubilation at the sight. Lodged against a pile of welcoming scree, his worldly goods smiled up at him. Now it was his turn.

Removing the rope from the curiously shaped outcrop that shouldn't have been there - he was still convinced that was the case - he double- checked the security of his anchorage...then checked again to make sure. Satisfied as far as he could possibly be, he threw the excess rope over the edge to take up the slack. He was ready. It was crunch time!

The instant his feet departed the security of solid ground he panicked. In reality it was for a few seconds, for him it was an eternity. Shoulder crying out for relief in his frantic search for a foothold, he crunched his injured leg against the unforgiving rock-face. The excruciating pain threatening to nullify his grip, he was rescued in the nick of time by the intervention of an uninvited stroke of luck fuelled by the desperation of the undisciplined. With no active guidance on his part, a flailing foot joined forces with a protruding ridge of rock and somehow managed to stay in contact.

For several minutes he didn't dare move, making use of the time to repair frayed nerves and rekindle earlier resolve. He was angry with himself. He'd acted like a complete idiot. Acrophobia given free rein, he very nearly paid the price. That mustn't happen again. He'd had his warning...there wouldn't be another.

The rest, if rest it could be called when huddled against a wall of rock a hundred feet from safety, instilled the will to carry on and the stamina to see it through. A stoic refusal to allow panic to dominate, he forced himself to stay calm before moving so much as his little finger. Catching nerves by the scruff of the neck before granting all moveable body-parts the freedom to progress.

Routine firmly embedded – seek foothold, move hand to match, next foothold - there was nothing to it! After having come close to ending it almost before it began, the rest of the climb was reasonably straightforward. He'd already established that the angled rock face provided help in abundance for the novice mountaineer, and so it proved. In an unbelievably short passage of time, and with no hiccups to speak of, he reached the bottom. Undamaged, untarnished and highly relieved.

Lying flat out on the sledge, he basked in sunshine that at last had some warmth to it. He'd swallowed what passed for a lunch, and the immediate intent was to do nothing. His body telling him it needed time to relax he closed his eyes. He could afford a few minutes...the clear blue sky, the gently massaging rays of the sun.

He woke. Annoyed at having fallen asleep, he was mollified to some extent by the sun having not noticeably moved. He couldn't have slept for long, so no harm done. His neck was sore...perhaps it was that which woke him. Seeking the cause of his discomfort his fingers made contact with the crucifix...he didn't remember the chain being this tight. It was digging hard into the softly yielding flesh, constricting his trachea. Concern turning to alarm, he started to choke. Tongue swelling and struggling to breathe, he strove to force a probing finger between the thin gold garrotte and the throbbing flesh. But there was no way through. Grabbing the crucifix with one hand, he stabbed furiously at the delicate but stubborn links with the fingernails of the other in a desperate attempt to defuse the python-like bondage. Fingers sliding uselessly across the skin of a blood-soaked neck, his efforts became manic. Head buzzing and consciousness fast fading he was thrown a lifeline. The tip of an overworked fingernail split, the half severed nail piercing a battered link to bring to an end its dogged resistance. Parting with barely a murmur, the high-carat alloy chain surrendered its lethal hold.

For fifteen minutes-or-so he lay prone, depleted energy supplies prioritised into replenishing oxygen-starved lungs. When finally able to take stock, he stared in perplexity at the crucifix dangling from still shaking fingers. An object with the power to protect that had come so close to ending his life.

"Bloody hell!" The impulsive shriek echoing back from the stark beauty of his surroundings. The chain was hot, too hot to hold. The jerking hand of an involuntary response sending the delicate piece of jewellery hurtling through the air. White hot as it hit the snow, it was swallowed in an instant. Struggling to his feet he half ran, half slid to where it had landed. He was too late. Having cornered its prey, the unblemished snow had no intention of giving it up. Knowing it to be a waste of time and energy, he didn't bother to search. Finding the lost crucifix wasn't part of the grand plan.

He knew damn well there was little likelihood of Membril's interest having waned with Kyle's death, but this he hadn't bargained for. If his chances had been slim to start with, they were now non-existent. Denied the protection of the crucifix he was left naked and exposed. When and where was irrelevant. They would meet up somewhere, sometime. When they did, Membril wouldn't want to hang around. Kyle was dead...he was defenceless. There was nothing he or anyone else could do to stop him. By depriving him of the precious talisman he had removed the last remaining obstacle to his success. His friend's demise had to have been a mistake. Membril had made it plain all along: it was the American who was special to his plans. There was no point kidding himself. Kyle might be beyond his reach, but it was pretty obvious whom he would choose for a substitute.

For reasons he couldn't explain he felt good, he'd even go as far as buoyant, as he shrugged the rope over his shoulder. He was somewhat at a loss as to why he should feel that way but he did, and he would make the most of it while it lasted. It probably had something to do with the realisation that his unplanned nap was Membril's doing and not negligence on his part. If it was that which cheered him up, so did the sight that confronted him. Gentle, snow covered slopes with not a rock to be seen. For all that, it didn't account for this sudden sense of well-being; why life had taken a different turn. Something else had taken a hand. No good guessing but too much sun was a likely culprit. Much more of this and he'd end up completely off his rocker. The idea he'd got one over on Membril for a start. Who did he think he was kidding? He'd still have his crucifix had that been the case. And that stupid panic attack when he thought he was being throttled? Should've known from the word go there was never any real danger of him choking. His death was already prearranged. Flat out on an altar in the not too distant foreseeable. Still, whatever and so what. He still felt good.

He spent the night sheltered by a cleft in a pinnacle of rock, a sturdy basaltic column sprouting incongruously from an otherwise un-littered slope. Patches of moss were beginning to appear through the snow, and although a welcome sight there was a worrying downside. Gliding across thick layers of snow the sledge had behaved admirably, but on solid ground it would be useless. The oxygen cylinders, now he was at an altitude that encouraged unassisted breathing, could be got rid of but the cases were a different matter. Two he could cope with, four would be two too many.

Up and ready at first light, he determined to make full use of the time at his disposal. He'd had nothing substantial to eat for close on four days, and if he didn't find help soon? The prospect of death by malnutrition prompted an unlikely smile. True he wouldn't be around to see it, but popping his clogs before the time appointed would wipe the smile off Membril's face. The thought put a whole new meaning to the saying, 'every cloud has a silver lining'.

Within an hour of setting off he came across a mountain stream. Although little more than a trickle rippling over stony ground, it was a sight to enthuse over. Fresh drinking water at last. He'd forgotten what it tasted like. Thankful for it though he'd been at the time, melted snow was at best unpalatable. Another advantage was that the stream would furnish him with a quick-route guide to the ground floor. For as long as the terrain allowed, that would be the path to follow.

Following the steadily expanding brook over open ground, he decided the time had come to abandon the sledge. It wasn't an easy decision. They had shared many anxious moments together and he and it had formed a close attachment; but what had to be, had to be. Apart from a few tenacious patches the snow had completely disappeared, and in his weakened state pulling it across an unhelpful surface was becoming ever more arduous. The allure of a well-earned rest beckoning, he sat staring at the flowing water that was by now quite deep. It had all been so black and white at the start but complications were now beginning to raise their ugly heads. For one thing he hadn't reckoned on losing so much energy quite so quickly. He had known the time would come when the sledge would have to be abandoned, but that was ok. The snow would've been left behind, he'd be able to breathe without assistance and the temperature would be more compatible. The original plan remained clear in his mind. When the time came to abandon the sledge he would carry as much as was necessary on his back. That was then. Now, in the full light of day, it was a different matter. There were no two ways about it. The cases would have to join the sledge in retirement.

About to move on, he had a rethink. It was possible...certainly worth a try. Divide the essentials between two cases as originally intended - Kyle's were of better quality so he'd go for those - and float them down the stream. Didn't matter if the contents got wet, they'd soon dry out if left in the sun for an hour-or-so..

At low ebb he plodded over broken ground interspersed with tufts of grass and an occasional lonely shrub: forced to stop ever more frequently to rest. There were trees to be seen on the not-too distant horizon, a welcome addition to the landscape and one that gave him hope. For some reason he tended to associate trees with habitat. Digging deep into increasingly meagre reserves, he added a tad more impetus to his steps. The extra effort proving worthwhile, he arrived at the edge of the tree-clad area sooner than expected. The sun filtering through the leafy mantle infused a warm contentment, so wonderfully different from the harsh beauty of the mountain peaks.

Walking a few yards into the forest he kept faith with his body. Dragging the cases from the stream by the rope to which they were tethered, he slumped to the ground exhausted; to sleep soundly for more than an hour. Returning slowly into the land of the living he stretched his arms above his head to aid circulation...about to curse the pain that shot through his shoulder as a result he stopped short. Failing to immediately recognise the smell that tickled his nostrils, he sniffed the air. Smoke...wood smoke. The dire possibility of a forest fire flickering through his mind, he scrambled to his feet. There was no mistaking the smell but, as it had been no more than a passing whiff, it couldn't be much of a blaze. Either that or it was a long way off. Keeping mounting excitement under wraps, he considered the alternative. If the forest wasn't ablaze someone, somewhere, had lit a fire. Tossing the cases back into the stream, he literally followed his nose.

A few yards further on he entered a grass-covered glade. Not much larger than a tennis court but sizeable enough for him to see above the trees. There it was. Straight ahead. A dense plume of white smoke infesting the clear blue sky.

In retrospect he should have been prepared. As it was he had given no active consideration to the possibility. Wisdom, however, seldom misses out on an opportunity arising after the event. Having come so far with surprisingly few difficulties, he was guilty of assuming that this was it. He'd made it! He'd damn well made it! Madam Nature however had other ideas. The onslaught was as silent as it was merciless, and it struck with frightening rapidity. Unaware and unprepared he'd reached the end of his tether. Unconscious before hitting the ground, he failed to see the man running to his aid.

He came to on a bed with two men pouring over him. One holding a damp cloth to his forehead, the other speaking in a language that sounded like Spanish. The mist that clouded his brain beginning to thin, he dimly recalled the phrase Kyle had used many times.

"Usted habla Inglés, Señor?"

"Hola! Inglés." Disappearing through a door on the far side of the room, he returned with another man hard on his heels.

"Don't have too many visitors up here..." he boomed, "but that don't mean you're not welcome. English I'm told and, according to Enrico, here, he reckons you're in a bad way. Leave it to you to tell me if he's hit the jackpot." He smiled, a happy-go-lucky twinkle of the eyes putting him completely at ease. "Nice to meet you by the way. Folks around here call me Willy: short for William, with Carter tagged on the end."

Despite feeling like death on the brink, he found a smile hard to suppress. The new arrival was a giant of a man, well over six feet tall and shoulders to match. Somehow 'Willy,' didn't seem to fit.

"Jack Sibley," offering a weak hand. "To say I'm pleased to meet you would be an understatement. But can I ask…what's an American's doing in this neck of the woods?"

"Canadian, Jack, but you're not the first to get it wrong and guess you won't be the last. What we have here is part of the Huascaran National Park. A centre for scientific research among other things. Put together by courtesy of the Peruvian government. Botany being my field of interest, I'm here to identify and catalogue the mountain flora. But enough of me, I'm itching to find out what you've been up to and how you come to turn up here in such a sorry state?"

"It's a long story."

"Oh don't worry about that, fellah. I've all the time in the world. You just carry on at a pace that suits."

Keeping mum about the events leading up to it, he told of the crash, Kyle's death and his own lucky escape. Going on to tell of his injuries and the trauma of the past few days.

"Some tale, Jack! And you getting here in one piece...bloody miracle if you ask me." Placing one enormous hand on the edge of the bed he spoke with sympathy and understanding. "Sorry about your friend. Must be a hard pill to swallow. But this crash? What happened? Airplanes don't drop out of the sky without good reason."

"No idea to be honest." he answered, keeping his guilt under wraps. "Mechanical failure I suppose…something along those lines. Just a guess, but can't see how it could be anything else. Flying along nicely one minute, everything going haywire the next. I remember seeing the ground rushing towards us…that was it. After that, nothing. All I remember, is waking up in the snow with a splitting headache, a bloody leg and a sore shoulder."

"Guess the boffins'll find out what went wrong - the authorities will have to be informed of course, but don't you worry about that - I'll see to it in the morning. Getting yourself immersed in bureaucracy won't do you any favours the condition you're in. All you need know is your friends remains will be taken care of. In the meantime we'll do our best to sort you out. So get your pants off." The sight of the pitiful surgery raising a cross between a grin and a grimace, the comment was straight and to the point. "Mm, not pretty. But hell, Jack, to have the guts to do it is something else. Now your shoulder." His first glance promoting a chuckle, it was more a statement than a question. "You're putting your money on a pulled muscle!"

"That…a break perhaps. One or the other. Don't see what else it could be."

"Wrong on both counts, Jack. A metal spike has buried itself just below your shoulder blade. Looks real nasty. Not much blood, so that's something."

"I'm happy to grit my teeth if you're game to pull it out." In a strange country, a lopsided bank balance and no health service? The thought of hospital treatment set his pulse racing.

"Not likely, mate. Too risky. When I said it looked nasty, I meant it." He stood, turning towards the door. "Cheer up, Bud," he grinned, responding to the crestfallen look, "I know a man who can. One of the advantages of a place like this, is we have all the medical facilities we're likely to need on tap. Stands to reason, cut off from the beaten track like we are. Miguel Sagan, the chief medic; knows his stuff and an all-round great guy...you'll get on well with him. He'll have you up and running before you know it. South American but speaks good English. Did his training at one of your big London hospitals he tells me. But that's for later. What you need right now is some nourishment inside you. Oh, and while I think of it, we rescued a couple of cases from the river…yours I guess; can't imagine how they could belong to anyone else. One of our chaps found 'em snarled up against the bank a few yards up stream. I'll get the laundry girls - yeah, another of our perks," he said, laughing at the incredulous expression, "- to do what they can with the contents."

"Willy wasn't wrong, Jack." Bolstered by a large bowl of hot soup followed by steamed fish and vegetables, he was being given the once over by Miguel Sagan. "There's a sliver of metal stuck between the left scapula and the upper ribs. Luckily for you it didn't puncture a lung. Won't know for sure till I see the X-rays, but must've come damn close. Any closer, you wouldn't be sitting here now."

"Could it have moved during my climb down the mountain? You wouldn't believe some of the contortions I got myself into."

"Possible, but wouldn't have thought so. Looks too embedded to have moved about much. However, no good looking at crystal balls. We'll know more when I get a look at the pictures. But that, my friend, is for tomorrow. You're in a low state, and before being put through any more mills you're going to need all the sleep you can get."

By the end of the fifth day he was aware of life returning to his ravaged body. Miguel had worked wonders in that time, removing the metal shard from his shoulder and repairing his sorry needlework. It had been a long time coming, but he was at last beginning to feel more like his old self. That was until the morning of day six. Beginning to think it was time to move on, Willy burst into the hut.

"Surprise, Jack. You have a visitor."

CHAPTER FORTEEN

The acting was superb. Thrusting Willy aside and wearing a warm smile he cried. "Jack! Oh words are not enough. When I heard the news I got here as fast as I could. I was so concerned...and, Kyle? I'm told he's dead. This is all so tragic. So very tragic. But you? Are you alright?"

The countenance thrust before him laid bare the mockery of his friendly approach, the synthetic facade of convenience replaced by the face of the real Membril. He tried to avoid the eyes but it was too late: his awareness unaffected, his movements in the hands of the aggressor. Not that he could have done anything about it, his hands were tied. He couldn't put his newfound friends at risk after all they'd done for him.

From there on in events moved rapidly, Membril making it clear he was in no mood for pleasantries, idle chitchat or any other delaying tactics. Despite the protestations of Miguel, who insisted Jack needed time to convalesce and Willy doing his best to persuade him to delay their departure until at least the following day, he remained adamant.

"I thank you for your courtesy, but we cannot afford more delay. I am due in conference early tomorrow and Jack's presence is essential to the progress of that meeting. It is a mere five-hours to Lima, and I'm sure he will cope with the journey. But beyond that, gentlemen, I assure you I would reconsider if I felt it would in any way jeopardise his recovery."

Finding it difficult not to retch at the unbridled hypocrisy, the words left a bitter taste in his mouth. The latent brutality of his portrayal, the lies and the conning of those who had tended his every need angered him. Making no attempt to hide his disgust, he met the triumphant smirk with one of his own. Membril might control his movements, but he wasn't going to dictate his sentiments.

Walking alongside as Membril led the way to his car, Willy asked. "You ok with this, Jack? I'm more'n happy to drive you to Lima, if that's what you want. Drop you at the airport...wherever. Only have to say."

That was interesting. So Willy hadn't been taken in after all and was voicing his doubts. Evidently Membril wasn't the polished raconteur he thought himself to be. But it didn't change anything. Tempting as it was he was barred from accepting Willy's offer. Membril pulled the strings; his role was to do as he was told.

"Thanks for the offer, but there really is no option, Willy. As Charles," - God, it stuck in his throat referring to him as if he were an intimate acquaintance - "explained, it's important we get to the meeting on time. I know what you're thinking. If things hadn't gone my way? But they did, and I have to face up to my responsibilities...even more so as Kyle can't be there. I hadn't given it a thought until now, what with one thing and another it completely slipped my mind...not surprising in the circumstances I guess. But, having returned to the world of the living, it's time to get back to earning a crust."

"Must be important...this meeting. What's it all about?"

He stuttered. Of all the questions? Willy was looking at him, awaiting his answer. Puzzled it was not readily forthcoming. He had to think of something, and quick. "Oh it's..." thought processes stagnating, he searched for an excuse. Thank heavens! Membril, making sure he didn't miss a word, came to his rescue.

"You must forgive us, Dr. Carter, but that is a question we are bound not to answer. The forthcoming discussions concern military matters and our lips are sealed by the official secrecy act. I trust you understand, and do not view our reticence as discourteous. Come Jack, shake a leg. It'll be dark by the time we get there if we don't get a move on."

Bundling him into a rear passenger seat, he drove off as if all the bats from hell threatened their existence.

"I assume we're not going to Lima."

"It is of little or no consequence to you where we are headed, but I will nevertheless satisfy your curiosity. Our destination is the small town of Camacarja. Set in the remoteness of the high Andes, it is almost unknown to the outside world. Although I have to say your late friend formed a cosy acquaintance with the place. He and I spent a most memorable few hours there. But of course you know all about that. I derived great pleasure listening to his narrative. That I was unable to gauge your reaction was unfortunate, but I would like to think you found it of interest."

Conscious of the gloating reflection in the rear-view mirror, he determined not to rise to the bait. He had no wish to leave himself open to further humiliation, but he was buggered if he was going to stay silent. He'd turn the tables. Have a go back at him. Challenge his ruddy hubris to the limit.

"You really are a slimy creature, Membril, but I can see why you find that hard to take on board. Your intellectual muscle is incapable of coping with such trite propaganda. So let me give you a rundown. With any luck it could open your eyes to what you really are. A conceited megalomaniac, nothing more than a foul raptor preying on the gullibility and fear of innocent people."

"You must learn to control your tongue, Sibley" giving vent to a laugh that sounded like a hammer drill on reinforced concrete, "it could get you into trouble one day." Pulling over onto a grassed embankment, he turned to face him.

"I am forced to ask yet again...why do you still live? And this time I want answers. Not another basinful of your pathetic humour."

The question, coming out of the blue as it did, left him cold. While trying to think of a suitable reply, he decided he'd be better off seated in the front of the car. A move apparently sanctioned, as no attempt was made to stoop him. Giving Jack the impression that he was wary of facing him full-on, Membril continued to stare trance-like through the windscreen. It didn't matter. His profile was quite capable of portraying the mix of confusion and underlying despair simmering beneath the surface. But beneath the facade of devastation lay the certainty of dire retribution.

"And how am I supposed to know? You're the one hell-bent on my demise. It was not of my choosing, that a man worth infinitely more than anything to which you can aspire lies dead. Murdered by your hand. And if you think I find humour in that you must be off your head. It was no action of mine that destined I should live." He changed his mind. It had been his intention to leave it at that. But what the hell? He'd take the piss. Goad him. Make him angry. "Do you not consider it strange, that every attempt to get rid of me has ended in failure. In your shoes I would find that rather worrying." A manufactured laugh mocking him without mercy, he went for the jugular. "Better make sure you get it right at the altar, Membril. Shouldn't think your master would be best pleased if there's another balls-up." He was enjoying this. He'd push him further. "It could of course be my phantom accomplice putting his oar in...you never know. Either way I wouldn't give much for your chances."

"Don't try me too far, Sibley," trembling lips registering rising anger, "persist in riling me and I'll take control of your mind as well your movement." He was rattled alright, the apprehension in his voice left Jack in no doubt. It wasn't fear exactly. More a wariness of the ground he trod. Nagging doubts creating anxiety within a much troubled mind.

He'd chance his arm. He was doomed anyway, so what difference did it make. If Membril was to have the final say he might as well make sure he got his pennyworth while he had the chance. "More claptrap," he spat with as much venom as he could muster. "As far as you're concerned my mind is a closed book, as you bloody well know. And that, I don't mind telling you, pleases me no end. You must find it frustrating to get the engaged signal every time you try to earwig in on my thoughts. Even more so when I'm having a chat with my special friend."

"So you admit it." His voice shook. His face paled. It was more than mistrust. This time it was genuine, unbridled fear.

"For me to know, for you to find out. But leave that for now. It's about time you gave me some answers. For a start you have all along made it clear Dr. Steinbeck was the important cog in your scheme, and I would like to know why. After all, as I'm to fill the gap left by his demise, I think you owe me that. And something else you can tell me. Why the muted interest in the statue? With what I've got coming, I don't think it's a lot to ask."

"You never fail to surprise me, Sibley. With so little time left I find it quite emotional that you should show such interest in my affairs. But as you have, it would be discourteous of me not to satisfy your curiosity. Something for you to reflect on...as you await the plunge of the sacred knife." Creating the impression he was loath to give too much away, he sat gathering his thoughts. Shaking hands, an inability to sit still for more than a few seconds at any one time...sure signs of nerves on edge. "Your second query puts the other into perspective, so I will deal with that first. The reason you believe my interest in the statue has waned stems from a change in circumstance. What you choose to believe is your prerogative, but I can assure you the statue is as important now as it ever was. The difference, is I no longer need to waste time in its pursuance. The statue will be returned to me upon its removal from your lifeless body. Which is why I made sure you rescued it from the remains of the aircraft."

"Thoughtful of you, but it doesn't answer my question. Why the change of heart?"

"It could be said the answer is in your own hands...pocket to be precise. Were you able to decipher the runes you would have found, as I later did, that, by itself, the statue is useless. You will no doubt be pleased to know that I too found translation difficult, and I was only part way through when the statuette was stolen from me. I had however gleaned sufficient to learn that the runes provide the basis of a spell to release Quetzalcoatl, from the tomb in which he was interred by an interfering catholic priest of the conquistador era. For reasons apparent I was anxious to complete the translation; hence my earlier determination to reclaim the statue. Luck however was on my side. I was able to retrieve the missing, vital as it turned out, information via an alternative source. It was then that I realised my mistake. The figurines role in the proceedings succeeds the sacrifice of an human to the Goat of Mendes, not instead of, as I was originally led to believe. As you will no doubt appreciate, that changed everything. As long as the sacrificial victim has the statue in his possession at the appropriate time I was home and dry. Does that answer your question?"

"If you say so, but are you sure you've got it right this time. You know what you're like. Your reputation goes ahead of you "

"Do not demean my ability, Sibley. Your good fortune" - the idea of a guardian evidently put on hold for the time being, - "will not last forever and, as will soon be made clear, forever is about to overtake you. Thanks to your forthcoming contribution my ultimate success is inevitable; which, in a way I suppose, makes you the guest honour. Such an exalted role must surely fill you with a sense of pride." The attempted humour producing a laugh resembling an old crones cackle.

"And if it all goes pear shaped? What then?"

"The outcome has been prophesied, there is no way it can be altered. Not by you, not by anyone. Fate is decreed and, once decreed, it cannot be undone."

"Mm, take your word for it. But in my own relatively short lifetime I've seen more than a few certainties go bottom-up. And you must have doubts yourself. If you hadn't, you wouldn't give a toss what I may or may not have hidden up my sleeve."

"I admit to you having been a thorn in my side and, on more than one occasion, to have caused me considerable aggravation. With that I have no argument. But don't underestimate me. It is true to say that your continuing disruption I found worrying for a time, to the extent that I wondered if it was something more than just luck that assisted you. Those concerns however are in the past. You have had your day, Sibley. It is now my turn." Leaning forward to turn on the ignition he added somewhat irritably, "I will answer your other question as we go along. We have delayed long enough."

"Soon after we met I came to the conclusion that it would be to my advantage if you and Steinbeck were to be separated," pulling onto the road as he carried on. "A decision triggered when all contact with your mind was denied me. I confess it bothered me at the time, mostly because I was unable to establish the cause...an enigma that continues to persecute me." He stopped abruptly. Expression close to pleading he turned his head to look at Jack, as if by beseeching compassion he would be granted pity. "But it was to get worse, a circumstance of which you are probably unaware. It was bad enough that your thoughts were screened from me, but it reached the point when the conversations between the two of you were, for want of a better word, scrambled. Barring me from Steinbeck's mind as well as yours. That was why disposing of you became a number one priority. But it wasn't the sole reason. Your late friend might have been an highly intelligent man, but you were the one with the appropriate know-how. Your association with the occult, albeit brief and at the lower end of the spectrum nevertheless posed problems. Without you to aid him, Steinbeck would be lost. All along you have been a constant irritation and even now, when almost at the end of the line, you continue to pester me beyond measure."

"Sorry about that, but offloading your troubles on to me won't do you any favours. It merely blinds you to your own inadequacies. An inbuilt refusal to accept responsibility for your mistakes passes you by and ignored as a consequence. Putting it bluntly it's yourself you should be castigating, not me. I've warned you in the past that conceit will one day be your downfall but you continue to treat my words with contempt. But it will happen. Believe me it will happen. Maybe not now, but sometime. More than likely when you least expect it. But for all that you seem to be either incapable or unwilling to do anything about it. So I suggest you listen to what I say and try to take my words on board. Every time - damn nearly every time - your plans have gone awry it was because of your own failings. I know it, Kyle Steinbeck knew it and, given half a chance, the entire bloody world would recognise it...but not you."

"Why you continue to persist with this delusion of yours baffles me, Sibley. Your opinion may be your prerogative, but be aware that ignorance can overshadow such liberty. My insistence that I am free from error is a statement of fact based on many years experience. It is not the fruit of wishful imagination and you would do well to get that into your thick head. However on this occasion you have no choice other than to accept the facts I am about to relate. That it was Steinbeck and not you killed in the crash was a direct result of your petty interference. With his protection in mind, I targeted the position he would be expected to occupy in the plane. As the pilot, he couldn't be anywhere else. But you, as per your maddening custom, opted to depart your seat and stand behind him at the crucial moment. You don't need me to spell it out. By choice or by chance, you occupied the one safe spot in the aircraft."

"Gave yourself away there, Membril. By choice or by chance? What you really mean, is was it my decision or did I have advice?" Smirking at the all-too transparent squirming of his adversary, he carried on, "But there's no good arguing over nothing. It won't change anything, so let's move on. You still haven't explained why Dr. Steinbeck, and not me. Does it matter whom you choose to murder? I'd have thought one sacrificial victim as good as any other."

"You have much to learn, Sibley. In certain circumstances it can matter a great deal. This you will come to appreciate with the story I am about to unfold. A tale of intrigue and revenge that will, perhaps, inspire an element of understanding. Although I have my reservations on that."

"The suspense is killing me."

"Sarcasm is uncalled for. I am doing my best to satisfy your curiosity; whether or not I continue to do so, is, on this occasion, my prerogative. So listen-up, or shut up. The choice is yours."

"And that's supposed to get my interest? No," a waving hand aborting the come-back, "I apologise, that was out of order. I need to find the reason behind all this, and the only way I'm going to find it is for you to tell me everything. The why's as well as the wherefores."

"As you wish." The tone hinted at anger simmering beneath the surface. A message telling him to belt up before he went too far. "We need to go back more than three hundred years, to the year of sixteen ninety-two to be precise. You are familiar with the Salem witch trials?"

"I've heard of them, but can't say I know much more than that."

"Then I will enlighten you. In that year nineteen people, a mix of both sexes, stood accused of practicing witchcraft. The trials, conducted by the small-minded hierarchy of Salem, a small town in Massachusetts, were a farce. Their guilt pre-ordained, each and every one of the accused were sentenced to death by hanging. Those executed included a witch by the name of Sarah Colcey, ironically the only true exponent of witchcraft amongst the rabble. The remainder were the innocent victims of a savage campaign."

"Without being rude and accepting this all very interesting, what has any of it got to do with Kyle Steinbeck?"

"If you care to curb your impatience it will become apparent. I will however add that the connection is to the Steinbeck family as a whole, not to any one individual. The meaning behind that statement will become clear as we proceed."

Wiping the back of his hand across his forehead, he adjusted the air conditioning. "Warming up, Sibley...now, where was I? Oh, yes. Sarah Colcey. Surprisingly not on the original list, she brought suspicion on herself by an act of wanton foolishness. Using her powers to advantage she seduced the fiancé of a near neighbour, a young girl by the name of, Dolly Proctor. Possessing a somewhat fiery personality, Proctor determined to have her revenge and the trials provided her with the opportunity. The mood in Salem at the time was such that a mere whisper of malpractice would lead to almost certain conviction. Thus it proved. Following Dolly Proctor's accusation, Colcey was found guilty and sentenced to death.

"Seems to me Dolly had good cause."

"That's as maybe, but it did her little good. Sarah Colcey was determined to exact her own, subtle vengeance. Poor Dolly. Certain her hearts desire would return to her once the sorceress was removed from the scene, she was to see her dreams vanish in front of her. She and her betrothed were among the crowd gathered to witness the executions. Gloating as her love assassin was dragged to the gallows, her joy was short-lived. The stool supporting her kicked away, Sarah fell to meet her slow death with a smile on her face. As the rope tightened round her neck a leg of the wooden stool shattered, a sharp and heavy splinter from the broken support arrowed towards Dolly's man: piercing his heart and killing him instantly. Sarah Colcey was, as to be expected, deemed to have used her powers for one final act. And who could say it wasn't so?"

"But it doesn't end there?"

"Not by a long chalk. At just thirteen years old, Dolly Proctor would have been looked upon as a grown woman back in the closing days of the seventeenth century. Of an age to make decisions of her own, she thought long and hard before making the move that was to change her life. Distraught at her loss she made for Boston, where she boarded a ship bound for Europe. Unable to pay her way she prostituted herself, spending the voyage in company of the ships captain. Following several gruelling weeks at sea, harbour was eventually made in Rotterdam where, now considered expendable, Proctor was put ashore to fend for herself."

"Not what you might call brimming with compassion, that captain. After sharing his bed for all that time, you would've thought he'd have seen her alright before dumping her."

"Women were used to it in those days, they knew their place and accepted it." With an expression that said nothing would have changed if he had his way, he carried on, "Dolly Proctor, you have to understand, was without compunction when it came to looking after herself. Aware she was attractive to men, she used her attributes to make her way across Germany and into Austria. Having by that time been on the move for close on three years, and liking the feel of the country, she decided that was where she would settle. And this is where we reach the climax, of a story that has no doubt bored you to distraction."

"Not at all. I admit to wondering where you're going, still do when it comes down to it, but you wouldn't be telling me all this if it doesn't go anywhere. In fact you've got me so intrigued, I can't help wondering if you would make a better narrator than you do a magician."

"Your infantile remarks no longer rile me, Sibley, so I suggest you stop wasting your breath and regard what I'm telling you with the respect it deserves. It will be of advantage to both of us if you do."

"Point taken. Alright, I'll behave myself. At least until you give me cause not to."

"I'll remember that, Sibley," the remark suggesting he wasn't quite sure how he should take what was said. "and, with the proviso that you keep your promise, I will continue. But one more word out of place…that's it. Understood?" A nod conveying the answer expected, he recommenced the archive from where he'd left off. "By then nearing her eighteenth birthday, Dolly Proctor ended her travels in the Austrian town of Tamsweg where she met and married a man many years older than herself. Despite her murky past and the quite considerable age gap the marriage was, by all accounts, successful; their contentment completed by the arrival of two children, both boys. That completes the narrative, Sibley, but not the saga. Ignoring the occasional spite, you have on the whole been an attentive listener and your perseverance is about to be rewarded. The name of the man Dolly married…Gunther Steinbeck."

"Ah, now I see where you're going. Gunther Steinbeck...long-time gone ancestor of the present-day Steinbecks'. Is that what you're telling me?"

"You're quick, Sibley."

"But how do you know all this? Or do you? For all I know it's nothing more than a juicy tale concocted by you and the rest of your perverted clan. The means to justify what you get up to at night."

"I've warned you before about your choice of words, but I'll not give you the satisfaction of indulging in another slanging match. Considering your earlier involvement with our association, brief though it was, I find your lack of knowledge hard to understand. I will, however, enlighten you. As far back as the time of Christ and beyond, every tiny detail, every mannerism, the most insignificant birthmark, of every past, present and, in some instances, future, follower of the left-hand path has been, and continues to be, reliably chronicled. No one, not even you, is exempt. Sarah Colcey, just nineteen years old when so cruelly executed, was a naturally imbued and powerful witch. During her short time in mortal form she was revered as one of the most able exponents of the dark arts to be found anywhere on this planet. Who knows what she might have gone on to achieve, had she not been so tragically betrayed? For more than three hundred years vengeance for her death has been sought, but for her to find true peace the act must reflect the circumstances of her demise."

"So that's it. The ancestral link to Dolly Proctor made Kyle Steinbeck the ideal foil for your seedy ambition. Why he was the main man, and me an irritating nuisance. A pest to be got rid of at the earliest. Can well imagine how the sacrifice of a direct descendent of the person responsible for the untimely death of one of your lot would boost your credibility rating."

"It was Steinbeck's lineage that was of importance, not my credibility. His sacrifice to the Goat of Mendes would have ensured the restoration of Quetzalcoatl to his former glory, having to use a substitute raises doubts. However I anticipate that your treacherous past, together with a close relationship to the Steinbecks', will balance matters out." A sickly leer presaged his next words. "Success is not an issue, Sibley. It is not that which worries me. It is that an extremely complex undertaking would have been that much simpler had you not got in the way."

"Although I can't claim to relish being a cog in your wheel of depravity, it's a comfort knowing I've made life difficult for you." It was his turn to sneer. "But while we're conversing like a couple of responsible adults for a change, you can satisfy my curiosity. This pact you've made with the Devil? What's that all about? I know what you can expect if you don't come up to scratch, but what's in it for you if you do turn up trumps? If I'm to have my lights extinguished to advance your cause, it's only right and proper I know what you hope to get out of it. You told Dr. Steinbeck it was your 'very being', but there must be more to it than that. Can't see you taking the risk unless there was a substantial incentive on the table."

"Immortality! That is to be my reward for releasing the serpent god from the bonds that imprison him. A worthy prize, for a worthy project."

"Immortality eh? Yep! I can imagine that would be right up your street. As for me...I wouldn't be so sure. Reckon I'd have had enough after a couple of thousand years-or-so. As I see it, this eternity thing might not be all it's cracked up to be. Too much of it could drive a man round the bend. But I suppose you know what you're doing. Something of a conundrum if you think about it. Snuff it if your efforts go awry, live too long if you get it right. From where I'm standing, you're stuck between the Devil and the deep blue...no pun intended. But there's something else I don't get. If your master, who must have a lot more going for him than you do, is that keen to have one of his buddies restored to his filthy clan why doesn't he do it himself?"

"He is barred from doing so, that is why. One of the demands of the Sermon on the Mount. An insidious restriction that will be rendered null and void upon the resurrection of, Quetzalcoatl."

"Now I..."

"No more Sibley. For the rest of the journey you will stay silent and leave me with my thoughts. We are still three hours from our destination and I've suffered enough of your endless curiosity."

About to respond he thought better of it, deciding instead to content himself by admiring the scenery. Simmering across lush wooded slopes, the shadows of the high peaks created a landscape of indescribable serenity. A tranquillity disturbed only by the sound of birds and the intrusive growl of the cars engine. The beauty and the sense of utter peace lulled him. Authorising his mind to reject his predicament, it conveyed him into the welcoming arms of untroubled slumber...woken by Membril shaking him back into the real world.

"Wake up, Sibley. We're here."

Bleary eyed, he looked about him. Low in the sky the sun glared through the windscreen, spreading the information that nightfall wasn't far off. Unfastening the seat belt, he stretched cramped limbs; yawning vigorously as he peered through the passenger window.

"This it? Thought you said it was some sort of town we were going to."

"And so we are, but this is as close as we can get by car. The rest must be done on foot. Come...see for yourself."

Escorted to the brim of a sheer precipice, he held back. Cliff edges made him nervous. "What am I supposed to be looking for?"

"You won't see anything from there. Get closer. Down below."

Refusing to give Membril satisfaction, he willed himself to within a couple of feet of the edge. It wasn't as unfriendly as he'd anticipated. A thick mist blanketing the ground going someway to nullifying his phobia. "I assume it's not the mist you're on about? I can't see anything else."

"A regular visitor at this time of day…but no matter." Pinching the bridge of his nose between thumb and forefinger, he was lost for a while in deep concentration. Eyes tight shut, mouthing inaudible words through barely moving lips. "It will clear. When it does, you will recognise the scene from your friend's description."

The mist rolled away to form a window framed by vaporous curtains. Unmasked, the lower slopes loomed up at him. Teasing him, instilling neural persecution. The immediate impulse was to shrink away from the edge, but he could feel Membril's impatience, sense his mounting irritation. Fighting the swimming sensation that threatened to engulf him, he forced his eyes downwards.

"Well?"

It was weird. He'd never before laid eyes on the sight below but there was nothing strange, nothing he didn't recognise, nothing unfamiliar…every square inch was indelibly etched in his mind. It was almost as if Kyle was standing next to him, describing the scene in minute detail. The town glistening white in the late afternoon sun, ant-size people slaving away in the fields many hundreds of feet below. The huge cathedral-like structure dominating the landscape. He knew where they were alright, there was no doubt about that. Kyle had visited in a dream. He was seeing it in the flesh.

"As if I could forget? The place where you put Kyle Steinbeck through hell with your foul practice." The response he expected not forthcoming he changed tack. "So ok! Now what? How do you propose we get there?"

"Patience, Sibley, patience. Shut up and listen, and I will enlighten you. There is no direct route to connect Camacarja with the sorry world of today. The only alternative to scaling these cliffs is to hill-walk from the far side of the valley. That would add a further two-hundred odd miles to the journey, consuming time I cannot afford."

"So what are you suggesting? Parachutes? Or is there a helicopter on standby?"

"For a man of your experience, Sibley, you can at times be remarkably naive. Watch...and learn."

It was worth watching, but apart from a grudging appreciation of the skill of his opponent it did little to enhance his education. It was clever, it was uncanny, but he couldn't see that it served any practical purpose. A twenty-four inch long stone block jutted from the face of the cliff a few inches from the top. If appearance was anything to go by it could have been taken from the staircase of a medieval castle. Membril stood silent, awaiting his comment: regarding him with the pompous look that was his trademark."

"Very clever but what's the point? assuming you're not about to impress me with your sky-diving expertise. Or are you having me on? Convincing me I'm to meet my maker on the altar, when the real plan is to have me jump from that lump of granite."

"Your petty jibes no longer bother me, Sibley, although I confess that has not always been the case. There is however an old proverb that springs to mind. One of which I am sure you will be cognisant. 'He who laughs last, etcetera'?" Grabbing him by the shoulder, he spun him round to face the void beyond the edge of the precipice. Adopting the air of an exasperated school master intent on instilling sense into a particularly thick pupil, he simmered. "That slab of stone is the first tread of a staircase that extends to ground level. The second tread is triggered by the raising of the foreleg preparatory to taking the next step...and so forth. Coincident with the removal of the second leg, the tread previous is returned from whence it came. Do you follow? Or are you more imbecilic than I take you for?"

Until that moment in time he had clung to the remote hope that an opportunity to turn the tables might come his way; a solitary chance to outmanoeuvre this madman. A tardy realisation of just how forlorn a dream that was now kicked in with frightening velocity. The power Membril had at his disposal was awesome. He'd known it from the time of their first meeting, but an inbuilt immunity had refused to embrace it. He had all along stressed the inevitability of success, but there was no longer any doubt that that had been an idle boast. For all that, he was damned if he was going to give him something else to gloat over.

"Ok, so you're a clever bastard. But what's the point? If you imagine for one moment you're going to persuade me to set one foot on that ludicrous contraption you couldn't be more wrong. You can do what you like, but count me out. And I mean that. To say I'm not happy with heights is the understatement to end all understatements. I get worried standing on a chair, so how d'you reckon I'll cope on a flimsy piece of stone half-way to the bloody moon?" Perhaps he was pushing it a bit, a touch of pleading might be prudent. "Honestly, Membril, I'm not kidding. I'll get down alright...a whole lot quicker than either of us would want."

"In case it has slipped your memory, Sibley, I decide what you do and what you don't do. But that aside, there is nothing for you to worry about. Were I able to attend your mind I could have erased your fears. However, you should find it consoling to know there will be no danger of you falling. On that, you have my word. After all said and done, you are all I have left. With no Steinbeck to assist me, I dare not run the risk of losing you as well."

"I somehow thought you'd say that. It would hardly be in your best interests to have to scrape my remains off the rocks. A small crumb of comfort, but there you go. Every little helps as they say. So how long does it take to get down...how many steps?"

"Three thousand, seven hundred and forty-four to be precise. A descent of around three thousand feet and yes, it does take a time. But there is a brighter side, Sibley. You won't have to face the climb back up. Once down...you stay down!"

"Thanks for the reminder." His entire being cried out; wanting to run. To free himself of this monster who threatened both his earthly life and his spiritual existence. Brutally shackled; every movement dictated in accord with his captor's wishes, it gnawed away at him. Biting into what little reserves he had left.

"It'll be pitch black in under an hour, so I suppose we're stuck up here for the night? Where and how do you suggest we spend it?"

"You yet again display your innocence. Did you learn nothing during your involvement with our movement? To lighten the darkness is simplicity itself...as I shall demonstrate." The smile reasserted itself. "Time to get a move on. Your big day tomorrow, Sibley, and you will no doubt want to make the most of it."

CHAPTER FIFTEEN

"Welcome to your sleeping quarters, Sibley."

The descent had taken its toll. Close on two hours of physical endeavour leaving him a drained and ragged bundle of nerves. It was all very well, Membril keeping on there was nothing to worry about. He was well acquainted with the damn contraption and could call on his mates if he ran into trouble. The energy with which he moved over the cloying snow suggested he must have already made use of their help. He wasn't so much as out of breath when they finally made it to the bottom of the phantom staircase.

He'd been made to go first. Doing little to calm his nerves, the reinstated mist was a mixed blessing. True it masked the ground below from his sight, but it did nothing to occlude the vision emblazoned in his mind. Membril demanding he stop pussyfooting and get on with it hadn't helped.

In retrospect he couldn't believe it had ever happened. That first step, from the assured security of terra firma to the doubtful solidity of a flimsy stone bar was his worst ever experience. In vain he battled his aggressor's command, resisting his will to the limit. For a short time it had worked, but it wasn't long before he was made to concede defeat. Mind in disarray and stress on the brink of erupting, he was forced to fling an uncoordinated foot onto the cold, mist-dampened slab. Then followed the more daunting task, that of persuading the second foot to join company with the first. It was a challenge too far. Straddled between the stone and solid ground he froze, unable to breath, physically paralysed. Aware of hot breath burning the nape of his neck, he half-turned...Membril, practically climbing up his back; impatience verging on fury. He wanted to obey. Wanted to wipe the smug leer from the mocking features confronting him, but escalating fear rendered him immune to his captor's demands.

Anger at fever pitch, Membril displayed a cruelty that would have had the Marquis de Sade screaming with delight. Venting an oath to defuse his mounting aggravation, he shoved him hard in the back. The blow aroused the dormant beast that had plagued him for as long as he could remember. The promise of meeting death in the way he dreaded most. The shock alone could have been enough to cause his heart to give up the struggle, but that had been the only danger. Snuggled into the diaphanous shrouds of an invisible net of gravity-defying succour, his safety was never under threat.

Membril had gloated until he was blue in the face. It was not in his makeup to either understand or be bothered by the horror of his action. He merely reminded him of what he had said, that he was in no danger of falling, and perhaps he would now have the common decency to believe what he was told. What he hadn't appreciated, was his callous stupidity only served to add to Jack's fears. Making it that much more difficult to conquer his nerves. As a result every one of the remaining three thousand, seven hundred and forty-three steps were viewed with deep suspicion and alarm. Thankfully that ordeal now behind him, he stood wondering why Membril should find a deep indentation in an otherwise plain and ordinary rock-face of such interest. On the tip of his tongue to ask, he decided it was perhaps better not to. Mumbling dark words to himself, his tormentor was off in a world of his own.

Billowing in wispy tendrils from the rear of the shallow cave, a mist began to form. Thickening rapidly, it oozed in enveloping waves to momentarily engulf them in dense cloud. For a few seconds he could barely make out the shadowy form of Membril, standing just a few feet away from him. On the tip of his tongue to query what was going on the near-to-opaque vapour shrank to clear his vision: the gaseous substance solidifying into the surround of an open portal.

With a curt, 'follow me', Membril entered the manifested gap at the back of the cave, the rock door re-sealing once they had crossed the threshold. The struggle to keep his jaw in place was almost more than he could cope with. He knew well enough what this man was capable of but this was something else. It wasn't exactly palatial, but it was more than adequate for a one-night stopover. The rough-hewn, undecorated stone walls were somewhat unfriendly but their forbidding appearance was offset by the subdued lighting that filled the emptiness with a warm, comforting glow. All that he took in at a glance, but it was the three doors set in the far wall that drew his interest. They hinted at the welcome prospect of some privacy. He prayed he wasn't wrong..

"We will eat before I show you to your room." Membril mumbled, interrupting his thoughts. "I want an early start tomorrow. It will take some time to show you all that Camacarja has to offer. But that apart, I want you to see for yourself why the reincarnation of Quetzalcoatl is absolutely vital to the continued existence of its populace." A lengthy pause followed, as if he was unsure of what to say. "You know, despite our differences, I have to admit to holding a certain admiration for you, Sibley. You have not made it easy for me, in fact there were times when you made things exceedingly difficult. There are not many who would have had the courage, or the will, to defy me as you have done and I take my hat off to you. If for no other reason, I regret having to make use of you in the way that I must. You probably deserve a better fate."

"If you expect me to fall for that load of sleazy crap," he seethed in return, "you're wasting your breath. You threaten us, Kyle and myself, you put us through hell, you murder a man in cold blood to satisfy your own selfish ends and now it's me in the firing line. How you have the gall to attempt to justify your obscene practice is beyond the pale. Well let me tell you this. You want to make amends? Then do so by keeping your slimy

301

sentiments under wraps. Leave me to spend what time I have left to dwell in memory of the truly nice people I have known, instead of being forced to listen to the empty spiel of a heap of shit."

Quivering lips making it plain he had difficulty controlling his temper, the reply was curt. "If that is to be your attitude, I withdraw what I said and accede to your wishes. When we have eaten, you will be left to your own devices until morning."

Whatever or wherever the source the food gave him no cause for complaint and, to add to his satisfaction, Membril kept his promise. Remaining mute until the meal was over, he broke the lengthy silence in curt tones. "You may retire if you wish. As I said, I shall be looking for an early start."

"Doubt I'll get much sleep anyway, and since your definition of an early start may not match mine how am I to know what time you want me up and about?"

"I appreciate you will find difficulty sleeping, Sibley...that will be attended to. I will also ensure you wake at the correct time." His manner abrupt, the tone unforgiving.

He slept well. The first really good sleep he'd had in quite a while and, however formatted, he was thankful for it. It could have otherwise been a very long night. Until now it was as if he lived in a dream. An unending fantasy, viewed by an outside looker-on with only a passing interest. It was weird the way the brain worked. How it could obliterate when prudent, ignore the march of time when obligatory. Impending perils treated as surrealistic and disregarded as a consequence. But he was well aware that pushing the truth aside was a mere temporary balm, one that would cease to exist with the passage of time...that time had arrived. It was when they stood together at the top of the cliff that it first made its presence known. In the guise of fearful inspiration it hit him penetratingly and without warning. From that moment on terror became his constant companion; an uninvited guest that had no intention of deserting him. That was, until it was beyond consideration.

The shout through the closed door, telling him to get a move on because he hadn't got all day, shook him from his reverie. If Membril hadn't got all day then what the hell was he left with? A thought that set him wondering, how much time *did* he have? Perhaps it was better not to know. But he'd never been one for surprises, so he'd get the answer straight from the horses mouth."

The full English breakfast looked appetising enough, and no doubt tasted as good as it looked: but he wasn't interested. On any other day he would have tackled it with relish...but not today.

"This so-called ceremony of yours. When does it get going? In other words, how long have I got? I've a right to know when my destiny is designed to overtake me."

"The proceedings will commence at around eleven o'clock, but your participation will not be required until shortly before midnight." Letting him know he hadn't forgotten the put-down of the day before, he added, "You should feel honoured, Sibley. Participation in a unique ritual that has not been enacted for many hundreds of years is, I should have thought, a privilege not to be scorned. It does strike as a shame though that, and despite having made such a major contribution, you will not be around to witness the finale. The resurrection of Quetzalcoatl will not occur until after your death. But if it is any consolation, Sibley, I am sure the Plumed Serpent will appreciate your input."

Refusing to give him the satisfaction of sinking to his level, he stayed silent. The time and effort would be better spent mulling over what he'd been told. What was preferable...sooner or later? Earlier would have given him less time to dwell on it, put a stop to his insides being torn apart that much sooner. On the other hand, was it not better to cling to life for as long as possible? Not that it mattered much either way. The time had been set, and that was it. In the meantime his only hope, if he wasn't to end up completely round the bend, was to shut the forthcoming terror from his mind. Try to give dignity a boost, accept what was in store with a brave face. That was the sensible thing to do but he wasn't in a particularly sensible frame of mind. It would be so much easier to play the role of a quivering coward...he could do that with neither qualm nor effort. But he'd try the dignity bit first - for all the good it would do him.

Deep down he'd known it wouldn't work. What had seemed a praiseworthy resolution evaporated before it had time to get going as Kyle's dream was brought brutally to life. Everything about the place was familiar. The farmhands slaving away in the fields, the busy city thoroughfares, the hustle and bustle of the town centre...nothing changed. The detail so deeply ingrained he found it hard to believe his memories were gleaned from a tale told, rather than from personal experience. There was nothing new, nothing to take him by surprise. Every turning opened a vista with which he was already acquainted. Uncanny to the extent of incredulity, he didn't under-stand. But then he wasn't meant to understand. He moved in a different world. A world not of his philosophy.

He jerked himself back to reality. The atmosphere was filling him with a cloying despair, a creeping disease sent to drain all hope, all expectation from a susceptible mind. But he wouldn't succumb. Not like the poor wretches that flocked these streets. He would dwell on the more pleasant aspects of his short life. Then he saw Julie. God, she's lovely! He wanted her. Wanted to take her in his arms, to hold her close. But it wasn't going to happen. He was going to die. By the time this day was over he would join Kyle in everlasting darkness. Two souls condemned for all eternity. He was aware of the tears running down his cheeks, the sorrow in his heart. Tortured by emotions threatening to explode, he sobbed uncontrollably...brought back to earth by the expression on the face alongside.

Vindictive mockery, contemptuous humour...it was all there. The sweeping depression that engulfed him was Membril's doing. A sordid reminder that he hadn't forgotten the put-down of the previous evening.

So his mind wasn't immune to Membril's intrusion after all...that was worrying. It was the one area where he'd felt safe. But on reflection, that must have always been the case. Had it been any different he wouldn't have been able to dictate his commands, his instructions telling him what he could and what he couldn't do. Deciphering his thoughts was a different matter entirely. In a way it was him reading Membril's mind, instead of the other way round. That was good, he could live with that. Mentally changing the subject, he sought an answer to a conundrum that had puzzled him for some time.

"Satisfy my curiosity, Membril. I don't need telling it was you who sabotaged my crucifix but, on a different note, was it also you who helped me get down that cliff face? If it was, then you'll know what I'm talking about. The spectacular spur of rock that appeared out of nowhere."

"I've no idea what you're talking about. Needless to say I kept my eye on you, but you appeared to be coping well enough without my assistance." He scoured his face, searching for clues before committing himself to an answer. "I'm intrigued. This rock...tell me more."

"It's just...well: I thought it was you up to your tricks. It was to your advantage that I survived the climb down the mountain, so it seemed obvious. But you had nothing to do with it?"

"I've already made that clear."

"Just checking, so keep your hair on. But if it wasn't you? I dunno. It gets ever more confusing. I was stuck on a ledge about a hundred feet up, and the only way I was going to get down was to abandon the sledge I'd made to carry my stuff. I didn't want to; in fact, at the time I'm talking about, it would've caused a few problems. But I had no option. There being only one anchoring point available meant I would have had to take the full weight of the sledge and its contents on my arms...more than I could cope with. While all this was going through my mind I came over dizzy: for a moment I had no idea where I was going or what I was doing. The giddiness didn't last long, and I put it down to altitude or exhaustion…perhaps a bit of both. It wasn't until I turned away from the edge that I saw it, the answer to all my prayers. A curiously configured rock protruding from the base of the cliff. Why I hadn't noticed it earlier was beyond me. Apart from it's odd shape, it was too big to miss. It wasn't there, that was why…the only answer that made any sense. Naturally enough my thoughts then turned to you. I knew we were destined to meet up in the final analysis and, when we did, you would prefer me to be in one piece."

"Then you were wrong, Sibley. For a start I can't imagine that your dizziness had anything to do with it. That was mere coincidence." His expression changed, from one of humouring to one of doubt. "It had to have been there all along. Seen but not observed…if you know what I mean. You were fooled into believing what you wanted to believe.

"Yeah, guess you're right. Had to have been I…" Belatedly the penny dropped…if that's what was going through his mind, he wouldn't disappoint him. "I still find it odd though, but if you had nothing to do with it?" Looking Membril in the eye, he shook his head, "No, probably not."

"Your playacting doesn't fool me, Sibley. The silly innuendos that may, or may not, have a degree of substance I find irritating…and I have had enough. All along you have blustered without proof, attempting to bewilder me into believing that you wallow in the protection of some phantom figure. I confess the possibility worried me for a time, but that is in the past. No, Sibley," butting in on the attempted interruption, "there is nothing more to be said. If I am wrong, then I am wrong. Time will tell." The wording strong, the delivery unimpressive.

The rest of the day passed boringly slowly. He could rake up little interest, either in what he saw or in Membril's non-stop preamble. He was sorry for the local inhabitants, their unhappiness and their all-consuming despair. But, and in this his certainty was paramount, the harsh life they led had nothing at all to do with a revered god of long ago. They were driven into their dire existence by a ruthless regime. That was how he saw it, and he had no intention of keeping his feelings to himself. Membril had laughed when he told him. Informing him his views were of little or no consequence. The rest of the time he spent trying to quell the fear that wouldn't leave him. It was a double whammy in a bizarre sort of way. Wanting the hours to pass to get it over with, while at the same time wishing the clock wouldn't move quite so fast. The hands of a chronometer are, however, constant and persistent movers: he had no say in the matter.

"It is nearly time, Sibley. If you wish to eat before we prepare, say so now."

Despite having not eaten since the previous night, he shook his head. He was hungry, in fact he was bloody starving, but the mere thought of food churned his insides. Membril's implication, that he hadn't much longer didn't exactly help matters; apart from reminding him there were still questions to ask.

The set-up here made no sense. Despite the ambience of doom and gloom, the town itself was vibrant and well populated. So how come it had remained so completely hidden from the outside world? This was the twenty-first century for chrissakes, and the Andes were not the formidable harbingers of death and destruction they might have been back when Quetzalcoatl and his gang of followers were running riot. Back-packers, mountaineers, hill walkers...travellers of all kinds must have passed this way over the years, yet Camacarja remained in isolation. An enigma yet to be discovered. He wanted to know why. More pertinently, he wanted to know how. Much to his surprise, Membril couldn't wait to tell him.

"There are frequently visitors who, as long as they are prepared to follow certain guidelines, are made welcome and enjoy the benefit of a conducted tour. They are then escorted, again with due chivalry, to the boundaries of the community. There they are deprived of all memory of Camacarja. Of what they have seen, of what they have heard. There are, however, occasions when those visiting are inclined to be, shall we say...obstinate? Meddlesome busybodies' who refuse to accept the imposed restrictions. Insisting on their right to wander unescorted, to take photographs and to make audio recordings. Such regrettable behaviour cannot be tolerated and is dealt with accordingly."

"The strange and unaccounted for disappearance of so-and-so in the remote regions of the Andes. Your methodology to a T."

"You have to appreciate the necessity of keeping secret the existence of these people to the outside world. Every visitor is treated with due respect. All that we ask is for that respect to be reciprocated. Is that not fair compromise?"

"I can see why you might think so but, and this time there's no doubt in my mind whatsoever: you've messed up again. Dug yourself a hole that even you will find it difficult to wriggle out of. You are probably not aware, but Dr. Carter contacted the Peruvian powers that be to inform them of the crash, the death of Dr. Steinbeck and my timely arrival at the camp. Not being the type to hang around, he will by now have added the information that you and I left yesterday: supposedly bound for Lima. Having made it painfully obvious that he mistrusted your motives when you carted me off, I don't think there can be any doubt about that. Moreover, if I'm right in the assumption that your car is rented – as I'm sure is the case - it will be a simple matter for the authorities to catch up with you. As they will do, eventually."

"Once again I must disappoint you, Sibley. When the investigators reached the scene of the supposed crash they could find no sign of the aircraft, no dead body, no indication that anyone or any thing had been anywhere near. Not so much as a footprint in the snow. I find it difficult to understand how they failed to discover at least a trace of what happened, but there you are. Nothing new under the sun, as they say." Throwing him a look that spelt 'it's me you're dealing with', he added salt to the callous wounding of his spite. "The authorities, none too pleased with your Dr. Carter, naturally enough wanted an explanation. Understandable in view of the cost and wasted resource. Surprisingly he denied all knowledge of the affair. Pleading total ignorance of any air accident and, by the same token, refuting having aided a survivor of the crash. In his view it had to be a sick hoax perpetrated by someone with nothing better to do. Do you not find it incongruous, that a man of such obvious intelligence should possess such a random memory?"

"You're an evil bastard, Membril, but I couldn't give a toss about the plane. It's Dr. Steinbeck's remains that concern me."

"You continue to query my birthright, Sibley, but it might make more sense to query my naivety. Can you for one moment imagine I would be stupid enough to leave a string of clues for a hustle of bureaucratic bigots to follow? That aside, however, you need have no fears for your friend. He lies safe beneath the snows of Nevado de Huascaran, where he will no doubt be discovered one day. At least...his mortal remains will be."

He didn't bother to respond, further argument would be a waste of breath. The last remaining vestiges of resistance blown away, he surrendered the will to carry on. Kyle's body left to rot in unconsecrated ground, his soul condemned for all eternity. Neither word nor prayer would bring comfort to him now. Pursued by the nauseous frustration of defeat, the tears moistening the corners of his eyes were on this occasion due to pent up emotions of his own making. His last dormant hope, the lingering possibility that something would go their way, was not about to materialise. Evil had triumphed. He and Kyle condemned to eternal damnation.

He was shoved into a small stone chamber, empty apart from a crude wooden bench and a white, hooded robe hanging from a hook in the wall. He had been given his instructions, sparse and to the point. The choice was his. He either did as he was told, or be forced to if he didn't. He was to strip naked, don the robe and hold the statue of Quetzalcoatl in his left hand. Having no wish to be mauled by some unknown piece of filth, he decided it would be better to swallow his pride and comply.

Changing quickly, he sat on the bench twiddling his thumbs. In danger of succumbing to rising terror, he leapt to his feet as two black-robed men barged into the cell. Ordered to put the hood in place, he was pushed to the front of a three-man triangle. That was ok. He could go along with that. He would take his time, dictate the pace. Exert what authority he could muster. But Membril had other ideas; making it clear that he didn't condone such mutinous practice. He could feel the strings tightening, forcing him to move at a faster pace. Letting him know it wasn't his place to make decisions.

He new the layout, Membril had made sure of that when he'd shown him around earlier. He referred to it as a cathedral, but it was nothing like any cathedral he'd ever come across. The atmosphere alone screamed the blasphemy in relating this den of evil to a house of God. The size didn't fit either. It was huge, massive...totally out of proportion with the rest of Camacarja. But then this was no normal town, this no normal temple of worship. This was the haunt of Satanists, a place of devilry where the good and the just were abjured. A fortress dedicated to Lucifer and his maleficent works.

He knew the way to go, Membril had mapped it out in fine detail. Not that there was any need. His personal puppeteer would make sure he didn't stray from the chosen path. As instructed he took the aisle to his left, toward the far-distant end of the building. Peering through the deep gloom his eyes focussed on the forbidding altar: six hooded figures in attendance...the priests: there to conduct the service. Clustered round the altar they were joined by another, taller man. A polished dignitary clad in lustrous robes of red and gold surmounted by a fur collar...Membril, basking in all his obnoxious glory.

Changes had been made since his last visit. The massive altar, now draped with a tapestry of dazzling colour, was illumined by a cluster of black candles at each of the four corners. Behind the altar hung a wooden crucifix, upside-down as in Kyle's dream. The throne below the inverted cross, if not the reincarnated article, was so frighteningly similar it rekindled dark thoughts of the night he'd witnessed the cure of the woman with acromegaly. A blistering reminder that stretched his nerves to breaking point. Blazing fear to levels beyond his ability to cope.

Lacking the will to carry on supporting his weight two jelly-like legs buckled in protest, to deposit him on the clammily cold stone floor. Brought to the threshold where all reason is lost, tears began to stream down his face. Sobbing in mindless torment he strove to shake off the demons tearing at his robe. Frantically waving arms imploring them to stop, to go away...to kill him and have done with it. Craving for life having departed, he prayed for death to strike. He couldn't care less how it came about...succour would be found at the end of this misery. But his prayers were to go unanswered. The foul things continued to pursue their purpose, pulling and shoving until they forced him to his feet.

Mentally deranged, he wasn't to know the imagined demons were his appointed minders reacting to Membril's command to get their arses in gear and shove the snivelling blight to humanity back on his feet. He was in no state to recall the given instruction, that it was essential he walked to the altar under his own steam.

Unhurriedly his senses began the reluctant journey back to somewhere near normality. Through a blanketing haze of mixed thoughts, emotions and distant memories he recalled his resolution. If he was going to die, then it would be with a modicum of dignity. In confirmation of that decree he struggled to coerce stubborn legs into movement, shrugging off the alien hands that supported him...his efforts were in vain. The more he tried, the more he staggered out of control and many the time would have fallen had it not been for his escort. Head spinning in disarray, he surveyed his surroundings through blurred eyes. Taking in the forbidding stone walls hung with ghastly tapestries that made for compulsive viewing. Changeless scenes of dreadful violence and merciless mockery. Foul entities hissed at him, demonic faces leered, barbed spears menaced and sensuous, naked women wove their spells of seduction.

Made to halt some twelve feet from the altar, his arrival was greeted with a contemptuous sneer. "You disappoint me, Sibley. My erstwhile, grudging esteem of your fortitude, your tenacity: a stupid man but a brave one...ground into dust. It would seem that you were not mistaken. I am after all prone to error, as you have just proved."

Aware of the enjoyment being had at his expense, he possessed neither the will nor the mental capacity to offer a response. He had only himself to blame. If he hadn't lost it, Membril would have nothing to crow about.

Turning away with a gesture of disgust, Membril signalled to one of the priests. No word was spoken, no order given; it was a routine familiarised by experience. Briefly melting into the shadows at the back of the altar, the man returned bearing a wicker basket.

Kyle's dream came flooding back as a sickening dress rehearsal to the act that followed. Their terrified squawking piercing the gloom two chickens, one black, one white, were dragged from the crate. Legs immobilised in a vice-like grip they demanded their release in vocal unison, but the depressing cries impinged on ears that refused to listen. Igniting the contents of a shallow dish, Membril lifted a heavy knife from the altar. Kissing the blade prior to sprinkling it with the burning ashes, he handed the weapon to the priest whose task it was to sever the thrashing heads. A wok-like metal bowl held in readiness, another priest stepped forward to collect the spurting blood. Purpose fulfilled, the poor beasts found their burial ground in a nearby waste receptacle.

Accompanied by a low, wailing chant, Membril sank to his knees. Accepting the proffered container, he held it aloft in token to the throne before lowering it to his lips. Voicing unintelligible words he rose, presenting the revolting contents to

312

each of the six priests in turn before swinging round to face Sibley. Slowly he walked towards him, sinister intent glowering in his piercing stare. It didn't dawn immediately. When it did …the horror struck. He was not to be left out of the proceedings.

It was an uncontrolled, natural reflex. The intention was to deflect the container away from his mouth, but in his panic he missed the target. It was no premeditated action on his part that decreed the upwardly flung hand should collide with the receptacle, no prior intent to drench Membril's face and gown with the repugnant contents. But the muttered apology fell on deaf ears. Hurling the empty dish to the ground his aggressor wiped a finger across a blood-soaked chin, forcing the grisly liquid into Sibley's mouth before slapping him hard across the cheek with the back of his hand.

"You will pay for that…on the altar. Your death will be as you cannot imagine. The agony, and the duration of that agony, will drive you insane long before life expires. And the pain will continue to plague you throughout your spiritual existence."

"You can do what you damn well like." Strangely, he felt stronger. Mentally more confident, for some reason less nervous. He could feel the change biting into him. "You're too blinkered to see it for yourself, but don't you find my clumsiness a touch worrying? If you care to remember, I'm supposed to be under your thumb. You're in charge...so you keep telling me. So what went haywire this time? Haven't put our foot in it again have we? Reckon I'd be real jittery in your shoes. What with me losing my marbles, and now this?" His words drew no response, but he took satisfaction from the doubt shadowing his would-be assassins eyes.

Unable to hide his confusion, Membril spun on his heel to face the altar. Arms spread wide he burst forth an incantation, a chant into which he put everything. A pleading, submissive oration aimed at an unseen audience. A summons to whoever waited in the wings. A deathly hush succeeding the culmination of his address, the priests sank to their knees; heads bowed.

Captured by a chillingly reminiscent sight from the corner of his eye, Jack looked towards the throne. Rising in a gaseous stream, a purple haze was rapidly solidifying into the evil embodiment with which he was all too familiar. Feet, hairless legs and thunderous thighs were first to materialise; followed by abdomen, hirsute torso, finally the abhorrent head. The Goat of Mendes...the malignity that had haunted him ever since that awful night. The monster fixed him with passionless eyes. Perhaps in remembrance of the inconsequence who had quailed before him on that previous occasion.

Prostrating himself before the demonic entity, Membril was quick to make sure Jack followed suit. He could offer no argument. His beliefs held no sway in this unholy dwelling. Obeisance was demanded, and it was beyond his ability to refute it. He tried, he struggled with everything he could muster, but it was wasted effort.

It was time. The telegraphed order to rise to his feet clear and precise. The fear that had temporarily deserted him returned with a vengeance but, strangely, he found compensation in the command. Albeit the preliminary to his execution, in a macabre way it was more acceptable than grovelling on his belly in mock obeisance to the fiend on the throne. He knew what was coming. How he handled it was up to him. It was a matter of pride. He take his terror by the scruff of the neck, or give Membril the pleasure of seeing him succumb in disarray.

The fear left him...as suddenly, as unexpectedly and as inexplicably as before. But this time it was stronger, more defined. Instilling a feeling of permanency, of growing confidence. Perhaps it was always like this when faced with certain death, resignation in acceptance of the inevitable. Calm to the level of serenity, he viewed the coming events in a way he would not have believed possible. Even the Goat of Mendes no longer posed a threat.

In pendulous step and accompanied by the inevitable chant, four priests walked towards him. The sound intensifying with their approach: a hymn of death, decay and, he supposed from their point of view, of celebration: an anthem to mark the imminent return of their errant god. The obtuse thought struck him that this was what Devil worship was all about. Death, particularly in the way it was coming to him, was a good excuse for a party.

He'd forgotten the statue clutched in his left hand. The state he'd got himself into earlier, when he had lost all reason and rolled around the floor like a demented lunatic, it was a miracle he still held on to the cursed thing. There was a message coming through...telling him to change hands. He didn't understand. Why would Membril want him to do that? The left hand was the prime mover in the occult world, always had been and, as sure as Monday followed Sunday, it always would be. Back in medieval times, a simple activity such as writing with the left hand was seen as the Devil's work. But it wasn't his prerogative to argue. Membril must know what he was doing.

Steaming anger exploding through mutated lips, Membril spun to face him. Shouting at the top of his voice, demanding to know what the hell he thought he was doing. His order had been specific. He was to hold the statue in his left hand at all times. Or was that too complicated for him to take on board?

Bewildered by the unfair accusation he was about to respond, but his words ground to a halt. Another message was coming through...a repeat of the last. Reiterating he was to transfer the statue to his right hand. Inwardly cursing the man for changing his bloody mind yet again, he did as instructed...to find himself on the receiving end of a reaction that carried even greater venom than before. Fire blazing from his fearsome, reddened eyes, Membril screeched expletives unbefitting a knight of the realm.

Tugged back and forth between the unidentified messages and, as he had thought, the verbal commands of his aggressor, his mind was in a total whirl. It couldn't be Membril barking instructions after all. Another, more persuasive presence, had taken over and he was caught in the crossfire. Strangely, and for reasons unknown, he knew he could pin his faith in this newcomer. It promised an alliance, the option to take matters into his own hands. Tensions easing, the last of his terror slipped away. Fuelling him with the confidence to counter the scarlet-orbed anger of Membril as he strove to reassert his authority. Smirking in memory of the times he had been made to grovel he held the statue, still firmly clasped in his right hand, in full view of his enemy. Basking in an inner euphoria that encouraged a sense of invincibility...in the knowledge that he was protected from harm.

Driven deep into the shadows by an ethereal glow of majestic intensity, the priests were in disarray. Panic stricken and confused, fear added to their torment, to their destruction. The Goat of Mendes raised its enormous hooves from the arms of the throne...eyes blazing, seeking his whereabouts. But he remained firm, calm and unafraid. Quivering in the horror of his own practice, the Devil's emissary stood transfixed by a sight prohibited to all but the most evil of men. A vision of awesome power sent to penetrate his dark and loathsome soul. Surrendering to the precursor of uncontrolled mania, Membril sank to the floor in violent spasm.

Interrupted only by the sound of agonised moaning emanating from where the priests had gathered, an eerie silence consumed the building. It was as if the whole world held its breath in the expectancy of a drama about to unfold. An act of grandeur in which he was to play the lead. He sensed a spiritual presence: there to guard his sanctity and to offer guidance. So this was what it was all about...the reason behind the continued persecution, the justification for Kyle's death. Why he had been protected...and the motive for his demise. That he would die this night was known and accepted. It had been planned. The way it had to be. His purpose was to rid the world of these decrepit disciples' of the Devil, in vengeful atonement of his embattled past.

Still clenched in his right hand, he lofted the effigy of Quetzalcoatl high above his head. The effect was both immediate and dramatic. There was no build up. No fanfare.

Metamorphosis instant. The familiar of a onetime great and powerful god, transformed into a fiery crucifix. The two-thousand year old emblem of the good and the just. Aimed at the monster on the throne, lance-like rays of lightning ferocity poured from the cross. Forced to shield its eyes from the holy radiance, the abomination abandoned its attempt to rise. Turning its attention instead to Membril...a man with nowhere to run. A broken man. A man certain in the knowledge that the deposit left with his master was about to be claimed. There was no way out. No sanctuary. No escape.

Wondrously restored to its rightful geometry, the cross on the wall burst forth a message. Such awesome power was beyond mere mortals and, Jack Sibley and the Goat of Mendes apart, all were thrown to the floor in the wake of its ferocity. Pleas for mercy gushed from hypocritical lips, hysterical demands for compassion not afforded to others but a different matter now their own skins were threatened. There was to be no mercy. This was their Armageddon.

Striding with great purpose he walked toward the creature on the throne, chanting words not of his recollection but accorded to him that it was the Apostles' Creed to which he gave voice. The verse of an unknown warrior, a battle hymn promising destruction to all who chose to follow Satan's path. He again recalled the wisdom of Father O'haloran, and it was therefore in pure Latin that the creed was propelled with thunder and with passion. Strident notes echoing into the farthest recesses. The bringer of vengeance flailing the ears of lost souls.

"Credo in Deum Patrem omnipotentem, Creatorem cæli et terræ. Et in Iesum Christum, Filium eius unicum, Dominum nostrum..."

He stepped over Membril's form, prostrate on the cold stone floor.

"qui conceptus est de Spiritu Sancto, natus ex Maria Virgine, passus sub Pontio Pilato, crucifixus, mortuus, et sepultus; descendit ad inferos; tertia die resurrexit a mortuis..."

The beast spread its hair-encrusted arms towards the body of the man to whom immortality was now a far distant dream. Gigantic hooves plucked him from the floor. Satanic eyes drenched him with a fearful malevolence.

Charles Membril screamed.

Jack Sibley continued.

"Ascendit ad cælos; sedet ad dexteram Dei Patris omnipotentis; inde venturus est iudicare vivos et mortuos."

Stonework crumbled from the ceiling, supporting pillars collapsed and the hung tapestries blazed. The floor beneath his feet heaved and splintered. His screams cannonading through the ether, the manifestation from hell grasped Membril by the thighs. Lifting his half-naked, blood-spattered body above the wickedly tapered horns it lowered him, slowly...prolonging the agony.

"Credo in Spiritum Sanctum, sanctam Ecclesiam catholicam, Sanctorum communionem, remissionem peccatorum, carnis resurrectionem, vitam æternam. Amen."

Mesmerized to a state of near-hypnosis, he was condemned to watch the bloody and terrible finale. To observe with his own eyes the cruel vengeance of a malignant entity. But there was another reason for his presence. He was there to witness the punishment of the man responsible for the death of his friend and his own imminent demise; to play the role of both judge and jury. But that was insignificant byplay. His main assignment was to confirm the ultimate triumph of good over evil. To know that he and Kyle did not die in vain.

Tearing what was left of the robe from Membril's body, the Goat of Mendes inserted the vicious tip of one of its horns into his rectum. Unmoved by the pain-wracked screams it lowered him...slowly. Mercilessly.

It would take a man with a heart of stone to not be torn apart in sympathy by the soulful cries, the frenetic entreaty for clemency...Jack Sibley was just that man. He felt no sorrow, no compassion. Membril's suffering was deserved, and none could say it was not of his own making.

Unsupported by crumbling columns, the roof began to cave in. Massive blocks of masonry falling in thunderous crashes from sixty feet above, holes appeared in the floor and walls sagged alarmingly. The Goat of Mendes, tossing aside the now lifeless body of the fruit of its vengeance, disappeared in the haze that had announced its arrival. It wouldn't be long now. The building was disintegrating on a grand scale and he, together with the six maddened priests, would soon be buried beneath the rubble. Yet in the midst of the carnage he remained calm and unafraid. Prepared to meet his fate, knowing that recompense had been paid. He had been granted the opportunity for atonement, and knew why his death was necessary. It couldn't be otherwise. The sights seen and the knowledge gained were for him alone. The wider broadcast of such wonders was prohibited. Secrecy paramount.

The end was quick and compassionate. A dull, rumbling explosion deep within the bowels of the temple heralded his last impression.

There was no pain, no discomfort...

EPILOGUE

"Well...good idea or not? What d'you reckon?" The piped music bellowing loudly, Kyle had to raise his voice. "Say something, Jack, for chrissakes. Not much fun sitting here all bloody night waiting for you to make your mind up."

"Sorry, but what you're suggesting? it's a lot to mull over in a few short minutes. Got to be worth a try though I suppose. But will Julie go for it? She might not like the idea of having me hanging around on a permanent basis."

"If I know my sister, she'll be over the moon."

"You should..." He broke off, peering hard at a nearby waiter: a puzzled look on his face. Carrying on from where he'd left off on coming back to earth. "there's many a slip etcetera. Still, whatever the outcome, it is a good idea and if it comes off...well? Let's just say I'll owe you one!"

"What I'm here for. But what the hell's bugging you tonight, Jack? You've done nothing but look over your shoulder ever since wc got here. Expecting someone I don't know about?"

"Doesn't it strike you that we've been through all this before? Nat King Cole crooning his heart out. The two of us discussing the possibility of me moving to America...interrupted before we finished. To me it's as clear as crystal. Don't you feel anything? Anything at all?"

"No idea what you're on about, but never you mind. Nothing you can do about it. It's an age thing...called senility for your education. Mind starts playing tricks, imagination runs riot and you end up spending your days in a care home with a lot of other old folks."

"Laugh all you like, but before you have me carted off to a home for the infirm take a look around. Can you say with any certainty that you recognise anyone who was here when we first arrived?" Raising a hand to brush aside the objection. "No of course I don't remember everyone, but there were one or two who stood out. Particularly if they were young, female and pretty. I noticed you eyeing a few in passing...where are they now? They can't all have upped and gone. And that waiter. The one who just walked past. He's not the same one we had earlier. And don't try telling me he'd come to the end of his shift. It's all hands on decks when a restaurant is this busy."

"You're hallucinating, Jack...hello," he broke off, "what's all this?" Retrieving a discarded newspaper from a nearby table, his face reddened with anger as he read the article that caught his eye. Thrusting the paper across to Jack he barked, "Take a look. Take a bloody good look. My God! Someone's gonna pay for this."

A MINDLESS HOAX

Representatives of the Peruvian Mountain Rescue Service, in conjunction with the Air Accident Investigation Board, vented their anger at the mindless stupidity behind what appears to have been a pathetic hoax. Acting on information received, a rescue team was despatched to the elevated altitudes of Nevado de Huascaran, the highest mountain in Peru, to investigate a reported
air accident. Aided by helicopters, little time was lost in reaching their objective but they could find no evidence of a crash. To rule out the possibility of their

informant having given the wrong bearings, the search was extended over a wider area but without success.

Dr. Kyle Steinbeck, an archaeologist from Nevada and reputed pilot of the airplane, was reported to have been killed in the accident. It was also claimed that a passenger in the aircraft, an Englishman by the name of Jack Sibley, survived the crash and managed to make his way to a scientific research centre located further down the mountain. Dr. William Carter, principle of the institute and initially believed to be the supplier of the erroneous information, denied any complicity: claiming he knew nothing of the affair. Meanwhile the relevant authorities are anxious to locate Dr. Steinbeck and Mr. Sibley. If any of our readers has knowledge of their whereabouts, they are asked to contact either the police or this newspaper.

"What the hell d'you make of that? Me...you...my God! Our lawyers are gonna be in for a hay day when they get a hold of this lot. Even if the guy who played the hoax ain't found out this rag's in trouble...putting our names in print like that. The family...in the name of Jesus Christ! Gotta ring home...can't leave it. They get to read this muck, they'll be torn apart. You'd better come along, Jack. Julie will be distraught and she'll need you to tell her you're ok. Hearing it from me won't be the same."

"Hang on, Kyle, before you dash off...I know it's important but take a peep at this. See what you make of it? Handing over the paper, an accusing finger pointing to the top margin. "September the thirteenth! The article might be cock-and-bull, but they wouldn't have got the date wrong."

"Course they've got it wrong...must have. Misprint I expect. Only left Tonopah a couple of weeks back. July the twenty-third, if you remember. Not much into August and they're telling us we're halfway through bloody September? Who they kidding?"

"Not likely they'd get the date wrong. Papers might print what they want to print, but I can't imagine a mistake of that magnitude getting past the editor. Let's ask him," beckoning to a passing waiter. "Señor? What's the date today. Can you tell me?"

"Si Señor, Septombre twenty-two."

Looking at Kyle with a drawn expression, he stated the obvious. "They didn't get it wrong. And to add to it, this paper is nine days old. You explain it. I can't."

"You kidding me? Something like six-or-seven weeks goes up in smoke and you expect me to say where it went. But how the..." He stopped, continuing in a voice not much above a whisper. "Jack...the crash, me dead. That report. You and me vanishing like it said. Chrissakes, Jack...tell me I'm not dead."

"Don't be daft. If you were dead we wouldn't be having this conversation. I'm supposed to have survived...remember? I might get up to all sorts of tricks, but talking to dead bodies isn't one of them." Initial shock dwindling, he began to think more clearly. "Listen, Kyle, I don't pretend to understand this any more than you, but guesswork will get us nowhere. You phone your family, I'll go and fetch my diary. That might give us some idea of what's gone wrong."

Crossing the lounge to where his friend fidgeted in the comfort of a plush armchair, he was met with a look spelling out a mixture of confusion, consternation and disbelief.

" More problems?"

"Too damn right there's problems…a long and complicated pile of sweet bugger-all. So it might pay to tell me how you got on before we try to make sense of this," patting the diary that lay open on his lap.

"The family don't read this rubbish, thank God. Not the most popular rag on the shelf in their eyes. What surprises me though, is news of our non-existent crash didn't appear anywhere else. Nothing on TV or radio, no mention in any other paper as far as they know. Stranger still, they weren't invaded by the paparazzi, as you can bet they would've been if the story had got around. The only hint they had that something might be wrong, was a phone call from someone in Peru demanding to know my whereabouts. My father took the call, but when he asked why they wanted to know the body at the other end rang off. Apparently Pop tried several times to get hold of us after that but, so he says, my phone was as dead as a dodo. Worried to hell, they couldn't understand why we didn't get in touch...only natural. What could I say when we don't know ourselves what's been happening? Managed to divert the conversation by saying I'd explain when we get back. Then it was Julie's turn. Miffed she didn't get to talk to you, I fobbed her off saying you were busy packing so we get back home pronto. But this you're not gonna believe. Her response was to say it was about time. We'd been away for nearly eleven weeks...getting on for five weeks longer than we told her we'd be. That flummoxed me, Jack. Only thing I could come up with was to say you send your love and we'd be leaving in a day-or-two. But it don't end there. Next off, I phoned the airport. After reading that article I wanted to know if my airplane was still there and in one piece. What I got was some jobsworth bending my ear so far back it was in danger of being parted from the rest of me. He couldn't have given a toss about my plane, all he was interested in was when he was gonna get paid for the extra eight weeks of hangar space. Having had to suffer him ranting on-and-on, I was kind of hoping you'd sorted it out but, from what you're telling me and if the look on your face is anything to go by, that's not gonna happen."

"See what you make of it," nodding in the direction of his diary, "it doesn't make much sense to me. That's not quite true. It has given me some ideas, but we'll talk about those later: you might come up with something more concrete."

"What am I supposed to be looking for?"

"Sixth of August is a good place to start. Take it from there. One day at a time. You should find the eighth particularly interesting."

Staring in disbelief, he bleated. "By God Jack, you're right! We did talk about you moving to the States...interrupted just like you said. But it don't say who did the interrupting."

"We'll come back to that. In the meantime thumb through the rest. One day at a time, up to the twenty-second of September."

"This gets us nowhere, Jack," throwing the book on the table in disgust. "Thought you were supposed to put everything down that mattered, but this tells us nothing. Absolute bloody nothing. No account of what we did or didn't do...not a snippet. Fair enough, you've got the irrelevant stuff down alright, but don't give us a clue to those missing weeks."

"In a nutshell! Every night before I let my head hit the pillow, I put everything down in my diary. A habit acquired when I was knee-high to a grasshopper, one that has been part and parcel of my existence ever since. So why, suddenly and without good reason, do I change the way of a lifetime? There is only one answer...I wouldn't have. Not just like that. What I did, people I met: conversations, ideas, incidents...anything remotely interesting. Each and every event, significant or otherwise, recorded in black and white. That's the puzzle, and until we can unravel it we'll remain in the dark." Retrieving the tome from the table, he held it out for Kyle to take. "I mentioned I have the murmurings of an answer but for all I know it could be miles off track and, because of that, I'm not going to attempt to put ideas in your head. So, if for nothing other than old times sake, humour me: look through my diary in detail. I suggest you Ignore what's there and concentrate on what isn't; that's the only way you're likely to get anywhere. At least, that's the way I see it. No, I haven't lost the plot," reacting to the bemused expression, "I've never been more serious in my life."

"Then convince me. Stop going round the houses, spill the beans and give me some sort of picture. You say you could have it all worked out, so why not pass the buck. Put me in the frame, talk your idea through like the educated grown-ups we kid ourselves we are."

"Bearing in mind your inbuilt scepticism, that might not be such a good idea. But, if it's what you want." Aware of the reception his admission would arouse, he hesitated before continuing. Preparing his banter with due care before putting it into words. "It's a theory, Kyle; nothing more than an educated guess. So please try and see it in that light. Based on past experience, but it's all I have to go on…I've got nothing else." He paused, licking his lips before carrying on. "I'm not forcing you to go along with me, so if you can suggest a better solution don't hesitate. I'm far from convinced myself that I've got it right and if you can put a more lucid, a more believable explanation on the table, then that's fine by me. In the meantime think about what I have to say. Give it some thought before discarding it as rubbish."

"Oh I get it. More weird goings-on from your murky past. Give us a break, Jack. I'm not sure I can handle any more of that funny stuff."

"Ok, so tell me what you think. As you're adamant you don't want to hear my version of what might've happened, I presume you must have an answer of your own."

"Course I ain't…and you damn-well know it. The whole thing's just goddamn crazy…don't bear thinking about, and I'm not gonna bother to try. The world – my world – has lost its way as far as I see it, and d'you know what? I don't give a toss."

"If you're going to adopt that attitude, then you've no right to take the piss out of what I think." Leaning his elbows on the table he spat, "what the hell's happened to the Kyle Steinbeck I used to know? He wouldn't have sat back and given up. He would've fought like mad to dig out the truth, battled his way through to the bitter end. Not content until he'd sorted it out to his own satisfaction."

"Alright clever Dick; as you've got everything sewn up all nice and dandy like, and I'm too bloody useless to try, put me out of my misery and give me something to laugh at."

"You're not making it easy for either of us, and losing your rag isn't helping." He responded. The words accompanied by a deep sigh. "But for Christ's sake, Kyle, drop the antagonism. I'm not forcing you to accept what I think could be the answer. All I want is for you do me the courtesy of listening and trying to understand. Is that too much to ask?"

"Do my best."

"That's all I ask. So, ok. First off, read aloud the diary entries for the eighth, twelfth and fifteenth of August, and the sixth of September."

"Not again! How many more times we gotta go over the same old baloney?"

"As many times as necessary, so cut the moans and groans and try me out. Use your imagination and, who knows? You could read a lot more into the bits that aren't there than you might think."

"Oh Jesus! This gets worse." He said, sounding like a truculent child made to recite his homework for the umpteenth time. "Ok, let's get it over with. Eighth August: 'spent the day walking round Oaxaca. Dinner in hotel. Kyle discussed possibility of me moving to America. Interrupted...'' Banging the diary down on his thighs, he blistered, "We know all that...what's the use of going over the same old thing again and again. Bloody stupid!"

"No, this is important, Kyle. Read that last bit again...word for word. Then tell me what's missing."

"Wish I knew where the hell you're going, but ok. I'll see if I can dig out what you're getting at."

"Well?"

"You didn't say who did the interrupting. Might've explained plenty if you had."

"Precisely. At last you're homing in on my way of thinking. The clues lie in what isn't there, not in what's left behind. I go upstairs to my room and, without exception, the first thing I do is enter the days events in my diary while they're still clear in my mind. I show an interest in your idea of me coming to live in America but, before we can reach a conclusion, we're interrupted...no idea by whom because I omitted to add his or her name. No reason, no explanation. Someone intrudes in the middle of a crucial discussion and I cant be bothered to say who it is. Even you must have doubts."

"Doubts? What bloody doubts? You got it wrong, Jack. Simple as that. Might've thought you put whosever's name down but you couldn't have. My only doubt is whether or not you believe what you're saying, or if you're having me on."

"Ok, then argue your way out of this. Twelfth of August...left hospital! What was I in hospital for? No idea. Couldn't be bothered to make a note of it. Does that make sense? Of course it doesn't" responding to the bemused expression facing him. "Unless you can tell me, we'll never know whether it was the result of an accident or some sort of malady."

"So what are you saying? Your precious diary's been got at? Is that what you're telling me? Come off it, Jack, I'm not buying that. If it had been tampered with in any way, shape or form we'd know it for sure. Even a pencil mark leaves a dent in the paper when it's rubbed out. And anyway, why the heck would anyone want to go to that sort of trouble? Say what you like, you won't convince me. Might've thought you'd written it all down but you couldn't have. If you had, it would still be there."

"Not tampered with in the physical sense, that's not what I'm getting at." Jack seethed, trying hard to contain his impatience. "But if you care to open your eyes and shed your scepticism, you might see it for yourself. To those with the right kind of know-how other methods are available. The ways and means to obliterate the written word without recourse to an eraser."

"You have an uncanny knack of shifting the goalposts, Jack. Every time I say it's not possible, you come back at me with the same old bullshit. The super-bloody-natural...that's what you're getting at.!"

"Seems I'm damned whatever I say. But if you can suggest something that doesn't include taking the piss, you can bet your life I'll listen." Smiling for the first time that evening, he grasped the advantage there for the taking. "That look you're giving me tells me you can't. Listen, Kyle, I've got my faults the same as everyone else, I know that, but omitting to include anything of such crucial importance from my diary isn't one of them. Scoff all you like. Without a shadow of doubt those notes have been doctored. Why? To prohibit our knowledge of certain specific events that happened during those missing weeks...it's the only explanation that fits."

"Ok, I admit it: don't pretend to understand and guess that's how it's always gonna be. So for the time being I'll go along with your fantasies, but that's only because I can't think up a tangible alternative. But what's it all about? Why would anyone not want us to know what we did with ourselves during those missing weeks for chrissakes?"

"I'm as much in the dark on that as you are, but we do have something to go on. We know we've discussed the possibility of me moving to America before, and in this very restaurant...of that we have proof. But this time there was no interruption. So, looked at objectively, this has to be the starting point. Whoever butted in on our conversation that night initiated the chain of events...and that could explain why the name was obliterated. It's not that we can't remember those missing weeks, Kyle. For us they never happened."

"You're right...you're damn well right! ...Gotta be. Those eight weeks didn't exist I; didn't get killed...can't have done."

"Oh but you were, at least I'm pretty sure you were, but not in a way that we can understand. Those missing weeks might not have happened in our consciousness, but that doesn't mean they didn't exist. They existed alright, and we must have lived through them. That's made obvious by what hasn't been removed from the diary...the trivial, inconsequential activities that bear no relation to what really went on. And this is where it gets complicated. It's not merely the inscriptions in my diary that were removed, our memories suffered the same fate."

"So the rag didn't lie? I was killed. So what the hell does that make me...a ruddy zombie? Oh this is getting damned stupid. No idea whether I'm coming or going. Not sure if I'm dead or alive."

"A zombie? Yeah I go along with that. Zombies' have a habit of wandering around with no idea what their doing or where their going, so you could be right." Grinning broadly he added, "See what you make of the last of those dates...sixth of September."

"Lima tomorrow. Kyle hopes to get away by ten-thirty. Nothing after..." Face white, it was more a statement than a query. "We didn't make it! We never got to Lima. That mountain...Huascaran. I did fly into it...why we didn't get there!" Hastily turning the pages he uttered the damning confirmation. "Nothing but blanks. That news report was spot-on. I was dead and you were on your way down the mountain; hence the blank pages...you wouldn't have given a monkeys toss about your diary."

"At last we're getting somewhere." Inwardly wincing at the forlorn expression on his friend's face, he chose his words carefully. If he found it hard, what must his friend be going through? "You were killed, Kyle, that, you - we - have to accept. But your death occurred in what was effectively a virtual world, a parallel universe of which we know very little...if anything at all. You were never dead in this world...the real world. Cling on to that and thank your lucky-stars. Had it been any different, you wouldn't be here now. But, if it's any consolation, you might not have been the only one it happened to. For all we know I could've fallen and broken my neck climbing down that ruddy mountain. My theory, and we both know how flirtatious theories can be, is something along these lines. For reasons I'm not going to attempt to fathom, we somehow became entangled with events too powerful for our understanding. Events of such unmitigated horror or stark magnificence, perhaps both, that our sanities were endangered. It may have been pre-destined, our involvement a necessary element in whatever it was that went on...that we'll never know. Could be utter crap of course. But it does tick all the boxes."

"Don't explain the time-gap."

"Oh but it does. To preserve our safety, we were wrapped in a time warp. Fast-forwarded through those weeks we can't account for. Had that not been the case you'd be six feet under and, as for me...who knows? Taken as a whole, it's the only solution that fits."

"Got no choice. As you say, it's the only logical answer. It's the illogical way you arrived at it that worries me. No, I'm not laughing, Jack. Don't pretend to know what went on, not even sure I want to. Just thinking about it terrifies me."

"You're not alone there but, if you're game, there is one clue it might be worth while to follow up. If you remember, I said there were four entries in my diary that were of especial interest; the one we haven't yet looked at is that of the fifteenth of August. No indication why or what it was all about, but, on that day, I apparently had a lengthy chat with a Reverend Osvaldo Martinez, the incumbent priest of 'La Iglesia del Sacramento Santo', a tiny church on the outskirts of Acapulco. According to this, I promised to return within twelve months...if we - the 'we', I presume, refers to you and me - are still alive!"

"Funny thing to say. Wonder what brought that about?"

"Precisely, and your guess is as good as mine. More significantly, why was an entry of such obvious potential not deleted with everything else? Most odd."

"Could be it was considered we had a right to know at least something of that part of our lives that was taken away from us. Forget me complaining I didn't want to know, I've changed my mind. We've gotta go back to Acapulco, Jack. Find out what it was you and this priest guy talked about. But we'll come back to that...what's really puzzling me at this moment is where'd I put the statue I got off that old fellah in Chichen-Itza? Searched through all my belongings but can't find the damn thing anywhere." Laughing at the thought, he chortled, "Perhaps it got itself erased with all the other stuff. Not over-bothered to tell the truth, just curious to know where it could've got to. For reasons I don't know about, I seem to have lost all interest in Quetzalcoatl and his band of worshippers."

"Can't help I'm afraid, but I've a funny feeling you've seen the last of that statue. I also have the notion that we're better off without it."

"Now that *is* strange, because it affects me the same way, and if I never see it again it'll be too soon. Anyway, Jack." Peering hard at his friend, he asked "What next then, mate? Acapulco and the priest, or back home to put the folks out of their misery?"

"Back home, Kyle. The vicar can wait...Julie can't.

16740225R00188

Printed in Poland
by Amazon Fulfillment
Poland Sp. z o.o., Wrocław